"Maybe I can help." Sloan motioned to her daughter.

"She doesn't go to strangers," Maggie said.

"It's worth a try." He held out his arms. "Hey, Shorty, what's up?"

The little girl silently stared at him, probably didn't know what to make of a man in the kitchen. Maggie braced for an ear-splitting protest, but after a moment's hesitation, Danielle went to him and settled her chubby little arm around his neck.

Maggie's heart melted at the sight of the big man carrying her little girl.

Gorgeous, charming and good with kids. Sloan Holden was a triple threat. But he must have a flaw.

Every man did.

* * *

The Bachelors of Blackwater Lake:
They won't be single for l~~ong~~

THE WIDOW'S BACHELOR BARGAIN

BY
TERESA SOUTHWICK

MILLS & BOON

First Published in Great Britain 2016
By Mills & Boon, an imprint of HarperCollins*Publishers*
1 London Bridge Street, London, SE1 9GF

© 2016 Teresa Southwick

ISBN: 978-0-263-91954-7

23-0116

Our policy is to use papers that are natural, renewable and recyclable products and made from wood grown in sustainable forests.The logging and manufacturing processes conform to the legal environmental regulations of the country of origin.

Printed and bound in Spain
by CPI Barcelona

Teresa Southwick lives with her husband in Las Vegas, the city that reinvents itself every day. An avid fan of romance novels, she is delighted to be living out her dream of writing for Mills & Boon.

To the men and women
of the United States Armed Forces and their
families. Your sacrifices have ensured our freedom,
and I am forever in your debt.

Chapter One

"You must be Mr. Holden. And—happily—you're not a serial killer."

Sloan Holden expected beautiful women to come on to him, but as pickup lines went, that one needed tweaking. He stared at the woman, who'd just opened the door to him. "Okay. And you know this how?"

"I had you investigated." Standing in the doorway of her log cabin home turned bed-and-breakfast, Maggie Potter held up her hand in a time-out gesture. "Wait. I'm a little new at this hospitality thing. Delete what I just said and insert welcome to Potter House. Please come in."

"Thanks." He walked past her and heard the door close. Turning, he asked, "So, FBI? CIA? DEA? NSA? Or Homeland Security?"

"Excuse me?"

"Which alphabet-soup agency did you get to check me out?"

"Actually, it was Hank Fletcher, the sheriff here in Blackwater Lake. I apologize for blurting that out. Guess I'm a little nervous. The thing is, I live here with my two-year-old daughter and another, older, woman who rents a room. It's my responsibility to check out anyone who will be living here."

Sloan studied the woman—Maggie Potter—dressed in jeans and a T-shirt covered by a pink-and-gray-plaid flannel shirt. Her shiny dark hair was pulled back into a ponytail and her big brown eyes snapped with intelligence and self-deprecating humor. She was pretty in a wholesome, down-to-earth way, and for some reason that surprised him. He'd assumed the widow renting out a room would be frumpy, silver haired and old enough to be his grandmother. It was possible when his secretary had said *widow*, he'd mentally inserted all the stereotypes.

"Still," he said, sliding his hands into his jeans' pockets, "a serial killer by definition gets away with murder and is clever enough to hide it. Maybe I'm hiding something."

"Everyone does. That just makes you human." The wisdom in that statement seemed profound for someone so young. "But you, Mr. Sloan Holden, can't even spit on the sidewalk without someone taking a picture. I doubt you could ditch photographers long enough to pull off a homicide, let alone hide the incriminating evidence."

"You're right about that."

"Even so, Hank assured me you are who you say you are and an upstanding businessman who won't stiff me for the rent. Again I say welcome." She smiled, and the effect was stunning. "I'll do everything possible to make your stay here as pleasant as possible, Mr. Holden."

"Please call me Sloan."

"Of course." When she turned away, he got a pretty good look at her work-of-art backside and shapely legs. They weren't as long as he usually liked, but that didn't stop all kinds of ideas on *how* to make his stay pleasant from popping into his mind. That was proof, as if he needed more, that he was going to hell. After all, she was a mother.

"I just need you to sign the standard guest agreement." She walked over to the desk in the far corner of the great room.

Sloan followed and managed to tear his gaze away from her butt long enough to get a look at her home. A multi-colored braided rug was the centerpiece for a conversation area facing the fireplace. It consisted of a brown leather sofa and a fabric-covered chair and ottoman. On the table beside it was a brass lamp and a photo of Maggie snuggled up to a smiling man. Must be the husband she'd lost.

Maggie handed over a piece of paper and he glanced through it, the normal contract regarding payment responsibilities, what was provided, dos and don'ts. He took the pen she handed him and signed his name where indicated.

"Do you need a credit card and ID?" That was standard procedure for a hotel.

"I recognize you from the magazines you seem to be in on a weekly basis. And I got all the pertinent financial information from your secretary. Elizabeth says you'll be staying in town for a while to work on the resort project."

"That's right."

"I know you're here at Potter House because Blackwater Lake Lodge had a major flood when a pipe burst and is now undergoing repairs and renovations. Elizabeth told me you do a lot of work outside the office and wouldn't be happy with all the pounding, hammering and drilling."

"She knows me well."

"I got that impression. And she said you're not a heartless jerk like most tabloid stories make you out to be."

"Did I mention she's loyal?"

He folded his arms over his chest and studied her. Elizabeth was the best assistant he'd ever had and an impeccable judge of character, even on the phone. She wasn't in the habit of sharing details about him. Not that she'd given away secrets to a competitor, but still… While taking care of his living arrangements for this stay in Blackwater Lake, Montana, she must have phone-bonded with Maggie Potter, meaning that she trusted this woman.

In any event, he didn't have a lot of choice about where to hang his hat. The lack of accommodations in this area, along with a beautiful lake and spectacular mountains, were the very reasons this resort project he and his cousin Burke had undertaken would be a phenomenal financial success. It was their luck that no one else had noticed the amazing potential of this area before now.

"It sounds as if you got to know my assistant pretty well," he finally said.

"Lovely woman. She invited me to her wedding."

"Wow. You really did make a good phone impression. I didn't even get an invitation," he teased.

"She's probably concerned that the kind of photographers who follow you around aren't the ones she wants documenting the most important day of her life."

Sloan knew she was joking, but that wasn't far from the truth. Because he had money, his every move seemed to generate a ridiculous amount of public interest—make that *female* interest. That would give a guy trust issues even if he hadn't been burned, but Sloan was a wealthy divorced bachelor and deliberately never stayed with the same woman for more than a couple of months.

A man in his position had social obligations and often needed a plus one. On the surface it looked like dating, but he knew it was never going anywhere. So the more women he went out with, the more interest his personal life generated. But he was ultimately an entrepreneur who knew getting his name in the paper was a positive. Even bad publicity could be good.

And interest continued to escalate about whether or not any woman could catch the most eligible bachelor who had said in more than one interview that he would never get married again. That it just wasn't for him. The remark, intended to snuff out attention, had really backfired on him and created the ultimate challenge for single women looking for a rich husband. He was like the love lottery.

"My assistant knows I'd never let anything spoil her special day."

"Because you respect the sanctity of marriage so much?" It sounded as if there was the barest hint of sarcasm in her question.

He didn't doubt that she knew the tabloid version of his disastrous foray into matrimony. It was well documented and also ancient history. "I do for other people," he answered sincerely.

"Just not for yourself."

"It's always good to know your own limitations."

"Seems smart. And wise," she agreed. "So how long will you be here?"

"Indefinitely." That was certainly an indefinite answer. "I handle the construction arm of the company, so it will probably be quite a while. And Blackwater Lake Lodge is undergoing renovations."

"True."

He glanced around and found he liked the idea of not living in a hotel for what would probably be months. "You have a nice place here."

"Thanks. My husband built it." There was fierce pride in her voice even as a shadow slid into her eyes. "It wasn't planned as a bed-and-breakfast. We opened a business in town."

"Oh?"

"Potter's Ice Cream Parlor on Main Street."

He nodded. "I saw it on my way here."

"Danny, my husband—" she glanced at the picture and

a softness slipped into her eyes "—thought everything through. Downstairs is the master bedroom with another room for a nursery. But he figured as the kids got older, into their teens, they'd need their privacy—bedrooms and separate baths. And a game room to hang out in. There's even an outside entrance for the upstairs. I'm not quite sure how he planned to deal with that when they were teenagers." She shrugged and the light dimmed in her dark eyes. "It didn't work out as he planned, but it works for my needs now."

He wouldn't have asked if she hadn't brought it up. And he probably shouldn't have asked anyway, but the question came out before he could stop it. "What *are* your needs?"

A slight narrowing of her eyes told him she didn't miss the double entendre, though he hadn't meant it that way. She answered the question directly. "I decided to expand the ice cream parlor to include a café, a little more healthy and upscale than a coffee shop. Even though I took on a partner, we needed an infusion of capital. The simple answer is that I need the money to pay back the business loan."

"I see."

"Josie, my other boarder, has been here for a few months. I've known her for a long time and this arrangement works for her. She's a widow and doesn't want the responsibility of a big house. When she wants to travel, she can go without worrying about the house she left behind. For the other room, you're my first. Tenant, I mean." A becoming flush crept into her cheeks. "Someone from your company who knows my brother contacted him about your housing dilemma and he put them in touch with me."

"And still you investigated me." One corner of his mouth curved up.

"It never hurts to be cautious."

Sloan couldn't argue with her about that. "So who is your brother?"

"Brady O'Keefe."

"Hmm."

She frowned. "Do you know him?"

"Not personally. But I know the name. He did some computer and website work for my company."

Sloan also knew the guy was pretty well off. The way Maggie had emphasized the word *need* when talking about money, he was pretty certain her brother hadn't been involved in raising the capital to expand her business.

"You look puzzled about something, Sloan."

"I am. But it's none of my business."

"Probably not." She shrugged. "Ask anyway."

He nodded. "I know your brother by reputation and he has a few bucks. Yet you didn't get the expansion loan from him."

One of her eyebrows rose. "How do you know that?"

"Because you said you *need* money to pay back the loan. I don't think your brother would pressure you or put you and his niece out on the street if you fell behind on payments."

"No." She smiled. "But I wanted to do this on my own. My way."

"And what way is that?" *Not the easy way*, Sloan thought.

She glanced at the photograph, then back at him. "When Danny and I opened the ice cream parlor, Brady wanted to help us, but my husband refused. He appreciated the offer, but it was important to him to do it on his own. A respect thing. Some might call it macho male pride."

"I see."

"He said it was human nature for people to not appreciate things they didn't have to work hard for. So we poured our heart, soul, blood, sweat and tears into the project.

Our phase one. The plan was always to expand and open the café, but there was a setback when he was killed in Afghanistan."

"I'm sorry." Stupid words. So automatic and useless. Why wasn't there something to say that would actually help?

"Thank you." She slid her fingers into her jeans' pockets. "Danny's gone, so I'm carrying on the dream. The way he would have wanted—without my brother's help."

"With three sisters, I can say with certainty that my instinct would be to write a check if they needed it. Brady probably feels that way, too. So how's he taking this loan thing?"

"You'd think I gave his computer a particularly nasty virus." She grinned. "Still, I think he's secretly proud of me."

Sloan didn't doubt that. What brother wouldn't be proud of a sister like her? It would have been easy to let herself be taken care of after losing her husband, but she hadn't. She was raising their child and running an expanded business plus taking in boarders. Doing things her way. And it was a good way.

She glanced at his empty hands. "I assume you have luggage. I'll show you to your room, then bring your things up."

"Thanks, but I'll get everything." His way wasn't to let a woman carry his stuff, especially when that woman looked as if the first stiff breeze would blow her away. He admired her independence, but he did things his way, too. "There's a lot and some of it is heavy."

"Okay. Follow me."

Now, *that* he didn't mind doing, because she had an exceptionally fine backside. Aside from her obvious external attributes, there was a lot to like about his new landlady.

Smart, straightforward, self-reliant. Salt of the earth. He would bet his last dime that she wasn't a gold digger.

He almost wished she was.

The next morning Maggie settled her crabby daughter in the high chair beside the round oak kitchen table. After giving the little girl a piece of banana, she whipped up a batch of biscuits and popped them in the oven. When the idea had taken hold to rent out the upstairs rooms, she'd come up with a different breakfast menu for each day of the week. Today was scrambled eggs with spinach, mushrooms, onion and tomato. Fried potatoes. Country gravy for the biscuits. And blueberries. This was one of Josie's favorites and made one wonder how the older woman stayed so trim. Could have something to do with her being tall and the brisk walk she took every morning after rolling out of bed.

Maggie hadn't seen Sloan yet this morning and was just the tiniest bit curious about what his favorite breakfast was and how he stayed in such good shape. The snug T-shirt he'd had on when checking in yesterday had left little to the imagination, and the man had a serious six-pack going on. Ever since she'd opened the door, her nerves had been tingling, some kind of spidey sense. It was like the princess-and-the-pea story she read to Danielle. Even when he wasn't near, she *knew* he was under her roof.

He wasn't model handsome, but there was something compelling in his eyes, which were light brown with flecks of green and gold.

"Mama—" The single word was followed by the sound of a splat.

Maggie looked up from stirring the country gravy and saw that Danielle had thrown her banana on the floor. Very little had been ingested, but the little girl had mangled the fruit pretty well.

"Want some Cheerios, sweetie?"

"Cookie—"

Some words came out of this child's mouth as mangled as that banana, but *cookie* wasn't one of them. It was tempting to give in and let her have a treat. Just this once keep her happy so the first breakfast with their VIP guest would go smoothly and convince him she knew what she was doing in the B and B business. But her maternal instincts told her that was a bad habit to start.

"Good morning." Josie walked into the kitchen freshly showered after her exercise. She was in her early sixties but looked at least ten years younger, in spite of her silver hair. The pixie cut suited her. She moved beside the high chair. "How are you, munchkin?"

The little girl babbled unintelligible sounds, which were no doubt a list of grievances about her mother being the food police.

"She's not her sunny little self today," Maggie apologized. "She was restless last night. Teething, I think. I hope she didn't disturb you."

"Not a bit. The insulation in these walls is amazing." She looked around, blue eyes brimming with understanding. "How can I help?"

"Go relax with a cup of coffee. You're a guest."

"Oh, please. We both know I'm your friend more than a paying customer. Besides the discount I get for emergency babysitting, it's a blessing to still be useful when you're as old as I am." She put a hand on her hip. "Now, what can I do?"

"You're doing it. Being a godsend." Maggie turned on the gas burner underneath the stainless-steel frying pan filled with potatoes. "If you could give Danielle a handful of that cereal, I'd be forever in your debt."

"Done." She grabbed the box from the pantry and did as requested. "Now I can get the eggs ready to scramble."

"Maybe I should change things up." Maggie grinned. "You know the menu by heart."

"How many eggs are you thinking with Sloan here? A man like that could be a big eater."

"So you met him?"

"Last night. We watched TV together in the upstairs game room. Some house-flipping program." The older woman opened the refrigerator and removed the containers of veggies that had been cut up the night before.

Maggie hadn't cooked breakfast for a man since the morning she'd said goodbye to her husband, before he deployed to Afghanistan. It wasn't the first time she'd made sure he ate before leaving the house but she'd never considered it would be her last meal with him. She'd never been able to decide whether or not she would have made the food more special if she'd known. Or if the not knowing had made the ordinary a final blessing.

"I think eight should be enough," Maggie said.

She couldn't remember how many Danny would have eaten and felt guilty about that. Every time she realized the recollections were getting fuzzier, she felt disloyal to his memory.

"With all the rest of the food," she continued, "it should be more than enough. If there are leftovers, I'll put some on a tortilla later and call it lunch."

"Okay." Josie started cracking eggs into a bowl. "He sure is a good-looking man."

"Who's that?"

"Your new boarder. Sloan. Unless there's another man you're hiding under the bed."

Just the sound of his name made Maggie's heart skip a beat. "I suppose he wouldn't have to wear a bag over his head in public."

"Not to be insensitive, Maggie. After all, I'm a widow, too. Also not blind. Take it from me, a man who looks like he does would have an almost nun thinking twice about taking final vows. You can't tell me you didn't notice."

"Of course I did." And even if she were blind, there would be no way not to notice the gravelly sex appeal lingering in his deep voice. "But you watched TV with him. What was that like?"

"He's not just a pretty face. I can tell you that. Seems to know his stuff and, quite frankly, he took a lot of the joy and mystery out of what those TV construction guys do."

"So it was like watching a medical show with a doctor who tells you how they're doing CPR all wrong?"

"Exactly." Josie grinned. "Still, he seems like a nice man. I wouldn't believe all that stuff about him in the tabloids."

"I sort of liked that story about him owning houses all over the world and swimming naked with the model."

"It does give one an image," Josie admitted.

"Did you ask him? Hanging out watching a house-flipping show seems like the perfect time to find out what inquiring minds want to know."

"It didn't occur to me, what with him talking about all the ways those TV guys could have reduced waste, pollution and environmental degradation."

A piercing wail from the high chair interrupted the fascinating conversation. What Josie had just said made Maggie even more curious than she'd already been, but now wasn't the time to pursue it. Danielle needed attention.

"Are you thirsty, baby girl?" She grabbed a sippy cup from the cupboard and filled it with milk. She handed it to her daughter, who eagerly stuck the spout in her mouth and drank. "So he's a green builder?"

"Who?" There was a twinkle in Josie's blue eyes as she stirred up eggs, veggies and seasoning in a bowl.

"Sloan. Unless there's a man *you're* hiding under the bed, Miss—"

"Good morning."

That gravelly, deep, sexy voice belonged to the man they'd just been talking about. Maggie exchanged a guilty glance with Josie but couldn't manage to come up with anything to say to him.

The sippy cup hit the wooden floor, interrupting the awkward silence. Maggie quickly stirred the potatoes before hurrying to her daughter, who was starting to squirm against the belt holding her in. Along with the high-pitched whining, it was clear the little girl wanted out. Maggie undid the strap and lifted the child from the high chair then tried to put her down. Danielle was having none of that and the screech kicked up a notch.

Please, not today, little one, Maggie silently begged. The man was accustomed to five-star hotels, and a two-year-old's temper tantrum wasn't the optimal way to put their best foot forward.

"Mommy has to finish cooking breakfast," she whispered. But Danielle shook her head and clung for all she was worth.

"I'll take her." Josie walked over with her arms outstretched, but the little girl buried her face against Maggie's shoulder.

She looked at Sloan. "I'm really sorry about this. I'll get her settled down and food will be on the table in no time."

"There's no rush. Although I'd love some coffee."

"It's made. I'll just put some in a carafe and you can

have it in the dining room. Cups and saucers are already out—"

"A mug is fine." He walked over to the coffeemaker and grabbed one of the mugs hanging from an under-the-cupboard hook. After pouring the steaming dark liquid, he blew on it, then took a sip. "Good."

Danielle had lifted her head at the sound of the deep voice and was intently studying the stranger. Her uncle Brady visited regularly, but other than him, a man in this house was a rare occurrence.

Maggie tried to put the little girl down again and got another strong, squealing protest. "Well, it's not the first time I've cooked with this little girl on my hip, and it probably won't be the last."

"Maybe I can help." Sloan set his mug on the granite island beside them and held out his arms.

"She doesn't go to strangers," Maggie said.

"It's worth a try." He held out his arms. "Hey, Shorty, what's up?"

The little girl silently stared at him, probably didn't know what to make of a man in the kitchen. Maggie braced for an earsplitting protest, but after a moment's hesitation, Danielle went to him and settled her chubby little arm around his neck. Then she touched the collar of his white cotton shirt. Obviously the man had a way with women of all ages. The shock had Maggie blinking at him, until she remembered that her daughter's hands were unwashed and still grubby.

"Oh, no—she's dirty. I'll get a washcloth—"

Sloan looked down at the banana streaks on his white shirt and shrugged. "Don't worry about it."

"I'll wash it for you."

"Whatever." He grinned when the child put her hands on his face and turned it to look at her. "You rang?"

She pointed in the general direction of the backyard. "Go 'side?"

Sloan met Maggie's gaze. "Is it okay if I take her out?"

"You don't have to—"

"I know. But I wouldn't have offered if I didn't want to. Is it all right with you?"

"Yes," she said helplessly.

"Okay, then. Let's go, Shorty."

Maggie's heart melted at the sight of the big man carrying her little girl out of the room.

"I don't remember any story in the tabloids about him having kids," Josie said. "But he sure is good with yours."

"I noticed."

Charming, good with kids and not hard on the eyes. Sloan Holden was a triple threat. But he must have a flaw. Every man did.

Chapter Two

In Sloan's opinion, Danielle Potter was the spitting image of her mother, minus the wariness in her big brown eyes. Or maybe it was sadness. Losing a husband must have been rough, especially the part where she was raising a child on her own. He set the little girl down on the patio and her feet had barely touched the ground before she headed for the grass, still wet with morning dew. It was early March, not quite spring, and a bit chilly. But the sun was shining in a clear blue sky that promised a beautiful day ahead.

He'd never before been responsible for a child. Ever. How hard could it be? Glancing around the big yard made him glad it was fenced in and the wrought iron bars were too close together for the toddler to squeeze through. He knew because that was the first thing she tried. After a quick check, he was satisfied that the gates on either side were secure and there would be no escape that way.

Sloan watched her squat and touch something with her tiny, probing finger. Bug? Snake? In two long strides he was beside her. "Whatcha got there, Shorty?"

She pointed to something he couldn't see and a stream of unintelligible sounds came out of her mouth. The expression on her face said she was looking for an appropriate response from him, but he had nothing. That happened when the party with whom you were conversing spoke a foreign language known only to herself, and possibly her mother.

"Is it grass?" He looked closer, hoping there was no dangerous, venomous creature lurking that would force him to do something manly, like deal with it.

She shook her head, then stood and toddled over to an area with bushes surrounded by bark chips to set it off from the grass. He was almost sure he'd heard somewhere that bugs collected in this environment, and it seemed like a bad idea to let her continue to explore unchaperoned.

Glancing around, he saw a brightly colored swing set with a slide and climbing equipment all rolled into one. Clearly it was there for Danielle's pleasure, so maybe he could channel her attention in that direction. And away from insect central.

He scooped her up in his arms, which set off instant rebellion. Sloan's response to this was a revelation. Size and strength were on his side and ought to count for something but really didn't. He would give her anything she wanted to make her happy.

"Want to go on the slide?" He held her high above him, pleased when she giggled. "I'll take that as a yes."

He set her at the top of the thing. It wasn't that high, but he was loath to let go and give her over to the unpredictability of gravity. It was remarkably astonishing to him how powerful his urge was to protect this small girl he'd voluntarily taken responsibility for. He held on to her as she slid down the short slide, then helped steady her at the bottom.

"Again," she said very clearly.

"Okay. And we have a winner." The sense of accomplishment he experienced at pleasing her wasn't all that dissimilar from the satisfaction he felt at overcoming a particularly challenging construction problem.

Sloan set her at the top of the structure and held on a little more loosely this time, although he was ready to scoop her up if the situation went south. Fortunately it didn't.

She grinned up at him and said, "Again."

"Your wish is my command, milady."

But before he could lift her up, the back door opened and Maggie stood there.

"Mama. Cookie," Danielle said, toddling over to her mother.

"Breakfast first." She met his gaze and there was a dash of respect in hers. "It's ready. Thanks to you for entertaining her."

"The pleasure was mine." He truly meant that. "I enjoyed hanging out with her."

"You're very good with her. Do you spend a lot of time with kids?"

"Actually, no. That was a first for me," he admitted.

"So you're a natural. Someone should alert the paparazzi," she teased.

"Oh, please no. I'll give you anything to keep my secret."

"You might change your mind after breakfast. And you must be starving. Everything is on the dining room table. Help yourself." She grabbed up her daughter and settled the child on her hip. "I'll get this one fed in the kitchen. So you can have some peace and quiet. If you're interested, I've set out newspapers—local and national."

"Thanks." Sloan was less interested in newsprint than he was the sight in front of him—the beautiful young mother snuggling her rosy-cheeked toddler close.

He understood her struggle to make a home for boarders while carving out a private space for her own family, but would rather have filled a plate and followed the two of them to the kitchen.

That was different.

An hour later, after changing out of his banana-slimed shirt into a clean one, Sloan drove into the parking lot of the O'Keefe Building, where his cousin Burke had rented office space. Maggie's brother, Brady, had built the place for his tech company's corporate office. At this point there was more room than he needed for his business, so he leased out the extra space. Sloan figured since he'd be working under the same roof as Brady, their paths would cross, and he was looking forward to meeting Maggie's brother.

Having visited on more than one occasion, Sloan knew where his cousin's office was located. After pushing the button for the correct floor, he rode the elevator up. The car stopped and the doors opened into a spacious waiting area. There was a reception desk straight ahead where Burke's assistant, Lydia, normally sat. She wasn't there now, so he walked over to the closed door, knocked once, then went inside.

"Hey, Burke, I—"

Sloan stopped dead in his tracks. His cousin was there, all right, holding a beautiful brunette in his arms while kissing her soundly. He recognized the lady. Sydney McKnight, Burke's fiancée. The scene in front of him was different from the usual all-work-all-the-time environment, and Sloan was beginning to wonder if he'd taken a tumble down the rabbit hole. His morning had started off with him entertaining a two-year-old before breakfast— not what normally happened in the five-star hotels he frequented, although not altogether objectionable, either. He'd been complimented on everything from his business expertise to the length of his eyelashes. But never had a flattering remark pleased him more than Maggie saying he was good with kids.

Now he'd accidentally intruded on a private moment. Instead of looking embarrassed, Burke proudly held on to his woman and grinned.

"Sloan," he said, "welcome to Blackwater Lake. You know Sydney."

"I do." He closed the door and moved closer to the desk, a little surprised his cousin hadn't brushed aside all the files and paperwork to have Sydney right there. Then again, Burke was a professional and would never do anything to compromise his employees or the woman he loved...no matter how much the intense expression in his blue eyes said he wanted her. "Hi, Syd."

"Sloan." She managed to wriggle out of Burke's arms and stood beside him, her cheeks a becoming shade of pink. "How are you?"

"Fine." Mostly. But he was feeling a little weird about this encounter and not entirely sure why. "Do I need to ask how you two are?"

"Spectacular," Sydney said, gazing up with love in her eyes at the man next to her, then back to him. "Very glad to see you."

"I doubt that," Sloan said, "but I'll play. Why are you glad to see me?"

"My reasons are purely selfish." She shrugged.

"You mean, it has nothing to do with you pining after me?" he teased.

"Sorry." She glanced up at her fiancé. "With you here, Burke will have help shouldering the workload and maybe have more time for me."

"Ah."

"You know if I were single I'd do it for you, cuz." Burke

looked and sounded like the soul of innocence, but it was an act.

"You're full of it." Sloan met his cousin's gaze. "But because I like Sydney, I'm happy to pick up any slack so the two of you can have couple time."

"Family time, really," Burke amended. "We try to include Liam as much as possible."

Sloan knew Burke and his son, Liam, had been through a rough patch when they moved to Blackwater Lake. Syd had been a bridge over troubled waters. But that had worked both ways when Burke had helped to convince her widower dad that she didn't have to be settled in a relationship before he could move on with his life. As it happened, the two of them had ended up falling in love and Burke had proposed a couple of months ago at her father's wedding to Loretta Goodson, the mayor of Blackwater Lake, Montana.

"How's Liam adjusting?" Sloan asked.

"Great." Burke looked thoughtful. "He's got friends. He's playing sports and doing well in school."

"That's good to hear." Sloan heard an edge to the words and hoped no one else had. It wasn't that he begrudged his cousin's happiness, but this whole perfect-life, happily-ever-after thing was starting to make his teeth hurt.

"Well," Syd said, "I have to get to work. My boss is very demanding."

Sloan knew she worked for her dad at the family-owned garage in downtown Blackwater Lake. Even if he hadn't, her khaki pants and matching shirt with a McKnight Automotive logo on the pocket would have been a clue.

Burke leaned down and kissed her lightly on the mouth. "Have a great day. Say hi to your dad for me."

"Will do." She walked to the door. "See you later, Sloan."

"Right. 'Bye, Syd."

When they were alone, he sat in one of the chairs facing his cousin's desk. "She's too good for you, Burke."

"Don't tell her that. I want to pull the wool over her eyes until we're married and she's stuck with me." He stared longingly at the door where she'd disappeared. "All I can do is my damnedest every day to be the best man I can be and make her happy."

If he had any doubts about his cousin's commitment to Sydney, they would have disappeared at the lovelorn expression on his face. Sloan had mixed feelings. On one hand, he was very glad to see Burke so happy. On the other, he knew this signaled the end of any bachelor-type fun with his best friend.

And suddenly it hit him what had been bothering him since walking in on Syd and Burke. He felt as if he was on the outside looking in. Alone. Lonely and a little bit envious. What a shallow bastard he was, with a healthy dose of selfishness thrown in for good measure.

Until this moment, he hadn't realized how much he'd been looking forward to hanging out with Burke and doing what bachelors did. Commitment changed everything and for Burke's sake, he hoped it was for the better. For Sloan's sake, it wasn't, but he couldn't help thinking about his luscious landlady and the until-death-do-us-part vow she'd made to the man she'd loved and lost. Had it been worth the price she'd paid and was still paying?

That thought made him more curious than he wanted to be about Maggie Potter.

In her office above the Harvest Café, Maggie stared at the spreadsheet displayed on her computer monitor. A few minutes ago the numbers had all looked good, but now she couldn't tell. Her eyes were starting to cross and everything blurred together.

When her vision cleared, she glanced at her watch and couldn't believe it was already two-thirty in the afternoon. On top of that, she hadn't eaten lunch. Downstairs the noon rush was probably over, making this a good time to grab some food.

She took the stairway right outside her office and walked down to the first floor, entering the café through a back entrance into the kitchen. The bowls, plates and utensils in the stainless-steel sink and on food preparation areas showed signs of exactly how rushed the rush had been, and it was good news for their bottom line. Her partner was standing in the doorway between front and back, keeping an eye out for customers.

"My head is about to explode," Maggie said. "Any chance of getting something to eat?"

Lucy Bishop smiled the smile that could have put her on magazine covers in swimsuits if her career path had taken her in that direction. Fortunately for Maggie, her friend was more interested in business than bikinis. She was a gorgeous, blue-eyed strawberry blonde who was forever being underestimated by men. It was immensely entertaining to watch them swallow their tongues and lose brain function in her presence.

"How about one of my world-famous chicken wraps with the secret sauce?"

"I don't expect you to wait on me. You've been busy, too. I'll make something myself."

"Keep protesting," Lucy said. "By the time you run out of steam I'll have your order up."

Maggie heard the words but they didn't register. Her attention was focused on the sidewalk outside the café and the man who'd just parked his Range Rover in a space out front.

Sloan Holden.

The problem with taking a break from hard work was that there wasn't anything to distract you from things you'd been deliberately not thinking about. Like seeing this big, strong man being gentle and protective with her daughter that morning. She couldn't reconcile that man with the one who was a global heartbreaker.

The real question was why she didn't want to think about him, and the best answer she could come up with was that he unsettled her.

"Maggie?"

"Hmm?" She looked at Lucy. "I'm sorry. What did you say?"

"I'm making you a wrap." Her partner automatically looked over when the door opened and Sloan walked in. She made a purring sound and said, "Right after I have that man's baby. Holy Toledo, he's a fifteen on a scale of one to ten."

"And he's my newest boarder."

"Sloan Holden?" Lucy lowered her voice but turned her back on the newcomer just to make sure he didn't hear.

"That's him," she confirmed.

"You have to introduce me."

"Of course," Maggie said, then the two of them walked over to where he stood by the sign that politely asked customers to wait to be seated. "Hi."

"Maggie." His gaze slid to her partner. "I've heard nothing but good things about the food here and decided to see for myself if the rumors are true."

"They're true," Maggie confirmed. "And that is all due to the culinary skills of my business partner. Sloan Holden, this is Lucy Bishop."

"Nice to meet you." He held out his hand.

Lucy shook it. "The pleasure is all mine. Isn't it a little late for lunch? Or is this an early dinner?"

"Lunch. I lost track of time."

"I always say it takes a special kind of stupid to forget to eat."

Maggie watched Lucy give him the smile that had made many a man putty in her hands, but Sloan didn't bat an eye.

"Then, label me a moron because that's the best excuse I can come up with," he said.

"You're in good company." Lucy met her gaze. "Maggie just surfaced, too, and realized she hadn't eaten."

"Then, you should keep me company. I hate to eat alone," he said. "And we dim-witted workaholics should stick together."

"Thanks," she said, "but I'm just going to take something back to my desk."

"I don't recommend that." He raised an eyebrow. "A break from work is food for the soul. That's just as important as nutrition for the body."

There was no graceful way out of this, so she was better off just sucking it up. "You're right. Let's sit over there."

The place was empty of customers at the moment and Maggie pointed to a table in a far corner that wasn't visible through the front window. She grabbed a couple of menus and followed him. He was wearing dark slacks and a pale yellow dress shirt, different from the one her daughter had streaked banana on early this morning.

She was very proud of the way the café had turned out. The interior was decorated in fall colors—orange, gold, green and brown. The walls had country touches: an old washboard, shelves with metal pitchers and pictures of fruit and vegetables. It was cozy and comfortable. But probably light-years from the places Sloan went to.

They sat at a small round table covered by a leaf-print tablecloth. Two sets of utensils wrapped in ginger-colored napkins rested on either side.

After looking over the choices, he met her gaze. "What do you recommend?"

"Everything." She smiled. "Obviously I'm prejudiced, but even the vegetarian selections are yummy. But my favorite is the chicken wrap. Lucy makes a dressing that is truly unbelievably good."

"Sold," he said.

When Lucy came over, they both ordered it and she promised to bring them out in a few minutes.

Maggie was watching Sloan's face when Lucy walked away and saw the barest flicker of male appreciation. She felt a flicker of something herself and wasn't sure what to call it. Envy? A visceral response? Whatever the label, she didn't especially like the feeling and wanted to counteract it.

"She's really pretty, isn't she?"

Sloan met her gaze. "Yes, she is."

"This small town is probably very different from what you're used to." Maggie knew that for a fact just from reading tabloid stories about him. "It can be lonely."

"There's lots of work to keep me busy."

"I heard somewhere that breaks from work are food for the soul as important as nutrition for the body."

His expression was wry. "Remind me to be careful what I say to you."

"My point is—and I do have one—you should ask Lucy out," she said.

"Oh?" There was curiosity in his expression, but he also looked amused.

"Yes. She's beautiful and smart. Not to mention an awesome cook."

"Until our food arrives, I'll have to take your word on her culinary ability. And we barely spoke, so it was hard to tell whether or not she's smart. But she is very pretty."

"So ask her out." The little bit Lucy had said was a big clue that she wouldn't say no. Maggie unrolled the silverware from her napkin and set it on the table.

"Why should I?" he asked.

"She's single. And so are you." She settled the cloth napkin in her lap. "Unless you're dating someone."

"I'm not." He met her gaze. "But it's a well-documented fact that I'm a confirmed bachelor."

"I have read that you have a reputation for quantity over commitment. But Lucy isn't looking for Mr. Right."

"Any particular reason?"

Yes, but Maggie had no intention of saying anything about that to Sloan, mostly because she didn't know why. Instead, she countered, "Any particular reason you won't commit?"

For the first time since he'd walked into the café the amiable and amused expression on his face cracked slightly. She'd struck a nerve, and that was annoying because she hadn't thought he had any.

"Why does any man resist committing?" he said, not really answering.

"Good question. Color me curious. And all the more determined to convince you to ask Lucy out on a date."

"For the life of me, I can't figure out what your stake is in my personal life."

"That's because you don't understand the fundamental dynamics of female friendship."

"Enlighten me."

"Communication and sharing," she said. "I'm curious about the man behind the tabloid headlines. Lucy could find out so much if you'd take her out to dinner. And she would tell me everything."

"Since you're the inquiring mind who wants to know,

why don't I cut out the middleman—or woman—and just take you out to dinner."

"Really?" She stared at him. "A widow with a small child?"

"Neither of those things means you can't go out with me. You may have heard. There are these handy-dandy people called babysitters."

That would only address the problem of what to do with Danielle when Maggie went out. She would still be a widow. But she had one irrefutable argument left.

"Look, Sloan, we both know I'm not the type of woman you go out with. In fact, just the opposite. I'm a business-woman and mother."

"True." His eyes narrowed on her. "But what if this is a conscious choice on my part to date a woman who is the polar opposite of my usual type? And I've simply used the tabloids and their stories to throw everyone off my real purpose? A deflection."

"You don't mean you're actually interested in some-one like me?"

"Don't I?"

Maggie had thought she had the upper hand in this ver-bal give-and-take. That she had him on the run. But his response stopped her cold. Of course, he was teasing. He had to be.

"Like I said—quantity over commitment. When would you have the time to troll for an ordinary woman?"

"You'd be surprised."

"We're talking about you," she said. "Nothing would surprise me."

"I'll take that as a challenge, Maggie Potter."

"If you're planning a campaign just to surprise me, I'd have to say that you have way too much time on your hands."

"Would it surprise you to know that I would really just like to get to know you?"

"Now you're simply trying to get a rise out of me. It's not going to work."

"We'll just have to wait and see." He studied her, and the intensity was disconcerting. "But I sense you pushing me away and can't help wondering about it. You don't go out, do you? Why is that? Why do you keep to yourself? Is there a reason you won't let yourself be happy?"

"I have priorities," she said. "And how do you know I don't go out? I'm perfectly capable of being happy. In fact, I am very happy."

And defensive, she realized. Pride went before a fall and it was a long way down when she'd thought she had him right where she wanted him.

Note to self, she thought. *Never underestimate this man.*

Chapter Three

"I love my daughter more than life itself, but I feel crushing shame for leaving her with my mom and enjoying myself with you guys."

Maggie was sitting at a bistro table in Bar None, Blackwater Lake's local drinking establishment, with her friends April Kennedy and Delanie Carlson. The latter had inherited the place from her dad, who had died the previous year.

"What you're experiencing is a curious phenomenon. It even has a name. Mom guilt," Delanie said.

She was another woman who made men turn into mindless idiots just by walking into a room. A blue-eyed redhead, she had just the right curves to fill out a pair of jeans. It was a weeknight and traditionally slow at Bar None, which made it ideal for their weekly evening out.

"I remember my mom saying the same thing." April tossed a strand of sun-streaked brown hair over her shoulder as a bittersweet expression slid into her hazel eyes. "She couldn't wait to get time to herself, but when it happened she missed me like crazy. I still miss her a lot."

"So it is a mom thing." Maggie took a sip of chardonnay, then looked at April, who had lost her mother to breast cancer. "And what you just said gives me hope and inspiration."

"How?"

"You were raised by a single mom. No dad in the picture. And you turned out okay. A successful businesswoman with your photography shop on Main Street."

"If I say I think my mother did a great job with me, does that sound conceited?"

"Of course not," Delanie answered. "It's just the truth."

Maggie looked forward to this night out with her friends. She'd cooked dinner for her boarders and Josie had agreed to get it on the table for Sloan. Whenever he was around, Maggie was jittery and nervous, so it was a relief to have an evening off.

"And what about you, Dee?" she asked. "How are you doing since your dad passed away? I know you two were close."

"I miss him." Delanie looked around the place she now owned.

The interior reflected the Montana pioneer spirit—rugged and rustic. Overhead, dark beams ran the length of the ceiling and the still-original floor was fashioned from wood planks. Lantern-shaped lights illuminated the booths lining the exterior and bistro tables scattered throughout. A rectangular oak bar with a brass foot rail dominated the center of the room, and pictures of the earliest Blackwater Lake settlers with shovels, axes and covered wagons hung on the walls.

Delanie glanced at her friends. "This may sound corny, but I can feel him here. Sort of a presence. It's comforting."

"That's good." Maggie envied her friend. She'd never experienced comfort or felt Danny's presence in the house he'd built for her. And when she looked at the daughter they'd made, sometimes she felt a guilt that had nothing to do with being a good mom and everything to do with a wife who'd let her husband down. He'd never had a chance to see his child.

"Okay, ladies," Dee said. "This conversation has taken a dark and twisty turn. I took the night off and am paying Savannah to pour drinks so that I can have a distraction from work."

April laughed. "Then, we picked the wrong place to distract you."

"There aren't a lot of places to go in a town this small," Maggie commented.

"That's going to change when the resort is built. Mark my words." April nodded knowingly. "Maybe you can convince your new boarder the builder to put up a movie theater."

"Or a shopping mall." Delanie's blue eyes took on a dreamy look. "I would happily indulge my love affair with shoes, especially the ones I didn't have to drive an hour to buy."

The other two thought about that and sighed dreamily.

"So what's he like?" Delanie asked. "I saw Lucy the other day and she said Sloan Holden came into the café and had lunch with you."

"What did Lucy say about him?" Maggie hedged.

"That he's charming and handsome."

Maggie's heart started beating just a little too fast as soon as his name came up. For the past couple of days she'd seen him at breakfast and dinner. And that one day for lunch. He was unfailingly polite, undemanding, and her daughter followed him around whenever she saw him. But what distracted Maggie most was what he'd said at lunch, the hint that he'd used serial dating as a cover until he found someone like her.

Surely he'd been teasing. Although, if he really was anticommitment, hooking up with a widow who wasn't interested in a relationship would certainly preserve his confirmed-bachelor status.

"So, is he?" April demanded.

Maggie blinked at her friends. "What?"

"Pay attention, Potter," Dee scolded. "Is he charming and handsome?"

"Oh, I'm not the best person to ask."

"Come on," April said. "You're a woman and you're breathing. We've watched movies together and rated the actors on a scale. If you can do that, you can give us an opinion."

"Since he's a paying customer, it seems unprofessional to talk about him like this."

Delanie frowned at her. "What's up? It isn't like you not to share."

"I'm uncomfortable with the one-to-ten thing."

"Okay. We'll compare him to actors and see how he holds up. I'll start." April took a sip of her wine. "Channing Tatum."

"Ooh," Maggie said. "But no. Sloan is in good shape, but more like a runner than a wrestler."

"Okay. How about Taylor Kitsch?" Delanie shrugged. "I just rented the movie *Battleship*. It was cheesy, but I loved it."

Maggie knew the actor and thought for a moment, then shook her head. "He and Chris Pratt are a similar type and both are fantasy-worthy, but I wouldn't say Sloan resembles them."

"Definitely fantasy material," April agreed. "I just saw the musical *Into the Woods* and I have to say that Chris Pine works for me in a big way as Prince Charming."

"Bingo," Maggie said. "He reminds me of Chris Pine, but with brown eyes and darker hair."

Delanie used her hand to fan herself. "Be still, my heart. And he's under your roof. How do you sleep at night?"

"Oh, you know. Exhausted after work, cooking for boarders and chasing after a toddler. I just close my eyes and…" *Think about being alone in my big bed while Sloan is alone in his on the second floor of my house.* "I'm sure you'll both get a chance to meet him. This is a small town and—"

The bell over the bar's front door tinkled and all three women looked over to see who'd walked in. Maggie instantly recognized Sloan, who smiled when he saw her.

"That's him," she whispered to her friends. "Sloan Holden."

Without hesitation, he walked over to their table. "Hi, Maggie. Mind if I join you ladies?"

Before Maggie could think of a way to discourage him, her two friends enthusiastically invited him to pull up a chair. He did and settled in right next to her.

"So you're Sloan Holden," Delanie said.

"Yes." He shook hands with her and April as they introduced themselves.

"What are you doing here?" Maggie asked. Then she realized that sounded just the tiniest bit abrupt and unwelcoming. "I mean, did you have dinner? Josie promised to put everything on the table for me. Since my mom has Danielle, it's a chance for me to have a night off."

"Yes, I did have dinner. Excellent pot roast, by the way. Josie mentioned that you were here and I felt like taking a night off myself."

The implication was that he'd come looking for her. Whether or not that was the case, the idea of it kicked up her pulse.

"Delanie owns Bar None," Maggie said.

He looked at the redhead. "I'm impressed. This is a nice place."

"Thanks. Would you like a drink?"

"Beer," he said. "Whatever you have on draft."

"Coming right up." Delanie slid off her chair and headed over to the bar, where the fill-in bartender was polishing glasses. She said something and the young woman grabbed a tall glass and filled it.

"April owns a photography studio," Maggie said, filling the silence.

"I've seen it." Sloan looked at the pretty brunette but gave no indication he noticed how pretty she was. "How's business?"

"A little slow when it's not ski or boating season. Tourism drops off then, but I diversify. Besides portraits and wedding pictures, I sell my photographs of landscapes and wildlife. I freelance for high school events and sometimes the sheriff's office needs photos taken."

"Sounds like you keep busy."

Delanie returned and set a glass on a napkin in front of him. "Welcome to Bar None. First one is on the house."

"Thank you."

For several moments, the four of them sipped their drinks in silence. Maggie could tell her friends felt a little uncomfortable after talking about him. Then he'd walked in and it was a little like getting caught with their hands in the cookie jar. She was preoccupied because his thigh kept brushing hers. He seemed bigger at this bistro table than he did in her dining room. She needed to act normal because her friends would notice, but she didn't feel at all normal around Sloan.

"So, Mr. Holden—"

"Sloan, please," he said.

"Sloan," April finally said. "I have a confession to make."

"Yeah. We need to come clean," Delanie chimed in, obviously aware of what her friend was going to say. "We were talking about you when you came in. Gossiping, really."

"Oh?" Sloan didn't look the least bit upset.

April nodded. "For the record, Maggie protected the privacy of her guest and wouldn't cooperate. The thing is, this is a small town and not much happens. People gossip anyway. But when we have a celebrity, there's going to be talk. And Bar None is gossip central, so we were doing our duty as loyal customers and citizens of Blackwater Lake."

"I see your point." Sloan held up his beer mug, signaling a toast. "To loyalty."

They all clinked glasses and sipped.

"What do you want to know about me?" Sloan asked.

"So many things, so little time." Delanie grinned. "Okay, since you volunteered… Why are you a confirmed bachelor?"

"Because I was married for fifteen minutes and found out I'm not good at it." The answer was straightforward, matter-of-fact. No tension or evidence he'd been deeply hurt.

And then his muscular thigh bumped against Maggie's and her nerves snapped, crackled and popped. Her gaze jumped to his and she saw laughter in his eyes. The table was small, but she would bet that he was deliberately touching her.

"What if you fall in love?" April wanted to know.

"I don't believe in it. Simple, uncomplicated and fun. That's all I'm looking for."

"You're honest. That's pretty cute." Delanie looked impressed. "But I think you should have that sentiment stitched on a sampler and mounted on the wall of your office."

"Great idea. I'll get my assistant right on that."

"Not if you want her to continue being your assistant," Maggie said.

"You're probably right. Next question."

"Can we talk you into building a movie theater in Blackwater Lake? Maybe a multiplex?"

"Why?"

"Someplace to go if we had a date," Delanie said.

"If?" He looked at each of them in turn, but his gaze settled on Maggie. "Now that I think about it, why are three beautiful ladies such as yourselves not on a date right now?"

"Who says we want to date?" Maggie answered, thinking about what he'd said to her, about her not wanting to be happy. "We are successful businesswomen—fulfilled and content without a man."

"Is it just me," he said to April and Delanie, "or does she sound defensive?"

Why was he going there? Maggie thought. The last time they'd talked, he'd agreed that she wasn't his type. So why was he zeroing in on her? She didn't for a second buy his story about using tabloid interviews referencing him being a confirmed bachelor as a cover to look for someone like her. And then it dawned on her that he was flirting. It took a while to recognize the behavior because no one had flirted with her in a very long time.

"Not defensive." She smiled at him and crossed one leg over the other. The movement brought their thighs into contact and she saw his eyes darken for a second. "Just telling it like it is."

"So that's what you say to all the guys?"

"No," she said. "Just the ones who sell newspapers because of their escapades with women."

The zinger made him grin and she felt that look all the

way to her toes. She smiled back at him and realized she'd forgotten how much fun flirting could be.

When Sloan got back to the house after leaving the bar, he poured himself a scotch from the bottle his assistant had requested for his room and took the tumbler outside. It was a beautiful March night—cool, crisp, clear. He didn't think he'd ever seen a more spectacular sky full of stars.

A little while ago he'd heard Maggie come home with Danielle. The open master-bedroom window backed up to the patio where he was sitting and the sounds of giggling and splashing drifted to him. It was bath time and all indications pointed to the fact that the girls were having a blast.

For some reason it made him feel lonely, again on the outside looking in. Especially after hanging out with Maggie at Bar None. She'd actually flirted with him and rubbed her leg against his, mostly, he suspected, because she was aware that he'd been deliberately doing that to her. He grinned at the memory even as his body grew hard with need. The attraction was unexpected and inconvenient, and he should have known better than to start something he had no intention of finishing. He'd been playing with fire and the burning inside him now was his punishment.

The voices inside the house became more subdued and then the light went off. Moonlight was now the only light source in the rear yard. He was almost sure Maggie was singing to her daughter, and then all was quiet. Moments later, he heard the microwave go on in the kitchen. The outside door opened and Maggie stepped onto the patio.

Sloan was pretty sure she didn't see him, because she stood still, looking at the sky and taking deep, cleansing breaths. He figured it would be best to warn her she wasn't alone.

"Maggie—"

"Dear God—" She jumped and let out a screech, pressing a hand to her chest. "You scared me."

"Sorry."

"I thought you'd be upstairs."

"No. I wanted some air," he explained.

"Me, too." She blew out a long breath then met his gaze.

She was close enough that he could reach out and touch her. He really wanted to, which meant it probably wasn't a very good idea.

"It's a beautiful night," he said.

"I don't want to intrude. And I didn't have dinner. I just put a plate in the microwave. You were here first."

"Is there anything in the Potter House rules that says we can't enjoy the fresh air together?"

"Of course not." Moonlight revealed her mouth curving up in a smile.

"Danielle is settled for the night?"

"She is."

"Then, you should take some time to enjoy the beauty of your own backyard." He saw her catch her bottom lip between her teeth and need sliced through him, sharp and deep. "I'll bet you don't do it very much."

"You'd win that bet."

"Take a chance, Potter. Throw caution to the wind. Five minutes to fill up your soul."

She sighed and he knew he'd won this round. There was a thickly padded chair at a right angle to his and she lowered herself into it.

"No guilt allowed." In front of him her friends had teased her about feeling guilty for enjoying an evening away from her daughter. "Whatever you have to do inside will still be there when your spirit is renewed."

"That's for sure," she agreed. "Somehow the B and B

fairies never make it here to get breakfast ready or do laundry."

"It's just sad. You can't get good fairy help these days."

She laughed. "You're very funny, Sloan."

"I'm glad you think so."

"April and Delanie thought so, too." She met his gaze. "They told me after you left."

"So that's why my ears were burning."

"Oh, please. A man who spends as much time as you do with a vast number of women couldn't possibly be surprised that we talked about you after you left."

"I'm not at all surprised. Especially since your friends came right out and copped to the fact that you were discussing me before I got there."

"You gotta love honest gossipmongers," she pointed out.

"It was refreshing. And I liked your friends very much."

"As I said, the feeling is mutual. You were exceptionally charming tonight, Holden."

"I did my best."

"Do you remember when you said we could ask you anything?"

"Yes."

"Well, you may also recall that I never asked a question at all."

He did. "I'm sensing that you would like to now. Am I right?"

"Yes. And I have several, if that's okay."

"Should I be afraid?"

"I promise it won't hurt," she said.

"Okay, then." He set his empty tumbler on the outside coffee table. "What would you like to know?"

"Did you follow me to Bar None tonight?"

"That makes me sound like a stalker," he hedged.

"Are you?"

"Wow. I'm not sure if going from serial killer to stalker is a step up."

She folded her arms over her chest. "You're very good at not answering questions."

"Lots of practice," he admitted. "Okay. It's a hard habit to break, but I'll stop sidestepping. When Josie mentioned that you were meeting friends it sounded like fun and I did deliberately crash the party."

He couldn't speak to how hard it was being a single mom and needing some downtime. But he knew how it felt to be a fish out of water, a big fish in a little pond and craving some social time. Not to mention being curious about Maggie. He braced himself for a grilling about following her.

"Why would you do that?"

"I needed to talk to someone about something other than work."

"Oh." She nodded. "I understand that. And then my friends asked you to build a movie theater."

"It's actually a great idea. The resort is going to bring in a lot of people. They'll be looking for entertainment involving something other than skiing or boating and water sports."

"Speaking of entertainment…" She tapped her lip. "Is it true that a woman once broke into your hotel room and waited in your bed? Naked?"

He groaned. "Don't remind me."

"So it is true." She leaned forward, warming to her subject. "You make it sound like a bad thing."

"By definition, breaking into my hotel room *is* bad."

"Surely not the naked part." Her tone was teasing.

"Whose side are you on? I was the injured party."

"You sound like an outraged spinster. I don't understand your problem. Was she fat? Cellulite? Abs weren't prime-time ready?"

"She had a lovely body. Hotel security thought so, too, as did the police. Why would this be okay because I'm a guy? She violated my personal space."

"I see what you mean." She scooted to the edge of her chair. "There was another story about you spending millions of dollars on breakup baubles."

"Baubles?" That's one he hadn't heard. Apparently he wasn't aware of all his publicity.

"Yes. Diamond tennis bracelets. Emerald pendants. Sapphire earrings. If this is true, it could explain why women throw themselves at you. Naked," she added.

"For the tasteful parting gift?"

"Yes. That's a heck of a consolation prize."

"Well, it's not true." The only woman who'd received a significant parting gift was his wife when he divorced her for cheating on him. Getting rid of her had been worth every penny it had cost him. He didn't care so much for himself. The mistake had been his, as were the consequences. But she'd hurt his family and he'd paid the price of protecting them. And he would do it again if necessary.

"There was another story that got a lot of attention. Something about you not being very good in bed. And a very bad kisser."

"Your friends didn't ask this many questions," he pointed out.

"Maybe their minds aren't as inquiring as mine. In all fairness, less-than-satisfied lady was one of the women scorned and the story had all the signs of being about revenge."

He stood. "How do you remember this stuff?"

"It's fascinating." She stood up, too.

"Well, I feel like an exhibit at the zoo." He was an inch

away from her, close enough to feel the warmth of her body and smell the sweet scent of her skin. "I think I hear the microwave signaling your plate of food is warm."

"So was it about revenge? Or are you lacking in the romance department?"

"Is there any way to make you stop this interrogation?"

"Feed me." She met his gaze and there was a sassy expression on her face. "Or kiss me."

It wasn't often that someone surprised Sloan, but Maggie did now. He remembered her saying this wouldn't hurt a bit, but now he wasn't so sure. The question was whether or not it would hurt more if he *didn't* kiss her. Hell and damnation, this was a dilemma. But he didn't get where he was in the business world by not taking a risk.

He curved his fingers around her upper arms and pulled her close, his gaze intent on her mouth. "I'll take door number two."

Chapter Four

Maggie had no idea why she'd dared Sloan to feed or kiss her, but when his lips touched hers she was really glad he'd picked the second option. His mouth was soft, gentle, tentative and tempting all at the same time. Her heart was racing and her knees were weak, but he was holding her and she trusted him not to let her go.

He whispered against her mouth, "Any more questions?"

"Hmm?" The only question on her mind was why he wasn't still kissing her. "I can't think of any."

"Okay, then." He slid his arms around her and pulled her close, then kissed her again.

It felt so good to be held and touched, wrapped in a pair of strong arms and pressed against a man's body. She was pretty sure her toes were actually curling, and it was the most wonderful thing that had happened to her for longer than she could remember.

Time seemed to stop and she wanted to stay suspended in this sensuous dimension. Right here, right now, while she kissed Sloan Holden on her patio under the stars, there was no guilt, worry or doubt about being a single mom. She was simply a woman enjoying everything about being female and savoring this bold man who wasn't afraid of a challenge. Sloan slid his fingers into her hair, cupping her head to make the pressure of their mouths more firm. His breathing was unsteady and it was thrilling to know she'd affected him, too.

And then she heard Danielle cry out. The sound came through the open window and reality rushed back like a slap in the face. She was a mother first and foremost. Maggie froze, waiting, and the sound came again, pouring in along with guilt, worry and even more doubt about her ability to do a decent job of raising her child alone. Look how easily this man had distracted her.

She took two steps back, away from the warmth of his body, and hating herself for missing it. "I need to check on my daughter."

"Right. Of course." He dragged his fingers through his hair. "Do I need to apologize for that?"

"Is that what your gut is telling you to do?"

He shook his head. "But the look on your face right now is making me think it might be a good idea."

What he was seeing on her face probably had more to do with astonishment. She had believed the part of her that could be turned on had died with her husband. But she was so wrong. Sloan had stirred something up and she wanted to settle it back down again.

"There's nothing to be sorry for. It was my fault." She played with her fingers, twisting them together nervously. "I have to go to Danielle."

And begin the process of forgetting about this kiss.

Several days went by and Maggie realized she was looking at time passing and putting it in two columns: before and after that kiss. She saw Sloan at breakfast and dinner, doing her best to go back to being his hospitable, professional but friendly landlady and not the woman who'd challenged him to kiss her. She talked to him as little as possible and he didn't push the issue by striking up a conversation. And there was a conclusion to be drawn from that. He regretted the kiss, too.

She set a platter of scrambled eggs and hash browns on the dining room table, where Sloan and Josie were sitting. The fruit and freshly baked muffins were already there.

"Can I freshen anyone's coffee?" she asked.

"I'm good." Sloan barely glanced up from the newspaper he was reading.

"Me, too." Josie was giving her a quizzical look.

"All right, then. Let me know if you need anything." She left the room.

Her daughter sat in the high chair eating half a banana. If she hadn't been, she would have been bugging Sloan. As if Maggie needed another one, that was a good reason to back off from him. And that was what she'd been doing, pretty successfully, in her opinion.

A half hour later, Sloan said goodbye and headed for the door. Danielle called out, "Bye-bye," and wiggled her fingers in her version of a wave. That earned the little girl a big grin from Sloan, but Maggie was the one who felt the power of it. And a pang of disappointment that he hadn't aimed the warmth at her.

Josie brought plates and platters into the kitchen. "Are you going to tell me what's going on?"

"I'd be happy to if you'd be more specific."

The other woman started rinsing off plates and putting them in the dishwasher. "I'm talking about you and Sloan. Since he arrived, there's been a nice friendly vibe going on between the two of you. And in the past couple days it's changed. You barely speak, and it can only be described as awkward. What the heck happened?"

That kiss happened, Maggie thought. She'd gone over it a thousand times. He never would have done it if she hadn't put the suggestion out there. Over and over she wondered why she had. Maybe the glass of wine. Possibly it was all the flirty talk and leg touching while sitting beside him at Bar None. The lingering effects of that might have made those fateful words come out of her mouth. Oh, how she wanted them back.

Josie was a friend as well as one of her boarders. But Maggie was proceeding on the hope that not talking about what happened on the patio would make it go away.

"You think we're acting awkward?"

"And how." Standing by the sink, Josie put a hand on her hip. "And don't think I didn't notice that you just answered a question with a question and gave no information at all."

Maggie was kind of hoping that one had slipped by, but no such luck. "Would I do that?"

"Seriously, Maggie? You just did it again. That only confirms my suspicion that there's something going on with the two of you."

"Knock, knock." The front door opened and in walked Maggie's mom, Maureen O'Keefe. She had brown eyes and dark hair shot through with silver, cut in a piecey style with the back flipped up. She smiled at Danielle, then walked over and cupped her granddaughter's small face in both hands before kissing her forehead. "Hello, my precious little girl."

"Hi, Mom." Maggie was grateful for the distraction. "Once upon a time I was your precious girl."

"You still are." Her mom walked over and cupped her face in her hands, then kissed her forehead. "Hi, Josie. Are we still on for shopping?"

"Just as soon as your precious girl—the grown-up one—comes clean about what's going on between her and the new guy."

Maureen's brown eyes turned wary. "There's something

going on? Between you and Sloan Holden? I'm going to have to meet him."

"Oh, please—" Maggie tried to look as innocent as possible.

"See?" Josie pointed at her. "That's the kind of answer I've been getting. Which is to say no answer at all. You're her mother. Surely you can get her to talk."

"Can you give me a little context?" Maureen said.

"I can see where that would help." Josie thought for a moment. "Like I just said to Maggie—since he got here things have been friendly and fun. Easy. That changed a couple of days ago and you'd think we're having another ice age the way these two act. Makes me want to put on a parka every time they're in the same room."

The two older women stared at her expectantly and Maggie squirmed. She felt like a kid caught doing something wrong when her only motive was to try to do the right thing. "It's all about being a professional. Creating a comfortable, uncomplicated space for my guests. I've never run a bed-and-breakfast before, so I'm experimenting with just the right feeling and mood."

Maggie saw a look on her mom's face and not for the first time wished the woman couldn't see through her like a piece of clear plastic.

"Really?" Maureen said skeptically. "I know you, Margaret Mary Potter."

Uh-oh. It was never good when her mom used all three names. Made her want to walk herself into a corner and face the wall until she was told her time-out was over. "Yes, you do."

"Josie's right. Something is up and you're avoiding it like the black death. What did that man do to you?"

Well, this was a fine mess. She wanted to bury her head in the sand and ignore what had happened. But she couldn't let them believe Sloan had harmed her. He'd shaken her up, but there was no permanent damage done. She would get back her perspective and all would be well. As long as these two women got an answer to their questions.

"It was nothing, really."

"Then, you won't mind sharing details," her mom said. "What was it, *really*?"

"He kissed me." Maggie shrugged.

"Well, then," Josie said, her tone full of approval. "When?"

"Where?" Maureen asked. "Here? In the bedroom?"

"That's not important," Maggie protested.

"It kind of is," her boarder said. "You know the only way this inquisition stops is when we get all the facts."

"That's not happening. And if you guys insist on pushing the issue, you're going to miss out on the early-bird specials at the mall."

"Come on, Maggie. I'm your mother. Put yourself in my shoes. What if Danielle wouldn't tell you about something going on in her life?"

Maggie nearly knuckled. Her mom was really good at applying just the right amount of motivational guilt. But she held back.

"You are my mother and I love you." She unstrapped Danielle from the high chair and lifted her out to toddle around the room. "But there really is nothing more than that to tell. He kissed me and we both realized it meant nothing."

"Not from the ice age I've been living in," Josie muttered. "Don't be too hasty about this."

"It's not a rush to judgment. It's reality. I'm a widow with a daughter to raise. He was in *People* magazine's 'most eligible millionaire bachelor' issue. If that doesn't make us incompatible enough, he has a playboy reputation. Love 'em and leave 'em."

"But he's so sweet with Danielle. Maybe he just hasn't met the right woman yet," Josie suggested.

"He's met dozens of women, and if none of them were right it's because he's not interested in making a commitment." Maggie looked at both women and sighed. "He's a nice man. And he seems good with children. But a good deal of evidence points to the fact that he's all flirt and no depth."

"Are you sure you're not just projecting that on him? Stereotyping him so he's not a threat?" her mom asked.

"I'm not labeling him that way. Magazines and newspapers have reported on his activities. It's all flash and no substance. A game. I'm too busy for games. So it's best if we avoid each other."

"But—"

"No, Mom. No buts. I'm a mother and a businesswoman. There's no room in my life for a man. Especially one like Sloan Holden."

She grabbed up her daughter and whisked her into the other room for a diaper change before the two older women could gang up on her again. It was for the best that she steer clear of Sloan, and thank goodness he was avoiding her, too.

Nearly a week after Sloan had kissed Maggie, he was pretty sure he was losing his mind. Up until that complete and utter failure of judgment when he'd touched his mouth to hers and found out she tasted even more amazing than he'd imagined, his business focus had been notorious, in a good way. His cousin had said more than once that he was like a computer, all circuits firing, efficiency central.

It had all changed after that kiss under the stars.

In the past couple of days he'd forgotten meetings, and in the ones he'd attended, his mind had wandered to the spectacular way Maggie's backside filled out a pair of jeans when she bent over the oven to pull out a pan of blueberry muffins. Then first thing this morning, his assistant had asked him for the quarterly reports he'd brought home last night to look over. And he had looked them over. Corrections were all neatly marked and initialed. But it didn't do her any good because he'd left the B and B without his briefcase that morning.

He'd been in a hurry to get out of there before someone noticed he was staring at Maggie. Couldn't seem to keep himself from looking at her when there were more muffins and bending over. Yeah, he was going to hell.

But first he had to go back and retrieve the briefcase full of work that his assistant needed. It was midmorning and he figured Josie was volunteering as usual at the library and Maggie was at the café by now. The coast would be clear and he was in his car and nearly there.

He turned right off the main road and followed the narrow street to the end, where the log home that was Potter House stood. In the semicircular driveway he saw her dark blue SUV with the tailgate open and the cargo area filled with grocery bags. Maggie was leaning into the rear passenger seat, filling out those jeans almost as nicely as when she took something out of the oven.

So much for the coast being clear.

He groaned and wondered what he'd done to tick off fate and what he could do to turn around his bad luck. In his opinion, the best option was to pretend nothing had happened. Just the way Maggie was doing.

He opened his car door and got out, prepared to say hello and pretend, for all he was worth, that the kiss had been no big deal and everything was normal. That was when he heard the high-pitched wails coming from the rear seat of her car.

"Come on, Danielle. Mommy doesn't have time for this. I have to unload the groceries. Food is melting."

The quietly spoken, utterly reasonable words had no effect on the completely unreasonable toddler, and the screaming continued. Sloan wanted to retrieve his briefcase and go back to his office. None of this was his problem. But he couldn't do it.

"Hi, Maggie," he said, walking up to the open tailgate. "I'll get those bags."

She straightened and met his gaze, a puzzled expression on her face. "Aren't you supposed to be at work? What are you doing here?"

And wasn't that the million-dollar question. Telling the truth was best. He didn't have to get into all of it. "I left some paperwork here and my assistant needs it today."

"Then, you should get it to her." Maggie's voice got a little louder in order to be heard above the wailing coming from the backseat of her car. "I've got this."

Not from where he was standing. "I'm sure you do, but since I'm here, it will just take a couple of minutes to get the groceries into the house. I'll do that while you take care of Shorty."

The look of stubborn independence on her face said she was going to push back. While he admired her character, arguing was a waste of breath. He was stubborn, too, and in the time it would take for a conversation, he could have all the groceries in the kitchen.

Without a word, he reached into the cargo area of the SUV and took as many bags as he could carry.

"Hold on," she said, racing past him and up the stairs to the front door. "I'll unlock it."

"Thanks," he said, moving past her.

"No. Thank you." And then she went back to the car and liberated her daughter from the car seat.

Sloan passed her in the living room on his way out for a second trip. Maggie had her child in one arm and a bag in the other. She tried to put the little girl down, but the toddler pulled her legs up, refusing to stand. And she was crying her eyes out. At that rate, it would have taken her all day to unload the car. Maybe it was a good thing he'd lost his mind and forgotten work material.

In a few minutes everything had been transferred from her car to the kitchen. Sloan was about to go upstairs to get the paperwork he'd forgotten when he realized Maggie was only using one hand to put things away because her other arm was full of little girl. So the secret was out. That was how she maintained her fantastic figure. No expensive gym membership for her. Being a working mom was how she stayed in shape.

Danielle had stopped crying, but she was taking deep, shuddering breaths that would tug at the hardest heart. Sloan just couldn't leave her like this.

He walked over to where Maggie was working on the other side of the island. "I have no idea where any of this stuff goes, but maybe she'll let me hold her."

Maggie shook her head. "She's really cranky. A very bad night. I think she's teething. But we were almost out of everything. I had to take her with me."

Sloan wondered if Maggie wasn't used to accepting help or if there was a chip on her shoulder about proving to the world she could do it alone. Either way, he was here right now and wouldn't leave without at least trying to give her a hand.

"I can see that she's cranky and I'm not afraid."

"I can't ask you to do that, Sloan."

"You didn't." He held out his arms to the kid. "What do you say, Shorty? Want to give your mom a break?"

"I don't think she'll go for it."

"Maybe not." He kept his arms extended while the child thought it over. Finally, hesitantly, Danielle leaned toward him and he took her. "What do you know."

"Wow." Maggie looked surprised, then determined. "I'll hurry and get everything put away so we don't keep you very long."

"No rush."

"But you have to get back to work," she pointed out.

"A few minutes one way or the other won't make much difference." He walked around, and the toddler's slight weight felt surprisingly good in his arms. Her face was wet, but she sighed, and the deep, hiccuping breaths stopped. "Feeling better, kiddo?"

She rubbed a chubby fist beneath her runny nose then dragged it over the front of his shirt. A very expensive tissue, he thought. When she calmed down, he set her on the great-room floor beside the toy basket pushed beneath an end table. He rummaged through it, looking for the talking thing, the one with the button beside an animal. When it was pushed, a voice named the critter and made the correct creature sound. He'd seen Maggie do this with her.

He pushed the cow and Danielle immediately said, "Moo."

"Right. Good job." He pushed the frog.

"Bet," she said.

"Pretty close. Ribbet," he told her.

She pushed the lion and made a roaring sound, or the two-year-old version of it. He sat on the floor and she plopped herself into his lap and held the toy out to him. It didn't take a PhD in parenting to realize what she wanted.

Sloan touched the horse and said, "Horse."

She tried to repeat the word and did a pretty good job. Then, plain as day, she said, "Cookie."

"Even I understood that," he said to Maggie.

"Of course." She glanced over her shoulder after shoving a box of cereal into a cupboard. "And she's very accomplished at saying no, too."

"Cookie," the little girl said again.

"You'll spoil your lunch, baby girl," her mother said. "And they're messy."

"If it was up to me," he said to the child, "you could have a whole bag. Fortunately, your mother is not a pushover." He looked at Maggie. "What do you say? Maybe just one for putting that little meltdown behind her?"

"Is that all it takes?" She was shaking her head at the same time she smiled at him. "A few tears and a woman can have whatever she wants?"

"You know how it is. Men are completely helpless when a female cries." He met her teasing gaze. "And I'm not ashamed to admit it."

"Cookie," Danielle said impatiently.

"I was sort of hoping she'd forget," he admitted.

Maggie laughed. "You are an optimist, aren't you? When it comes to *c-o-o-k-i-e-s*—" she spelled the word "—my daughter has single-minded determination that is legendary."

"Okay." He looked at the little girl, who was staring back at him with an expression he interpreted as expecting him to go to battle for her. "It's up to your mom, kid."

"No, it's up to you," Maggie said. "If I give her one, that pretty white shirt of yours won't be so pretty and white anymore."

"Well—" he looked at the stain already streaking his chest "—she already used it to wipe her nose. A few crumbs can hardly do too much more damage."

"For the record, I'm sorry about your shirt and I will wash it." Maggie sighed. "But if you think it can't get much worse, you really are a rookie."

"No big deal on the shirt. My point is that I have to change it anyway. So I vote in favor of a *c-o-o-k-i-e*."

"Okay, then." She opened the brand-new bag of chocolate-chip cookies on the counter beside her, then reached in to grab one. Absently, she picked up the bag and walked over to him. She held up the treat and said to her daughter, "What's this, baby girl?"

"Cookie!" Happily she snatched it out of her mother's hand and shoved it in her mouth.

That made Sloan a little nervous. "Is she going to choke on that?"

"It scared me, too, the first time, but she'll be fine." She held out the bag to him. "Cookie?"

"Thanks." He reached in and took one.

There was an odd expression on Maggie's face. "Don't look now, but your playboy image is taking a direct hit. If they could see you eating cookies with a two-year-old, what would your women say?"

"It's not so much what they would say as what they might do," he said.

"No more scantily clad babes hiding in your room?"

"If that were the case, I'd put a picture on social media myself. But me with a child would ratchet up the marriage minded, and speculation would run rampant about the end of my eligible-bachelor days. Stalking would be off the chart."

"Really?" Maggie looked genuinely surprised.

"Yes. Do you have any idea how inconvenient and annoying it is to have a stranger show up in your bed uninvited?"

"So you want to personally invite your women into your bed?"

Sloan would personally invite Maggie there in a heartbeat, and the instantaneous thought sent a sliver of need straight through him. Clearly she was joking or he would have extended an invitation right then and there. Then Danielle wiped a grubby hand over his chest, leaving a trail of chocolate and crumbs. That brought him down to earth. Even if Maggie was willing to accept an invitation into his bed, there was no way anything could happen with this little one to take care of.

Oddly enough, that didn't bother him. And it wasn't his bachelor-playboy image he was concerned about. He realized how much he liked being a part of this scenario, entertaining a child and hanging out with her mother. It filled up a part of his soul that he'd put aside for a long time. Since his divorce, he'd consciously avoided personal complications. After a failed marriage, the last thing he wanted was to get serious about a woman who was still in love with the man she'd lost.

He needed work and lots of it to focus more completely on the resort project. No more thinking about kissing Maggie.

Or inviting her into his bed.

Chapter Five

Maggie thought she had put that kiss with Sloan into perspective and had her life back under control until he had come to the house unexpectedly a couple of days ago. It had been an awful morning with a fussy toddler, but she'd had business responsibilities. Things needed to be done, whether Danielle had wanted to come along or not. And she definitely had *not* wanted to.

After the grocery store, Maggie had had one nerve left from the nonstop crying all the way home. She'd never expected Sloan to come riding in like a white knight to the rescue, but white knight was a fitting description for a man who hauled in all those grocery bags in half the time it would have taken her. And she didn't think it was possible for him to be any sweeter to her daughter than he'd been that day. Watching the two of them was heartwarming, and at the same time it made her deeply sad that her husband had never had a chance to spend time with his daughter.

The problem wasn't Sloan; it was her. The threads of her life were delicately intertwined, but they fit together and were working. If one of those strings came loose and pulled free, it would all come apart. She was on an even keel and trying to stay that way. She didn't need a man coming in to unbalance her canoe, to mix a metaphor.

Her B and B was Sloan's temporary home and he had every right to come and go. So the lesson from his drop-in was to have her guard up at the house. In town she could probably avoid him. He was working, as was she, and the odds of their schedules intersecting were slim.

Still, she was vigilant on her way down Main Street from her office to the Grizzly Bear Diner, where she planned to meet her friend Jill Stone for lunch. Some would call it supporting her competition, but the two eating establishments provided very different dining experiences.

She walked into the diner and didn't see anyone at the podium displaying a sign that read, Please Wait to be Seated. The hostess must be busy somewhere else at the moment. Glancing into the area with booths and tables, she didn't see her friend, either. It would be hard to miss Jill's red hair, so obviously Maggie was the first to arrive.

She heard her cell phone ring and fished it out of her purse. "Hello."

"Maggie? It's Jill. I'm so sorry, but I can't make it. The school called just as I was on my way out the door to meet you. C.J. is sick and I have to pick him up."

C.J. was Jill's ten-year-old son. She also had a daughter about Danielle's age. Maggie knew how hard it was when a child was sick, and suspected it made no difference whether the child in question was two or ten.

"I'm so sorry to hear that," she said.

"I feel awful standing you up like this. But he's running a fever and has a sore throat. It came on suddenly, because he was fine when he went to school this morning."

"Don't worry about it, Jill. We'll put another date on the calendar when he's feeling better. I hope that's soon."

"Me, too," the worried mom said. "I might just drop in at the clinic and let Adam look him over."

Adam Stone was her husband, a family-practice doctor

at Mercy Medical Clinic here in town. He'd adopted the boy after marrying Jill. Come to think of it, her friend had been a single mom when the doctor had rented the apartment she owned that was upstairs from hers. The two had fallen in love, but any similarity between Jill's situation and Maggie's ended there.

C.J.'s dad had abandoned him and Danielle's father had died. If given the choice, Danny would have devoted himself to his child. Since he couldn't, Maggie would devote herself to the little girl enough for two parents.

"I think it's a good idea for C.J. to see a doctor," Maggie said. "If only to reassure you that there's nothing to worry about."

"It's very handy being married to a doctor," Jill said.

"I bet it is." Maggie laughed. "Don't let me keep you. Do me a favor. In a day or so give me a call and let me know how C.J. is doing."

"Will do. 'Bye, Maggie."

"Take care." Maggie pressed the stop button on her phone and turned to leave the diner. No point in staying. She would grab a sandwich at the café and eat it at her desk. Even though she'd been craving a burger and fries.

She reached out to push open the door, but it moved before she touched it. Sloan Holden walked in, backing her up several steps.

"This is a surprise," he said, smiling. "A nice one."

Her heart rate increased, just to let her know she thought it was nice, too. And ironic. Just minutes ago she'd been thinking that in town it would be much easier to avoid him. Not so much, apparently.

"I was just leaving," she said.

He looked at his watch. "Have you eaten already?"

"No. I was supposed to meet a friend, but she couldn't make it. Her son is sick."

"That's too bad."

They were standing a foot away from the hostess podium and a female voice said, "Two for lunch?"

Sloan hesitated just a moment before saying, "Yes."

Before Maggie could say they weren't together, he took her elbow and steered her after the hostess, who was leading the way. The next thing she knew, they were being seated at a secluded booth in the back.

"Brandon will be your server today. If there's anything I can get you, please don't hesitate to ask." She smiled at both of them. "Enjoy your lunch."

"Thanks." Sloan looked at her across the table. "This is unexpected, in a good way. I thought I was going to have to eat alone."

"You don't have to do this."

"What? Eat?" His mouth turned up at the corners. "Yeah, I kind of do."

"No. I meant you don't have to eat with me. Or keep me company. I'll just grab a sandwich and eat in my office."

"Oh, come on. You were planning to eat with someone. Why not me?"

So many reasons. "You might be planning to work." Since he wasn't carrying a briefcase or anything that looked remotely like work, it was a pretty weak excuse.

"I was planning to sit at the counter and chat up whoever was behind it. But a quiet booth with you is a lot more appealing." His dark brown eyes took on a pleading expression. "Come on. Do a lonely bachelor a favor. Be spontaneous. Have lunch with me."

"Lonely bachelor, my as-paragus," she teased. "If you're alone, it's only because this is Blackwater Lake and it's off the radar for your women."

"I'm going to ignore the 'my women' part of that statement and take the rest of it as affirmative that you'll join me for lunch."

"Okay. It's a yes. But only because I was looking forward to the Mama Bear burger combo."

"Good." He looked around, taking in the decor. Pictures of bears on the walls. Wallpaper with black paw prints on a cream background. The wild-animal ambience had everything but a stuffed grizzly in the corner. "This place has a lot of local color."

"That it does."

A nice-looking young man with brown hair and blue eyes who was in his late teens walked up with menus. "Hi. I'm Brandon and I'll be your server today."

Sloan held up a hand to stop him from leaving the menus. "I think we're ready to order."

"What can I get you?"

"I'll have a Mama Bear burger combo. Diet cola with lemon," Maggie said.

"Make mine a Papa Bear combo and coffee. Black."

"Coming right up," Brandon said.

Sloan watched the young man walk away and there were questions in his eyes. "Shouldn't he be in school?"

"He graduated from Blackwater Lake High School in June. He's taking some online classes while working to save money for college so he can go away in the fall."

"How do you know that?"

"His dad is a carpenter and works for McKnight Construction, not to be confused with McKnight Automotive where your cousin's fiancée works. Brandon's mom works at the grocery store and comes into the café. I hear things," she explained. "And it's a small town. So everyone hears things."

"I guess it's hard to keep a secret around here."

"Yes."

But no one knew Maggie's secret because she kept it to herself. No one knew Danny had wanted kids right after they'd married but Maggie had refused. She'd wanted to wait until his National Guard commitment was fulfilled. But she'd gotten pregnant and it hadn't been planned. That was the reason she had Danielle. And thank goodness she did. Best mistake ever. Or she would have nothing left of Danny.

"This town is very different from my stomping grounds."

"How?" She unwrapped eating utensils from the napkin and spread it in her lap. "Everything you do ends up in a newspaper, which means even more people know things."

"True. So tell me. Since there are no small-town tabloids, how does information spread in Blackwater Lake? Jungle drums?"

"Almost." She laughed. "But it works pretty much the way it does in the big city. Phone. Social media. Word of mouth."

His eyes darkened as it settled on *her* mouth. "Don't look now, but you're having a better time than you would have eating alone in your office."

"Says who? I really like my office and what I do."

"Me, too," he allowed. "But as I told you once before, everyone needs a break. Recharge your batteries. Let your hair down. Have a little fun."

"If you say so."

He studied her. "What do you have against having fun?"

"Nothing."

"That's not the impression I get," he said.

Although she had very little time for it, Maggie was completely open to having fun. As long as that fun didn't include a relationship. Maybe running into him was actually a sign. A good thing. They'd never talked about that kiss and probably should. Might be a good idea to clarify it, make sure he understood that she had boundaries.

"Believe me, Sloan, I like having fun as much as the next person. But…"

"What?" he asked when she hesitated.

"As long as it doesn't include kissing." Before he could say anything, she added, "I take full responsibility for what happened that night. What I said comes under the heading of not thinking it through."

"Your sense of accountability is extraordinarily acute. Last time I checked, it takes two to make a kiss." He met her gaze and there was amusement in his. "I believe I initiated that kiss and no one twisted my arm."

"All right. If you insist on splitting hairs, you can take half the blame. But you're flirting. Maybe you can't help yourself. It just comes naturally when you're around women. I need to be honest and straightforward. Just in case you're thinking about a repeat, I'm not going to kiss you again."

His eyebrows rose. "Really? You're absolutely certain about that?"

Maggie wasn't sure what kind of reaction she'd expected, but it probably included him looking more serious than amused. "Yes, really. I'm very serious about this."

"You're serious about everything," he pointed out. "But if we're being straightforward and honest with each other, I feel the need to share that I also had decided kissing you again wasn't a good idea."

"Oh." Was that disappointment trickling through her? How could it be? This was what she wanted. "Okay, then. We're both on the same page about this—"

"Not anymore. Now you've accused me of being a serial flirter. I'm feeling as if you just threw down the gauntlet, and my honor is at stake. Your declaration hits me as a challenge. A dare to see if I can do it again."

"No." She shook her head even as excitement coiled inside her. "That's not what I meant—"

Brandon stopped at the end of the table carrying two plates and their drinks, then set the appropriate items in front of each of them. "One Mama Bear. One Papa Bear. Cola with lemon and black coffee. Anything else I can get you?"

Maggie shook her head. All she wanted was to rewind and delete that ill-advised kiss and this whole conversation about it not happening again.

She'd just made everything worse.

Maggie glanced up from the spreadsheet on her computer monitor when the office door opened and Lucy Bishop walked in. "Hey, partner."

"Hey, yourself." The strawberry blonde lowered her skinny little self into one of the chairs in front of the desk. "You're back from lunch."

"Nothing gets by you." Maggie hoped the playful remark would cover her involuntary reaction to memories of that lunch. She felt a little shimmy in her tummy at the memory of Sloan's eyes when he'd all but said there would be another kiss. But now she was back at work and needed to get her head in the game.

"Did you have a good time?" Lucy asked.

"I did." Unfortunately, she had, but not in the "girlfriends catching up" way she'd expected. And that was really all she wanted to say about that. "How's everything in the café?"

"Good. We were busy today." She leaned back in the chair and sighed. "And I've been thinking."

"That's dangerous."

"You have no idea." Lucy grinned. "Seriously, though. Suddenly it's April and summer will be here before you know it. That means tourists and—fingers crossed—a jump in business, which we need to prepare for. We should talk about possible additions and changes to the café menu and an increase in supplies."

"Not to mention hiring extra staff," Maggie pointed out.

"Probably high school and college students looking for summer jobs."

"I have a list of kids who worked in the ice cream parlor," Maggie said. "Most of them are smart and hard workers. Conscientious. I can start making calls to see who might be interested in coming back. Line up the standouts."

"It's going to be a tough call to decide how many we need for the ice-cream side and the food-service side."

"A delicate balance, for sure," Maggie agreed.

"We have no idea how busy it's going to be our first summer." There were shadows in Lucy's bright blue eyes. "If we don't have enough staff, customers will be kept waiting for food and not inclined to give us their repeat business. But we don't want to pay employees for standing around doing nothing."

"Yeah, it's definitely a numbers-and-luck game," Maggie agreed. "I'm pretty sure the mayor's office keeps statistics on summer visitors from year to year. We can probably get a copy and work out a reasonable guess at the percentage of customers to expect. I'd be inclined to lowball the staffing ratio. If we get swamped, I'll help out. And I have some emergency reinforcements in mind."

"It's a good place to start." Lucy nodded. "Wow, I never realized being the boss would be so hard. I'm very glad we're in this together."

"Me, too."

Maggie remembered the pressure of handling just Potter's Ice Cream Parlor all alone. She and Danny had opened it together. When his National Guard unit had been called up and deployed to Afghanistan, her solo engagement had only supposed to have been temporary. Then he'd been killed in action and she was pregnant. All the responsibility of the business, as well as the baby, had fallen to her.

On top of that, or maybe because of the stress and trauma, there were complications with her pregnancy and the obstetrician ordered her to stay off her feet. If it hadn't been for friends and family, she would never have made it through that terrible time.

Lucy Bishop had been a summer visitor to Blackwater Lake a couple of years ago and fell in love with the town. She'd finished culinary school and eventually relocated, working at the Grizzly Bear Diner for a while. She and Maggie had become friends because Lucy had a notorious sweet tooth and was the best ice-cream-parlor customer.

She never said much about her background and Maggie still didn't know anything about her personal life. But she liked Lucy and was aware that she had a passion for cooking good healthy food. Instead of throwing out what they couldn't use at the end of the day, her friend made sure less fortunate people in town had enough to eat.

She'd confided to Maggie her dream of opening her own restaurant and then a couple of things had fallen into place. The shop space next to Maggie's business had become available and Lucy had inherited some money.

They had partnership papers drawn up and opened the Harvest Café last Labor Day weekend. At first, they'd broken even and revenue from the ice cream parlor, along with a busy winter season, had kept them afloat. Now they were making a small profit. This would be their first summer and, hopefully, it would be a good one.

Lucy looked thoughtful. "I've heard that the resort project is going to be constructed on two fronts simultaneously—

the condos at the base of the mountain at the same time as the hotel with retail shops a little farther up."

Sloan hadn't said anything to Maggie about that, but they didn't talk business. She'd been concentrating so hard on avoiding him and keeping conversation to a minimum that she never asked.

"If that's true," she said, "it could be really positive news for our business. You're talking a good-size workforce, and those people need to eat."

"Plus, more permanent and part-time residents will live here when the condos are finished. The hotel will cater to skiers in the winter and fishing and lake-oriented tourists in summer."

"That's true." Maggie leaned back in her chair. "Who told you about this? Is it a reliable source?"

"It was someone who works for McKnight Construction. One of the cabinetmakers, I think. He said Sloan Holden is bringing in his own contractor, who will coordinate with Alex McKnight."

"That would be great."

Maggie wondered if Sloan would be around until the project was completed. The scope of it was pretty big, which could keep him in Blackwater Lake for a long time. On the one hand, that would mean having a stable boarder and a reliable income source, which was important for paying her small-business loan. On the other hand, he could be under her roof indefinitely. That would make her life complicated.

"You could ask Sloan," Lucy suggested.

"About what?"

"How he's planning to approach the building project. After all, you see him every day. He lives in your house."

"True."

"So it seems like a reasonable question. When you see him at home," Lucy said.

"And sometimes not at home."

"Hmm. That sounds interesting. I sense a story there."

"Not really. I just ran into him at the diner. Jill cancelled because C.J. was sick. Sloan walked in while I was there and we had lunch together."

"So when you said it was good, that didn't exactly cover all the facts. How was it?" Lucy asked again. "You look a lot more relaxed than before you left."

Warmth crept into Maggie's cheeks. "I had a good time."

And, God help her, that was the truth. When Sloan walked into the diner, or any room for that matter, things were definitely not dull.

Lucy studied her. "Now that I think about it, there's something different about you. And I don't just mean because you're not the stressed-out partner I sent off to lunch with orders to have a good time."

"It was nice to get out for a little while." It was even nicer to know a man was interested enough in her not to take no for an answer in terms of another kiss. That was different from wanting him to kiss her. It was just nice to know a man thought she was attractive.

It had been a long time since any man had been interested and Maggie preferred it that way. She'd had her great love and had made peace with that. When Sloan got the message, he would be glad he was off the hook.

She noticed Lucy was looking at her funny. "What's wrong?"

"You're blushing." The other woman leaned forward in her chair. "Methinks there's more to this story."

"Not really."

"You should be aware that your answer has no conviction whatsoever."

"He's a flirt. That's all."

"Aha." Lucy nodded as if that explained everything.

"No aha," Maggie protested. "What does that mean anyway?"

"It means that you left here looking uptight and stressed out. My guess is that he's responsible for the fact that you are no longer looking as though you want to bend steel with your bare hands. You're glowing."

"No I'm not."

"I can get you a mirror." Lucy looked very certain of her observation. "You definitely are glowing."

"You make me sound as if I came in contact with radioactive material." Come to think of it, that wasn't far from the truth. Sloan was too hot for her to handle, even if she wanted to.

"It's just that I've never seen you look like this before. The only difference now is him." Lucy shrugged.

"That's weird because I don't feel any different. He rents a room from me. It's a mutually beneficial arrangement. Nothing more. We're barely even friends. He suggested we eat together only because he didn't want to sit at the diner counter and chat up a stranger behind it."

"Okay." But there was a gleam in her friend's eyes. "Then, I guess you wouldn't mind if I flirt with him a little?"

"Of course not." Maggie's tone was adamant—and automatic.

"Seriously? You have no objections to me going after him? And if he asks me out?"

"Absolutely none." That was stubbornness talking. "Go with my blessing."

"Okay, then." Lucy stood. "He is an exceptionally good-looking guy. And quite the charmer. If I get the chance, I'm going to let him know I'm interested."

"Remember, he's divorced." At her friend's questioning look, she added, "He told April, Delanie and I. Keep in mind that he might be disillusioned and have no intention of settling down."

"Good. Neither do I." She looked at her watch. "I have to get back downstairs."

"Okay. I'll see you later."

When Maggie was alone, she let out a long breath and felt like a two-faced witch. She'd given Lucy, her partner and friend, the okay to show interest in Sloan. The problem was, Maggie wasn't at all sure she meant it. Oh, God. Was she one of those friends? The "I can't have him but I don't want her to have him" kind of woman?

It would mean she had feelings for Sloan.

Chapter Six

Maggie parked in the lot at O'Keefe Technologies where her brother, Brady, had built the corporate headquarters for his company. He'd chosen a beautiful spot for it. From his office window he had a spectacular view of the mountains in the distance. If Maggie worked there, not much would be accomplished what with her looking out the window all day.

After getting out of the SUV, she walked toward the glass double-door entry and the hair on the back of her neck stood up. There was a parking area reserved for people who worked in the building, and she spotted Sloan's silver Range Rover.

It had been a week since their chance meeting at the diner. During that time she'd only seen him at the house for meals and hadn't really made more than small talk with him. Nothing like the intimate nature of their conversation at lunch.

Her skin had tingled and burned just talking with him about kissing. She really hoped to get in and out of the building without running into him, or anything else that would test her ultimatum about kissing him again.

She walked into the lobby and automatically looked at the directory, even though she knew that her brother's office was located on the fourth floor. The fifth was leased to Holden Property Development, where Sloan and his cousin Burke had their offices. Again her skin prickled just knowing Sloan was here somewhere. Part of her wanted to see him, but the survival-instinct part of her knew that wasn't a good idea.

Maggie pushed the elevator up button, and when the doors opened, a sigh of relief escaped her. Sloan hadn't taken this one to the lobby and she was getting off before his floor. She was halfway home free in Operation Avoid Sloan.

The car went up and the doors opened to a reception area where Olivia Lawson, her brother's executive assistant and fiancée, sat behind her desk. The pretty, blue-eyed blonde smiled warmly. "Hi, Maggie. How are you?"

"Great. You?"

"Fabulous. And how is that precious little girl of yours?"

"Good. But you know the terrible twos everyone talks about? It really is terrible." She shuddered, recalling that nightmarish trip to the grocery store then Sloan unexpectedly coming to her rescue.

"She has a mind of her own, doesn't she?" Her sister-in-law-to-be looked sympathetic.

"That's putting it mildly. Intellectually I know it's a good thing and just a speed bump on the road to independence, which is every parent's goal for their child." She sighed. "I just wish that the learning curve on this would play out somewhere private, where no one could see and give you a look that says you were nowhere to be found when maternal competence was being handed out."

"You're doing a fabulous job," Olivia protested. "Danielle is lucky you're her mom."

"You have to say that. You're marrying my brother and you want me to like you because I'm his sister."

"Busted." The other woman shrugged then grinned. "It's all about diplomacy and kissing up to the sister."

"I knew it." Nothing could be further from the truth.

"Seriously, Mags, when Brady and I have babies, I hope I'm even half as good a mom as you are."

Their kids would be lucky because the two of them would be a whole parenting team, Maggie thought, envying the couple. It was hard raising a child, but as the saying went, many hands made light work. Two against one had to be easier. She'd seen it herself the day Sloan had helped her with groceries and her little girl. As grateful as she'd been to him, the experience had left her with an empty and sad feeling that her daughter wouldn't know the security of having a father in her world.

"Speaking of babies, Danielle needs a cousin," she said. "When are you and Brady going to get on that whole baby-making thing?"

"Who's making babies?" That was her brother's voice.

Maggie hadn't noticed him in the doorway to his office. "Hi, big brother."

"Little sister." He walked over to hug her. "So who's making babies?"

"I'm hoping you and your beautiful bride-to-be."

He gave his fiancée a lecherous look. "We are practicing all the time."

"That's a very unsatisfactory answer," Maggie retorted.

"On the contrary—" he winked at Olivia, who was blushing "—it's very satisfying."

"Okay, then. Let me ask another question. No nuance, just yes or no. Have you set a date for the wedding?"

"As a matter of fact, we have." Brady had a smug look on his handsome face.

"Do you plan to share?" she asked.

"Olivia, you do the honors."

There was an adoring look in her eyes as she gazed at her fiancé. She'd looked at him like that a long time before Brady had realized that he was in love with her, too. "Saturday, June 25."

"Oh, my gosh. That's only a couple months." Maggie hugged Brady, then his fiancée. "That's fantastic. I'm so happy for you guys."

"And I have a favor to ask you," Olivia said. "Will you be my matron of honor?"

Maggie didn't know what it was about engagements and weddings, but tears filled her eyes and emotion choked off her words so that she could only nod. When she could finally speak, she said, "I would absolutely love that."

"And we want Danielle to be a flower girl." Brady put his arm around Olivia's waist.

"You do know that she'll only be two and a half and doesn't follow directions very well, if at all?"

"We don't care about that," her brother said. "She's our niece and we want her in the wedding."

Olivia nodded. "Whatever happens is fine. Everything she does is perfect to us. The best part is the spontaneous, adorable factor that will make our day unique and special."

Maggie's eyes filled with tears again when she looked at her brother. "You do know that Olivia is too good for you."

"I do," he said solemnly, then grinned as if he'd performed a new trick. "See? I'm already practicing."

"This news is so awesome," Maggie said. "Does Mom know?"

"Not yet. We're taking her to dinner tonight to break the news. You had to go and ask your yes-or-no question, so there was no dodging an answer. You'd have known something was up and hounded us until we broke." He pointed at her. "But if you spill it to Mom before we can, you'll be demoted from matron of honor to guest-book duty."

"My lips are sealed. This is so cool," she gushed.

Maggie was ecstatic for them. But she also felt the tiniest bit of envy and hated herself for it. They deserved every happiness. But she was only human and wished her life had worked out the way she'd planned.

"As much as I hate to kill the buzz," she said to her brother, "can I steal you away for a little work?"

"Right," Brady said. "You wanted to talk about updating your website."

"Yeah."

"No problem." He held out a hand, indicating she should go into his office. "Right this way."

"See you later, bride-to-be." She smiled at Olivia.

"Count on it. We have a lot to talk about and I'm going to need your help."

Maggie nodded, then followed her brother and he closed the office door behind them. There were two barrel-backed chairs facing his desk and she took the right one while he sat down behind the desk.

"What can I do for you?"

"Lucy and I were talking last week about the business. Our first summer since combining the ice cream parlor and café is coming up. With tourist season on the horizon, it's a good time to overhaul the website. We were too busy after the café launch to do it during the winter, but now things are running more smoothly."

"A new Facebook page wouldn't hurt, either," he said absently, typing on his keyboard.

"You're the computer guru, so I bow to your expertise and judgment. And hope you'll give me a break on your normally exorbitant charges."

"I should inflate my fee." Brady gave her a pointed look. Maggie knew he was still smarting because she hadn't come to him for a business loan, but decided to play innocent. "But you won't."

"Give me one good reason why not. I still haven't forgiven you for not consulting me before you decided to open a B and B to make payments. I could have helped with the financing."

"You know why I didn't," she protested. "If Danny were here, that's the way he would have handled it."

"And if he were still here, he'd be around in that house where you're renting rooms to strangers."

"It's working out great. Josie is a huge help and I love having her there."

"What about Sloan Holden?" he asked while staring at his computer monitor, where her current outdated website was displayed.

"He pays his rent on time and doesn't bring wild women back to his room."

Brady glanced at her. "What does that mean?"

"Just what I said. He's an ideal guest." Except for the inconvenient fact that he'd kissed her. But because of her part in it, she'd decided not to hold that against him.

Her brother's eyes narrowed on her. "He hasn't gotten out of line, has he?"

No, she thought, that would describe her. "He's very nice and I'm grateful to have the income."

Brady studied her for a moment then nodded. "So what changes are you looking for?"

"That's your area. What do you think I should change?"

"I can come up with a new design, but I'd suggest current pictures of you and Lucy that show both the ice cream parlor and café. April Kennedy can help you with that."

Maggie made a mental note to visit her photography studio just down the street from the café and across from the sheriff's office. "Okay, what else?"

"Put up menus for meals and desserts. Maybe a pairing like some restaurants do for wines. Advertise coupons, giveaways. Like kids-eat-free Mondays. Or two-for-one Tuesdays. Things like that."

"I'll talk to Lucy and pick her brain," Maggie promised.

"Then I think a little plug for Blackwater Lake as the perfect tourist destination," Brady said.

"That all sounds good."

"Okay. Get back to me as soon as possible with the material and I'll put it all together." He met her gaze. "No charge."

"Have I told you that you're the best brother in the whole world?"

"Yeah, yeah. Talk is cheap." There was phony little-boy petulance in his tone. "Actions speak louder than words."

"Don't be that way," she pleaded. "I know if I needed you that you'd be there for me and Danielle. But I found out how unpredictable life is when I lost Danny. That made me realize I need to do things on my own. Not count on anyone."

"I really do get it," he said gently. "But it's in the big brother's handbook to never miss a chance to needle your little sister."

"And you're very good at that." She smiled and stood up. After blowing him a kiss, she said, "I'll be in touch. Have fun with Mom tonight. Isn't it about quitting time?"

"You're my last appointment. Now get out of here so Liv and I can shut everything down and go pick up Mom."

"I'm so gone."

Maggie left his office and said goodbye to Olivia. She pushed the down button and when the doors opened, Sloan Holden was the sole occupant of the elevator.

A slow smile curved up the corners of his mouth. "This is an unexpected surprise."

Maggie wasn't often speechless. She took pride in being queen of the smart-aleck comeback or witty retort. She should have been prepared to see him and had been ready when she'd walked into the building. But wedding news pushed it out of her mind and now she had nothing. This was a particularly bad time to lose her words. Olivia was sitting right behind her and there was no way she wouldn't notice weird or unusual behavior in her matron-of-honor-to-be.

"Hi," she finally said, then walked into the elevator and watched the doors close.

"What brings you here? Just a wild guess—it has something to do with your brother."

"Yes." They stopped on the first floor and the elevator doors opened to the marble floor of the lobby. She stepped out. "I want to update my website and that's what Brady does. It's quite handy to have a computer nerd in the family."

"Is business good?"

"Very. And our plan is to give it a little nudge so it will be even better come summer."

"You and your partner must be pleased."

"We are."

"Your success doesn't surprise me. The food is great and the atmosphere friendly and inviting. Linking the café and ice cream parlor is smart. I can only speak for myself, but I'm never too full for ice cream."

That was so boyishly charming she couldn't help smiling. "I should get you to star in a commercial."

The elevator dinged and the doors opened. Burke Holden stepped out and smiled at them. The cousins were similarly built, and a facial resemblance pegged them as family. But Burke's eyes were vivid blue and his hair was a little lighter than Sloan's.

"Hi, Maggie." Burke exited the elevator and stopped beside her. He and his fiancée, Sydney McKnight, were frequent visitors to the café. "How are you?"

"Good. You?"

"Never better. On my way home to pick up Syd." He looked at Sloan. "Hey, you're still going to meet us for dinner, right?"

"That's the plan." He met her gaze. "I'm not sure how much notice my landlady needs that I won't be dining at the boardinghouse."

"No problem. It's spaghetti night."

"Maggie," Burke said, looking at her. "You should come, too. Syd would love to see you."

"I wish I could," she said politely. "But I don't have a babysitter for Danielle."

"Bring her along. I'm good with kids. Just ask Syd."

Maggie glanced at Sloan, who wasn't saying much, mostly looking interested in what she was going to say. Probably amused about how she would wiggle out of this invitation. Well, she would show him.

"It really sounds like fun. You're sure you don't mind a two-year-old at dinner?"

"Not at all. We'd love it."

"Have you ever had dinner in a restaurant with a two-year-old?"

"No," Burke answered. "But how bad can it be?"

"You'd be surprised," she said mysteriously. "I'll try to get a sitter, but…"

"If you can't, don't worry about it," Burke assured her. "We're going to a place near the mall and it's not fancy. With the lodge renovations, the Fireside Restaurant won't be back open for a while. Sloan has all the information. You guys should come together."

He waved, then headed for the double glass doors. She

and Sloan silently watched him walk out of the building before looking at each other.

"I sure hope he's not matchmaking, because you and I have already agreed that I'm not your type," she reminded him.

He smiled serenely. "Isn't it handy that I don't have to pick you up?"

Then he walked out the door and Maggie stood there alone, wondering what train had just mowed her down. Fate had a weird sense of humor, putting him on that down elevator at the same time she was getting on. And then Burke had found them chatting. Maggie had come here for a business meeting and was leaving with a dinner engagement.

She refused to call it a date.

"So you and Sloan?" Sydney McKnight was washing her hands in the ladies' room at Don Jose's, a Mexican restaurant about forty-five minutes from Blackwater Lake.

"It's not what you think," Maggie answered. "He's renting a room from me. We're friends. I think."

She and Sloan, along with Danielle, had met Syd and Burke at the restaurant. Strapped in the car seat, her daughter had napped the whole way and the two adults had chatted. It had been—nice. But that was all.

After being seated at a table, they'd ordered, then Sydney announced a trip to the powder room. The men had assumed Maggie would go, too, and teased them about women traveling together in platoons. So Maggie had taken them up on their offer to watch her toddler. Even though she knew Sydney was curious about her relationship with Sloan and, when they were alone, would grill her like a kebab.

So here they were in the ladies' room.

"Friends? You think? That's it?" Sydney persisted.

"Yes." Maggie glanced at her reflection in the mirror. The red sweater and black slacks looked good. Her brown hair was shiny and fell in layers past her shoulders in a flattering style. She was okay, but not in the same league as the models and actresses Sloan dated. "You know I like a romance as much as the next woman, but there just isn't one going on between Sloan and me."

Then it hit her that maybe Holden men didn't necessarily settle down with high-profile women. Sydney was a mechanic and worked with her dad at McKnight Automotive. She'd met Burke when he'd brought his car in for service and now they were engaged to be married. A beautiful brunette with dark eyes, she really cleaned up well in her skinny jeans, white silk blouse and red blazer. Burke didn't seem to care that she didn't have a glamorous profession. Theirs was a lovely romance and Maggie was happy for them. But before panic set in, she remembered that Sloan had enthusiastically agreed with Maggie that she wasn't his type.

"He's awfully good with your daughter." Syd brushed a smudge of mascara from beneath her left eye. "Not just any man would volunteer to watch her while her mom goes to the powder room."

Syd didn't know it, but this wasn't the first time he'd volunteered. That very first morning in her house he'd taken Danielle outside.

"He's great with her" was all she said.

"So he's good-looking. Nice. Funny. Charming. An eligible bachelor. And pretty decent father material. Where's the downside?" Syd folded her arms over her chest.

"It's obvious that you and Burke are in love. When that happens, you want to see everyone around you in love, too.

But maybe a relationship isn't the right thing for someone else," she said gently.

"You're talking about you," Syd said.

Maggie shrugged. "Everyone's path is different. Sloan might be a wonderful husband and father, but not for me or Danielle. It's my job and mine alone to raise her the way her father would have wanted."

"I hear what you're saying." Syd nodded her understanding. "But I knew Danny and he was a good man. He used to bring the cars into the garage all the time, so we got to know each other pretty well. I'm not so sure he would have minded another good man stepping in when he couldn't be there for his wife and daughter."

Maggie couldn't say the other woman was wrong about that. Because of his military service, Danny faced danger the average man didn't. He thought about things other husbands and fathers didn't have to. Just before his final deployment, he'd asked her if she would remarry should something happen to him. She'd tried to make light of it, never really believing he wouldn't come home. She'd said something glib about not wanting to train another man, but Danny had been serious. He'd told her he trusted her and to do what was right for her and the baby. All he wanted was for her to be happy.

Maggie knew the deeper issue was *her*. "The thing is, I'm going to have to be enough for my little girl because I don't want another romance. Not ever again."

"You obviously loved him very much. I'm sorry, Maggie. I didn't mean to push." There was regret in Syd's dark eyes.

"It's okay."

"No, it isn't, but you're sweet to say that." The other woman shook her head. "And I understand. Everyone's past puts them in a place where they're open to love. Or not."

"Right." It was a lonely place not being open, Maggie

thought, but that was where she was. "I'm starting to feel guilty about being gone this long."

"I'm sure Danielle is fine with Burke and Sloan."

"They're the ones I'm worried about."

Syd laughed, and any tension, real or imagined, disappeared. "It's good for them."

"Builds character," Maggie agreed.

They left the ladies' room and walked over the tile floor through the restaurant decorated like a Mexican hacienda. The walls were painted to look like adobe and had sombreros hanging on them. Sloan and Burke were seated at a table for four with a high chair for Danielle. Maggie always carried antiseptic wipes in the diaper bag and had thoroughly cleaned the chair before putting her daughter in it.

She wasn't in it when they returned to the table, because Sloan was holding her and looking as if he didn't mind.

Maggie stood on the other side of the high chair. "Is she fussy?"

"No. Good as gold," he said.

"Does she need a diaper change?"

He looked at the child in his arms. "I'm no expert, but she seems fresh as a daisy. Right, Shorty?"

Danielle nodded, but Maggie figured he had this little girl so completely charmed that if he said, "Let's jump off a bridge," she would enthusiastically agree.

"So she hasn't been a problem at all?"

"No. She just held out her arms and I felt sorry for her all restricted in that contraption," Sloan explained.

"You are a completely spineless pushover." Syd gave him a pitying look, then her gaze rested on Burke. "Does that spineless streak run in the family? Will our children have you wrapped around their tiny little fingers?"

"No." His tone was adamant. Then he looked at the little girl and his expression grew soft. "Yes."

"Which is it?" Sloan was unselfconsciously holding Danielle in her long-sleeved pink dress, white tights and Mary Janes. She had ribbons in her hair. "Yes or no?"

"Maybe." Burke shrugged. "I will rationally assess each situation and react to it in whatever way my wife says I should."

"Oh, please. You're so full of it," Syd scoffed. "You've done a great job with Liam, which is more parenting experience than I've got."

"Where is he tonight?" Sloan asked.

"At his friend Todd's house," Syd said. His mother, Violet, was her best friend. They'd had a falling-out when Syd's boyfriend had fallen in love with Violet and eloped, but the two women had put it behind them and now the boys were besties. "We gave him a choice and he said he'd rather put up with Bailey, Todd's little sister, than a bunch of grown-ups." She shrugged. "What can I say? He's ten."

"Ouch." Sloan looked at Danielle. "How old will you be when having dinner with anyone over ten is worse than a root canal?"

"She probably feels that way right now," Maggie said, "but she can't verbalize it yet. I swear there are times when she looks at me and is thinking, 'If I could talk and dial the phone, Grandma would get an earful and you'd be sorry you didn't give me a c-o-o-k-i-e.'"

They all laughed, including Danielle, who clapped her hands for good measure.

"She is really cute," Burke said.

"Are you feeling your biological clock ticking?" Syd teased.

"Not the clock so much," he answered seriously. "Just that I'd really like having a mini-you."

"Aw." She touched his arm and the love shining in her eyes was obvious. "You're a keeper."

Sloan studied the child then looked at Maggie. "Speaking of minis… She looks a lot like you."

"That's the consensus," she agreed. "Poor kid."

"I don't think so." Sloan met her gaze and there was something in his eyes that sent a shiver down her spine. "Before you know it, boys are going to notice, and then you'll have your hands full."

"Don't remind me."

Just then a waiter arrived with a tray full of steaming plates. Sloan put Danielle back in the high chair as if he'd been doing it for years and the child went without protest. What was wrong with this picture?

Maggie hadn't tried very hard to find a babysitter. She'd secretly hoped her daughter would make dinner a challenge like any respectable two-year-old would. Not that she wanted to spoil Burke and Syd's evening. Her plan had been to take the fussy toddler outside, but it would be a warning to Sloan if he had any illusions about tempting her into a fling.

But if there was anything a mother could count on, it was that a child would make a liar out of her. Tonight was no exception. Her little girl had been practically perfect, the poster child for any couple considering whether or not to have children.

It turned out to be a wonderful evening. If there was a downside, it had to do with her and feelings that scratched at the wall she'd put up around her heart when her husband died. This was where she reminded herself that it wasn't just about her. She had to think about Danielle. Anything casual with a man was out of the question.

There were many things in life Maggie couldn't control, but getting involved with Sloan wasn't one of them.

Chapter Seven

After work Sloan returned to Maggie's house and went straight to his room via the outside stairway. As a paying guest, he had a key to the front door but preferred to come in the back way. Especially for the past three weeks, after taking Maggie and Danielle to dinner with Burke and Sydney.

They'd had a great time—at least he had. That little two-year-old charmer could wrap herself around his heart if he wasn't careful. And so could her beautiful mom. But if Burke hadn't invited them, Sloan certainly wouldn't have asked them along. It fell into personal territory. Every time the scales tipped in that direction, Maggie nudged him back over the line into neutral, and he didn't do neutral very well. It made him want to shake her up—in a very personal way.

All he had to do was look at her and he wanted to get very personal. But the woman had emotional baggage and he didn't want to unpack it, so he was keeping his distance—hence he was using his outside access to get to his room. That way he didn't have to see Maggie until dinner, and avoiding her seemed best for both of them.

He dropped off the paperwork he planned to look at later and changed out of his suit. He was a jeans and T-shirt kind of guy at heart, but sometimes a suit and tie was required.

Now he was at loose ends. After a long day, he wanted a break before diving into more work. He wondered if Josie was watching TV in the upstairs family room. After exiting his room, he walked down the hall to the garage-size common area and found it empty.

"She must be downstairs." Great. Talking to himself. That was why he needed someone else to talk to. And going to the first floor meant seeing Maggie. "At least Josie and Danielle will take the pressure off."

When he was alone with Maggie, his willpower and common sense seemed to go missing in action.

Sloan descended the stairs and wondered what was going on. It was way too quiet. Until rooming here at Potter House, quiet had always been his preference, but he'd gotten used to background noise. Right now there was a disquieting, no pun intended, lack of it. No female voices exchanging the latest town gossip. No screeching, chattering or crying from Shorty. In the six weeks he'd been here this had never happened.

At the bottom of the stairs Sloan heard noises but couldn't identify them. He walked through the great room and didn't see anyone, then got closer to the kitchen—and sounds he still couldn't place. After rounding the island, he saw Maggie. She was on her back, half in and half out of the cupboard underneath the sink. It happened to be a great view of her legs, and he felt that familiar tightening in his gut.

He was pretty sure she hadn't heard him and didn't want to startle her. Quietly he said, "Hi, Maggie."

"Sloan? Oh, gosh. I didn't know you were here already. What time is it?"

"Almost six."

"Rats," she mumbled.

"I can leave," he offered.

"No. I just lost track of time trying to deal with this stupid thing."

Now that he wasn't quite so preoccupied with the shape of her legs in those snug jeans, he noticed there was an open pink toolbox on the floor beside her. Next to that was a brown box containing a new faucet. It looked to him as if she was planning to replace the existing fixture.

"Is there a problem?" he asked.

"Leaky spigot."

"Have you ever changed one before?"

"It never dripped before."

She'd said her husband had built the house, and it was probable that all of the plumbing fixtures were original. "How old is this place?"

"Let me think." She grunted and there was a noise that sounded like a metal tool hitting bottom inside the cabinet. "Hell and damnation!"

"Are you all right?"

"Yes. Sort of." She wiggled her way out from under the sink, holding her left hand.

"What happened?" He went down on one knee beside her and saw blood.

"The wrench slipped. I tried to catch it. A sharp edge caught my finger."

"Let me take a look," he offered.

"I'm sure it's fine. I'll just put a bandage on it, then get dinner—"

"That can wait." He met her gaze. "Let me see your hand."

She stared at him for several moments, then correctly realized that he wasn't going to back off. She opened her right hand and he could see a gash on her left index finger that was oozing blood.

"Where are the clean dish towels?" he demanded.

"Top drawer next to the sink."

He reached over and opened it, grabbed a terry-cloth towel and pressed the material onto the wound. "I don't think it's deep. The bleeding should stop in a minute." He settled their hands on his thigh and saw something flicker in her eyes.

"I'm sure it's fine." And there was the push back to neutral land. But the words came out a little breathy. "I need to get dinner on the table."

"Maybe Josie can help," he suggested.

"She's not here. Dinner plans."

That explained why he hadn't heard them talking, but not the lack of little-girl activity. "Where's Danielle? Napping?"

"My mom has her."

So he was alone with Maggie. That was inconvenient. And Sloan was pretty sure his pulse spiked as the implications of it all sank in.

"Let me guess. You had a window of opportunity without a toddler around and decided to tackle a DIY project."

"Good guess," she said.

He lifted the towel to check her finger and missed the sensation of her hand on his thigh. "It's still bleeding a little, but I don't think it needs stitches."

"Sloan, I can take care of this."

"Probably. But it's not easy to bandage yourself with only one good hand." All he wanted to do was help and she brought down the cone of independence. It was annoying and offended his sense of chivalry. He didn't give her a choice but kept her injured hand in his and stood, then curved his fingers around her upper arm to help her stand.

"It's really not that big a deal."

"So give me two minutes to patch you up. Do you have peroxide, Band-Aids and antibiotic cream?"

"Yes." She nodded toward the upper cupboard by the sink.

"Okay. Hold this while I get everything."

Surprisingly she did as ordered without argument. He set the supplies on the granite, then took her hand and lifted the towel. "Looks as if the bleeding stopped."

"I concur."

"I'm going to hold your hand under the water to wash it off, then pour the peroxide on it. After that, ointment and a Band-Aid."

"Yeah. I kind of figured that." She smiled.

"Right." Their eyes met and it felt too much like a moment, so he got busy.

He turned on the faucet and saw a stream of water squirting out from the base of the spigot. "Ah, I can see why this needs changing."

"Yeah. The guy at the hardware store said it would be a piece of cake. I don't know what kind he eats, but he was dead wrong about this job." There was frustration and annoyance in her voice.

As promised, Sloan poured the cleansing agent over the gash and watched it bubble for several moments. Then he took a paper towel and blotted the moisture so the bandage would stick. He finished up the job and met her gaze.

"You're good as new," he said.

"Thank you. Wish I could say the same about my faucet."

"What's the problem? In changing it, I mean."

"The bolts holding the old one in place are on really tight. I couldn't budge them."

"Let me give it a try."

She shook her head with a bit more enthusiasm than necessary. "You're a paying guest. I can't ask you to do that."

"You didn't ask. I offered."

"And I appreciate that." She thought for a moment. "But if you were staying at Blackwater Lake Lodge and there was something wrong with the faucet in your bathroom, would you offer to help change it?"

"Probably not," he said.

"Okay, then. This is my problem and I will handle it. Until the plumber can fit me in, I'll have to live with it." She shrugged.

"In the meantime, that fixture is wasting water. I'm a green builder and well aware that water is life and saving it is important."

"I couldn't agree more. I'll get someone out here to fix it first thing tomorrow."

"A plumbing professional is a good idea."

"Why?" There was uneasiness in her eyes, as if she expected the other shoe to fall.

"If this one needs attention, there's a better than even chance that they all do."

"Is there a problem with the one in your room?"

"Not yet."

Her expression turned stubborn. "And the master bathroom is fine."

"I wouldn't know. I've never been in your bedroom."

Sloan gave himself a mental slap as soon as the words were out of his mouth. For days he'd been keeping his distance from her and everything had been fine. But something about the way she deflected him at every turn tapped into his stubborn streak and pushed him into baiting her.

It happened this time, too.

Her dark eyes flashed with temper and something else hot and exciting. Something smoky and sexy. "If you're looking for an invitation, you'll be waiting for a very long time."

She was saying he would never be invited into her bed. Just like the promise she'd made that hell would freeze over before she kissed him again.

"That sounds like another challenge, Maggie."

Her full lips pressed into a straight line for a moment. "You can twist my words any way you want, but we agreed that the idea of anything serious between us just isn't very smart."

"Maybe intelligent choices are highly overrated."

"Not for me," she said quietly. "I have Danielle to think about. Every choice I make is with her welfare in mind."

As it should be, he thought. "You're a terrific mother, Maggie."

"Thanks."

"And really, while I'm here, I don't mind helping you out when you need a little muscle."

"I appreciate that." She smiled and the tension was gone.

But it would be back unless somehow he could get a handle on his tendency to tease and challenge her.

Maggie walked into her mom's house without knocking. It was where she'd grown up and coming here was completely natural and normal.

After shutting the door, she called out, "Hi, Mom."

"In the family room, sweetie." The voice was soft and that meant her daughter had fallen asleep.

She walked past the living and dining rooms, which were across from each other, then into the family room that was open to the kitchen. Maureen O'Keefe was sitting on her floral sofa in front of the flat-screen TV where an animated movie was showing. As suspected, Danielle was asleep beside her.

Maggie looked tenderly at her daughter then bent to kiss her mother's cheek. "Thanks for watching her. Sorry I'm so late picking her up."

"Did you get the faucet changed?"

"No."

Since it was her mother's regular day to watch Danielle, Maggie had called to ask if she could give the little girl dinner. The project would have been impossible with a toddler climbing all over her under the sink. As it turned out, the project was impossible anyway. Mostly because she refused to let Sloan help.

"What happened?" her mom asked.

"The bolts holding the fixture in place were on so tight I couldn't budge them."

Sloan had offered his muscle, and since then all she could think about was what he looked like with his shirt off. Her imagination went out of control picturing his broad chest, muscular arms and that made her want to touch...

"Maggie?"

"Hmm?" She blinked away the seductive vision in her head and tried her best to focus.

"Did you hear what I said?" There was the mom voice Maureen had always used when she wanted undivided attention from her children.

"I confess," Maggie said. "My mind was wandering."

Dark eyes very like her own assessed her. "Did your mind wandering have anything to do with Sloan Holden?"

Maggie sat down at the end of the sofa with Danielle between them. It was a calculated action designed to stall the conversation and give her time to come up with an answer that would end this third degree.

She didn't want to talk about Sloan because it would make her feelings bigger than they were, give them more importance than she wanted them to have. By the same token, lying to her mother was something that wouldn't end well. Maggie knew this for a fact because she'd tried it as a child and the woman *always* knew. It didn't matter that she was now a grown woman. Telling Mom a falsehood flirted with bad karma.

The best she could come up with was a flanking maneuver. "Sloan rendered first aid when I hurt myself with the wrench." She held up her bandaged index finger.

"Is it bad?" The stern look slipped from her mom's face, replaced by maternal concern.

"No. Superficial. He didn't think I needed stitches and it's not bleeding anymore."

"Good. So if he was there to patch you up, why didn't you ask him to help get the old faucet off?"

"Oh, you know." *Think, Maggie.* How could she lie without telling a lie? Nothing succeeded like the truth. She had just the thing. "He's a high-powered executive with a multimillion-dollar company. A man like him doesn't get his hands dirty."

"Did you ask him for help?"

"Of course not. He's a paying guest. I couldn't ask him to do that. I'd look like the world's most unprofessional bed-and-breakfast owner. Not a reputation I want to have."

"I see your point." When her granddaughter sighed in her sleep, Maureen smiled softly. "So did he offer to help?"

Crap. This was a yes-or-no question. Not an inch of wiggle room. "Yes. I really need to get Danielle home—"

"Not so fast." Her mom held up a hand to stop her. "You've been tap dancing since I mentioned his name. What's up with that?"

"Nothing." *Liar, liar, pants on fire.*

"I don't believe you, but let's leave that for the moment. I'm more curious about the fact that he offered to help and you turned him down when you were so determined to get that job done. Why would you do that?"

"Like I said, Mom, it would be unprofessional because he's a paying guest at my bed-and-breakfast. I'll call the plumber." It would be highly unlikely that Harvey Abernathy, a fifty-year-old happily married father of two, would say anything about getting an invitation into her bedroom.

Her mom's eyes narrowed. "You turned down his help because you wanted him to kiss you again."

"How in the world did you get that from what I just said?" No matter that it was true.

"Maggie…" Her mother smiled at her the way she had at her granddaughter just a minute before. "You're a mother now. How did you know when your child was thirsty or hungry before she could talk even a little? Or when she needs reassurance or just to be left alone? Or when she's not feeling well even before there are signs that she's sick?"

Maggie shrugged. "Don't know how. I just do."

"And I just know, too, because I know you. Kissing Sloan was lovely in the moment, but then it felt uncomfortable and for that reason you're pushing him away."

Maggie wondered when she would learn not to question the power of maternal mind reading. "You're right. I'm not comfortable with all this man/woman weirdness. It's been a few weeks and nothing more happened with him."

"Are you disappointed or relieved?"

"Both," Maggie admitted. "It was exciting and that's tempting. But then I realized it's a bad idea on many levels and figured he did, too. Then when I refused his help, he pointed out that it was probably a good idea to get a plumber and have him check out all the fixtures because they're original and might need work."

"He's right."

"Maybe. But during this discussion I pointed out that

the one in my bedroom was fine. He said he wouldn't know about that because he's never been in my bedroom. And I said if he was waiting for an invitation he'd be waiting a long time."

"Oh, dear…"

"Yeah. He said that sounded a lot like I was challenging him to take me to bed." She hated to admit it, but getting her there wouldn't be much of a challenge.

"He's obviously interested in you, sweetie." There were questions and a whole lot of concern in her mother's eyes.

"I get that, Mom. But I can't trust it." Or herself, for that matter. "And I'm not looking."

"You're sure?"

"I missed Daddy when he died." Maggie would never forget that awful day when her father had collapsed in this house. It had been a massive heart attack and suddenly he was gone. For a long time this place had felt sad and lonely but that had passed and laughter had come back. "I know you were devastated after losing the man you loved. And you never remarried. I lost Danny suddenly, so if there's anyone who understands why you didn't, it's me."

There was a sad look in her mother's eyes. "So pushing Sloan away has nothing to do with the fact that he uses women, then discards them like tissues?" Her mother shrugged. "After you told Josie and me about that kiss we Googled him."

"His reputation is a consideration," Maggie admitted.

"Doesn't it just suck that the first man you're attracted to since your husband died is—how did you phrase it? Oh, yes, all flirt and no depth. A playboy."

"Yes, there are pictures and stories verifying that he has been photographed with many women." The statement neither confirmed nor denied that she was attracted to Sloan.

"I'm so torn, sweetie. On one hand I'm glad there's a

man in the house and you, Danielle and Josie aren't there all alone. Call me old-fashioned, but in my day women weren't so hell-bent on proving they can run the world without a man." She sighed. "On the other hand, I wish he looked like a garden gnome and had the personality of a troll."

"I see you've met him," Maggie teased.

"You bet. I stopped by your brother's office on the pretext of him taking me to lunch, then insisted he introduce me to Sloan." Suddenly her mother looked fierce, ready to rip someone's head off. Possibly Sloan's. "He's handsome, wealthy and has too much charm for my peace of mind. That makes me nervous for you."

"Don't worry, Mom. I'll be careful."

"Sometimes being careful isn't enough. That type of man can draw you in before you even know what's happening. He's a wolf and you're a vulnerable widow."

She was a widow. That was a fact. But vulnerable? Not so much. She could tell the good guys from the bad. Maggie felt the most ridiculous urge to defend him. Or throw herself at him. The complete opposite of what her mom was telling her to do.

What was she? Sixteen? Where was this rebellion coming from?

"It's getting late, Mom. I need to get my baby girl home now."

"I hate to see you wake her. Are you sure you don't want to leave her here tonight?"

"Thanks, but no. You've got your volunteer work at the library tomorrow with Josie. It's better if I keep to her morning routine."

"Okay. Everything's packed up in the diaper bag. Her shoes are in there, too."

Maggie thought about that. "I don't think I'll put them

on her. It will be hard enough not to wake her when I slip her sweater on. Then there's getting her in the car seat. If she sleeps through that, it will be a miracle. After this nap, if she wakes up, she won't be ready for bed until midnight."

And that would be Maggie's penance for not accomplishing the mission for which she'd asked her mother to babysit. If she'd taken Sloan up on his offer, that new faucet would be in. But she might have ended up with the playboy in her bed.

Danielle stirred but didn't awaken when Maggie picked her up, slid the diaper bag over her shoulder and headed for the front door.

Her mother opened it and smiled lovingly at both of them. "Good night, baby girl."

"Thanks again, Mom. I don't know what I'd do without you." She kissed the woman's cheek. "I love you."

"Love you, too."

On the drive to her house, Maggie thought about the conversation with her mom and her own defiant reaction. Maybe it was knee-jerk, a habit of pushing back because her mother was always right. That would imply this time she hoped Maureen was wrong.

Did the reaction have anything to do with how close Maggie was to crossing a line with Sloan? If she did, there was no going back. So staying far from that line seemed like the best plan.

The truth was that she wouldn't have to work very hard to keep her distance after the inhospitable way she'd behaved when he'd offered his help. It was unlikely he would be inclined to ask her out.

That thought was far more disappointing than it should be.

Chapter Eight

Sloan was in position behind a lectern that faced a packed town hall in order to give a presentation to the chamber of commerce and all interested citizens about the virtues of green building. The standing-room-only crowd was proof that these people really cared about their town, and he was here to convince them that he did, too.

He didn't have time right now to wonder about the why of it, but in this capacity crowd Maggie was the first person he spotted. Had he subconsciously been searching only for her? What with leaving before breakfast and not returning until late, he hadn't seen her for a few days. He'd been putting a lot of hours in preparing this talk. It was important to convince the community to trust him. That he was committed to reducing the environmental impact in building a project that would benefit the town.

And it was time to start.

"Good evening, ladies and gentlemen. For those of you who don't know me, my name is Sloan Holden. I'm with the Holden Development Company and in charge of construction on the condominium, hotel and retail resort project." He looked around the room, then let his gaze rest on Maggie, sitting on a folding chair, dead center in the third row. "It's obvious from this amazing turnout that each and every one of you is intensely interested in the project and how it will affect your town and quality of life here in Blackwater Lake."

As he gazed around the room, he saw people in the audience nodding their agreement. "I've provided a packet of information so you can follow my remarks and take it with you for further review at your leisure.

"What's new about green building is that costs can be the same, or less, than building a conventional structure with far less consequences for the environment. When you consider the energy savings, construction quality and lower maintenance over time, a sustainable building really is paying you back. This will benefit businesses that lease retail space and condominium owners.

"But I suspect most of you are here to get a sense of how this venture will impact the mountain site and the breathtaking scenery surrounding it. Holden Development specializes in minimizing site impact and construction waste. That starts with a design that uses less land. We've hired a local architect. I'm sure most of you know Ellie McKnight, and her work is brilliant. Who has more skin in the game than someone who lives right here in Blackwater Lake?"

Sloan went on for another fifteen minutes explaining the company's objective of conserving energy and natural resources. He'd worked hard to include the right amount of detail and information but not so much that it would make their heads explode.

"In conclusion, I want to assure you that we are committed to building smart, building green. Not only to preserve the beauty and natural resources here, but in a global way."

He looked around, trying to gauge the reaction, and again his gaze settled on Maggie. Big mistake. That pretty face made him think about kissing her, and he couldn't afford to be distracted.

"There's more information in the material I provided, including the phone number of my office. If there are any questions after you've thoroughly reviewed everything, feel free to contact me. Also, I encourage everyone to research Holden Development. I'm confident our outstanding reputation will withstand intense scrutiny and ease any misgivings. Thank you for your time and attention."

There was polite applause and then Sloan gathered up his notes from the lectern. Mayor Loretta Goodson-McKnight made a few remarks in support of the building project before ending the meeting. With so many people standing at the back of the room, it took a few minutes for the rows of people in the chairs to file out toward the rear exit.

In the center aisle, Sloan was waiting his turn to merge with everyone. As it happened, that turned out to be perfect timing. He was there just as Maggie made her way to the end of her row.

"Hi." He held his hand out. "After you."

"Thanks." She smiled and moved in front of him.

And there it was, that tightening in the gut that always happened whenever she was near. Somehow it seemed stronger tonight. Maybe because he hadn't seen her for a few days. Even so, that didn't mean he could get her out of his thoughts.

He'd really missed the sound of her voice, the scent of her skin. The way her eyes sparkled. Her sense of humor. From where he stood, there was a pretty nice view of her sunny yellow cardigan, faded blue jeans and navy flats. Those jeans hugged the curve of her butt in the best possible way.

Finally they made it outside, where the cool, fresh air chilled the heat his thoughts had generated. "Where are you parked?"

"In the lot by city hall," she said.

He knew it was a couple blocks from here. "Me, too. Mind if I walk with you?"

"No."

He'd half expected her to shut him down and was glad she hadn't. Above them, old-fashioned streetlights illuminated the sidewalk in front of the town's community center. People headed in different directions, so the crowd was melting away. The echo of voices faded and soon there was just the sound of their footsteps on concrete.

Sloan fell into step next to her, walking on the street side. "What did you think of my presentation?"

"Very informative." She glanced up at him and the moonlight revealed her teasing smile. "On the plus side, I didn't hear anyone around me snoring."

"Ouch. That boring?" He slid his right hand into his slacks pocket to minimize the temptation of linking his fingers with hers. "Or are you mocking me?"

"What do you think?"

"I think I don't want to know," he said.

"Actually, you did a good job of giving the facts without too much embellishment. Short and sweet." She held up the packet of material that had been handed out. "This was a good move. If anyone wants to know more, they can read it or Google Holden Development as you suggested. Because everyone absorbs information differently."

"How so?"

"Some people are auditory and a speech works for them. Some are visual and need to read things in order to internalize it. I'm one of those."

"Oh?" He liked that she seemed in the mood to talk, and he was content to listen, hear the sound of her voice.

"And here's an example. Have you ever made the mistake of agreeing to take one of those phone surveys?"

"Can't say that I have."

"Right," she said drily. "You have a layer of protection from annoying calls. Okay. I'll explain. Someone asks you to take a survey, then reads several paragraphs and wants you to evaluate it on a scale of one to ten, one being very likely and ten being highly unlikely. By the time they're finished reading, I can't even remember the rating system."

"I'll have to tell my assistant never to put one of those calls through to me."

She laughed. "I suspect she doesn't really need a directive from you."

"Probably not." Still, as someone who'd lived here all her life, he valued her opinion and wanted her thoughts on tonight. "How do you think the audience in general responded?"

"Favorably. The people around me were smiling and nodding." She looked up at him. "But they were women who could just be taken in by your charm and good looks."

"You think I'm charming?"

She turned right into the city hall parking lot. "Do you really want me to answer that? Are you a quart low on ego?"

"Maybe." He laughed and realized that was what he'd missed most. Her making him laugh.

"All I'll say is that you are pleasant company." She stopped by the familiar SUV. "Here's my car."

Sloan realized he wasn't ready to give up her company and go back to the impersonal landlady/boarder existence they'd settled into. He wanted to talk to her, but the idea of asking her to spend time with him was a little nerve-racking. It felt a lot like being a teenager and asking a girl you had a crush on to the prom.

Maybe he *was* a little low on ego.

All she could do was say no.

"Would you like to get a quick bite to eat before going back to the house? Or a drink if you already had dinner?"

She had her keys out but stopped before pressing the button on the fob that would unlock the doors. Hesitantly, she met his gaze.

When a few seconds passed without an answer, he filled the silence and gave her an out if she wanted one. "You probably have to get back to Danielle."

"Actually, Josie is with her. And I didn't have a chance to eat before the meeting." She smiled and said, "I'm pretty hungry."

He was, too, but not necessarily for food. Being with Maggie in the moonlight brought back memories of kissing her and the yearning to do it again. "Good."

"Really? You're happy that I'm starving and could eat a horse?"

"No. Of course not. I just meant good that you want to have something to eat with me." Dear God, now he sounded like an overeager, inexperienced teenager in addition to feeling like one.

"I know what you meant." She thought for a moment. "What about Bar None? It will be less crowded than the diner and no one under twenty-one is allowed inside. Don't get me wrong, I adore my daughter, but on the rare occasions she's not with me, it's kind of nice to go somewhere only grown-ups are allowed."

"Bar None it is." He opened her car door for her. "See you there."

"Okay." She smiled and shut herself inside.

Sloan jogged to his car; he was in a hurry. Partly because he was looking forward to seeing her, but mostly because he was afraid she would change her mind.

But ten minutes later they were sitting at a bistro table in the establishment on Main Street. Cardboard menus stood up on the table and they each took one. He studied the listed items and still managed to glance at Maggie when she wasn't looking. She probably wouldn't make the list of the world's ten most beautiful women, unlike most of the ones he'd dated, but there was something about her that drew him.

"I think I'll have the soup-and-salad combo," she said. "And a glass of white wine."

"A sensible choice."

There was a twinkle in her eyes when she said, "I bet you're going for the B and B—burger and beer."

"What gave me away?"

"It was the sensible part. And the fact that you're a guy."

Just then, a waitress came over and took their orders. She told them she'd be back with their drinks and the food was coming right up. Then they were alone again.

"What does being a guy have to do with ordering a hamburger?" he asked.

"Don't forget the sensible part. It implies that you are fully aware of more nutritional choices you could make. But nine times out of ten a man will get red meat and the only hint of healthy is the lettuce, tomato and onion that comes on it."

"You do realize that's negatively profiling men," he pointed out.

"Profiles exist for a reason. Think about your guy friends. Tell me I'm wrong."

"It's as if you're psychic," he teased.

"Hardly. Danny used to—" Suddenly she stopped, as if she'd just revealed national secrets, and all the merriment disappeared. The expression on her face could only be described as guilt. "Never mind."

If it would help, he would encourage her to talk about the husband she'd lost. Because after she mentioned him, the carefree young woman who'd been enjoying herself was gone.

He might be a selfish bastard, but Sloan wanted that young woman back.

Maggie had always enjoyed busy, mindless chores like cutting up vegetables for the following morning's omelets. Tonight she realized it gave her too much time to think. She was doing that now as she put sliced mushrooms into a container, then pressed the lid on it.

She should never have accepted Sloan's dinner invitation.

He'd caught her at a weak moment. The problem was that every moment around Sloan made her weak. Not only that, she hadn't been ready when he'd asked her to get a bite to eat. She'd been so sure that he wouldn't waste any more time on her. Then he'd surprised her and the word *yes* had come out of her mouth before she could think it through.

At Bar None things had been going well. She'd been relaxed and that was when it happened. She'd started to tell Sloan that Danny had never listened to her warnings about limiting hamburgers. It felt wrong to talk to another man about him, especially because she felt something for Sloan. But it was as if she'd turned her back on her husband. If she and Sloan hadn't already ordered food, she would have made an excuse and walked out. A hasty exit would have been better than the awkward conversation that had followed. Still, it was her punishment for saying yes in the first place.

The only thing that saved her more awkwardness on the drive home was having her own car. Sloan had followed her, and when they'd arrived at the house, he'd said good-night and used the outside stairs to go to his room.

Danielle was peacefully sleeping and Josie had gone to bed. Maggie was alone and couldn't shut off her thoughts.

"Maggie, I—"

"Dear God—" She started at the unexpected male voice behind her. Her pulse throbbed when she turned around to face Sloan. "You scared me."

"Sorry. Next time I'll whistle. Or clear my throat. Or something."

"Yeah. Something."

She saw that he'd changed out of his expensive dark suit and silk, charcoal tie. The jeans and cotton shirt with its sleeves rolled up made him look every bit as attractive. Sexy, in a rugged way. That just proved dangerous thinking could happen even when you were cutting up vegetables.

They stared uneasily at each other for several moments, then finally she remembered he was a paying guest. She'd freshened his room that morning and replaced the towels.

"Is there something you need?"

"Yes."

"I'll get it for you right away. How can I help you?"

"You can talk to me." He moved closer, stopping at the kitchen island that separated them. His light brown eyes darkened and began to smolder as he stared at her.

Her heart started pounding again and it had nothing to do with being startled. He didn't want to discuss sheets, towels, the B and B's choice of body lotion or lack of a chocolate on his pillow. This was personal and didn't come under the heading of hospitality.

"It's late, Sloan. I have a busy day tomorrow and you probably do, too. Can we talk another time?"

"I'd prefer to have a conversation now. If you don't mind." He folded his arms over his chest. "While you're vulnerable."

"Excuse me?"

"It's not what you're thinking. I'd never take advantage of you. But I need to understand what happened tonight at Bar None." He didn't look confused as much as determined not to let her off the hook.

"Okay." She gave him points for being straightforward. It was a little unexpected, given his well-publicized dating history. "But I'm not sure what you mean about something happening tonight."

"Have you ever heard the expression when you bury your head in the sand you leave your backside exposed?"

"No. But I get it."

"Do you?" he challenged. "If you think there wasn't a thing tonight, then you've got more than your head buried in the sand."

"Maybe you should define it for me," she suggested. It could be something else, although that thought was proof of her attempting to bury her head in said sand.

"Okay." Intensity shone in his eyes. "Tonight at the bar I was having a good time. Things were easy between us. Joking, laughing. Unless I miss my guess, you were enjoying yourself. Or am I wrong?"

She couldn't tell a lie. "You're not wrong."

Some of the tension eased in his jaw and he looked a little surprised. As if he hadn't expected her to admit he was right. "The truth is, I'd very much like to take you out again."

Once more she had to be honest. "I can't do it."

"What? Have fun?"

"I have nothing against fun," she said. "It's going out with you I have a problem with."

"Why?"

"It's not fair to you. I have a child—"

"You can't hide behind Danielle forever." Sloan shook his head and the muscle in his jaw jerked. "Things were fine tonight until you mentioned your husband and realized you were having fun. Then it was as if you'd committed an unforgivable sin because for a little while you were a woman who was having a good time with a man and forgot to be a widow."

"You make it sound as if I pull out that designation to wear as a Halloween mask."

"Your words."

"You don't know me well enough to make that call," she accused.

"I'll tell you what I do know." He put his palms flat on the granite island and leaned toward her. "I get that you lost your husband, the man you loved and built a life with. The father of your child. I also admit that I have no idea what you went through. But I do know that it's been several years."

"What does that have to do with anything?"

"I'm getting to that," he said. "The night we kissed, you kissed me back."

"How do you—"

He held up a hand to stop her. "You are forever bringing up my reputation with women. Even if only half of the stories are true, it implies that I have a certain level of understanding and familiarity with the fairer sex. I know when there's a spark and when there isn't." His gaze held hers. "You and I could have started a forest fire with all the sparks swirling around us."

Maggie realized he had a point. And she knew her own romantic history could never compete with his in terms of experience. She wasn't good at pretending and wished she could take back that kiss. The fact that he had a point took a lot of the starch out of her comeback choices.

The best she could do was "An out-of-control fire leaves nothing but scorched earth behind."

"That sounds like an Asian proverb and brings me to my point. I do have one," he said. "Either you're still in love with the husband you lost and there's no room in your heart for another man. Or—"

She realized she'd been holding her breath, waiting for him to say the rest. Part of her was afraid to hear the or, but she couldn't stop herself from asking, "Or what?"

"Or you don't believe you deserve to be happy."

That struck a nerve. "Since when does a building contractor dabble in psychobabble?"

"Almost never. But, for some reason, I can't help it with you. So sue me." He dragged his fingers through his hair. "If you're still in love with your husband, that's the end of it. But if you're afraid to be happy, there's something I can do about that."

"Like what?"

Sloan stared at her for several moments without saying anything. Then he just smiled before turning away and walking out of the room.

Maggie had thought there was a lot to think about before. Now her mind was humming with questions about what Sloan planned to do about making her happy.

Chapter Nine

"Sorry I'm late, Maggie." Jill Stone slid into the booth and let out a sigh. The redhead smiled across the table. "Bet you thought I was going to cancel again."

"When one has children, plans are automatically subject to change at a moment's notice. And I was so confident and optimistic that you would be here, I let the hostess seat me." She grinned at her friend. "I'm just glad you made it this time. Let's call it diner lunch, take two."

"Works for me."

"I know C.J. is in school. Where's Sarah? I'm sure you didn't leave her by herself," Maggie said.

Jill laughed at the very idea of it. "My daughter is with her nana and papa. Adam's folks are here from Texas for a visit. They love babysitting."

"Aren't grandparents the best thing ever?" Maggie was lucky to still have her mom. Unfortunately Danny's parents had both passed away even before their son got married. It was sad that Danielle wouldn't have a chance to meet the Potter side of her family. Again there was a stab of guilt over putting off children and the wish that she could change the past.

"The best ever," Jill agreed.

"I guess C.J. is feeling better now?"

Jill shuddered. "It was a nasty virus. Went through the whole family. We ran out of tissues and poor Adam was blowing his nose on toilet paper. At least I never made it here and exposed you. You're lucky."

Maggie's luck was open to interpretation. She'd had lunch with Sloan the day Jill had canceled on her and it had been fun. But he'd also said that her declaration about no more kissing sounded like a challenge. One he'd so far resisted. And the other night he'd implied that he planned to do something to convince her to not be afraid to be happy.

"How's Danielle?" Jill asked.

"Great. Growing too fast. Does it sound horrible if I say that she's the most beautiful, brilliant, sweet, adorable child in the whole world?"

Jill pretended to be shocked. "She can't be. My Sarah is the most stunning, smart, kind—"

"Yeah, yeah." Maggie laughed. "I guess every mom feels that way about her kids."

The server, Brandon Sherman, walked over. "Hi, Maggie. Jill. I see you two made the lunch date work this time. Everyone's okay?"

"My children cooperated by staying healthy," her friend said. "How are you, Brandon? What's going on in your life? Not that we don't enjoy hearing about everything, but it helps us remember what it was like to be young."

"Yeah, you guys are pretty old. Just saying…" He grinned, then said, "I'm great. My online classes are okay. Getting some units out of the way." The teen shrugged. "Just socking away money for school in the fall."

"Where are you planning to go?" Maggie asked. "Somewhere warm?"

"I wish." He grinned. "The University of Montana."

"Do you know what you want to study?" Jill looked at the young man.

"Chemical engineering, I think."

"Wow. Good luck with that," Maggie said. "I guess you're not going to follow your father's footsteps into construction."

Brandon winced. "I have two left thumbs where tools are concerned. And anyway, my dad would be a tough act to follow. He's an artist."

"It's true," Jill chimed in. "When Adam and I had our house built in the Lake Shore subdivision, your dad made the cabinets and they're perfect. He works with Alex McKnight."

"Aren't they involved in the renovations at Blackwater Lake Lodge?" Maggie asked.

"They are," Brandon confirmed. "And with the resort project breaking ground soon, there's some job security for him. Plus, an added financial source for me if necessary."

"You're going places, Brandon. Your parents must be very proud of you." Maggie admired the whole hardworking family.

"Not so much when it comes to cleaning my room or taking out the trash." He grinned and it made him look impossibly young. "I'm glad you guys finally got together for lunch. Although, speaking of that, Maggie did okay when you canceled. She ended up eating with Sloan Holden."

"Oh?" Jill's eyes glittered with the need to know more.

"I'll tell you later." Maggie looked at Brandon. "As you probably already are aware, we don't need menus. I'll have the chicken salad with oil and vinegar dressing. And a diet cola."

"Not me." Jill was looking superior. "I lost weight when I was sick and have room to be bad. I'd like the Mama Bear combo and iced tea."

The teen wrote it on his pad. "Coming right up, ladies."

Maggie watched him walk away. "He's so cute. Someday in the not too distant future he's going to be a heart-breaker."

"You're so right."

"But let's talk about that burger and fries. You're really going to eat it in front of me?" Maggie grumbled.

"Oh, yes. And I plan to savor every bite."

"I may have to steal one, maybe two, of your fries."

"Of course. What are friends for? On one condition," Jill added.

"What?" Here we go, Maggie thought.

"You have to tell me how you ended up with Sloan. What happened?"

"Nothing." Not that day anyway. "When you canceled, I started to leave just as he was coming in. We said hello and the hostess assumed we were two for lunch." She shrugged. "So he insisted we sit at the same table."

"Insisted? You didn't want to?" Jill gave her a "what the heck is wrong with you" look. "I saw him at the chamber of commerce meeting last week. He's gorgeous."

"Looks aren't everything."

"No, but it's not a bad start. And he's renting a room from you. Is he a jerk?"

"Not so far." It would be easier if he were. "He seems like a nice guy. He's not around much, but when he is, Danielle won't leave him alone."

"Oh?"

"On his very first morning at Potter House she was fussy and didn't want either Josie or me. Plus, I was trying to get breakfast on the table." Maggie remembered how he'd jumped in to help. Like a white knight to the rescue. "He made the mistake of taking her outside, which is her favorite place to be. Now he's her hero. The way she acts, you'd think he walks on water."

"So put a check mark in the good-with-kids column."

Clearly Jill was being a loyal friend and wearing her matchmaker's hat.

Still, Maggie was relieved when Brandon arrived with their food, salad for her, burger and fries for Jill. Then he set the drinks in front of them.

"Ketchup is on the table." They gave him a really-this-is-us look and he shrugged. "I know you know, but it's habit. Anything else I can get you?"

"No," they both said.

"Enjoy your lunch."

Maggie knew her friend well and was aware that she would go back to digging for information on Sloan unless she changed the subject. "How are things with you and Adam?"

Jill glowed, and it had nothing to do with her red hair. Quite simply she radiated happiness. "I don't want to say perfect, but it's pretty darn close. Adam is a wonderful man. Handsome, smart, funny, kind. Great with the kids."

"This is coming perilously close to mom bragging," Maggie teased.

"It's different. Trust me."

"How so?"

Jill looked thoughtful, as if trying to find the words to explain. "With kids you love them unconditionally because they come into your life tiny, sweet, innocent. Their future is a blank slate. But when a man becomes part of the equation it's complicated. Everyone comes with flaws and baggage."

"But it's worked out for you." Maggie wasn't asking. She didn't need to. The truth was there on Jill's face, the happiness that made her glow.

"Yes, it worked out pretty darn well." She picked up a fry and bit into it. "We love the new house. It's big and beautiful, but the best part is that Adam has an office right off the family room. I don't mean I like that he has to do paperwork, just that he's home when he does it. Close to the activity."

"Must be nice having him there." Maggie speared some lettuce with her fork.

"It is. He helps C.J. with his homework, and when the weather's nice they play ball outside. My son adores Adam and I'm glad C.J. has a positive role model."

"That's so great."

Smiling, she said, "And he's so sweet with Sarah. He plays with her, whether it's a tea party, dolls or just tickling to make her giggle. That makes us all laugh. It's the cutest thing."

"Children laughing is the sweetest sound."

Maggie felt regret stab her in the heart. Danny never had the chance to see his daughter, let alone play dolls with her or hear her laugh. The sadness that was never far away welled up and stole her appetite. She picked at her salad and sipped her cola. Jill went to town on her burger and ate most of it, but left a few bites.

"I'm so full." She looked across the table and frowned. "Don't you want some of these fries?"

Maggie shook her head. "No, thanks."

"Are you sure?" Jill pushed. "I thought we'd have to arm wrestle for them."

"Actually, I'm not that hungry."

"Is everything all right?" Jill leaned forward a little. "We've been friends for a long time, so I'll know if you're just putting on a brave face."

"Okay, then, I'll come clean." Maggie knew her friend was right and would see through her. "I envy you. I'm not proud of it, and I don't want to say jealous because somehow that sounds resentful and spiteful. So I'll say it this way. I'm envious of the fact that you have such a beautiful family."

"I know you mean it in the nicest possible way and are happy for me," Jill said.

"Absolutely true. You have everything that I ever wanted."

Jill reached over and squeezed her hand. "You can still have it. The right man will come along. Maybe he already has. Sloan seems—"

"No. A person gets one shot at happy-ever-after, and mine died with Danny."

"Maggie, keep an open mind. You just never know what's going to happen."

True. If she had, she would have agreed to have the child her husband had so intensely wanted. Her chest tightened with sadness, regret and a healthy dose of guilt. If he could have known his daughter she might feel differently, but right now she felt that she owed a debt that could never be repaid.

Guilt was turning out to be Maggie's new best friend. It pricked her now because she'd turned this lunch into a slushy, mushy outing and her friend needed lighthearted. Subject change pronto.

"Speaking of not knowing what's going to happen, what can you tell me about the man who bought your old place by the marina on the lake?"

"His name is Jack Garner and he's a writer. His first book was a runaway bestseller. Apparently he's working on the second one and was looking for a quiet place. He liked that mine had an apartment for his office and one for living space. Plus, views of the lake and mountains."

"Did you meet him? How old is he?"

"We did. I'd say he's somewhere in his midthirties. Handsome. Dark. Brooding."

"And reclusive," Maggie said. "As far as I know, no one in town sees him. At least not anyone I know."

"You should go out there, march up to the front door and introduce yourself," Jill suggested.

"Are you playing matchmaker again?"

"What gave me away?" her friend teased.

"Your big, generous heart."

That and the fact that they'd been friends for a long time. Jill had taken shifts at the ice cream parlor when Maggie had experienced a problem in her pregnancy with Danielle and was ordered to stay off her feet. It had made the difference in keeping her business afloat through a very difficult time. And her friend was just interested in helping her now. If only scooping ice cream could fix her current problem.

"I love you for it, Jill." She smiled. "But matchmaking for me is doomed to failure."

"I think your mom is home, Shorty."

Sloan heard a car drive up, but Danielle was completely oblivious. She continued talking to her doll in a language no one but her could understand. It looked as if every toy she owned was on the floor. If there was a way to harness her energy and market it, he could make a fortune. He'd been with her for about an hour and the closest she'd come to stopping was putting her head on his shoulder in a sort of hug. The kid was a hoot and a half.

The front door opened and Maggie walked in carrying a couple of grocery bags. She did a double take, and he figured that had more to do with Josie not being here than the fact that her living room looked as if a toy store exploded inside it.

"Where's Josie?"

Before he could explain, her little girl said, "Mama!"

Maggie smiled. "Hi, baby girl."

The toddler let loose with another stream of unintelligible sounds and an occasional word that was clear. But it was the weirdest thing. The tone, inflection and gesturing looked as if she was explaining that for the past hour he'd been sitting on the floor, playing when encouraged and generally just making sure she was okay.

Maggie set the bags just inside the door and walked over to hug her child. Then she looked down at him and asked again, "Where's Josie?"

"Ah, you don't understand her, either."

"What do you mean?"

"Danielle was just telling you what's going on. It's clearly exposition, but average humans like you and me can't understand."

"Very observant of you, Sloan. But I'd still like to know what's going on. Preferably in exposition that a run-of-the-mill human like myself can comprehend."

"Josie had a date for dinner. The early-bird special, I guess."

"With who?"

A hint of romance brought out the curiosity in a woman, he noted. "She didn't say. It came up suddenly and she was going to call you. I happened to be here working. Mostly to get away from the phone."

"That's what you get for volunteering your number at a town meeting," she pointed out.

"Lesson learned." He watched the little girl tug on her mother's hand, then pat the rug next to him. The message was as clear as Maggie's reluctance to take the hint. Danielle wanted her mother to sit beside him. He was all in favor but Maggie was still waiting for the rest of his explanation. "I told Josie not to bother you to come home early. I needed a break from the work and volunteered to watch Shorty."

"That's very nice of you, Sloan. I hope she hasn't been too much of a bother."

"No trouble at all. I feel like one of those dancers who just stands there while his partner does cartwheels and dances circles around him, making him look like a world-class hoofer." He shrugged. "I just sat here."

"So you were simply keeping her safe."

There was a soft look in Maggie's eyes, the kind of look that made a guy feel like a hero.

"Yeah. I didn't want her to stick her finger in a light socket or invite boys over."

Maggie laughed. "I think that's a few years off. But I can't help wondering what you'd have done if you had to change a diaper. One of *those*."

"One of what?" Then it hit him. "*Oh*. Well… Hmm."

"Yeah. Hmm." She grinned.

"Smart aleck."

"Rookie." She was still smiling. "Have you ever changed a dirty diaper?"

"I've never changed one at all," he said. "But I like to think I'd have rallied to the occasion. Risen to the challenge."

"Oh, how I would have loved to be there for that. I can see the magazine headline now—Dapper Bazillionaire Bachelor on Diaper Duty." This time when her little girl tugged on her hand and patted the rug, Maggie sat beside him. Danielle sat on his thigh, between them.

"I'm sure you would," he said drily.

"Is there anything more irresistible to a woman than a big strong man caring for a child?"

"I don't know. You tell me."

Right here in this house he'd told her that he could do

something about showing her she deserved to be happy and had meant every word. He would bet his last nickel that she hadn't been with anyone since her husband died. That probably should have warned him off, but he couldn't stop himself from wanting her. He wanted to be the man who showed her that life was good and there was nothing wrong with living it to the fullest.

Hell, he wasn't a saint. The fact was, they had chemistry and he couldn't let it go.

"I think one picture of you being nice to a child would have women all over the world throwing themselves at your feet. And breaking into your hotel room."

"Writing their phone number on my cardboard coffee cup?"

"Buying your coffee," she said.

"The thing is, I wasn't asking about whether or not women in general would find me irresistible. I was asking if you do."

A flush crept into her cheeks and she didn't quite meet his gaze. "It doesn't matter what I think."

It did, oddly enough, and the fact that she wouldn't answer directly meant he got the answer he wanted. She might have a problem resisting him. But he sensed that pushing her too far too fast would drive her away.

"Maggie, the truth is that I enjoyed hanging out with your little girl. She's very good company."

"Interesting." She met his gaze now. "Considering the fact that, as you so accurately pointed out, she's not exactly a gifted conversationalist just yet."

"In reality, it was the perfect dialogue. She spilled her secrets in code so I can't rat her out to you. And I ran construction numbers past her while she trashed the room with toys. Everyone is happy." He glanced around and picked up the pink car she'd dropped beside him. "Did you buy her all of these?"

"No way. Most of them came from her uncle."

"Way to go, Brady." Sloan could see himself spoiling a niece or nephew shamelessly.

Then Danielle stood, walked over to a soft stuffed doll and picked it up before wandering around the room with it in her arms as she chattered away.

"Can I ask you a question, Sloan?"

"That was a question."

"You're impossible. I'd hate to be a reporter who was trying to interview you." She made a frustrated sound.

"Okay. Sorry. It's a firmly embedded deflection technique." He'd noticed the tone of her voice had become serious and that made him wonder what she was thinking. If he didn't want to answer, he'd find a way not to. "Ask me anything."

"You're so good with kids." She met his gaze directly and didn't glance away. "Why aren't you married with a family of your own?"

Curious, he thought. It had taken Maggie a while to ask what was usually one of the first things a woman wanted to know about him. Since he was divorced, he would simply tell everyone that he wasn't very good husband material. That had backfired and he was dealing with the consequences and ducking the truth in interviews.

But he didn't want to avoid it with Maggie.

"My mother's Italian. Antonia Delvecchio Holden is outgoing, loving and an incurable romantic."

"She sounds wonderful."

"She is—a force of nature." He couldn't help smiling. "Also pushy, determined and bossy. She believes with every fiber of her being that she knows best. I think it was at my college graduation that she started dropping not-so-subtle hints about me taking a wife and having babies. I just laughed it off, assuming she was joking."

"She wasn't?"

"My mother doesn't joke about that sort of thing," he said ruefully. "The more I ignored her, the more she pressed. Resisting the suggestion of settling down became a reflex for me, automatic."

"But that changed?" Maggie asked.

He nodded. "I met Leigh at a children's hospital charity event. She was a personal trainer. To this day I'm not sure how she scored a ticket to the affair and at the time I really didn't care. I was blown away and thought I'd found *the one*. Just shows how screwed up my judgment is. Then I made the mistake of marrying her first and asking questions later."

"Why?"

Sloan didn't think Maggie was judging him at all, let alone as hard as he was criticizing himself. He remembered his disillusionment and thought about how different his ex-wife was from Maggie. She'd insisted on taking out a small-business loan and turned her home into a B and B to pay for it instead of taking interest-free money from her brother. He looked into her dark brown eyes and knew integrity was staring back at him.

"Shopping and status were more important to my bride than having a family. I ignored the credit card bills coming in, assuming the retail thrill would wear off. But a year later it still hadn't and I thought maybe she needed a different focus." When Maggie opened her mouth to say something, Sloan held up a hand to stop the words. "I know. If the relationship already had problems, bringing a child into it was just going to make it worse. At that point I hadn't admitted it was a mistake."

"What convinced you?"

"I jumped in with both feet and suggested we start a family." A familiar knot of anger and bitterness coiled inside him at the memory. "She laughed and said that it had taken too much work to keep her body in perfect shape. If I wanted her to ruin it, I would have to pay her the big bucks."

"I can't believe anyone would do that." Maggie's eyes grew wide with disbelief. "I assume that before the wedding she understood that you wanted a family."

"Yes. And she claimed to want that, too." He stared at Danielle sitting in the center of the room fitting together plastic blocks that were as big as her tiny hands. This child had been conceived out of love, the way it should be. "She lied to me."

"That's really low." There was sympathy in Maggie's gaze and something else that wasn't as clear.

"I took the failure of my marriage badly, but the breakup hit my mother even harder. She'd grown attached to Leigh and treated her like one of her own daughters."

"That doesn't make you bad husband material," Maggie pointed out.

"It's proof that my judgment is flawed, which is almost the same thing."

"I see. And now you have trust issues."

"Yes." That was part of it. The other part was being made a fool of. Sloan wouldn't let it happen again.

"That's too bad. You'd have made a terrific father."

"Back at you." At her blank look he said, "It's too bad you're standing in your own way, because you're a terrific mom and should have more children."

Her existing child had disappeared from sight and there was a suspicious rustling of bags by the front door.

Maggie didn't seem to hear it. She was looking at him

intently. "Aren't we a pair. Both of us with so much baggage we're tripping over it."

Sloan was almost sure there was regret in her comment, a chink in her armor. Before he could ask, Danielle toddled over to them with a box in her hands.

"Cookie," she said.

Maggie laughed, then looked at Sloan. "What was that you said about not understanding her?"

"I believe I said an occasional word was comprehensible."

"Why did it have to be this one?" She took the box from her daughter, who started to protest loudly. "Just one. You'll spoil your appetite."

Sloan definitely felt regret when she stood and walked away because he missed the warmth of her body and the sweetness of her that was like sunshine to the soul. But he didn't regret answering her question about why he'd vowed never to marry again. He was glad he'd given her the facts. She should know what she was getting into when she slept with him.

And she would. He would bet his last nickel on it.

Chapter Ten

Sloan was having trouble concentrating on work. Maggie was on his mind, more specifically her reaction to learning why he never planned to marry again. The problem was, he'd been unable to gauge her reaction. Would that strengthen her resistance to anything personal between them?

With an effort, he pushed that problem to the side for right now. He and Burke were in his cousin's office with Ellie McKnight, their local architect. She was sitting in the chair behind the desk while they stood on either side of her, going over preliminary plans for the new resort complex near the base of the mountain.

Sloan was intently studying the blueprints and zeroed in on the hotel walls. "You know there's a plastic wrap that can be put around the building to reduce the amount of air leakage through the envelope, that barrier between inside and outside."

"I'm aware of it." Ellie tucked a strand of long brown hair behind her ear then made a note on the plans. "I've included an initial materials list for your consideration, alteration and approval."

Burke nodded absently as he studied the top paper on the thick stack that was nearly as wide as his desk. "At the risk of sending you screaming from the room, Ellie, can we round these walls that face north? It's more self-contained that way. The interior temperature is comfortably maintained without an increase in energy usage."

"I can do anything you want," she said cheerfully. "You've both made it clear that it isn't just the construction process that needs to be green, but the energy sustainability of the building itself."

Sloan was glancing through the list Ellie had provided. "I don't see it on here, but I can provide you the information. There's an innovation for elevators. A company has put a high-friction polyurethane coating over a carbon-fiber core to create a lighter and stronger conventional steel rope. It eliminates the disadvantages of the material currently being used, and the efficiency reduces energy consumption."

"Can you make a note of that on the list?" Ellie asked.

"Of course." He grabbed a pencil from Burke's desk and did as requested.

Sloan knew that the foundation of any construction project was rooted in the concept and design stages. Building, as a process, wasn't streamlined and changed from project to project. Each one was complex, composed of a multitude of materials and components, each constituting various design variables. Any difference in one of them could affect the environment during the building's relevant life cycle. It was important to get this right, and they plowed through the details for the rest of the morning.

"I think we've got this," Sloan finally said, glancing at his watch. Noting that it was just after one, he picked up the phone and asked his assistant to order in some food from the Harvest Café. "I don't know about anyone else but I'm starving."

"Right there with you," Burke said.

"I hope the café sandwiches are all right with you two?"

"I love the food there," Ellie chimed in.

"Me, too." Burke straightened and looked at the architect. "This is really good work."

She flashed a pleased smile and said in her charming Texas drawl, "Aw, you're just sayin' that because you're engaged to my sister-in-law and would rather walk on hot coals than have her mad at you for hurting my feelings."

"No offense," his cousin said, "but this is business and I can't worry about your emotional well-being. That's your husband's job."

"And Alex is really good at it, but you're talkin' awfully brave," she teased. "Seriously, I'm glad you're happy with the overall design. I will incorporate all the changes you've mentioned. And it has to be said that I'm thrilled to have the opportunity to work with your firm. It will be an impressive addition to my résumé."

"You're very talented and we're lucky to have you," Burke said. "And I'm impressed by your conscientious attention to detail, your punctuality and, most important, you really listen."

"Thank you for saying so. My goal is always to be as professional as possible."

"It may not be completely professional, but I believe it falls under the heading of friendliness to ask about someone's family. So I'm going to," Burke said. "You have a little girl, don't you?"

"Yes. Leah."

Sloan had heard about pregnancy glow, but nothing about the glow of pride on a mother's face when talking about her child. Although he'd seen Maggie wear that look every time she glanced at her daughter. "How old is Leah?"

"A little over two. A challenging age for sure."

Right around the same age as Danielle, and he wouldn't

describe her as challenging. Cute as could be, maybe, but not difficult. But he wasn't her primary parent and didn't feel the weight of responsibility for her whole life. If it were up to him, he would give her a cookie whenever she wanted one, so it was probably a good thing it wasn't up to him.

Burke's blue eyes twinkled as he looked down at Ellie. "Syd has promised me that our first child will be a boy, to put a halt to pink domination in the younger generation of her family."

"Don't look now," Ellie said, "but she really has no control over that."

"The truth is that I don't really care about the gender of our children. A little girl as beautiful as her mother would be fine with me."

"That's what I thought. Trust me when I say you weren't fooling anyone." She leaned back in the desk chair and studied his cousin. "But all this talk about children makes me wonder. Is there an imminent announcement on that front?"

"No," Burke said. "We've discussed it, of course. Syd wants to wait awhile. Have some time for just the two of us. And I want what she wants. Making her happy is the most important thing."

"She's a lucky girl," Ellie said. "She's also right. After kids come along everything will be different forever. There's no more being selfish, doing what you want anytime you feel like it. There's another little human whose needs come first." She smiled and her green eyes grew tender. "The weird thing is, you don't really mind. There's an overwhelming compulsion to do anything and everything to make your child's life as perfect as possible."

Sloan listened to his cousin and their architect discuss relationships with present family and future expansions of it. Again he felt as if he was on the outside looking in, a little empty. No personal experiences to share. Well, that wasn't completely true. A time or two he almost jumped in with a comment about Maggie, her daughter and the obvious maternal devotion.

What stopped him was that any interjection would change the dynamic of this conversation and shift attention to him. And Maggie. He would push back and say there was no him and Maggie. Not because he was against the idea. And maybe she was beginning to weaken. Last night, after he made sure she understood that he wasn't a forever-after kind of guy, he'd seen her regret and possibly a decline in her resistance. He couldn't help contemplating his next move and wasn't willing to discuss it.

"Right, Sloan?"

"Hmm?" He heard his name and knew a question was being asked, but had no idea what it was.

"I said, the partial closing of Blackwater Lake Lodge has really affected you."

"Yes. Right."

If he'd been able to get a room there, things would be different. He would probably have met Maggie, but doubted he'd have kissed her in the moonlight. The problem with kissing her was that it made him want more. Living in the same house, looking without touching, was skewering his focus and cranking up a need that grew more intense every day.

"How has it affected you?" Ellie asked. "Good or bad?"

"Both," he answered honestly.

"Specifically?" Burke pushed.

"Home-cooked meals go in the good column. And not living in a hotel for this extended assignment is great."

"What are the negatives?" Ellie wondered.

Maggie. Getting sucked in and captivated by her. Distracted every time he looked at or thought about her mouth, which led to contemplating what she looked like naked. He wasn't going to say any of that, however.

"I don't know. It's just different, I guess."

"Alex is doing the repairs and renovations," Ellie volunteered. "He says it will only be a few more weeks until the cosmetic details are complete. Soon everything will be shiny, new and ready to resume full operations. The rooms are up and running and I know they're taking reservations and accepting guests. And the restaurant is back in business. It's the lobby area and reception/banquet rooms he's concentrating on now."

"So." Burke sat on the corner of the desk. "It should be ready for my engagement party."

"Yes," Ellie answered.

"What party?" Sloan didn't know about this.

"Didn't I tell you?" His cousin frowned. "Damn, I meant to. Syd and I are having a party to celebrate our engagement. Don't you ever talk to your family?"

"Yes." But Sloan realized it had been a while. "Why?"

"I invited your folks and siblings. They would have said something to you if you ever got in touch with them."

"They're not coming, are they?" he teased.

Burke laughed. "Unless they cancel at the last minute, they said to count them in."

"Oh, boy. Do you think Syd is ready for that?"

"She has brothers," the other man said confidently. "She's ready for anything. Besides, you have a terrific family. I spent a lot of time at your house growing up and I know this for a fact."

"I can't wait to meet them," Ellie commented.

"Well, I hope it will be fun for everyone who got an invitation." Sloan folded his arms over his chest.

"Aren't you coming?" his cousin asked.

"I wasn't invited."

"Technically you are. I just forgot to tell you." He shrugged. "I've been busy."

"Yeah, I hear that." Sloan grinned. "Of course I'll be there. You're the brother I never had."

"Good. Feel free to bring a plus one."

Ellie's ears perked up. There was no visual confirmation of that fact, but her next statement proved it. "I heard you've been seeing Maggie."

Sloan only wanted to shoot down that rumor because Maggie was so skittish about dating. But there was visual evidence to back up Ellie's statement because the two of them had been out to dinner with Burke and Syd. Then there had been lunch at the diner and a bite to eat at Bar None after the chamber of commerce meeting. All of the above had been in full view of anyone in Blackwater Lake who cared to spread rumors. And that pretty much encompassed everyone in Blackwater Lake.

As far as Maggie was concerned, *date* was a four-letter word that she adamantly refused to use.

"Are you going out with Maggie?" Burke asked.

"I've been trying. But she doesn't make it easy."

At noon Sloan jumped into his car and headed to Maureen O'Keefe's house. Maggie's mom had called that morning and invited him to lunch at her home. She wouldn't hear of him taking her out, so he was on his way. He'd met her briefly in Brady's office, but today's invitation had initially surprised him. Then he'd figured it out. People were talking about him and Maggie and word had reached her mother.

He turned onto the street where Maggie had lived and drove slowly, checking out her old neighborhood. There were well-maintained yards in front of one- and two-story houses. When the GPS told him he was in front of the right one, he parked in front of it and got out. There was a pine tree in the center of the grass with pansies planted around it. He took the brick walkway leading to the wrap-around porch and front door. Almost immediately after he knocked it was answered.

"Sloan. Hello. Thank you for coming on such short notice."

"Thanks for inviting me. It's nice to see you again, Maureen."

"You, as well." She pulled the door open wider. "Please come in."

He did, then sniffed. "Something smells good."

She smiled a little tensely as she closed the door, then said, "I hope you like quiche."

Because real men eat it. There was a message, and now he knew this meeting was going to be a thing.

"Please come into the kitchen. Can I get you something to drink? Iced tea? Water? Soda? Wine? Beer?"

"I have a busy afternoon, so iced tea would be great."

While she got his drink, Sloan looked around. A granite-topped bar lined with stools separated the kitchen and family room. In it there was a fireplace with a man-tel and above it was a flat-screen TV. Wood floors were broken up by area rugs scattered throughout the room. On the walls were beautiful framed pictures of scenes that looked familiar.

Maureen set a tall glass on the bar in front of him. "Here you are."

"Thanks." He glanced around the family room. "Are those pictures on the walls of the mountains and lake here in town?"

"Yes, they are." Her tone indicated surprise and maybe that she was a tiny bit impressed that he'd recognized the subject matter. "They were taken by April Kennedy, a local photographer."

"I've seen her store on Main Street. The composition of the shots is wonderful and the shadows and reflection of mountains on water gives them a black-and-white sort of haunting look."

"Obviously you like them. You should stop by the store and see her. She has a lot more for sale."

"Right now I have nowhere to hang them."

"Because you're staying at my daughter's B and B." Dark eyes—Maggie's eyes—narrowed slightly, indicating a transition into her real reason for inviting him to lunch.

Sloan didn't get to be a successful businessman by dodging the tough issues. And there was no doubt in his mind that Maureen O'Keefe was tough. What surprised him was his unexpected reaction to the third degree he knew was coming. He really cared what Maggie's mom thought of him. Judging by what he knew of her daughter, this woman wouldn't respect anyone who didn't deal with her in a blunt, outspoken and honest way. Fortunately that's the only way he would deal.

"You didn't invite me to lunch just to be neighborly," he said. "This is about Maggie."

"And Danielle." Standing on the other side of the bar, she studied him for a moment, her hands gripping a coffee mug. "My daughter told me about you watching my granddaughter the night before last."

Sloan felt like a sixteen-year-old being interrogated about his intentions. He was so tempted to babble about his motivations being pure to convince her he wasn't a bad guy. But long ago he'd learned it was always best not to embellish. In everything you said there could be something to use against you. So he forced himself to respond only to the question.

"I did."

"You volunteered?"

"Yes."

"Why would you?" The look she gave him said "convince me you're sincere."

"I was just trying to help out. Josie had to leave before Maggie got home from work. I was there doing paperwork and needed a break." He shrugged. "It was a win for everyone."

"And you got to look like a hero." Maureen studied him for any sign that she was right.

"That wasn't my intention. It was knee-jerk. Just responding to the situation in a helpful way." He'd told her the truth; now it was time to push back a little. "Do you have a problem with that?"

"What I have a problem with is a playboy prancing into Maggie's life and sweeping her off her feet."

"Okay. Let's get something straight. I almost never prance."

One corner of Maureen's mouth curved up for a moment, then the humor faded. "But you didn't deny that you're a playboy."

"I am a male. But I don't appreciate being labeled as a man who toys with a woman's emotions."

"There are a lot of stories in newspapers that beg to differ with you about that." She took a sip of coffee. "Seems to me if there wasn't some truth in them, you would be filing lawsuits right and left."

"I have sued when lies were printed that hurt someone's reputation," he said.

"What about yours?"

Sloan could live with it mostly by ignoring what was printed. Number one: getting his name in the paper was a plug for his company. Number two: the sensational nature of the stories actually did him a favor. The women who came on to him because he was a wealthy, eligible bachelor were the ones he had no interest in. To anyone else, the articles were a horrible warning to avoid him like nuclear waste. It saved him from any temptation to break his no-commitment vow.

"My reputation," he said, "is what it is. Anyone I care about who really knows me is aware that's not who I am. The rest—" he shrugged "—I don't really give a rat's behind what they think."

"I guess I fall into the latter category."

"No, that's not what I meant—"

She held up a hand to stop him. "Whether you did or not doesn't change what I have to say. You're a paying customer at my daughter's bed-and-breakfast. I understand that's business. But things seemed to have taken a personal turn when you volunteered to babysit my granddaughter. I feel compelled to protect the two of them and warn you that if you're playing games with their affections it would be a very good idea for you to back off now."

"I assure you that's not what I'm doing."

"Maggie has been hurt enough."

Sloan met her gaze. "I understand what you're saying. I get it."

"Do you?" One of her eyebrows rose questioningly.

"Yes. I can't force you to believe me, but I would never deliberately cause Maggie distress."

"I truly hope you mean that."

"I've never meant anything more in my life. She's a special woman."

Maureen's face softened. "You'll get no argument from me about that."

He ran a finger through the condensation on the outside of his iced-tea glass. "The thing is, Maggie doesn't want another relationship. She's deliberately pushing me away. And before you say anything, I'm almost certain it's not only about losing her husband."

She frowned at him. "Why would you say that? How can you possibly know?"

"I kissed her."

"I know. She told me."

"She did?"

"It was two against one. Josie was on my side. Maggie said the kiss was nothing and both of you realized it meant nothing. Then she told us that you're a womanizer who's not interested in a commitment. That you're a nice man. Good with kids, but all flirt and no depth." Maureen shrugged. "I have perfect recall."

"I can see that." He was impressed. "What she may or may not have told you is that it was kind of her idea. She was going on about outrageous tabloid stories I was featured in and I jokingly asked if there was any way to stop her. She said, and I quote, 'feed me or kiss me.'" He shrugged. "So I did and she kissed me back. It affected her and meant something. But ever since it happened, she's been keeping me at arm's length."

"Maybe you're wrong about the kiss."

"I'm not."

He met her gaze, trying to decide whether or not he should tell her how he could be so sure. Then he realized he had to. This woman cared about her family and wanted to protect them. Sloan wanted that, too, even if it meant doing something to protect her from herself.

"I know she's attracted to me, Maureen. You're probably thinking that's ego talking, but that's not the case. It's experience. I'm not a playboy. I don't lead women on, but I do have a—what should I call it?"

"Active social life?" Maureen suggested wryly.

"That works. The thing is, I've met a lot of women and I can tell when someone is just pretending or when she's sincere. Your daughter doesn't have a dishonest cell in her body. She's open and honest. What she's feeling is right there on her face. Anyone who takes the time to look can see what's inside her." He met her gaze. "Believe me when I tell you that she kissed me back, then retreated from what she was feeling."

"Josie said she didn't believe Maggie when she said it was nothing." Concern replaced distrust on the older woman's face. "It doesn't take a gifted psychologist to realize she was devastated after losing Danny and doesn't want to fall in love and risk being hurt again."

Sloan figured she didn't pretend any more than her daughter did and was starting to believe him. "It feels to me as if she's refusing to let herself be happy. Like a punishment for something."

"What?"

"I wish I knew."

"If you're right," her mom said, "I have no idea why she would do that."

"You know her better than anyone."

"I used to think so, but it seems you know more about her than I do." She smiled, the first genuine warmth she'd exhibited since opening the door. "You're finding out things I didn't even suspect."

"I have a feeling she's buried whatever it is pretty deep. You have no reason to look for it."

"But I'm her mother."

"And she doesn't want to disappoint you," he said, knowing the feeling all too well.

"She never could do that. But I get it." Maureen sighed. "We should eat. You have a busy afternoon and I promised you lunch."

"It smells good," he said again. This time he grinned. "And I happen to like quiche very much."

She looked uncomfortable. "Don't hold it against me. I planned the menu when I was sure you were a heartless jerk."

"I have a heart," he told her. "But there are people who would tell you that there's no question I'm a jerk."

"I'm not one of them." She nodded resolutely. "I'll put the food on the table."

Sloan insisted on helping her. He needed something to keep his hands busy while his mind raced. And he came to a decision.

Since he was the one who'd discovered Maggie wouldn't let herself be happy, it seemed like his responsibility to find out why.

Chapter Eleven

After lunch with Maureen O'Keefe, Sloan returned to work. When he exited the elevator into the reception area on his floor he found Brady O'Keefe waiting for him. And the man didn't look happy.

"You're scowling. Did your computer hard drive crash? Or come up with a particularly nasty virus? Maybe someone didn't pay rent on their office space? I'll check with my assistant about that." Sloan looked at her empty chair. "When she gets back from lunch."

"That's not why I'm here. Can we talk? In your office? Where it's private?"

Sloan glanced around the obviously empty room. "What's wrong with this?"

"Trust me. You're going to want to have this conversation behind closed doors."

This had to be about Maggie. First her mother and now this. Sloan recognized the protective-big-brother look that was all over the other man, from the tension in his body to the hostility in his eyes.

"Okay." He walked into his office and shut the door after the other man followed. It was probably a good idea to put the desk between them, just in case. Sloan moved around it and sat in his chair. "It might save time if you knew that your mother already gave me the 'I'll hurt you if you hurt my daughter' talk."

Brady looked surprised. "When?"

"A little while ago. She invited me over for lunch. It was enlightening."

"So you're going to back off my sister?"

Sloan leaned forward and rested his forearms on the desk. "Again, in the interest of time, you should know that I don't respond well to threats."

Brady's eyes narrowed. "Since we're baring our souls here, you should know that I don't respond well when a publicity-obsessed playboy uses my niece. Clearly stepping in like a conquering hero was your attempt to get on my sister's good side in order to seduce her."

"You couldn't be more wrong."

"So you didn't babysit Danielle until Maggie got home when Josie had to leave?"

"No. I did."

"So you admit you're trying to get my sister in your bed?" Brady braced his feet wide apart and folded his arms over his chest.

Sloan *wanted* Maggie in his bed, but he hadn't watched Danielle to manipulate the situation in his favor. Still, he knew Brady didn't want an answer quite that blunt. Every woman could be a guy's sister, and being protective was just what brothers did. But there was no fighting the chemistry between women and men, and if your sister wanted to sleep with a guy, she would do it whether you approved of her actions or not. Sloan knew about these things.

"I will admit that I like Maggie. A lot," he added emphatically.

"If you like her, then leave her alone."

Sloan blew out a long breath. "Look, I'm not the heartless bastard the tabloids make me out to be."

"What does that mean?"

"It means that I'm photographed with a lot of women and the facts get twisted and embellished to sell magazines. If I'd really been serious about even half the women they say…"

"What?" Brady prodded.

"Let's just say I don't have that much stamina."

"I'm only concerned about one woman. Are you in love with my sister?" Brady moved closer to the desk and settled his palms flat on top of it, his eyes flashing angrily.

"I've never been in love," Sloan answered honestly. "I've never experienced it. I admire and respect Maggie—raising a child and building a business without help."

"No help? What am I? Chopped liver? I built her new website."

"I'm aware that she's got you and Maureen as backup. And Josie is there. Lucy is her partner. But she's a single mother and doing a great job. At the same time, her business is growing. She's an amazing woman. I can tell you without a doubt that I want to get to know her better. I look forward to finding out what makes her tick."

Sloan had never met anyone like her. He'd dated actresses and models who all had "people" to help them. Maggie was a superwoman and made it look easy. He meant every single word he'd just said, and the truth of it was even more clear to him now that her family was on his case to leave her alone.

"Why should I believe you?" Brady demanded.

"I could give you a PowerPoint presentation, but you know as well as I do that talk is cheap." He met the other man's gaze. "But you can take what I'm about to tell you to the bank. I won't say anything to her that I don't mean. I will never make a promise that I don't intend to keep, then walk away. I understand that she has an impressionable child, and whatever affects Maggie impacts her daughter."

"Very true." The other man nodded, then straightened away from the desk. "Danielle is little now, but she'll be affected even more when she gets older."

"I know." The idea of that little girl being used by a guy to get to her mom made Sloan really angry. "Look, Brady, I don't have any clue where this is going with Maggie. Maybe nowhere, because your sister is as stubborn as they come."

"Tell me about it." Brady sat in one of the chairs facing the desk. "I'm the guy she didn't come to for a business loan."

"Maggie has a mind of her own, so your guess is as good as mine about her. Probably better since she's your sister and you grew up with her." Sloan met the other man's gaze. "I can't promise she won't get hurt, but you can count on this. I will never lie to her or treat her with less than the utmost respect."

Brady nodded his understanding, then said, "Damn you."

"Excuse me? Now what's your problem?" Sloan didn't know what else to say. "So you want me to cut my wrist and sign something in blood?"

"As appealing as that sounds…" Brady grinned. "No. I'm ticked off because you were honest."

"What?" Sloan shook his head. "Now you've lost me."

"Okay, then, let me explain. If you were a low-down, lying, cheating, shallow bastard, it would give me an excuse to beat you up."

"Ah. Understood." Sloan smiled slowly. "Well, if it's any consolation, your mother made me eat salad and quiche for lunch."

"Dude—" Brady shook his head sympathetically. "Girl food. That's harsh."

"I'll survive."

"But that's going to leave a scar on your man card."

Sloan shrugged. "Chicks dig scars."

"I've heard that rumor." The other man stood. "I'll have to ask Olivia, my significant other and so much better half, whether or not that's true."

"Let me know the verdict."

"Will do." Brady headed for the door and opened it, then hesitated before leaving. "I hope you're not offended that I interfered. Another guy might—"

"I have three sisters."

"Dude," he said again in that sympathetic tone. "Tell me they're married."

Sloan shook his head. "All single."

"Harsh."

"Well said." He grinned. "And don't worry. We're good. I'd have done the same thing if I were in your shoes."

"Okay. And now I'm going to call my mother and give her a stern lecture about keeping me up-to-date so that I don't pile on when not absolutely necessary."

"Give Maureen my best."

Brady nodded. "Will do."

Alone in his office, Sloan thought about the conversations with Maggie's mother and brother. Commendable loyalty. There was a lot to admire about her whole family. If any of his sisters were in a situation like Maggie's, he would have done exactly what Maureen and Brady O'Keefe had done.

The thing was, he'd meant every single word he'd said to both of them. And that brought him to the law of unintended consequences. They'd forced him to put his intentions into words, made him really think about him and

Maggie and the price of his actions. Not only for him and Maggie, but Danielle, too.

His life would be much less complicated if he'd agreed to back off, but he just couldn't bring himself to do it. He thought about her, dreamed about her, ached to kiss her again and touch her everywhere.

When he gave his word, he kept it and took great pride in that. If he'd promised not to get personal with Maggie, it would have been a lie. Oh, he'd have tried his best, but the forces drawing them together seemed to have other ideas. So he couldn't tell her family that she was off-limits to him.

He really hoped he didn't come to regret that decision.

Maggie had just turned on her office computer and opened a business spreadsheet when she heard her cell phone. It was Josie's ring and she answered.

"Hey, Josie. I just left you. Is my little angel driving you crazy already?"

"I'm so sorry to call, Maggie. But I can't watch her today. There's an emergency. It's Hank Fletcher."

"The sheriff?" This was almost unbelievable; the man was barely sixty and in great physical shape. "What's wrong?"

"He was taken to Mercy Medical Clinic here in town. Adam thinks he had a heart attack."

"Oh, my God."

"He's being taken to the hospital in Copper Hill. I'm going to drive his daughter, Kim, there. She's pretty upset."

Maggie knew the trauma center was an hour away. She was supposed to have given birth to Danielle there but had gone into labor a little earlier than expected and Adam had delivered her. "I can imagine how she feels."

"She called her brother, Will. You remember him, he's

a detective with Chicago PD now." Josie was normally un-flappable, but she was rambling and sounded really shaken.

"I've heard about him."

"Anyway, I don't know how long I'll be. They're going to do tests and Kim will need support until her brother can get here."

"Of course she will. I'll come home right now—"

"I can drop Danielle off on my way to pick up Kim. That will be faster."

"If you're sure. That would be great."

"Okay. See you soon."

"Josie, don't worry about this. I'll manage."

"I know you will, sweetheart. 'Bye, Maggie."

"'Bye." She hit the off button and set her phone on the desk.

The spreadsheet on the computer monitor caught her eye and she sighed. There was no point in starting any-thing because as soon as her daughter got here there would be no work. This whole office would become fodder for exploration. There was nothing Danielle liked more than investigating, aka getting into everything.

Maggie shut off the computer and decided to go down to the café for a cup of coffee. Maybe she could be of help until Josie dropped off Danielle. After taking the rear stairs and walking through the kitchen, she found Lucy circulat-ing around the few tables that were occupied, topping off coffee and making sure no one needed anything.

Her partner saw her and walked over, the empty glass coffeepot in hand. "Hey, I thought you were going to be up to your eyeballs in numbers and budget projections."

"That was the plan. It changed." She looked at Lucy. "Josie called. The sheriff may have had a heart attack. She's going to drive his daughter to the hospital and stay with her."

"Oh, no. I hope he'll be okay." As the situation sank in, Lucy's blue eyes widened. "What are you going to do with Danielle?"

"Good question. I thought I'd have a cup of coffee and contemplate my options while I wait for Josie to drop her off here."

"Have a seat over there by the window," Lucy said. "The breakfast crowd has run its course. Now there are just a few moms who dropped kids at school and came in to eat. They're all taken care of, so I think I'll join you."

"That would be great. An unexpected treat. When life gives you lemons."

"Be right back."

Maggie sat by the window and watched the activity on Main Street. The grocery store was across the way. She'd be willing to bet that after breakfast the moms in here would head over there. Four tables were occupied, two ladies at each of them. She felt a pang of guilt sprinkled with envy about having to work and not be a stay-at-home mom.

The reality was that if Danny had made it back from the war, she would still be a working mom. The difference was that her work time would be more flexible with two people to run the business.

Lucy walked toward her with a steaming mug of coffee in each hand. She put one in front of Maggie then sat across from her. "So this is a good chance to catch up. How are things?"

There was a slight emphasis on the last word, just enough that Maggie knew she wanted to know about Sloan. That was difficult to put into words. The night she'd come home and found him watching Danielle, it was all she could do not to… What? Swoon? Melt into a puddle at his feet? Throw her panties at him?

She didn't know how to reconcile the man who went

through beautiful women like tissues with the one who had volunteered to watch her daughter. She would have thought ten minutes with a toddler would make him curl into the fetal position, but he hadn't done that. He'd actually seemed to enjoy it.

She hadn't known what to make of him and had talked to her mom for the maternal perspective and her brother for the male point of view. Both had said not to worry, but neither knew she *was* teetering on the edge of throwing her panties at him.

She blew on her coffee and finally said, "Things are fine."

"Really? That's all you've got?"

"If you're talking about Sloan, there's really nothing interesting." When did she get to be such a good liar?

"Too bad." Lucy sipped her coffee. "He's got that pretty face, great butt and seems very nice."

He *was* nice, Maggie thought. The other two things were true, too. But between them there were so many reasons not to get involved it was best to ignore all his appealing qualities. It was on the tip of her tongue to suggest again that Lucy chat him up if she had the chance. Again that idea put a knot in her tummy, so she kept her mouth shut.

"So are you seeing anyone?" she asked instead. Best to take the spotlight off herself.

"Oh, no." Lucy seemed more adamant about that than was necessary.

"Wow, that was emphatic." Maggie glanced out the window and saw a Range Rover stop at the curb and park. "Do you want to explain?"

"I know I asked if you'd mind if I flirted with Sloan, but you know better than anyone that I talk the talk but don't walk the walk. And mostly I was testing you out, to see if you were interested. Which, by the way, you are. But suffice it to say, I'm taking a break from men."

"Taking a break or sworn off?"

"Both."

Before she could ask more, Maggie saw Sloan get out of the car that had just pulled up. She'd thought it looked familiar but had been distracted. Her heart stuttered and thumped the way it always did when she saw him, but this time the sighting was unexpected. There hadn't been time to brace herself. He moved to the sidewalk and opened the rear passenger door.

"Speaking of the devil," Lucy said. "There he is now."

"Yeah." Maggie watched him bend over to lean into the backseat.

"Nice butt," her partner observed.

Then he lifted something out of the car and she realized it was a child. Her child.

"What in the world…" She started to get up, but her partner stopped her.

"Wait. Let's see what he does."

"Josie must have asked him to drop her off."

Before she could get up, he walked to the back of the SUV, pressed a button on the key fob and the rear door went up. He pulled out the familiar pink stroller and unfolded it until the thing locked in the open position. He was still holding Danielle when an older couple stopped. Norm and Diane Schurr were regular customers at the ice cream parlor. They stood there for a few moments, smiling and chatting.

Then Sloan started for the café door and Mayor Goodson-McKnight paused beside him to say hello. Danielle had her little arm around his neck and he seemed comfortable, confident and completely unselfconscious.

Maggie noticed that conversation in the café had grown

louder. She caught snippets of "how cute" and "so ador-able." The ladies were smiling as they watched the hand-some man holding her little girl. A chorus of "aw" drifted to her and she understood the sentiment. She felt the same way.

"There's a sight that could almost change a girl's mind about swearing off men." Lucy was practically drooling.

Maggie knew how she felt. That thought pushed her into action and she stood. "I have to go."

"Me, too." Her partner sighed. "When these women in here come to their senses, they're going to want their checks."

Paying a check would be easy compared to Mag-gie's problem. She hurried over to the door just as Sloan was walking inside, pushing the empty stroller. Danielle seemed very comfortable in his arms.

She spotted Maggie and held out her arms. "Mama!"

"Hey, baby girl." Maggie took her and hugged her close for a moment, breathing in the sweet, little-girl scent of her. "Did you go for a ride?"

"Car," she said, pointing to the one at the curb. "Go bye-bye."

"Yes, you did." She looked at Sloan. "I guess Josie asked you to bring her?"

"I volunteered," he said. "I overheard her telling you about what happened to the sheriff and I could see she was in a hurry to get on the road."

"Yeah, I got that feeling, too."

"So here's Danielle," he said. "What are you going to do with her?"

"Call Grandma."

"Gamma?" the toddler said.

"Yes, love. Thank you for bringing her here, Sloan. Hopefully, Grandma is free today." She looked at the man in front of her, whose reputation was completely at odds with his behavior. "And don't worry. I won't tell her about your good deed."

"So you know she talked to me?"

"Yeah, about your ulterior motive in looking after Danielle."

"She invited me to lunch at her house to chat." There was a twinkle in his eyes.

"Sloan, I'm so sorry. She shouldn't have done that."

"It gets better," he said.

His expression was wry and she got it right away. "Brady, too?"

"Man to man," he confirmed.

"That, I didn't know about. Tell me he didn't hit you," she said, a little horrified.

"I was more concerned about him hacking into the company computers and giving us a virus that would wipe out everything. But we talked it through."

"Hugged it out?" she asked.

"And sang, 'Kumbaya,'" he teased.

"Seriously, Sloan, I'm so embarrassed. It never occurred to me that they would interfere and bother you."

"No bother." He smiled at the child in her arms, squirming to get down. "They're concerned about you. I respect that."

"There's concern and then there's meddling. I'll talk to them. Make sure they don't bother you again."

"It's no bother, Maggie. Forget about it."

"As if that's going to happen." She set Danielle on the floor but held on to her. The little girl was pulling against the grip, practically quivering to get into trouble. "I apologize again. And thanks for dropping her off."

"I was coming into town anyway. Maybe the spirit of

this town and helping your neighbors is rubbing off on me." He shrugged. "Now I have to get to work."

"Right." There was a frustrated wail from her daughter, who was still desperately trying to get away. "And I have to see if Mom can watch her."

"I'll see you for dinner?"

"You will. It's chicken piccata night."

"My favorite. Later, then." He looked at her and, just before he walked out the door, something smoldered in his eyes. Something that had her quivering from head to toe, some parts more than others.

Maggie felt the quivers give way to goose bumps as she watched him through the window. She wasn't sure if the neighborliness of this town was rubbing off on him, but he was certainly rubbing off on her.

She felt cracks in her resistance to him and was fairly certain that surrender couldn't be far behind.

Chapter Twelve

"So the sheriff is holding his own?" With the phone to her ear, Maggie leaned back against the kitchen island and waited for Josie to answer.

"They did tests and he's resting comfortably. Doctors will talk to him tomorrow about the results. Will Fletcher is flying in from Chicago," her friend said. "But he can't get here until morning. So I'm going to stay with Kim until then."

"How's her son?" Maggie knew Tim was fourteen and probably worried about his grandfather.

"He's staying with a friend because he's in school. But she calls him or texts all the time. So he's hanging in there."

"Good." Maggie knew that was the best thing. "And thanks for letting me know you won't be back tonight. I would worry."

"You're sweet. I'm so sorry about not being able to watch Danielle. Did it mess you up a lot?"

Only where Sloan was concerned. Seeing him effortlessly handling her daughter had flipped a switch inside her. She glanced at him carrying dishes into the kitchen from the dining room.

Grandma had not been free today, which meant Danielle had hung out in her office. Dinner had been later than usual tonight because the work schedule had fallen apart. It had just been her and Sloan, what with Josie at the hospital and Danielle in bed early for lack of a nap. Now Sloan was helping with dishes instead of leaving it to her like any respectable paying guest would.

How was a girl supposed to resist that?

"Maggie?"

"I'm here." Although her mind was on how sexy Sloan looked in his worn jeans.

"Good, I thought I'd lost you," Josie said. "Did everything work out all right with Danielle?"

"It's fine." That was one good thing about being your own boss. Things worked out; it just took a little longer sometimes than others. "Don't worry about us. Just concentrate on Kim, and if she needs anything let me know. Give her hugs from us."

"Will do. Talk to you tomorrow. 'Bye, Maggie."

"'Bye." The phone went dead and she set it back on the charger.

"What's up?" Sloan set glasses in the sink then met her gaze.

"Hank Fletcher is stable. In the morning the doctors are going to give him test results. There will be more news then."

He nodded and went back to the dining room, returning with leftovers. "So right now it's no news is good news."

"Yes." She stared at him displaying his domestic side. "If I didn't know better, I'd say you're getting ready to do the dishes."

"Look at you. Miss Observant." He grinned. "Not just another pretty face."

The compliment, teasing though it was, warmed a cold,

dark place inside her that hadn't been touched in a long time. She didn't have the energy or will to seal it off now.

"You do know that being charming doesn't mean you get to have your way here in my kitchen."

"Okay." He nodded thoughtfully, but his eyes were twinkling. "Then, let's just go with the fact that hospitality is your goal and it would be hospitable to just give in and let me help."

"I can't talk you out of this, can I?"

"No."

"Then, let's go with hospitality." *Be still my heart*, she thought. "I'll put the food away."

"Teamwork," he said. "I like it."

And she liked him. So much more than she wanted to. Maggie's hands were busy and so was her mind. As she put leftover chicken, mashed potatoes and green beans into containers, she was trying to figure out Sloan Holden's deal. He must have a flaw. Everyone did. No one was this nice, this perfect.

More than that, no man that nice and so nearly perfect should still be an eligible bachelor. Except he'd told her why he would never get married again. So she was pretty far gone that even his honesty was sexy to her. How could she not admire that he'd put his cards on the table and let a woman decide whether or not to play when she knew what the game was?

So far, Maggie had resisted him, but the longer they were alone, the more she believed *him* being alone was somehow wrong.

"It's been one of those days for you," he said when the kitchen chores were finished. "What do you think about you and I having a glass of wine?"

Her head was warning danger, but her hormones were telling her head to shut the heck up.

The hormones won. "Great ideas like that are responsible for your business success."

"Nice to be appreciated. And I have another world-class suggestion."

"What would that be?" she asked.

"We should turn on the gas log in the fireplace and have our wine in the great room." Flecks of gold in his brown eyes glowed with a hint of challenge.

God help her, that dare sounded wonderful and she couldn't walk away from it tonight. "Another great idea."

Look at her—all grown-up and sophisticated. No nerves in her voice, at least none that she could detect. This was just too much temptation to defend against. Talking with a handsome man in front of a fire. There was no harm in that, right?

She retrieved a bottle of cabernet from the center island's built-in wine rack, then Sloan expertly opened it with the corkscrew she handed him. After she pulled two stemmed glasses from the china hutch in the dining room, he poured and then held one out to her.

"Let's go sit." She turned off all but the beneath-the-cabinet lights to dim the brightness.

He followed her into the other room. Beside the river-rock fireplace was a switch, and when she flipped it, flames instantly danced around the gas log, which was behind glass doors.

Sloan waited until she sat on the sofa, then lowered himself beside her, not too close, but close enough to touch her without moving.

Maggie was suddenly nervous and took a sip of wine. "This is—nice."

"Out of all possible words to use, *nice* is the best you could come up with?"

"Do we need to have another stern talk about your ego, Mr. Holden?"

He laughed. "With you there's never a risk of it getting out of control. I was just hoping for a little more detail about what you're feeling."

"Okay." She took another sip of the deep red liquid. "I can't remember the last time I had a relaxing evening stretching in front of me. Usually it's bath time, then a battle to convince a reluctant toddler she should get some sleep."

"It's a lot of work." He drank his wine and watched her.

"That's an understatement." Maggie would never be sure why the next words came out of her mouth, but once said there was no putting them back. "Danny wanted children right away. He said it would make him the happiest man on earth if I got pregnant on our honeymoon."

"But you didn't agree." He shrugged as if to say it was a no-brainer. "You said he wanted it. Not that the two of you did."

"You're observant, too." Maggie met his gaze. Flames reflected in the green flecks in his brown eyes, but there was no judgment in his expression. "I wanted to wait. We had a lot going on with getting the ice cream parlor opened. And I just wanted time for the two of us alone."

"That's understandable. A child changes everything forever." He half turned toward her, his long legs just inches away now. "It's practical. Syd and Burke are waiting."

"And you know all this how?" She sipped from her glass.

"There was a meeting about the resort hotel plans in Burke's office not long ago and Ellie McKnight was there. The subject just came up."

That made her smile. "Is having children a normal topic of conversation during a meeting about blueprints?"

He shook his head and managed to look only a little sheepish. "It's what I like to call the Blackwater Lake Effect."

"What's that?"

"There's something about this town. Some enchanted thing that makes you break the rules of business that would apply anywhere else. And somehow it works."

"Well said." She finished her wine and set the empty glass on the coffee table. "Danny and I agreed on pretty much everything but having a baby right away. We hardly ever fought, but we did about that. Before the wedding we were in agreement on having kids but never talked about the time frame for doing it."

"Do you know why he felt that way?"

"He didn't say, but my theory is that he had a feeling he was going to die."

"He was in the military and knew he could deploy to a war zone. It makes sense that he would think about the possibility."

"I didn't. I wouldn't ever consider that he might not come home to me." She felt the familiar self-blame welling up inside her. "He really loved kids and wanted to see his child before he had to leave." There was a catch in her voice and she swallowed. "But he never did."

"And you feel guilty about it."

"Of course. Because I was selfish, he never had a chance to see his daughter."

"So that's what you've been carrying around," he said.

"Pretty much. How can I not?"

"Maggie..." His tone was scolding and sympathetic at the same time. Sloan set his glass on the table beside hers, then moved close and cupped her face in his hands. "Don't do this to yourself."

"I did it to him. Don't you see?"

"It's not your fault," he said gently. "A person can't really be true to herself if she's making decisions based on the fact that her partner might not be around tomorrow. Sure, it's a variable you factor in because of his military service, but you have nothing to feel guilty about. It's stopping you from being happy."

"How can I? I'm here and he's not."

"By all accounts, your husband was a good guy. He would want you to go on living. Have a full and satisfying life."

Danny had said as much to her, but she was curious about Sloan's perspective. "How can you be so sure?"

"Because if I loved someone and couldn't be there for them, I wouldn't want that person to be lonely and unhappy. I think Danny would feel the same."

Having another man's point of view seemed to validate what her husband had said, and the words struck a chord with her. Either they were exactly the right thing to say, or maybe she was just ready to hear them. Either way, Maggie felt something inside her shift and a great weight lifted from her heart.

"Danny *was* a good guy," she said softly.

"Of course he was." His voice was emphatic. "You wouldn't have chosen him if he wasn't."

"That's very nice of you to say." Maggie looked into his eyes and saw something smoldering there, something sizzling and incredibly exciting. "Are you going to kiss me?"

"You have no idea how badly I want to."

"I'd like that very much."

"Are you sure?" His gaze searched hers.

"Yes."

She'd barely spoken when he claimed her mouth. It was like touching a match to dry grass, and heat exploded inside her. He pulled her onto his lap and settled a big hand at her waist. While their mouths teased and taunted, his thumb brushed over her midriff and grazed the underside of her breast. The touch, so tentative and tantalizing, made her want more.

She linked her arms around his neck and pressed her breasts to his chest. There was a hitch in his breathing and it grew ragged. He folded her in his strong arms and held her tight. Sliding his fingers into her hair, he gently cupped the back of her head to make the contact of their mouths more firm.

When he traced her bottom lip with his tongue, she opened her mouth, inviting him inside. Without hesitation he entered and explored, caressed and coaxed. She felt there was a very real promise of going up in flames, and was so ready for that to happen.

Sloan pulled back, his mouth an inch from hers. He was breathing hard, but managed to say, "What are the chances of getting an invitation into your bedroom to see if the faucet is okay?"

She knew he was referring to her warning not to expect to be invited. Now he knew it had been an empty threat. "The plumber has been here, so I'm sure it's fine."

"It could still be leaking."

"I'm not worried about it." Then she grinned. "But if you'd like to come into my bedroom and check out the thread count of my sheets, that would be all right with me."

"Just all right?" His gaze was hooded, smoky, sexy.

"More than all right—"

"If you're sure…"

"Absolutely." She slid off his lap and took his hand in hers. "I really want you to see my bedroom."

"So this is all about me?"

"Yes."

He stood and smiled like a man who'd just gotten everything he wanted for Christmas. "That works for me."

Hand in hand they walked through the house to the double-door entry of her room. She turned on the hall light and glanced at the room across from them, where Danielle was soundly sleeping in her crib.

Maggie opened her bedroom door, revealing the king-size bed with the wedding ring–patterned spread and a lot of pink-and-green throw pillows. In the far shadows there was an oak dresser and matching armoire. A glider chair, which she'd almost worn out when her daughter was a newborn, sat in the corner. A right-hand turn led to the master bath with its two sinks.

"Maggie?" There was concern on his face and it was incredibly sweet.

She felt Sloan's hesitation and looked up. "I'm okay."

"Are you really sure about this?"

"Yes."

He nodded. "Then, while you turn down the bed, I need to go upstairs and get something."

With that, he turned and hurried back the way he'd come. What in the world? She hadn't done this for a long time, but it didn't sound as if he'd changed his mind. Even if he had, the bed still needed to be undressed. As she stowed the throw pillows on the glider chair and rolled the spread to the end of the bed, she thought about that word. *Undressed.*

The bed wasn't all that needed undressing. She would have to take off her clothes. And get naked.

Just then a large shape filled the doorway. It was obvious because the light was cut off. "I'm back."

"Okay."

Sloan walked to the nightstand and set a small packet there. A condom. Maybe more. But of course. How could she have forgotten? They would need that after getting naked. He no doubt looked like a Greek god. But she… *Eek!*

"Maggie?" He walked over to her and cupped her face in his hands then tenderly touched his mouth to hers. Pulling away slightly, he said, "What's wrong?"

"Nothing." She was facing the hall and her features were illuminated, showing him what she knew was probably an anxious expression.

"Don't do that." He was in shadow but there was pleading in his tone. "Don't shut me out. Talk to me."

"You'll think I'm crazy. Or worse."

"There's something worse?" He tilted up her face and was obviously studying her. "Tell me what's going on in that mind of yours."

"It's silly. Unimportant. It's—"

He touched a finger to her lips. "I'm not giving up, so you might as well get it over with."

"Okay. It's— I—" She sighed and looked away. "It's been a long time for me. Sex, I mean."

"I knew that."

"I've had a baby."

"Yeah. I met her. Cute kid," he said.

"The thing is, you're a man—"

"Actually, I knew that, too." There was a smile in his tone.

"Now you're laughing at me. Forget it." This was so humiliating. She started to walk past him, but he gently took her arm to stop her.

"I think your cute daughter has a very cute mom. I'm not laughing, Maggie. I'm listening."

She blew out a breath. "Here's the deal. I have stretch marks. My tummy isn't flat. These are childbearing hips."

"If you're trying to turn me on, it's working." His voice was low, uneven, rough.

"You don't get it, so let me spell this out. I'm saying you shouldn't have high expectations, because I'm not like the perfect women you date. You should prepare yourself for a big disappointment."

"Maggie…" He reached out a finger and touched her collarbone then lightly dragged the touch over her chest to her breast. He stopped at her waist and undid the button on her jeans. "There's no way you're talking me out of this."

"I'm only being honest—"

He kissed her, then whispered against her mouth, "Stop talking. More important, stop thinking. You are a beautiful woman. So hot. I've wanted you since the first time I saw you."

"Wow." Her heart pounded. "You can keep talking."

"Actions speak louder." His tone was full of the need to possess and a whole lot of pent-up passion.

Then he kissed her again and she kissed him back. Flames licked through her, setting her on fire with the need to touch his skin. She tugged his cotton shirt from the waistband of his jeans and started undoing the buttons, but her hands were shaking. He brushed them aside and impatiently yanked the thing over his head.

She settled her hands on his chest, one over his hammering heart. The light dusting of hair tickled her palms and made her savor his masculinity. Her breath caught and yearning welled up inside her. It had been so damn long since a man had held her, told her she was beautiful and wanted her.

Sloan pulled off her T-shirt, then unhooked her bra and slid it off. After that, he lowered the zipper on her jeans. In moments she was naked, and held her breath. Instinctively she crossed her arms over her breasts, but he shook his head and gently pulled them away.

"Beautiful," he breathed.

She put her back to the lit hall in order to see his expression. It was everything she could have hoped for and more. "You have to say that."

"No. I don't have to say anything." He shook his head. "I'll tell you a secret. Remember that presentation I did at the chamber of commerce meeting about green building? You were sitting in the third row and seriously messing with my concentration."

"How?" She ran a finger over his chest and grazed a nipple, then smiled when he groaned.

"I kept picturing you like this. And you are even more beautiful than I imagined."

Maggie knew he had a lot of experience to fuel his imagination and if he was lying she didn't care. The compliment did a lot to shore up her female confidence and her shattered soul. "And you, sir, have too many clothes on."

That was all it took for him to set a record for getting out of them. Maggie looked at him the way he'd looked at her. "Better than I imagined, too."

"You thought about me in the altogether? Ms. Potter, I'm shocked."

"Oh, please…"

"Please what?"

She saw the need in his eyes and knew it was a match for her own. "Please take me to bed."

And he did just that, then pulled her against him. They were on their sides facing each other and he ran his palm over the dip at her waist and down her thigh. It felt like magic and moonlight. But he didn't stop there. His fingers brushed her inner thigh and strayed between her legs. She couldn't stop the moan of delight, and unconsciously opened to his exploration. He touched the sensitive bundle of nerves at the heart of her femininity and she nearly shot off the bed from the electric pleasure of it.

"Sloan—" She could hardly talk, her breathing was so uneven. "I want you. Sloan—"

"I know, sweetheart." He was already reaching for the condom and tore open the package. In seconds he had it on, then covered her body with his own.

Slowly he entered her and let her get used to the feel of him. Impatient, Maggie instinctively tilted her hips up, signaling what she wanted. He obliged, pushing into her, moving in and out, taking her higher and higher until sensation blasted through her and shock waves claimed her body.

He held her, stroked her hair until she stilled. Then he moved inside her again. Several moments later he groaned and went still, burying his face where her neck and shoulder met. It was her turn to hold him and she did, loving the way he felt in her arms. They stayed that way for a long time.

Finally he said, "I don't want to move, ever, but I'm afraid I'm crushing you."

"I don't mind." She liked holding him.

But he rolled away and smiled down at her. "In case you were wondering, I am in no way disappointed." He cupped her cheek in his hand and kissed her. "That was perfect."

Maggie appreciated the words. What she didn't appreciate was the way reality had a way of creeping in and obliterating the glow. Sex had been fantastic and he was even more wonderful than she'd thought. She hadn't realized how much she'd missed this intimacy.

But none of that changed her situation. She was still a single mom with a daughter to raise.

After Sloan came back to bed, he pulled her into his arms and they dozed for a little while. Then Maggie rolled away and said she had to check on Danielle. He waited for her to return to him, but she didn't and he knew something was up. Most likely she was thinking too much again. It was time to put a stop to that.

He got up and quickly dressed before going in search of her. He found her on the couch in front of the fire where she'd told him about the guilt she'd carried since her husband died.

He sat down beside her and knew there was nothing on under her navy blue terry-cloth robe. Pushing aside the fact that he wanted her again, just as much as he had earlier, he asked, "Is Danielle okay?"

"Sleeping like a baby." There was a tender smile curving up those full lips. "This probably isn't the best time to tell you, although we used protection, but my little girl is here because of an oops."

"Oh?"

"I was busy, tired, stressed what with getting the business up and running. I forgot that I had to see the doctor to renew my birth control prescription and didn't have time to go. Before you ask, Danny knew and we were careful." She shrugged. "But one night we got carried away. I have to say—best mistake ever."

"If only we could say that about all mistakes," he said.

"She's what got me through the worst time in my life, right after Danny died. I had to take care of myself, not for me but for the baby Danny wanted so much. She's the only part of him that I have left. Then she was born and I fell in love with her. I had to get out of bed whether I wanted to or not."

"I can see how that would be the case." Sloan sensed that she wasn't saying this because he'd asked about her little girl. Maggie had a point and he wanted to know what it was. "What are you trying to tell me?"

"I didn't plan to sleep with you, Sloan. But it happened. And it was wonderful."

If he had to guess, he'd say she didn't want to admit that. Points to her for honesty. It was refreshing. "I hear a *but* coming."

"No." Her lips curved up, but there was the same sadness in her eyes that had been there when they first met, when she'd looked at a picture of her husband. "I just want to clarify. And make sure you don't have an expectation of anything permanent. I mean, you've told me you don't, but that was before we…"

"Slept together," he finished.

"Yes. I wouldn't want you to think I'm leading you on."

"Hey, that's my line." And Sloan was annoyed that she'd stolen it from him.

"So you understand where I'm coming from."

"Yes." But that didn't mean he liked it.

"Good. I'm glad we cleared that up."

It was clear to Sloan that even confessing her secret hadn't eased the guilt she felt. She was holding her emotions close, and he wasn't happy about the distance she'd put between them. That declaration of not wanting to lead him on was particularly annoying because it was the way he'd acted ever since his divorce. How disconcerting to realize that taking Maggie to bed was more than just for fun. It meant something.

He wasn't at all sure how he felt about that. But she was waiting for a response. "I appreciate the warning. It's always good to have things spelled out. What do you say we take things one day at a time?"

"Sounds sensible to me."

For the first time in his life, sensible was about as appealing as banging his head against the wall.

Chapter Thirteen

"It's really above and beyond the call of duty for you to do this," Sloan said.

This being to have his family over for dinner tonight, Maggie thought. He was trying to help her in the kitchen and Danielle was clinging to her leg. Josie was staying in Copper Hill near Hank Fletcher and his family after his heart-bypass surgery a week ago. And in a little while there would be five extra people around her dining room table.

"Not a duty. It's the Blackwater Lake Effect." She shrugged. "We're neighborly."

"Still, you didn't have to and I really appreciate it."

The Holdens were due in about thirty minutes, and as the time ticked by, Maggie wondered if she was a glutton for punishment. Just plain crazy. Or both. Feeding her paying guests was her responsibility, and that didn't technically extend to their relatives.

But she knew they'd been in town for several days, having come early to visit with their son before their nephew's engagement party. Technically they were Burke and Sydney's responsibility. They were staying at the newly renovated Blackwater Lake Lodge, and Sloan had had dinner with them a couple of nights ago at Fireside, the five-star on-site restaurant.

At breakfast the next morning he'd casually mentioned his folks would like to see where he was staying. Maggie was afraid sleeping with Sloan had fueled her curiosity about his family. It didn't matter that she'd agreed with him about not getting serious; she was still curious about his parents and sisters. Whatever the reason, she'd suggested he invite them to dinner and now she was a little intimidated and a lot nervous because they'd accepted. This reaction proved that their positive opinion mattered to her no matter how much she tried to convince herself it didn't.

She'd made most of the simple meal ahead of time, planning to serve roast, mashed potatoes, rolls and broccoli salad, a yummy recipe with onion, raisins and fabulous dressing. Most people were either firmly in the pro or con column on broccoli, but not even one hater had ever complained about her dish. The meat was done and wrapped in aluminum foil to stay warm. Gravy was made and the potatoes needed a final warming up in the microwave. There was only one more thing to do.

Maggie picked up her child. "I have to make biscuits, sweetie, and I can't do that with you glued to my thigh."

The little girl smiled and clapped her hands. "Cookie?"

"How do you always know when to push your advantage?" She sighed, but couldn't help smiling and kissing that precious face.

"What can I do to help?" Sloan asked.

"If you can mix up dough, roll it out and cut circles out of it to put on a baking sheet and into the oven, that would be pretty awesome."

"Sorry," he said. "That's above my pay grade."

"Too bad." She tried to set the little girl on her feet but the toddler pulled her legs up and refused to be put down. "What we have here is a standoff."

"Maybe she'll come to me. We can play with the toys."
He held out his arms and Danielle eagerly went into them.

"Dolly?" she asked.

"Let's go find her." He grinned. "And just like that, tensions are resolved."

"Thank you," she said gratefully.

Maggie was mesmerized by the sight of his broad back before he left the room. The memory of being in his arms was never far from her mind, especially at night in her big bed all alone. She knew if he kissed her again it would happen again. But the thought of giving in again gave her pause. Once wasn't serious; twice was a pattern.

The problem was, he'd awakened the need in her that she'd so carefully folded up and put away when her husband died. Even if Sloan changed his mind about taking a chance on a relationship, she couldn't risk it. Raising her daughter the way Danny would have wanted was her job and hers alone.

It only took her about ten minutes to whip up the made-from-scratch rolls, and she put the cookie sheet in the oven. She could keep them warm and fresh, but baking them at the last minute with the distraction of total strangers could be a recipe for disaster.

When the timer dinged, she removed them and placed the steaming rolls in a cloth-lined basket on the stove. She was as ready as possible, and as if that was the cue, the doorbell sounded. Perfect so far, she thought.

She went to greet the newcomers and saw Sloan headed for the door, Danielle hot on his heels. When the little girl stopped and grabbed his leg, the trusting gesture tugged at Maggie's heart. Then he opened the door and chaos erupted when his family walked in.

"Hi, Mom." He hugged the older woman who had

dark hair and eyes. Then he held out his hand to the distinguished-looking, blue-eyed man. "Dad."

"Son." His hair was the same color as Sloan's but shot through with silver.

Three young women who looked to be in their twenties followed the older couple inside and Sloan hugged each one before closing the door. "Mom, Dad, I'd like you to meet Maggie Potter, my landlady." He looked at her, then his parents. "Maggie, this is my mother, Antonia, and my father, Campbell."

She smiled and shook hands with each of them. "It's a pleasure to meet you both."

"Likewise." His mother sized her up. "And please call me Annie. Everyone does."

"Not everyone. We call you Mom," one of his sisters said.

Sloan held out his hand, indicating the young women. "And these three smart alecks are the curse of my existence. My sisters—Carla, Gina and Isabella."

Maggie shook their hands and made mental notes to remember who was who. Carla had dark hair and blue eyes. Gina was a green-eyed redhead. Blonde Isabella's eyes were brown like Sloan's and her mother's.

Danielle had backed away from the invasion of Holdens, looking decidedly uncertain about this turn of events. Now she moved forward and grabbed Sloan's leg again. He picked her up as if the movement was automatic.

"And who's this little angel?" Annie asked.

"Maggie's daughter, Danielle." The look Sloan sent her said he'd clued them in about her being a single mom and why.

"She's gorgeous." Annie glanced at Maggie. "Like her mother."

"She is beautiful," Maggie answered, making this all about her little girl. "But I'm definitely prejudiced."

"Can I get everyone something to drink?" Sloan asked his family.

He'd told her not to worry about that part of the evening's hospitality, that he would handle it. Now she realized how much of the stress it took off her. On the other hand, it added a different kind. This felt so much like being a couple. They weren't, but a pleasurable sensation moved and stretched a little painfully inside her, like muscles that hadn't been used in a long time.

Before filling drink orders, Sloan gave them a tour of the house. Afterward, they all gathered around the kitchen island while he poured a scotch for his father and himself. The women, including Maggie, had wine. Then he handed Danielle a sippy cup with watered-down apple juice. How sweet and thoughtful to make sure she wasn't left out.

"What should we drink to?" Campbell asked.

"To Maggie," his wife said. "And giving our son a home away from home."

Before she could protest that this was part of her business, they were all saying, "To Maggie."

"You're very sweet," she said. "But Sloan is a paying guest and hospitality is my job."

"It's not your job to put up with his family," Annie said. "Thank you for your warmth, kindness and generosity. I think I speak for all of us when I say that."

"You don't speak for me, Mom," Isabella said. "Personally I think Maggie needs to have her head examined for letting my brother stay here. He's a pain in the neck." The young woman was clearly teasing.

"Hey," he protested.

"Izzy, you always were the most headstrong child," her mother scolded.

"Ignore my sister," Sloan advised.

"She's right, though. What if we were horrible to you?" Gina asked.

"There's no what-if about it," Sloan shot back. "You *are* horrible. I warned her but she refused to listen."

"You did not," Maggie said. "What he actually told me was that if anyone got out of line he would take care of them the Chicago way. Do you have any idea what that means?" she teased.

"Not specifically." Campbell's blue eyes twinkled. "But I understand it's not pretty. So you girls better behave yourselves."

"Us?" The three of them spoke together, innocent and outraged at the same time.

"You realize that's sexist, right, Dad?" Carla asked. "What about Sloan? And you?"

Her dad shrugged. "It's four against two. That means the odds favor one of you ladies messing up. And I'm too charming for that."

"No one is going to be mean because they answer to me," Annie assured her. "Do you think Danielle would come to me?"

Maggie studied her daughter, in Sloan's arms because he'd picked her up again. The little girl looked comfortable and Maggie thought if it was her, she wouldn't willingly leave the safety he offered. But that wasn't the question.

"You've raised four children and I don't have to tell you how unpredictable they can be. Give it a try. But please don't be offended if she's shy."

"You're right about unpredictable. Raising these troublemakers prepared me for anything." The older woman walked over to her son and held out her arms to the little girl. She went willingly and Annie cuddled her close. "You are a sweet girl."

"Sometimes yes, sometimes no," Maggie qualified. "But my mother would tell you that she's always perfect."

"Your mother is very fortunate to have a grandchild." She gave her four children a look. "I'm still waiting."

Sloan cleared his throat. "I think it's time for dinner, don't you, Maggie?"

She wanted to laugh but didn't. He so clearly wanted a distraction. "Everything is ready. If you'll all have a seat in the dining room, I'll put the food out."

"I'll help." Sloan's expression pleaded to be kept busy.

"That would be great," she said. "You can settle Danielle in her high chair."

"Remind me to ask about you knowing how to do that," Annie said. "But would you mind if I put her in?"

"That would be great. Thanks."

Maggie found herself liking these people a lot. Meeting them explained how Sloan was so down-to-earth in spite of all his money and the playboy reputation. This family would never let him get too full of himself. It would be so much easier if she found him annoyingly pompous and egotistical.

Dinner went better than she'd hoped, and it seemed everyone was having a good time. When they finished eating, Sloan and his mother offered to help her clean up and wouldn't take no for an answer. They were rinsing off dishes while the other Holdens played with Danielle.

"It's so nice that you didn't have to stay in a hotel while working on the resort," his mother said.

Sloan was looking at Maggie when he answered, "There's definitely an upside."

Annie glanced between them, a pleased look shining in her eyes. "You're a lucky man. Finding someone as pretty and wholesome as Maggie is a plus."

"You mean, finding my bed-and-breakfast," Maggie clarified.

Dishcloth in hand, Annie stood with her back to the sink. "No, I meant *you*. I like you very much."

"That's awfully nice of you to say." Maggie recalled Sloan telling her how much his mom had been hurt when he'd split from his wife. This woman wore her heart on her sleeve, and part of his commitment avoidance had to do with protecting her.

"I'm not that nice," Annie teased. "We could be good friends. You're the sort of person I could grow fond of, Maggie."

She met Sloan's gaze, waiting for him to jump in and warn this woman not to get attached. That the two of them had agreed not to get serious. He remained conspicuously silent as he carefully watched to see how she would react.

"I appreciate you saying that."

"It's the truth. I tell it like I see it. And what I see is that my son hit the jackpot with you."

"We're just friends." Maggie put a finer point on it. "Friendly."

"Are we that generic?" His look and tone clearly said he was irritated at the bland description of what they were.

"Yes." She turned away from the flash of protest in his eyes. "We have pie for dessert."

Maggie knew he was thinking that he'd been in her bed and that made them more than friends. But his family didn't need to know about that, because neither of them was willing to take it to the next level.

Her problem was that since sleeping with him, she was a little less sure about *not* wanting forever after.

* * *

"Mama go bye-bye?"

"Yes, love." Maggie stooped to her daughter's level. "Mommy's going to a party."

"Me bye-bye?" Her eyes grew big, hopeful.

"Not this time, sweetie. You're going to have fun with Aunt Josie."

Her friend was standing by for a possible tantrum. "We're going to have a good time, cutie. We'll watch *Frozen* for the billionth time."

"Maybe you can talk her into a SpongeBob video."

"And hell might freeze over. No pun intended." Josie laughed. "If anyone can do it, Elsa can."

Tonight was Sydney and Burke's engagement party. She and Sloan had both been invited and were going to ride together. He'd pointed out that carpooling was the "green" thing to do. It was hard to argue with that even though she'd wanted to.

Just then he walked into the kitchen and her heart nearly stopped beating. In his dark suit, snow-white shirt and red tie he was so handsome she could hardly breathe.

Danielle toddled over to him. "You go bye-bye?"

He looked at Maggie. "How does she know? Is it the suit?"

"Must be." She smoothed the front of her black dress. It was a lace column with a peplum and cap sleeves. Simple and elegant. The four-inch heels were new, too, and the whole ensemble was way different from her everyday work clothes. "She doesn't miss much and figured something was up by the way I'm dressed."

Sloan didn't say anything. He just looked her up and down and stared. It was a good stare, the kind a man gave a woman when he enthusiastically approved of what she was wearing. And how much he wanted to take it off.

"Say something, Holden," Josie prompted.

"First I have to make sure I didn't swallow my tongue." There was a glow in his eyes. "You look beautiful."

"Thanks." Her brain was shorting out from the vibe he was giving off and heating her hormones to the boiling point. But she finally recovered enough to say, "You look very nice, too."

"Thanks."

"I guess we should go." She stooped to her daughter's level again, not easy in the tight skirt. "Give mommy a hug."

"Hug." Danielle moved into her arms and pressed her head to Maggie's chest.

"Good one, baby girl. Mommy loves you."

"'Ove you." She walked over to Sloan and held out her arms. "Hug?"

He bent down and grabbed her up, tickling until she was giggling hysterically. "'Bye, Shorty. Be nice to Josie."

Watching the big man and little girl made something shift inside Maggie. It wasn't him, but the fact that her daughter had initiated the hug. The fact that she'd automatically gone to him for a goodbye had Maggie's maternal instincts humming protectively.

"You two have fun," Josie said. "Be home by the stroke of midnight or that really expensive car he drives could turn into a pumpkin. And I don't think orange is his color."

Sloan opened the front door and settled his palm at her waist, letting her precede him. They made it outside without Danielle having a meltdown, but that was where the good news stopped. This was starting to feel an awful lot like a date. It would probably be better when they got to the party and she could mingle.

The drive didn't take long, so there wasn't too much time to fill with small talk. It also made for only a short period of trying to ignore the awareness sizzling between them. Before she knew it, Sloan drove into the Blackwater Lake Lodge parking lot and pulled into a space. He turned off the car, then got out and came around to open her door. But she'd already done it, so he offered his hand.

She took it and that was an error in judgment. His palm was warm and wide, strong and secure. The brief touch made her ache to be in his arms again.

She cleared her throat. "The lodge is lit up like this is a grand reopening or something."

"You must have seen the banner over the front door."

"It's pretty hard to miss." An uneven spot on the parking surface made her wobble in her high heels, and he took her elbow to steady her.

"You okay?"

"Fine. Just not used to these shoes."

"They're probably not very comfortable, but I meant what I said at the house. You look incredible tonight."

They were just walking under an outside light and she saw the intensity in his gaze. Knowing she was wanted was intoxicating, but too much of it impaired common sense and that was never a good thing.

"Here's the lobby." *Thank goodness*, she thought.

Automatic doors whispered open and they walked inside. There was a new wood-plank floor with an area rug and leather chairs for conversation in front of the smooth stone fireplace. Walls were newly painted a pale gold and held framed photographs of the lake and mountains. Maggie recognized the pictures from the front window of April Kennedy's photography studio.

She pointed them out to Sloan. "I like to see a business utilize local work."

"Me, too," he said. "We're doing that with labor and materials for the resort. I'll keep this in mind when we start planning the decorating phase."

There was a notice directing them to one of the lodge's banquet rooms. Walking down a cushy carpeted hallway after passing the registration desk, they heard the sound of voices drifting to them, indicating they were headed in the right direction.

They stood in the doorway and checked out the room. Tables set for dinner and covered with flowers and candles were off to the side. Overhead lights were set on romantic and contributed to that mood. People stood around talking and most had drinks in their hands. Maggie was just about to excuse herself and go mingle on her own when Sloan slid his arm around her waist.

"Let's go congratulate the happy couple," he said, indicating Burke and Sydney standing at the far end of the room.

His breath stirred her hair and tickled her ear, sending sparks dancing through her and she was simply swept along.

Sydney was already smiling happily, but it widened when they approached. She looked from Sloan to Maggie and one dark eyebrow rose. Apparently she approved of what she saw. "Well, well… So the two of you are officially an item now."

"No, we just rode together. And congratulations on your engagement." Maggie deliberately changed the subject.

"Really? Not an item?" Burke shook his cousin's hand. "I've heard rumors that your bachelormobile actually had a car seat in it. With a certain little girl strapped in."

"That's true." Sloan didn't look the least bit needled by the statement.

Maggie waited for him to clarify and when he didn't,

she said, "It's not what you're thinking. Josie couldn't watch her that day and Sloan was doing her a favor by bringing Danielle to me at the café."

"I know what you're doing," Syd said. "That was code for 'it's really new and just for us.'"

"And I think you two are high on romance and seeing it where there isn't any." Again Maggie looked at Sloan to refute the claim, but he just shrugged.

"We're very happy," Syd confirmed. "And we do want everyone else happy, too. So after the wedding, at the reception, I'll make sure to throw you the bouquet."

"That's not necessary—"

"Congrats, you two. We're going to get a drink now." Sloan took her hand in his and led her to the bar set up in a back corner. "What would you like?"

"For people to stop assuming we're together." A vision of her daughter holding out her little arms to Sloan ran through Maggie's mind. It was the cutest thing ever yet had so much potential for pain.

"I meant, what would you like to drink?"

"Wine. White."

He gave their order to the bartender and put some bills in the tip jar when the drinks were ready. Then he handed her one before picking up his scotch. He touched the rim of his tumbler to her glass. "Here's to the happy couple."

Just then Dr. and Mrs. Adam Stone walked up beside them. "And speaking of happy couples…" Jill smiled at them as if they were particularly bright. "I heard you two are dating. Adam and I think that's wonderful."

Her tall, good-looking husband nodded. "I don't listen to rumors as a rule, but you're here together, and that elevates gossip to it-must-be-true status."

"Not really," Maggie said. This man had delivered her daughter. He knew the emotional trauma and tragedy she'd gone through and the toll it had taken on her pregnancy. She couldn't let him get the wrong idea. "We carpooled tonight. That's all."

"So this isn't a date?" Jill looked disappointed.

"No, it's not." Maggie felt as if she'd just spit in Cupid's eye.

And the rest of the evening went pretty much the same way, even though she finally managed to mingle and separate herself from Sloan. His family was there and were completely charming to her again. When the party was winding down, she was more than ready to leave. They rode back to the house without either of them saying a word. He parked in the driveway beside her SUV and turned off the car. The interior was dark, the only illumination came from the front-porch light.

"You've been awfully quiet—"

"I have to tell you something—"

They both spoke at the same time and, ever the gentleman, Sloan said, "Ladies first."

"Okay." She took a deep breath. "About us... I've changed my mind. I can't take it one day at a time any more and wait to see what happens. I know what *can't* happen."

"And that is?" Wariness laced the words.

"Sleeping with you again. I can't."

"Why?"

"Everyone thinks we're dating. That we're a couple."

"What we are is no one else's business."

"That's true except when it comes to my daughter." She glanced at the driver's seat, but his expression was hidden in shadow. "She's too little to even realize this, but you're becoming a father figure to her. I first noticed it when your family came to dinner."

"What? How?"

"They were strangers invading her world and she was

uneasy about the situation. She moved to you for protection. It was instinctive." She took a breath. "And tonight when we left, she insisted on giving you a hug, too."

"It was sweet."

"Yes. And also evidence that she's getting attached to you. But you're not going to stay, and when you're gone it will break her heart."

"You can't know for sure what I'm going to do," he protested.

"I can. Your life isn't here in Blackwater Lake. If it were, you wouldn't be renting a room from me."

"That's not what this is about. You're putting up one more wall to protect yourself."

His tone challenged her to push back on that assertion, but there was no point. "You could be right, but that doesn't change anything. In spite of what the whole town thinks, we're not dating. And like you once said, it's good to have things spelled out. So I need to tell you that I'm closing the door on anything personal between us. Sleeping with you was a mistake and it can't happen again."

"That's a problem, Maggie." He shifted toward her and a shaft of porch light showed the dark passion in his eyes. "Every morning I see you at breakfast and want you. Before dinner each night I hope the wanting has gone away, but it's only stronger." He stared at her. "And I dare you to deny that you feel the same way."

"You're wrong," she lied. "But this isn't about you and me. It's about Danielle. She has to come first. I'm all she has to protect her and I will not risk her being hurt. Please, Sloan, I'm asking you to keep your distance."

"I don't think I can live in your house and honor that request." His voice was oddly calm, like the eye of a storm.

"Then, I'm going to have to ask you to leave. According to the rental agreement you signed, I have discretion to do that."

"It's a shame you feel you have to use that contract. I guess it's a good thing that Blackwater Lake Lodge is back in business. I'll move there tomorrow morning."

That was for the best, and what she'd hoped he would say. But Maggie hadn't expected the words to hit her heart like a sledgehammer.

Chapter Fourteen

The next morning Sloan booked a suite at Blackwater Lake Lodge and started packing his things. He was going to miss this room, the house—Maggie. This move didn't make him happy, and part of the reason was that *he* was always the one who walked away from a relationship, not the one who was given his walking papers. If he said that out loud, Maggie would tease him about his ego, and the thought tightened like a fist in his chest.

He wanted to fight her decision to distance herself from him. She said that was about protecting her daughter and was probably part of it, but her reasoning felt an awful lot like an excuse not to take a chance. Almost certainly, if it wasn't Danielle, Maggie would have found another reason to push him away.

His suitcase was open on the tufted stool at the foot of the king-size bed, and he threw his leather bag filled with toiletries into it. Before he could start emptying the dresser, there was a knock on the door, and hope that it was Maggie with a change of heart jumped into his mind.

But when he answered, the disappointment at finding Josie there was immediate. "Hi, what's up?"

"That's what I'm here to find out." She glanced past him to the open suitcase. "You're leaving?"

"Maggie didn't tell you?"

"No. She didn't say much at all, and you were conspicuously not present at breakfast." She shrugged. "I knew something was going on."

"I'm going, so you're right about that."

"Call me nosy, but I'm here to find out what the heck happened." She looked puzzled. "Why are you moving?"

"Maggie threw me out." That was a tad dramatic, but he was feeling that way.

"Why would she do that?" Josie's blue eyes narrowed on him. "What did you do, mister?"

"Nothing." He couldn't suppress a small smile at her tone and figured he should explain. "You sound like my mother and make me feel twelve years old again."

"That's a relief. I thought I'd lost my mojo." The older woman stood a little taller. "But something must have spooked her into evicting a stable, paying customer."

"If this was only business between us, I'd be at my office right now and not throwing my stuff into a suitcase."

Josie pushed the door wide and walked into the room. "You're saying there was something personal between you?"

"Yes." That was all he was prepared to divulge.

"I knew it!" The older woman pumped her arm in triumph.

"What exactly did you know?"

"Here's the thing. Maggie is an open book." She met his gaze, and her own had a spark of intelligence that hinted she missed very little. "You're a bit more guarded, but not much. You kissed her. I knew right away. Not because I was doing covert surveillance or anything. It was the way you acted around each other."

"How was that?"

She laughed. "Both of you worked so hard at being casual and cool. Before the kiss there was an easy give-and-take. Afterward, you acted as if an accidental touch would cause spontaneous combustion."

Eventually that was exactly what had happened, Sloan thought. And if it was up to him they would spontaneously combust again.

Often.

But after the engagement party last night, Maggie made it clear that wasn't ever going to happen. "Okay," he said grudgingly. "So we kissed."

"I also confirmed it with Maggie. I'm not proud of it, but her mother and I got her to admit it."

"So I heard." He remembered lunch with her mother.

"Maureen meant well." It was as if Josie could read his mind. "Then after a while you and Maggie sort of relaxed. Although anyone could see the sparks between you. The way you looked at her when you thought no one was watching. And Maggie did the same to you, in case you were wondering."

"I was," he admitted.

"So you care about her." She wasn't asking a question.

"Yes." Again, he wasn't prepared to say more, although he had the distinct impression this woman already knew his secrets.

"You're in love with her." Again, it wasn't a question.

Why did his feelings need a label? Couldn't they just be whatever they were? He liked spending time with Maggie. Sex was awesome and left him aching to have her again. She was beautiful, smart, hardworking, nurturing. He could go on, but that felt a lot like digging a hole he wouldn't be able to crawl out of.

And Josie was waiting for him to comment, watching him like a hawk and probably reading his mind. In case that was a power she didn't possess, he said, "I'm going to tell you what I told her brother. I've never been in love, never experienced it. So I wouldn't recognize it if it walked up and shook my hand."

"Aha," she said. "Baggage."

"Yeah." Good. She got it. Maybe she'd back off now.

"That's just an excuse for running away."

So much for cutting him some slack.

"You should be telling Maggie that, not me." He was getting irritated at taking the blame for having to move out. "I suggested to her that we take things one day at a time and see what happens."

"She didn't agree?"

"Her initial reaction was that it was sensible." He'd hated how bland she'd made the exploratory phase of a relationship sound. "But last night, just before we left, Danielle insisted on giving me a hug."

"I saw Maggie's face when that happened and hoped it wouldn't be a problem." Josie looked troubled. "I guess it was."

"Maggie said her daughter was getting attached to me and she didn't want her hurt by someone who wasn't sticking around."

"How does she know you won't?" the older woman demanded.

"That's what I said. But she refused to discuss it. Her mind was made up."

"There's more, isn't there?" She was studying him intently. "Maggie knows as well as I do that there are ways to handle Danielle's attachment if that was the only issue. But you're determined to move out. Did she ask you to?"

"Yes."

"Why?"

"She said there couldn't be anything physical between us." Sloan wasn't quite sure how she'd gotten so much information out of him, but, oddly enough, he didn't mind all that much. So what did he have to lose by telling her what she probably already knew? "I told her that every time I see her I want her again and couldn't promise that it wasn't going to happen."

"Good for you!" Then Josie frowned. "I don't understand. Why are you giving up? You wouldn't handle your business that way. What the heck is making you run away from this fight?"

Her tone clearly said she was disappointed in him, and Sloan was surprised at how much losing her good opinion bothered him. It put him even more on the defensive. "Look, Josie, you can't call me any name I haven't called myself. But this was Maggie's decision. She has enough to deal with and I don't want to make things harder for her."

"I didn't peg you for the cop-out type, Sloan."

"It's pretty easy to pass judgment when you don't have skin in the game," he said angrily.

"It is." She wasn't the least bit intimidated by his accusation and outburst. "But you're wrong. I do have a stake in this. Maggie is like the daughter I never had. Opportunities for happiness don't come along every day and second chances are even harder to find. I don't want to see Maggie blow it like I did."

"What—"

She held up a hand. "I'm not finished. You're not the only one with baggage. If you stack yours up next to hers, she'll win hands down. She lost the man she loved and is raising his child alone. That baby has to be at the top of her concern list if she considers letting a man into their lives. The thing is, you passed the test. You're terrific with Danielle, obviously a natural with kids. Danielle responded to you in the best possible way. So there's one wall down." She blew out a breath. "But now Maggie has to face the fact that she's just plain scared to let herself care for some-one again and risk getting hurt a second time."

"If I could make her take a chance, I would." Frustra-tion laced his words and had his hands curling into fists. "But only she can do that."

"For you she just might try," Josie said. "And if you were here every day right under her nose, if she had to look at you, interact with you, it would be easier to wear down her resistance. It would be a lot harder for her to ig-nore her feelings."

"And if it doesn't work, where does that leave me?" he demanded.

"You're tough. Smart. Not just a pretty face. A big boy who would never have to say he gave up."

"What if I want to throw in the towel?"

Josie sighed. "You're hiding behind self-righteous anger to keep the hurt from leaking through."

"My choice." His stubborn was coming out.

"It is. But sooner or later you're going to have to face your feelings and be honest about them."

"Maybe." The bullheaded streak wasn't going to let him admit she had a point.

"Or you could decide to continue ignoring the obvious."

"There are benefits," he maintained.

Josie nodded as if to say she felt sorry for him. She smiled sadly and met his gaze. "I'm going to miss watch-ing TV with you."

"Come to the lodge. The suite has a TV."

"It won't be the same." She walked over and hugged him. "Goodbye, Sloan."

"Take care of her, Josie."

She nodded, then left him to his packing.

He threw things into the suitcase and wallowed in his self-righteous indignation. When there was nothing left to pack, the bubble of anger and resentment popped. It was time to face walking away from Maggie and this brief but wonderful glimpse into a life that could have been everything he'd ever wanted. Josie's words drifted through his mind about being a quitter. They stung, but he didn't see any future in taking his head out of the sand.

The problem with leaving it there was that it left his ass exposed.

Two days. Forty-eight hours.

Maggie couldn't stop herself from marking time in terms of before and after Sloan. It had been two days since he'd moved out of her house. Correction: her B and B. He'd been a paying guest and it wasn't supposed to get personal. So she'd fixed the problem and now he was gone. If only her house would stop feeling so empty without him in it.

Speaking of empty—her stomach growled, a reminder that she hadn't eaten lunch and it was nearly two o'clock in the afternoon. Food hadn't been high on her list for the past couple of days, but she needed something or she'd get sick. That wasn't an option.

She left her office and went downstairs to the café. The lunch rush was over and only a few customers were in the place. Lucy was ringing up a couple's bill, and after paying it they left. She picked up the half-filled coffeepot and strolled over to the table where the lone customer sat and topped off his mug. There was a flirty expression on her partner's face, then Maggie noticed that the guy was very cute. Brown hair, blue eyes and broad shoulders—a triple threat. He also had a nice smile.

When she finally looked up and spotted Maggie, Lucy waved her over. "I was wondering when you'd surface for lunch."

"I guess that would be now." Maggie shrugged.

"Have you two met?" Lucy indicated the thirtysomething man she'd been chatting up. "He works for Sloan."

"We haven't run into each other." Although just hearing Sloan's name made Maggie feel as if she'd run into a brick wall. "I'm Maggie Potter."

"Dalton Sparks. It's nice to meet you, Maggie." He shook her hand.

"I was just telling Dalton about all the fantastic things Blackwater Lake has to offer," her partner gushed.

"It's a pretty little place," he responded, his eyes never leaving Lucy.

"It would be hard to find more spectacular scenery anywhere." The woman was practically purring. She rested the half-full pot on the table. "And you can't beat the people. Salt of the earth. Best anywhere. Friendly, hardworking. Always there if you need them."

Maggie wondered if her friend should be on the town's tourism and public relations committee. She was doing quite a sales pitch on the man. It was obvious because everything she'd said was what Maggie would have pitched to Sloan in order to talk him into staying. But she never had.

There were times when Maggie envied her partner. By taking a break from men, and apparently no emotional baggage, Lucy could be carefree. The only person she had to think about was herself. If she met a good-looking man there was nothing to stop her from pulling out all the stops. Maggie could barely remember a time when she didn't have to consider a little girl, whose welfare came first. The love for her child was tremendously big and all consuming, but it didn't quite fill up the lonely places inside her, the places that missed Sloan.

"How do you like Blackwater Lake?" she asked the newcomer to town.

"Seems like a great place," he said.

"Do you enjoy working here?" Lucy wanted to know.

"If you'd asked me that two days ago I'd have answered yes without hesitation. But my boss has developed a bad case of surly and it's showing no sign of letting up anytime soon."

Two days? That was when Maggie had asked him to leave the bed-and-breakfast. It probably wasn't a coincidence. Part of her wanted to believe he was crabby because he missed her, too. The practical part shut down that thought. And before she could figure out how to delicately phrase a question, the café's front door opened. Automatically she turned to look and saw her brother, Brady, walk in. He glanced around, then spotted her and came over.

"Ladies. How's it going, Dalton?" He obviously had met the man who worked with Sloan.

Dalton stood and shook hands. "Good to see you, Brady. I was just saying that things could be better."

"What's wrong?"

"Sloan. His attitude stinks. It's as if someone told him he has to paint the outside of the new resort pink or something." Dalton shook his head. "And speaking of work, I better get back to it. You know what they say about poking an angry bear."

"I'll ring up your check." Lucy led him over to the cash register.

Maggie watched the other woman smile up at the new guy, then met her brother's gaze. "Hi, there. Are you here for lunch?"

"Yeah."

"It's kind of late."

"I've been kind of busy," he said.

"Me, too. I just came down for a quick bite myself."

"Good. Join me," he invited. "I hate to eat alone."

"Since when?" she asked. "After you met a computer, you made a friend."

"Very funny. Although kind of true." He grinned. "Maybe falling in love with Olivia changed me for the better."

"Definitely better. You had nowhere to go but up," Maggie teased. She led him to a table for two by the front window and they sat down across from each other. "That's the thing. Because she's your executive assistant you took her for granted. You took advantage of her for years. But I don't think you suddenly fell for her. You just always loved her."

"I see that now. But it wasn't until she gave me notice that she was quitting and leaving town for another job that I started to pay closer attention."

"She shook you up."

His eyes narrowed. "As I recall, you had a little to do with that."

"Oh, who can remember." Maggie waved her hand dismissively.

"I do, as a matter of fact. It was your idea for her to quit."

"She tried to give her notice more than once, but you dangled more money in front of her. All she wanted was for you to love her."

Brady's expression turned serious. "I don't know what I would have done without her."

"You would have gone after her. Just like you did when she took that trip to Florida." Maggie grabbed two menus stacked beside the salt-and-pepper shakers and handed one to him. "Olivia said you proposed to her right there on the beach."

"What can I say? I'm spontaneous. A man of action."

Maggie scoffed. "It only took you five years."

"I had issues," he defended.

Lucy walked over to them, order pad in hand. "Hi, Brady. How are you?"

"Good. You?"

"Can't complain." She glanced over her shoulder to the door where Dalton had just exited. "I have to say that the resort project is bringing in a lot of interesting men to deepen the dating pool."

As far as Maggie was concerned, the pool could be a puddle and that would be deep enough for her. Her experience with Sloan had shown her the wisdom of not dipping her toe in the water. If only she'd listened to her own warnings and stuck to her guns when she'd blathered to him about not inviting him into her bedroom. Now she missed him so much she ached from it.

"So what'll you two have?" Lucy asked.

"Hamburger." Brady hadn't even looked at the menu.

"If that's what you had your heart set on, you should have gone to the Grizzly Bear Diner," Maggie said.

"Excuse me," Lucy objected. "But in Building a Business 101, it says that you should encourage people to come into your establishment, not send them to the competition."

"He's not people. He's my brother. And he doesn't pay anyway," Maggie reminded her.

"Wait a second. I'm not a freeloader," he protested. "I did your website at no charge. And I'm here because the beef you serve is grass fed and comes with a side of field greens or fruit. Organic and healthy. My woman will be so proud."

"Okay, then." Lucy looked at her. "Maggie?"

"Vegetable soup."

"And?" Lucy and Brady said together.

"That's it. I'm not very hungry." Her stomach growled

in spite of the knot that told her she would have trouble getting the soup down.

"I'll throw half a tuna-salad sandwich on the plate." Lucy turned away.

"She's a gigantic pain in the neck," Maggie said fondly.

"And she cares about you," her brother reminded her. "A lot of people do. So what's wrong, Maggie?"

Ah. This was why he hadn't gone to the diner. There was an ulterior motive for showing up at the Harvest Café.

"Nothing's wrong. I'm fine."

"Let's leave that for now. I'll come back to it because you're not fine." Brady met her gaze. "But it's important for you to know that Sloan has been like the walking dead since the night of Burke and Sydney's engagement party, And from what Dalton just said and my own observations, it's clear something happened between you two that night, because the rumor is that the next morning he moved into Blackwater Lake Lodge."

"He did."

Brady waited for more. When it didn't come, he prodded, "And?"

"Nothing. He moved out of the bed-and-breakfast."

"Why?"

Maggie recognized the stubborn look on his face and knew he wouldn't let this go unless she explained. "I asked him to leave."

"Why?" Then he frowned. "Did he do something?"

The only thing he did was be his charming, irresistible self, she thought. "Nothing like you're thinking. He's great with Danielle, and that's a problem."

He stared at her for a moment, then shook his head. "I'm not seeing the issue."

"He's not staying and she's getting attached to him."

"Her? Or you?" Brady asked.

"She's a little girl. I'm not. I understand that he's temporary but Danielle doesn't. I have to protect her."

"Really?" One dark eyebrow rose. "Or is it yourself you're protecting?"

"She's my number one priority," Maggie snapped. "It's my job to raise her the way Danny would have."

"I get that. But raising your daughter doesn't mean you can't have a life, too." Brady reached across the table and covered her hand with his own. "It's obvious to anyone who sees you and Sloan together that you care about each other."

It would be so much easier if she didn't like him so much. Her determination to keep him at a distance had been no match for the power of her attraction to him.

"Brady, if you don't mind, I would rather not talk about this."

He squeezed her fingers then let go of her hand. "I just have one more thing to say."

"It better be short and sweet."

"You once lectured me about getting over loss, moving on and making the most of every day. It's about time you took your own advice."

"It's not that easy," she protested.

"That's where you're wrong. Falling in love is easy. It's taking a leap of faith that's hard. Trust me, I know. And you're the one who gave me the kick in the butt I needed to get out of my own way."

"Look, Brady, I must have sounded like an annoying know-it-all. I didn't mean to. But you and Olivia have known each other forever. It was a very different situation between the two of you. Mine is complicated—"

He held up a hand to stop her. "Don't apologize. Not to me. I couldn't be more grateful that you made me see the light. I love Olivia more than anything and I'm grateful for every single second that we spend together. I'm deliriously happy with her. And that's why I'm here. I want you to be deliriously happy, too."

"I know." She tried to smile but tears were right there. It wasn't so easy putting on a brave front to someone who knew you almost as well as you knew yourself. "Thanks for caring about me."

"And that's code for you're finished with this conversation." He sighed. "Just keep in mind that cowards always have regrets."

"Okay, then. Good talk, Brady."

Not.

Coward? That seemed a little harsh. *Don't sugarcoat it*, Maggie thought. *Tell me how you really feel.* And that was the problem. Feelings. She didn't want them.

Not ever again.

But she didn't know how to make them go away.

Chapter Fifteen

Maggie came home from work, parked in front of the house and tried her new attitude, which was to feel nothing at all. Normally spending time with her brother lifted her spirits, but not today. And her spirits would sink even further when she walked in the door. That was all about the fact that Sloan had done as she'd asked and no longer lived under her roof. She looked at the place and couldn't help thinking it looked as sad as she felt.

She braced herself for the overpowering emptiness waiting for her inside. That morning Josie had said she wouldn't be there for dinner, and Danielle was with her mom, due here shortly. But right this minute the house was deserted. Sloan was never coming back, and in spite of trying to feel nothing, Maggie swore she could feel her heart crack.

She exited the car and walked to the rear to retrieve the two small bags of groceries she'd picked up on the way home. Milk, bread, fruit, eggs and her daughter's favorite cookies. It made Maggie probably the world's worst mother, but she'd been a little lax with the cookie rules in the past couple of days.

After unlocking the front door, Maggie went inside and turned on lights as she made her way to the kitchen, then settled the bags along with her purse on the island. She busied herself putting groceries away. Busy was good. It would keep her from missing his cheerful, charming disposition along with the broad shoulders and brown eyes. Not to mention her own sense of security and support. If she needed him he'd be there—or he would have been if she hadn't thrown him out.

The sound of a car door slamming drifted to her. "Oh, thank God."

Moments later the bell rang and the door opened, followed by her mother's voice. "Maggie?"

"In the kitchen."

"Mama!" Danielle's little feet sounded on the wood floor.

Maggie went down on one knee and opened her arms, grabbing that little warm body in a hug and holding her close. "Hi, baby girl. Did you have fun with Grandma?"

"Book. 'Bary."

"Library," her mother enunciated. "I took her for story time. We were in the car anyway and it was easier for me to drop her off than have you pick her up."

Maybe that was the reason her mom had called and said she'd drop Danielle off, but Maggie wasn't so sure. "I hate to have you go out of your way, Mom. You're doing me a favor."

"It's not a favor. I love spending time with my grandchild. You know that." Maureen watched the little girl toddle toward the stairs, obviously calling for someone. "What is she doing?"

Maggie sighed and met her mom's gaze. "She's looking for Sloan. Been doing it since he left. She's too little to understand why he's not here."

"That makes two of us. I don't understand and I'm a lot older than she is."

Maggie caught up with her daughter before she could climb the stairs. "It's complicated, Mom."

"I've got time." Maureen took off her sweater and hung it on one of the bar stools at the island and set her purse on the seat. "Explain it to me."

Maggie put her squirming-to-get-down daughter in the high chair and warmed some cut-up chicken and green beans, then put it on the tray. Danielle instantly grabbed a piece in her chubby fingers. She put it in her mouth, then took another, in a not very ladylike way. One of these days, they would work on manners.

The explain-it-to-me remark had been a clue, and now Maggie knew for sure that dropping Danielle off at home was a contrived excuse. Her mother's real purpose was to interfere in her personal life. "You talked to Brady, didn't you?"

"What makes you say that?" her mom hedged.

"Oh, please. Nothing happens in this family that doesn't get relayed to all at light speed." She rested her hands on her hips. "He came into the café for lunch today and I explained everything to him. I'm sure he shared the high points with you."

"He did." Her mother sighed. "But the explanation doesn't make sense to me."

"I can't help that. It makes perfect sense to me." *Mostly.*

"I'll admit to having doubts about Sloan at first. After all, he can't help that he's handsome and wealthy and women are drawn to him like—well, the nicest metaphor is bees to honey."

Maggie wished she was the exceptional woman who successfully ignored his appeal, but unfortunately she'd succumbed. And it wasn't about those qualities. She'd been drawn to them as much as the fact that he was a really good guy. "What's your point, Mom?"

"My point is that he proved me wrong. He manned up and came to my house for lunch. He ate quiche and said he enjoyed it." Her mom took a breath. "And while he was being a real man and choking down that quiche, I grilled him like raw meat. About his women. He said the stories were exaggerated and he wasn't that guy. I believed him when he told me he would never deliberately hurt you, that you're a special woman. It shows he has good taste."

It was the "deliberately" part, Maggie thought. He might not mean for it to happen, but as soon as you let someone into your heart you left yourself open to hurt. "You saw the way Danielle was looking for him. She was getting used to him. What happens to her when he leaves town? I won't let her be hurt."

"Oh, Maggie—" Her mom pressed her lips together. "A mother's job is to protect her babies, but we can't do that all the time. If it was possible, I'd have done that for you. With Danny—"

"I know."

"The only positive thing I can say is that what doesn't kill you makes you stronger. A cliché, I know, but that doesn't make it any less true. You're strong and you have to move on with your life."

"I have."

"You're raising a child and working at your business." Maureen shook her head. "But you have no joy in a personal relationship with a man. I saw a flash of it when Sloan was here, but it's gone now."

"Mom—"

"I hear a patronizing tone and we'll nip that in the bud." Speaking of flashes, there was one in her mother's eyes. "No one knows you as well as your mother. On top of that, the two of us are members of an exclusive club no woman wants to belong to. We're widows. We both lost the man we loved. And it sucks. I know. I recognized your pain when you got the news and the light went out of your eyes. I saw when it came back on—when Sloan was here."

"I don't want Danielle to get attached to him," Maggie said stubbornly.

"You mean the way you were to your dad?" A sad look slid into her mom's eyes.

"Yeah." Maggie would never forget the shock of her father's sudden heart attack, the pain of finding out he was gone.

"You were older when he died, but there were still things you missed out on. Seeing the look of amazement in your father's eyes when you were all dressed up for your first formal dance. You didn't have the man whose mere presence in the house told all those boys who came calling not to mess with his daughter." There was a hitch in her voice before she said, "Giving you away on your wedding day."

"Danielle won't miss what she never had," Maggie protested.

"That's just it. She could have all of that. She could have a man in her life to be the best kind of role model. She wouldn't be missing Sloan now if he hadn't shown that he was ready and up to the challenge of being a father. The kind of man who would navigate the complex world of car seats and strollers to help you out is looking for family. He's ready to support you because he cares about you and your daughter. But you have to meet him halfway, baby girl."

"Oh, Mom—"

"Cookie?"

Maggie looked at her daughter's messy high chair tray. There was food sticking to it and some on the floor. Guessing the little girl had consumed enough, she gave her a cookie from the brand-new box sitting on the island. Happily, Danielle shoved it into her mouth.

Maggie looked back at her own mother and recognized hope and pain in her expression. "I don't know if I can move on. You never did."

"I would have—if I'd met anyone who made me want to," Maureen admitted.

"Josie lost her husband and she hasn't moved on." Maggie was grasping at straws to make an argument, support her decision to push Sloan away.

"Are you sure about that?"

Something in her mother's voice got her attention. "Is she seeing someone? Who?"

"You don't think she went all that way to the hospital in Copper Hill when Hank Fletcher had his heart attack and only stayed there just for his daughter, Kim, do you?"

"She's dating the sheriff?"

"Hank is a widower. And technically he's not the sheriff right now, what with being on medical leave. But, yes. They have been discreetly hanging out, or whatever it's called these days." Her mother smiled. "She's moving on."

"I'm happy for her."

"Me, too." She released a big sigh. "I know what loneliness feels like. No one knows better than me that it takes a toll. I can see what it's doing to you, Maggie, and it breaks my heart. Especially when there's a chance to change it."

"Mom, I—"

"Get back out there, Maggie. Sloan is a good man. But if you don't love him, that's a different story."

"It's not that," she whispered. "I'm afraid."

Maureen moved close and wrapped Maggie in her arms. "I know, baby girl. I get it."

"What if I lose him, too, Mom?"

"What if you don't?" There was steel in her mother's

voice. "The choices you make in life don't come with a money-back guarantee. You can put a wall around your heart to protect it, but that's not really living. Or you can take a chance and make the choice to live every day to the fullest."

Maggie's eyes filled with tears. "What if I blew my chance?"

"Well—" Her mother's expression turned fiercely protective. "You know what love feels like and I expect you would recognize it if that's what you have with Sloan. This may come as a surprise, but he can't read your mind. If you love him, you have to tell him."

"What if—"

"No. Don't borrow trouble. You tell him what's on your mind. It will either work out or it won't. But you'll never have to wonder what might have been. You'll never have to say, 'if only.'"

Maggie nodded. "Good talk, Mom."

And this time she meant those words with all her heart.

Later, after putting Danielle to bed, Maggie waited for Josie to come home. She was hoping her friend would babysit because there was something important she had to do.

Unable to sit still, she paced the length of the house, rehearsing what she wanted to say. A jumble of thoughts went through her mind but she couldn't pull them together. Then finally she heard a car pull into the driveway, and at this time of night it wouldn't be anyone but Josie. Her friend always used the front door instead of the outside stairs and Maggie waited for her to come in.

Josie unlocked the door and opened it. When she saw Maggie, her eyes widened. "Is everything okay?"

"Yes. Fine." If you didn't factor in that she'd been a stubborn coward. "I was just wondering if you could keep an eye on Danielle for me."

"Of course. I can give her a bath—"

"She's in bed already. Mom wore her out today at the library and she didn't have a nap." Maggie twisted her fingers together. "If you could just listen for her I'd really appreciate it."

"Sure." Josie looked at her watch. "It's after eight. Must be pretty important."

"I have an—errand."

"Kind of late, isn't it?" There was a knowing look on her friend's face. "This errand isn't by any chance the handsome and charming man who, until recently, lived here, is it?"

Maggie sighed. It was too much to hope that she could pull this off without anyone else knowing about it. In her defense, it was difficult to pull off a covert operation when you had a two-year-old. But Josie was guessing.

"Why would you think that?"

"I talked to your mother." Josie's expression grew firm. "Before you get huffy, you should know that she's worried about you. She needed to unburden herself to someone."

Maggie fought a smile. "Unburdening oneself sounds so much more tasteful than gossiping."

"It does. Thank you for noticing. But it's also true. Maureen could see how distracted and unhappy you've been and, frankly, I did, too."

"I didn't mean to worry anyone."

"It comes with the territory. We love you." Her friend turned serious. "Just keep in mind that he was hurt and angry when he left here."

"You talked to him?"

"Yes."

"So am I wasting my time? Maybe he won't see me—"

Josie held up a hand. "I'm sure he's cooled off by now. And just remember, if you don't try, you'll never forgive yourself."

"Yeah. That seems to be the majority opinion." Her wise family had made her see the truth of it. And she knew from personal experience that what might have been was more painful than facing up to what was going on right now.

"Okay, then. And before you leave, I just want to say that you need to remember when he left here he was running away, too."

"From what?"

"That's something you need to ask him. But trust me, honey, it's an even playing field."

"Okay." She hugged her friend. "Thanks."

"Anytime. Now go run your errand. And put on your raincoat. It's drizzly and cold outside."

Maggie did as ordered, then grabbed her keys and purse and drove to Blackwater Lake Lodge, where her "errand" was currently residing. *Nervous* didn't adequately describe how she was feeling. Her nerves had nerves. And it would be ridiculously easy to turn the car around and go home. But Brady and her mom were right. She'd lost her husband in a situation that was completely beyond her control. With Sloan... Well, she would regret it forever if she didn't at least talk to him one last time.

She exited her car and headed for the lodge's bright lights. When the lobby doors automatically whispered open, she stopped short. Obviously she hadn't thought this completely through.

She had no idea what room he was staying in.

As the owner of a B and B, she was well aware of a guest's safety and privacy rights. Now that she was here, there was only one thing she could do.

She walked up to the reception desk and smiled at the young man there, whose name tag said Ron.

"Hi, Ron. I'm here to see one of your guests. Sloan Holden." The guy looked uncomfortable and started to say something, but her patience and nerves were on thin ice. She interrupted. "I'm aware that you're not permitted to give out room numbers. I was hoping you could call and just let him know Maggie Potter is here to see him."

"Of course." Ron looked relieved that she didn't push the issue.

Maggie's heart pounded as he picked up the phone, dialed and waited for an answer. She pulled the belt a little tighter on her water-resistant coat with sweaty hands and realized her pulse was racing. How had all those women sneaked into his room and stripped naked to wait in his bed? It would take more nerve than she had. Obviously she wasn't cut out to be a stalker groupie.

Finally she heard Ron say, "Yes, sir. I'll send her right up." The guy replaced the phone and said, "He's in the suite on the top floor."

"What's the room number?"

"He said he'll be waiting for you."

Maggie wanted to grill this young man like raw hamburger. Did Sloan sound happy that she was here? Angry? Or worse—annoyed? There was only one way to find out and she wasn't hiding from it anymore. She braced herself and stiffened her spine, then walked around the corner to the elevator and rode it to the top floor of the lodge.

When the doors opened, she saw an arrow on the wall directing visitors to the rooms. She followed the hall to the suite and found out why she didn't need to know a number.

Sloan was standing in the doorway.

Maggie's breath caught and she couldn't look at him hard enough. It felt like a lifetime since she'd last seen him. The sleeves of his white shirt were rolled up and his gray slacks were wrinkled, indicating a lot of sitting behind a desk. His dark hair looked as if he'd dragged his fingers through it countless times. Most of all, there were lines in his face, deeper than she'd ever noticed. He looked tired and she badly wanted to smooth the weariness away.

"Maggie." His voice wasn't as enthusiastic as she would have liked.

"Hi." She met his gaze. "I thought about being naked under this coat, but showing up here at all makes me feel really vulnerable."

When he didn't say anything, she started talking. "You were right about me. I was carrying around a lot of baggage about my husband's death and subconsciously felt it was wrong for me to be happy. Survivor's guilt and regrets that he died before his daughter was born. That makes me sound a little crazy, but it's really more complicated than that. I was afraid to let anyone in. I was terrified of caring again and being hurt. And not just me this time. Danielle, too. She wouldn't miss her father because she never had a chance to know him. But she was getting to know you.

"What if you left me? She would be devastated, too." Maggie took a deep breath and prayed that he would say something. But he just stared at her, intensity darkening his eyes. Fortunately she was almost finished, because he probably wanted her gone.

"I tried so hard to keep you out. For Danielle's sake, but mostly for me. The thing is, I just couldn't keep you out. I fell in love with you, Sloan."

Maggie looked at him and waited. And waited some more. Then her heart squeezed tight to hold back the pain.

"Okay, then. I'll take your silence as a sign that you aren't on the same page. I'm sorry I bothered you." She stepped back and started to turn away.

Sloan reached out, took her arm to stop her and simply said, "Stay."

"Why? You have nothing to say to me."

With his index finger, he traced the collar of her raincoat. "I just got an image of you naked under this coat and words failed me."

"I'm not sure I believe that." But hope blossomed inside her. "You're probably the most smooth-talking man I've ever met."

"Normally I am, but not where you're concerned." He pulled her into the suite and closed the door. "If you hadn't come to me, I was going to you. Prepared to wear you down with sheer persistence."

"Josie said you left because you were running away. Why?"

"I didn't want to be hurt. Just like you." He sighed. "But the longer I was away, the more I knew I had to fight for you. I couldn't let you go without trying."

"Really?"

"God's honest truth." He curled his fingers around her arms. "I love you, Maggie. Pretty much since I showed up on your doorstep. You're everything I ever wanted and thought I'd never find. If I'd known my dream was here in Blackwater Lake, I would have come to town sooner."

Happiness flooded through her. "I think things happened exactly the way they were supposed to. I might not have been ready for love before now. And missing out on loving you would have broken my heart. Sooner? Later?" She shrugged. "It doesn't matter because we have the rest of our lives to be together."

"Starting now," he said, his gaze on hers. "I want a family with you. I love that little girl of yours as if she was my own."

"She's missed you terribly. Keeps trying to go upstairs to find you." She smiled. "It was watching her turn to you like she would a father that freaked me out."

"Don't be," he pleaded. "I'll be the best father to her that I know how to be. Marry me, Maggie."

"You're willing to give up your standing as one of the world's most eligible bachelors?" She grinned up at him.

"More than you will ever know," he said fervently. "Marry me."

"You're not going to miss the women showing up in your room?"

"The only woman I'd miss if she didn't show up in my room is you. Please say you'll marry me, Maggie."

"On one condition."

"Anything," he said.

"You'll move back into the house." She met his gaze. "Into my room."

"Wow. You drive a hard bargain." He grinned. "Done. Now please put me out of my misery, because I want more than anything to marry you."

"Yes," she said.

He breathed a sigh of relief and pulled her against him. "Is Josie with Danielle?"

"She is."

"Do you think she would mind giving her breakfast in the morning?" There was a gleam in his eyes that was both passion and promise.

"I think that could be arranged. Why?"

"Because I'd really like to unbutton that coat and find you naked."

"All night?"

"And for the rest of our lives," he said.

And so much for their bargain not to get personal. This one worked for her so much better.

* * * * *

The main lights in the room were set low, and a large glitter ball revolved slowly from the ceiling, scattering the floor and the walls with shards of silver light.

Max watched them dance over Cara's face in fascination, thinking that she looked like some kind of ethereal seraph with her bright eyes and pale, creamy skin against the glowing silver of her dress.

A strange elation twisted through him, triggering a lifting sensation throughout his whole body—as if all the things that had dragged him down in the last eighteen months were losing their weight and slowly drifting upwards. The sadness he'd expected to keep on hitting him throughout the day was still notably absent, and instead there was a weird sense of rightness about being here.

With her.

UNLOCKING HER BOSS'S HEART

BY
CHRISTY McKELLEN

MILLS &
BOON®

First Published in Great Britain 2016
By Mills & Boon, an imprint of HarperCollins*Publishers*
1 London Bridge Street, London, SE1 9GF

© 2016 Christy McKellen

ISBN: 978-0-263-91954-7

23-0116

Our policy is to use papers that are natural, renewable and recyclable products and made from wood grown in sustainable forests.The logging and manufacturing processes conform to the legal environmental regulations of the country of origin.

Printed and bound in Spain
by CPI, Barcelona

Formerly a video and radio producer, **Christy McKellen** now spends her time writing fun, impassioned and emotive romance with an undercurrent of sensual tension. When she's not writing she can be found enjoying life with her husband and three children, walking for pleasure and researching other people's deepest secrets and desires.

Christy loves to hear from readers. You can get hold of her at www.christymckellen.com.

This one is for Babs and Phil, the most generous,
loving and supportive parents in the world.
You've seen me through all my ups and downs
(and there have been a few), and always picked me up,
dusted me off and cheered me on.

I love you. I hope you know that.

CHAPTER ONE

CARA WINSTONE CLIMBED the smooth slate steps to the shiny black front door of the town house in South Kensington and tried hard not to be awed by its imposing elegance.

This place was exactly the sort of house she'd dreamed about living in during her naïve but hopeful youth. In her fantasies, the four-storey Victorian house would be alive with happy, mischievous children, whom she and her handsome husband would firmly but lovingly keep in line and laugh about in the evenings once they'd gone to bed. Each room would have a beautiful display of fresh seasonal flowers and light would pour in through the large picture windows, reflecting off the tasteful but comfortable furnishings.

Back in real life, her topsy-turvy one-bed flat in Islington was a million miles away from this grand goddess of a mansion.

Not that it was going to be her flat for much longer if she didn't make good on this opportunity today.

The triple espresso she'd had for breakfast lurched around in her stomach as she thought about how close she was to being evicted from the place she'd called home for the past six years by her greedy landlord. If she didn't find another job soon she was going to have to slink back to Cornwall, to the village that time forgot, and beg to share her parents' box room with the dogs until she got back on her feet.

She loved her parents dearly, but the thought of them all bumping elbows again in their tiny isolated house made her shudder. Especially after they'd been so excited when she'd called six months ago to tell them about landing her dream job as Executive Assistant to the CEO of one of the largest conglomerates in the country. Thanks to her mother's prodigious grapevine, word had quickly spread through both the family and her parents' local community and she'd been inundated with texts and emails of congratulations.

The thought of having to call them again now and explain why she'd been forced to hand in her notice after only three months made her queasy with shame. She couldn't do it. Not after the sacrifices they'd made in order to pay for her expensive private education, so she'd have the opportunities they'd never had. No, she owed them more than that.

But, with any luck, she'd never be forced to have that humiliating conversation because this chance today could be the ideal opportunity to get her feet back under the table. If she could secure this job, she was sure that everything else would fall into place.

Shifting the folder that contained her CV and the glowing references she'd accumulated over the years under her arm, she pressed the shiny brass bell next to the door and waited to be greeted by the owner of the house.

And waited.

Tapping her foot, she smoothed down her hair again, then straightened the skirt of her best suit, wanting to look her most professional and together self when the door finally swung open.

Except that it didn't.

Perhaps the occupier hadn't heard her ring.

Fighting the urge to chew on the nails she'd only just grown out, she rang again, for longer this time and was just about to give up and come back later when the door swung open to reveal a tall, shockingly handsome man with a long-limbed, powerful physique and the kind of self-possessed air that made her heart beat a little faster. His chocolate-brown hair looked as though it could do with a cut, but it fell across his forehead into his striking gold-shot hazel eyes in the most becoming manner. If she had to sum him up in one word it would be *dashing*—an old-fashioned-sounding term, but somehow it suited him down to the ground.

His disgruntled gaze dropped from her face to the folder under her arm.

'Yes?' he barked, his tone so fierce she took a pace backwards and nearly fell off the top step.

'Max Firebrace?' To her chagrin, her voice came out a little wobbly in the face of his unexpected hostility.

His frown deepened. 'I don't donate to charities at the door.'

Taking a deep breath, she plastered an assertive smile

onto her face and said in her most patient voice, 'I'm not working for a charity. I'm here for the job.'

His antagonism seemed to crackle like a brooding lightning storm between them. 'What are you talking about? I'm not hiring for a job.'

Prickly heat rushed across her skin as she blinked at him in panicky confusion. 'Really? But my cousin Poppy said you needed a personal assistant because you're snowed under with work.'

He crossed his arms and shook his head as an expression of beleaguered understanding flashed across his face.

'I only told Poppy I'd look into hiring someone to get her off my back,' he said irritably.

She frowned at him in confusion, fighting the sinking feeling in her gut. 'So you don't need a PA?'

Closing his eyes, he rubbed a hand across his face and let out a short, sharp sigh. 'I'm very busy, yes, but I don't have time to even interview for a PA right now, let alone train them up, so if you'll excuse me—'

He made as if to shut the door, but before he could get it halfway closed she dashed forwards, throwing up both hands in a desperate attempt to stall him and dropping her folder onto the floor with a loud clatter. 'Wait! Please!'

A look of agitated surprise crossed his face at the cacophony, but at least he paused, then opened the door a precious few inches again.

Taking that as a sign from the gods of perseverance, Cara scooped up her folder from the floor, threw back her shoulders and launched into the sales pitch she'd been practising since Poppy's email had landed in her inbox last night, letting her know about this golden opportunity.

'I'm *very* good at what I do and I'm a quick learner— I have six years of experience as a PA so you won't need to show me much at all.' Her voice had taken on an embarrassing squeaky quality, but she soldiered on regardless.

'I'm excellent at working on my own initiative and I'm precise and thorough. You'll see when you hire me,' she said, forcing a confidence she didn't feel any more into her voice.

He continued to scowl at her, his hand still gripping the door as if he was seriously contemplating shutting it in her face, but she was not about to leave this doorstep without a fight. She'd had *enough* of feeling like a failure.

'Give me a chance to show you what I can do, free of charge, today, then if you like what you see I can start properly tomorrow.' Her forced smile was beginning to make her cheeks ache now.

His eyes narrowed as he appeared to consider her proposal.

After a few tense seconds of silence, where she thought her heart might beat its way out of her chest, he nodded towards the folder she was still clutching in her hand.

'Is that your CV?' he asked.

'Yes.' She handed it to him and watched with bated breath as he flipped through it.

'Okay,' he said finally, sighing hard and shoving the

folder back towards her. 'Show me what you can do today, then if I'm satisfied I'll offer you a paid one-month trial period. After *that* I'll decide whether it's going to work out as a full-time position or not.'

'Done.' She stuck out a hand, which he looked at with a bemused expression, before enveloping it in his own large, warm one.

Relief, chased by an unnerving hot tingle, rushed through her as he squeezed her fingers, causing every nerve-ending on her body to spring to life.

'You'd better come in,' he said, dropping the hand-shake and turning his broad back on her to disappear into the house.

Judging by his abrupt manner, it seemed she had her work cut out if she was going to impress him. Still, she was up for the challenge—even if the man did make her stomach flip in the most disconcerting way.

Shaking off her nerves, she hurried inside after him, closing the heavy door behind her and swivelling back just in time to see him march into a doorway at the end of the hall.

And what a hall. It had more square footage than her entire flat put together. The high, pale cream walls were lined with abstract works of art on real canvases, not clip-framed prints like she had at her place, and the colourful mosaic-tiled floor ran for what must have been a good fifty metres before it joined the bottom of a wide oak staircase which led up to a similarly grand stairwell, where soft light flooded in through a huge stained-glass window.

Stopping by a marble-topped hall table, which, she

noted, was sadly devoid of flowers, she took a deep calming breath before striding down the hallway to the room he'd vanished into.

Okay, she could do this. She could be impressive. Because she *was* impressive.

Right, Cara? *Right?*

The room she entered was just as spacious as the hall, but this time the walls were painted a soft duck-egg blue below the picture rail and a crisp, fresh white above it, which made the corniced ceiling feel as if it was a million miles above her and that she was very small indeed in comparison.

Max was standing in the middle of the polished parquet floor with a look of distracted impatience on his face. Despite her nerves, Cara couldn't help but be aware of how dauntingly charismatic he was. The man seemed to give off waves of pure sexual energy.

'My name's Cara, by the way,' she said, swallowing her apprehension and giving him a friendly smile.

He just nodded and held out a laptop. 'This is a spare. You can use it today. Once you've set it up, you can get started on scanning and filing those documents over there,' he said, pointing to a teetering pile of paper on a table by the window. 'There's the filing cabinet—' he swung his finger to point at it '—there's the scanner.' Another swing of his finger. 'The filing system should be self-explanatory,' he concluded with barely concealed agitation in his voice.

So he wasn't a people person then.

'Okay, thank you,' she said, taking the laptop from him and going to sit on a long, low sofa that was pushed up against the wall on the opposite side of the room to a large oak desk with a computer and huge monitor on top of it.

Tamping down on the nervous tension that had plagued her ever since she'd walked away from her last job, she booted up the laptop, opened the internet browser and set up her email account and a folder called 'Firebrace Management Solutions' in a remote file-saving app. Spotting a stack of business cards on the coffee table next to the sofa, she swiped one and programmed Max's mobile number into her phone, then added his email address to her contacts.

Throughout all this, he sat at his desk with his back to her, deeply absorbed in writing the document she must have stopped him from working on when she'd knocked on his door.

Okay. The first thing she was going to do was make them both a hot drink, then she'd make a start on the mountain of paperwork to be digitally backed up and filed.

Not wanting to speak up and disturb him with questions at this point, she decided to do a bit of investigative work. Placing the laptop carefully onto the sofa, she stood up and made for the door, intent on searching out the kitchen.

He didn't stir from his computer screen as she walked past him.

Well, if nothing else, at least this was going to be a very different experience to her last job. By the end of her time there she could barely move without feeling a set of judging eyes burning into her.

The kitchen was in the room directly opposite and she stood for a moment to survey the lie of it. There was a big glass-topped table in the middle with six chairs pushed in around it and an expanse of cream-coloured marble work surface, which ran the length of two sides of the room. The whole place was sleek and new-looking, with not a thing out of place.

Opening up the dishwasher, she peered inside and saw one mug and one cereal bowl sitting in the rack. *Hmm.* So it was just Max living here? Unless his partner was away at the moment. Glancing round, she scanned the place for photographs, but there weren't any, not even one stuck to the enormous American fridge. In fact, this place was so devoid of personalised knick-knacks it could have been a kitchen in a show home.

Lifting the mug out of the dishwasher, she checked it for remnants of his last drink, noting from the smell that it was coffee, no sugar, and from the colour that he took it without milk. There was a technical-looking coffee maker on the counter which flummoxed her for a moment or two, but she soon figured out how to set it up and went about finding coffee grounds in the sparsely filled fridge and making them both a drink, adding plenty of milk to hers.

Walking back into the room, she saw that Max hadn't budged a centimetre since she'd left and was still busy tapping away on the keyboard.

After placing his drink carefully onto the desk, which he acknowledged with a grunt, she took a look through the filing cabinet till she figured out which system he was using, then squared up to the mountain of paperwork on the sideboard, took a breath and dived in.

Well, she was certainly the most *determined* woman he'd met in a long time.

Max Firebrace watched Cara out of the corner of his eye as she manhandled the pile of documents over to the sofa and heard her put them down with a thump on the floor.

Glancing at the drink she'd brought him, he noticed she'd made him a black coffee without even asking what he wanted.

Huh. He wasn't expecting that. The PAs he'd had in the past had asked a lot of questions when they'd first started working with him, but Cara seemed content to use her initiative and just get on with things.

Perhaps this wasn't going to be as much of a trial as he'd assumed when he'd agreed to their bargain on the doorstep.

It was typical of Poppy to send someone over here without letting him know. His friend was a shrewd operator all right. She'd known he was blowing her off when he promised to get someone in to help him and had clearly taken it upon herself to make it happen anyway.

Irritation made his skin prickle.

He was busy, sure, but, as he'd told Poppy at the time, it wasn't anything he couldn't handle. He'd allow Cara to work her one-month trial period to placate his friend, but then he'd let her go. He wasn't ready to hire someone else full-time yet; there wasn't enough for her to do day-to-day, and he didn't need someone hanging around, distracting him.

Leaning back into the leather swivel chair that had practically become his home in the past few months, he rubbed the heels of his hands across his eyes before picking up the drink and taking a sip.

He'd been working more and more at the weekends now that his management consultancy was starting to grow some roots, and he was beginning to feel it. It had been a slog since he'd set up on his own, but he'd been glad of the distraction and it was finally starting to pay dividends. If things carried on in the same vein, at some point in the future he'd be in a position to rent an office, hire some employees and start expanding. *Then* he could relax a little and things would get back to a more even keel.

The thought buoyed him. After working for other people since graduating from university, he was enjoying having full control over who he worked for and when; it seemed to bring about a modicum of peace— something that had eluded him for the past eighteen months. Ever since Jemima had gone.

No, *died.*

He really needed to allow the word into his interior monologue now. No one else had wanted to say it at the time, so he'd become used to employing all the gentler euphemisms himself, but there was no point pretending it was anything else. She'd died, so suddenly and unexpectedly it had left him reeling for months, and he still wasn't used to living in this great big empty house without her. The house Jemima had inherited from her great-aunt. The home she'd wanted to fill with children—which he'd asked her to wait for—until *he* felt ready.

Pain twisted in his stomach as he thought about all that he'd lost—his beautiful, compassionate wife and their future family. Recently he'd been waking up at night in a cold sweat, reaching out to try and save a phantom child with Jemima's eyes from a fall, or a fire—the shock and anguish of it often staying with him for the rest of the following day.

No wonder he was tired.

A movement in the corner of his eye broke his train of thought and he turned to watch Cara as she opened up the filing cabinet to the right of him and began to deftly slide documents into the manila folders inside.

Now that he looked at her properly, he could see the family resemblance to Poppy. She had the same shiny coal-black hair as his friend, which cascaded over her slim shoulders, and a very short blunt-cut fringe above bright blue almond-shaped eyes.

She was pretty. Very pretty, in fact.

Not that he had any interest in her romantically. It was purely an observation.

Cara looked round and caught him watching her, her cheeks flushing in response to his scrutiny.

Feeling uncomfortable with the atmosphere he'd created by staring at her, he sat up straighter, crossing his arms and adopting a more businesslike posture. 'So, Cara, tell me about the last place you worked. Why did you leave?'

Her rosy cheeks seemed to pale under his direct gaze.

Rocking back on her heels, she cleared her throat, her gaze skittering away from his to stare down at the papers in her hands, as if she was priming herself to give him an answer she thought he'd want to hear.

What was *that* about? The incongruity made him frown.

'Or were you fired?'

Her gaze snapped back to his. 'No, no, I left. At least, I opted for voluntary redundancy. The business I was working for took a big financial hit last year and, because I was the last in, it felt only right that I should be the first out. There were lots of people who worked there with families to support, whereas I'm only me—I mean I don't have anyone depending on me.'

Her voice had risen throughout that little monologue and the colour had returned to her cheeks to the point where she looked uncomfortably flushed. There was something not quite right about the way she'd delivered her answer, but he couldn't put his finger on what it was.

Perhaps she was just nervous? He knew he could come across as fierce sometimes, though usually only when someone did something to displease him.

He didn't suffer fools gladly.

But she'd been fine whilst persuading him to give her a shot at the PA job.

'That's it? You took voluntary redundancy?'

She nodded and gave him a smile that didn't quite reach her eyes. 'That's it.'

'So why come begging for this job? Surely, with your six years of experience, you could snap up a senior position in another blue-chip firm and earn a lot more money.'

Crossing her arms, she pulled her posture up straighter, as if preparing to face off with him. 'I wouldn't say I *begged* you for this job—'

He widened his eyes, taken aback by the defensiveness in her tone.

Noting this, she sank back into her former posture and swept a conciliatory hand towards him. '—but I take your point. To be honest, I've been looking for a change of scene from the corporate workplace and when Poppy mailed me about this opportunity it seemed to fit with exactly what I was looking for. I like the idea of working in a small, dedicated team and being an intrinsic part of the growth of a new business. Poppy says you're brilliant at what you do and I like working for brilliant people.' She flashed him another smile, this time with a lot more warmth in it.

He narrowed his eyes and gave her an approving nod. 'Okay. Good answer. You're an excellent ambassador for yourself and that's a skill I rate highly.'

Her eyes seemed to take on an odd shine in the bright mid-morning light, as if they'd welled up with tears.

Surely not.

Breaking eye contact, she looked down at the papers in her hand and blinked a couple of times, giving the floor a small nod. 'Well, that's good to hear.' When she looked back up, her eyes were clear again and the bravado in her expression made him wonder what was going on in her head.

Not that he should concern himself with such things.

An odd moment passed between them as their gazes caught and he became uncomfortably aware of the silence in the room. He'd been on his own in this house for longer than he wanted to think about, and having her here was evidently messing with his head. Which was exactly what he didn't need.

Cara looked away first, turning to open one of the lower filing cabinet drawers. After dropping the documents into it, she turned back to face him with a bright smile. 'Okay, well, it won't take me too much longer to finish this so I'll nip out in a bit and get us some lunch from the café a couple of streets away. When I walked past earlier there was an amazing smell of fresh bread wafting out of there, and they had a fantastic selection of deli meats and cheeses and some delicious-looking salads.'

Max's stomach rumbled as he pictured the scene she'd so artfully drawn in his mind. He was always too busy to go out and fetch lunch for himself, so ended up eating whatever he could forage from the kitchen, which usually wasn't much.

'Then, if you have a spare minute later on, you can give me access to your online diary,' Cara continued, not waiting for his response. 'I'll take a look through it and organise any transport and overnight stays you need booking.'

'Okay. That would be useful,' he said, giving her a nod. It would be great to have the small daily inconveniences taken care of so he could concentrate on getting this report knocked into shape today.

Hmm. Perhaps it would prove more advantageous than he'd thought to have her around for a while.

He'd have to make sure he fully reaped the benefit of her time here before letting her go.

CHAPTER TWO

SHE WAS A terrible liar.

The expression on Max's face had been sceptical at best when she'd reeled out the line about leaving her last job, but Cara thought she'd pulled it off. At least he hadn't told her to sling her hook.

Yet.

She got the impression he was the type of person who wouldn't tolerate any kind of emotional weakness—something she was particularly sensitive to after her last boyfriend, Ewan, left her three months ago because he was fed up with her 'moaning and mood swings'. So she was going to have to be careful not to let any more momentary wobbles show on her face. It was going to be happy, happy, joy, joy! from here on in.

After slipping the last document into the filing cabinet, taking care not to let him see how much her hands were still shaking, she grabbed her coat and bag and, after taking a great gulp of crisp city air into her lungs, went to the café to pick up some lunch for them both, leaving the door off the latch so she wouldn't have to disturb Max by ringing the bell on her return.

Inevitably, she bought a much bigger selection of deli wares than the two of them could possibly eat in one session, but she told herself that Max could finish off whatever remained for his supper. Judging by the emptiness of his cavernous fridge, he'd probably be glad of it later.

This made her wonder again about his personal situation. Poppy had told her very little in the email—which she'd sent in a rare five minutes off from her crazy-sounding filming schedule in the African desert. Cara didn't want to bother her cousin with those kinds of questions when she was so busy, so it was up to her to find out the answers herself. For purely professional reasons, of course. It would make her working life much easier if she knew whether she needed to take a partner's feelings into consideration when making bookings away from the office.

Surprisingly, Max didn't put up much resistance to being dragged away from his computer with the promise of lunch and came into the kitchen just as she'd finished laying out the last small pot of pimento-stuffed olives, which she hadn't been able to resist buying.

'Good timing,' she said as he sat down. 'That deli is incredible. I wasn't sure what you'd prefer so I got just about everything they had—hopefully, there'll be something you like—and there should be plenty left over for tomorrow, or this evening if you don't already have dinner plans.'

Good grief—could she jabber more?

Clearly, this had occurred to Max too because he raised his eyebrows, but didn't say a word.

Trying not to let his silence intimidate her, Cara passed him a plate, which he took with an abrupt nod of thanks, and she watched him load it up with food before tucking in.

'So, Max,' she said, taking a plate for herself and filling it with small triangular-cut sandwiches stuffed with soft cheese and prosciutto and a spoonful of fluffy couscous speckled with herbs and tiny pieces of red pepper. 'How do you know Poppy? She didn't tell me anything about you—other than that you're friends.'

He gave a small shrug. 'We met at university.'

Cara waited for him to elaborate.

He didn't. He just kept on eating.

Okay, so he wasn't the sort to offer up personal details about himself and liked to keep things super professional with colleagues, but perhaps she'd be able to get more out of him once they'd built up a rapport between them.

That was okay. It was early days yet. She could bide her time.

At least she had some company for lunch, even if he wasn't interested in talking much. She'd spent all her lunchtimes at her last place of work alone, either sitting in the local park or eating a sandwich at her desk, forcing the food past her constricted throat, trying not to care about being excluded from the raucous group of PAs who regularly lunched together. The Cobra Clique, she'd called them in her head.

Not to their faces.

Never to their faces.

Because, after making the mistake of assuming she'd

be welcomed into their group when she'd first started working there—still riding on a wave of pride and excitement about landing such a coveted job—she'd soon realised that she'd stepped right into the middle of a viper's nest. Especially after the backlash began to snap its tail a couple of days into her first week.

Fighting the roll of nausea that always assaulted her when she thought about it, she took a large bite of sandwich and chewed hard, forcing herself to swallow, determined not to let what had happened bother her any more. They'd won and she was not going to let them keep on winning.

'It's a beautiful house you have, Max,' she said, to distract herself from the memories still determinedly circling her head. 'Have you been here long?'

His gaze shot to hers and she was alarmed to see him frown. 'Three years,' he said, with a clip of finality to his voice, as if wanting to make it clear he didn't want to discuss the subject any more.

Okay then.

From the atmosphere that now hummed between them, you'd have thought she'd asked him how much cold hard cash he'd laid down for the place. Perhaps people did ask him that regularly and he was fed up with answering it. Or maybe he thought she'd ask for a bigger wage if she thought he was loaded.

Whatever the reason, his frostiness had now totally destroyed her appetite, so she was pushing the couscous around her plate when Max stood up, making her jump in her seat.

'Let me know how much I owe you for lunch and I'll

get it out of petty cash before you leave,' he said, turning abruptly on the spot and heading over to the dishwasher to load his empty plate into it.

His movements were jerky and fast, as if he was really irritated about something now.

It couldn't be her, could it?

No.

Could it?

He must just be keen to get back to work.

As soon as he left the room, she let out the breath she'd been holding, feeling the tension in her neck muscles release a little.

The words *frying pan* and *fire* flitted through her head, but she dismissed them. If he was a friend of Poppy's he couldn't be that bad. She must have just caught him on a bad day. And, as her friend Sarah had pointed out after she'd cried on her shoulder about making a mess of her recent job interviews, she was bound to be prone to paranoia after her last experience.

Once she'd cleared up in the kitchen, Cara got straight back to work, using the link Max gave her to log in to his online diary and work through his travel requirements for the next month. His former ire seemed to have abated somewhat and their interaction from that point onwards was more relaxed, but still very professional. Blessedly, concentrating on the work soothed her and the headache that had started at the end of lunch began to lift as she worked methodically through her tasks.

Mid-afternoon, Max broke off from writing his document for a couple of minutes to outline some research he wanted her to do on a few businesses he was considering targeting. To her frustration, she had to throw every molecule of energy into making scrupulous notes in order to keep focused on the task in hand and not on the way Max's masculine scent made her senses reel and her skin heat with awareness every time he leaned closer to point something out on the computer they were huddled around.

That was something she was going to have to conquer if they continued to work together, which hopefully they would. She definitely couldn't afford a crush on her boss to get in the way of her recuperating future.

After finally being released from the duress of his unnerving presence, she spent the remainder of the day happily surfing the internet and collating the information into a handy crib sheet for him, revelling in the relief of getting back into a mindset she'd taken for granted until about six months ago, before her whole working life had been turned inside out.

At five-thirty she both printed out the document and emailed it to him, then gathered up her coat and bag, feeling as though she'd done her first good day's work in a long time.

Approaching his desk, she cleared her throat and laid the printout onto it, trying not to stare at the way his muscles moved beneath his slim-fitting shirt while she waited for him to finish what he was typing. Tearing her eyes away from his broad back, she took the opportunity to look at his hands instead, noting with a strange satisfaction that he wasn't wearing a wedding ring on his long, strong-looking fingers.

Okay, not married then. But surely he must have a girlfriend. She couldn't imagine someone as attractive as Max being single.

He stopped typing and swivelled round in his chair to face her, startling her out of her musings and triggering a strange throb, low in her body.

'You've done well today; I'm impressed,' he said, giving her a slow nod.

She couldn't stop her mouth from springing up into a full-on grin. It had been a long while since she'd been complimented on her work and it felt ridiculously good.

'Thank you—I've really enjoyed it.'

His raised eyebrow told her she'd been a bit over-effusive with that statement, but he unfolded his arms and dipped his head thoughtfully.

'If you're still interested, I'm willing to go ahead with the one-month trial.'

Her squeak of delight made him blink. 'I can't promise there'll be a full-time job at the end of it, though,' he added quickly.

She nodded. 'Okay, I understand.' She'd just have to make sure she'd made herself indispensable by the end of the month.

He then named a weekly wage that made her heart leap with excitement. With money like that she could afford to stay in London and keep on renting her flat.

'I'll see you here at nine tomorrow then,' he concluded, turning back to his computer screen.

'Great. Nine o'clock tomorrow,' she repeated, smiling at the back of his head and retreating out of the room.

She floated out of the house on a cloud of joy, desperate to get home so she could phone her landlord and tell him she was going to be able to make next month's rent so he didn't need to find a new tenant for her flat.

It was all going to be okay now; she could feel it.

Back in her flat, she dialled her landlord's number and he answered with a brusque, 'Yes.'

'Dominic—it's Cara Winstone. I'm calling with good news. I've just started at a new job so I'll be able to renew my lease on your property in Islington.'

There was a silence at the end of the phone, followed by a long sigh. 'Sorry, Cara, but I've already promised my nephew he can move in at the end of the week. I got the impression you wouldn't be able to afford the rent any more and I've kept it pitifully low for the last couple of years already. I can't afford to sub you any more.'

Fear and anger made her stomach sink and a suffocating heat race over her skin as she fully took in what he'd just said. He was such a liar. He'd been hiking the rent up year on year until she'd felt as if she was being totally fleeced, but she hadn't wanted the hassle of moving out of her comfortable little flat so she'd sucked it up. Until she wasn't able to any more.

'Can't you tell your nephew that your current tenant has changed her mind?' Even as she said it she knew what his answer was going to be.

'No. I can't. You had your chance to renew. I couldn't wait any longer and my nephew was having trouble finding somewhere suitable to live. It's a cut-throat rental market in London at the moment.'

That was something she was about to find out herself, she felt sure of it.

'Do you have anywhere else available to rent at the moment?' she asked, desperately grasping for some glimmer of a solution.

'No. Sorry.'

He didn't sound sorry, she noted with another sting of anger.

'You've got till the end of the week, then I want you out,' he continued. 'Make sure the place is in a good state when you leave or I'll have to withhold your damage deposit.' And, with that, he put the phone down on her.

It took a few minutes of hanging her head between her knees for the dizziness to abate and for her erratic heartbeat to return to normal.

Okay, this was just a setback. She could handle it.

Just because it would be hard to find a decent flat to rent in London at short notice didn't mean she wouldn't find somewhere else. She'd have to be proactive though and make sure to put all her feelers out, then respond quickly to any leads.

That could prove tricky now that she was working so closely with Max and she was going to have to be very careful not to mess up on the job, because it looked as though she was going to need things to work out there more than ever now.

The rest of the week flew by for Max, with Cara turning up exactly when she said she would and working diligently and efficiently through the tasks he gave her.

Whilst it was useful having her around to take care of some of the more mundane jobs that he'd been ignoring for far too long, he also found her presence was disrupting his ability to lose himself in his work, which he'd come to rely on in order to get through the fiercely busy days.

She was just so *jolly* all the time.

And she was making the place smell different. Every morning when he came downstairs for his breakfast he noticed her light floral perfume in the air. It was as though she was beginning to permeate the walls of his house and even the furniture with her scent.

It made him uncomfortable.

He knew he'd been rude during their first lunch together when Cara had asked him about the house and that he'd been unforthcoming about anything of a personal nature ever since—preferring to spend his lunchtimes in companionable silence—but he was concerned that any questions about himself would inevitably lead on to him having to talk about Jemima.

Work was supposed to be sanctuary from thinking about what had happened and he really didn't want to discuss it with Cara.

He also didn't want them to become too sociable because it would only make it harder for him to let her go after the promised month of employment.

Clearly she was very good at her job, so he had no concerns about her finding another position quickly after her time was up, but it might still prove awkward when it came down to saying no to full-time employment if they were on friendly terms. He suspected Cara's story about taking voluntary redundancy wasn't entirely based on truth and that she and Poppy had cooked up the story to play on his sympathy in order to get him to agree to take her on. While he was fine with allowing his errant friend to push him into a temporary arrangement to appease her mollycoddling nature, he wasn't going to allow her to bully him into keeping Cara on full-time.

He didn't need her.

After waking late on Friday morning and having to let an ebullient Cara in whilst still not yet ready to face the day, he had to rush his shower and hustle down to the kitchen with a pounding headache from not sleeping well the night before. Opening the fridge, he found that Cara had stocked it with all sorts of alien-looking food—things he would never have picked out himself. He knew he was bad at getting round to food shopping, but Cara's choices were clearly suggesting he wasn't looking after himself properly. There were superfoods galore in there.

He slammed the fridge door shut in disgust.

The damn woman was taking over the place.

Cara was in the hallway when he came out of the kitchen a few minutes later with a cup of coffee so strong he could have stood his spoon up in it. She waved a cheery hello, then gestured to a vase of brightly coloured flowers that she'd put onto the hall table, giving him a jaunty smile as if to say, *That's better, right?* which really set his teeth on edge. How was it possible for her to be so damn happy all the time? Did the woman live with her head permanently in the clouds?

They'd never had fresh flowers in the house when Jemima was alive because she'd suffered with bad hay

fever from the pollen, and he was just about to tell Cara
that when he caught himself and clamped his mouth
shut. It wasn't a discussion he wanted to have this morning, with a head that felt as if it was about to explode.
The very last thing he needed right now was Cara's
fervent pity.

'I thought it would be nice to have a bit of colour in
here,' she said brightly, oblivious to his displeasure. 'I
walked past the most amazing florist's on my way over
here and I just couldn't resist popping in. Flowers are
so good for lifting your mood.'

'That's fine,' he said through gritted teeth, hoping
she wasn't going to be this chipper all day. He didn't
think his head could stand it.

'I'll just grab myself a cup of tea, then I'll be in,'
she said.

Only managing to summon a grunt in response, he
walked into the morning room that he'd turned into an
office. He'd chosen it because it was away from the dis-
tractions of the street and in the odd moment of pause
he found that staring out into the neatly laid garden
soothed him. There was a particular brightly coloured
bird that came back day after day and hopped about on
the lawn, looking for worms, which captivated him. It
wasn't there today, though.

After going through his ever-growing inbox and
dealing with the quick and easy things, he opened up
his diary to check what was going on that day. He had
a conference call starting in ten minutes that would
probably last till lunchtime, which meant he'd need to
brief Cara now about what he wanted her to get on with.

Where was she, anyway?

She'd only been going to make herself a hot drink. Surely she must have done that by now?

Getting up from his chair with a sigh of irritation, he walked through to the kitchen to find her. The last thing he needed was to have to chase his PA down. It was going to be a demanding day which required some intense concentration and he needed her to be on the ball and ready to knuckle down.

She was leaning against the table with her back to the door when he walked into the kitchen, her head cocked to one side as if she was fascinated by something on the other side of the room.

He frowned at her back, wondering what in the heck could be so absorbing, until she spoke in a hushed tone and he realised she was on the phone.

'I don't know whether I'll be able to get away at lunchtime. I have to fetch my boss's lunch and there's a ton of other stuff I have to wade through. His systems are a mess. Unfortunately, Max isn't the type you can ask for a favour either; he's not exactly approachable. I could make it over for about six o'clock, though,' she muttered into the phone.

The hairs rose on the back of his neck. She was making arrangements to see her friends on his time?

He cleared his throat loudly, acutely aware of the rough harshness of his tone in the quiet of the room.

Spinning around at the noise, Cara gave him a look of horror, plainly embarrassed to be caught out.

Definitely a personal call then.

Frustration rattled through him, heating his blood.

How could he have been so gullible as to think it would be easy having her as an employee? Apparently she was going to be just as hard work to manage as all the other PAs he'd had.

'Are you sure you took redundancy at your last place? Or did they let you go for taking liberties on the job?' he said, unable to keep the angry disappointment out of his voice.

She swallowed hard and he found his gaze drawn to the long column of her throat, its smooth elegance distracting him for a second. Shaking off his momentary befuddlement, he snapped his gaze back to hers, annoyed with himself for losing concentration.

'I do not expect behaviour like this from someone with six years of experience as a personal assistant. This isn't the canteen where you waste time gossiping with your mates instead of doing the job you're being paid to do. Things like this make you look stupid and amateurish.'

She nodded jerkily but didn't say anything as her cheeks flushed with colour and a tight little frown appeared in the centre of her forehead.

Fighting a twist of unease, he took another step forwards and pointed a finger at her. 'You do not take personal phone calls on my time. Is that understood? Otherwise, you and I are going to have a problem, and problems are the last thing I need right now. I took a chance on you because you came recommended by Poppy. Do not make a fool out of my friend. Or out of me.'

'I'm sorry—it won't ever happen again. I promise,' she said, her voice barely above a whisper.

The look in her eyes disturbed him. It was such a change from her usual cheery countenance that it sat uncomfortably with him. In fact, to witness her reaction you'd have thought he'd just slapped her around the face, not given her a dressing-down.

'See that it doesn't,' he concluded with a curt nod, an unnerving throb beginning to beat in his throat.

As he walked back into his office, he found he couldn't wipe the haunted expression in her eyes from his mind, his pace faltering as he allowed himself to reflect fully on what had just happened.

Perhaps he'd been a bit too hard on her.

Running a hand over his tired eyes, he shook his head at himself. Who was he kidding—he'd definitely overreacted. For all he knew, it could have been a sick relative on the phone whom she needed to visit urgently.

The trouble was, he'd been so careful to keep her at arm's length and not to let any of his own personal details slip he'd totally failed to ask her anything about herself.

And he was tired. So tired it was making him cranky.

Swivelling on the spot, he went back out of the room to find her, not entirely sure what he was going to say, but knowing he should probably smooth things over between them. He needed her on his side today.

Walking back towards the kitchen, he met her as she was coming out, a cup of tea in her hand.

Instead of the look of sheepish upset he'd expected to see, she gave him a bright smile.

'I know you have a conference call in a couple of

minutes, so if you can walk me through what I need to tackle today I'll get straight on it,' she said, her voice steady and true as if the past few minutes hadn't happened.

He stared at her in surprise, unnerved by the one hundred and eighty degree turn in her demeanour.

Had he imagined the look in her eyes that had disturbed him so much?

No, it had definitely been there; he was sure of it.

Still, at least this showed she wasn't one to hold grudges and let an atmosphere linger after being reprimanded. He appreciated that. He certainly couldn't work with someone who struggled to maintain a professional front when something didn't go their way.

But her level of nonchalance confused him, leaving him a little unsure of where they now stood with each other. Should he mention that he felt he'd been a bit hard on her? Or should he just leave it and sweep it under the carpet as she seemed keen to do?

What was the matter with him? This was ridiculous. He didn't have time for semantics today.

Giving her a firm nod, he turned around and walked back towards the office. 'Good, let's get started then.'

Determined to keep her hand from shaking and not slop hot tea all over herself, Cara followed Max back into the office, ready to be given instructions for the day.

She knew she couldn't afford to show any weakness right now.

Based on her experiences with Max so far, she was pretty damn sure if he thought she wasn't up to the job he'd fire her on the spot and then she'd be left with absolutely nothing.

That was not going to happen to her today.

She needed this job, with its excellent wage and the prospect of a good reference from a well-respected businessman, to be able to stay here in London. All she had to do was keep her head down and stick it out here with him until she found another permanent position somewhere else. She had CVs out at a couple more places and with any luck another opportunity might present itself soon. Until then she'd just have to make sure she didn't allow his blunt manner and sharp tongue to erode her delicate confidence any further.

The trouble was, she'd allowed herself to be lulled into a false sense of security on her first day here after Max's compliment about her being a good ambassador for herself, only for him to pull the rug out from under her regrouping confidence later with his moods and quick temper.

The very last thing she needed was to work with another bully.

Not that she could really blame him for being angry in this instance. It must have looked really bad, her taking a personal phone call at the beginning of the working day. The really frustrating thing was that she'd never done anything like that before in her life. She was a rule follower to the core and very strict with herself about not surfing the Net or making personal calls on her employer's time, even in a big office where those kinds of things could go unnoticed.

Putting her drink down carefully, she wheeled her

chair nearer to Max's desk and prepared to take notes, keeping her chin up and a benign smile fixed firmly on her face.

His own professional manner seemingly restored, Max outlined what he wanted her to do throughout the day, which she jotted down in her notebook. Once he appeared to be satisfied that he'd covered everything he leaned back in his chair and studied her, the intensity of his gaze making the hairs stand up on her arms.

'Listen, Cara, I'm finishing early for the day today,' he said, surprising her with the warmth in his voice. 'I'm meeting a friend in town for an early dinner, so feel free to leave here at four o'clock.'

She blinked at him in shock before pulling herself together. 'That would be great. Thank you.'

There was an uncomfortable pause, where he continued to look at her, his brows drawn together and his lips set in a firm line. He opened his mouth, as if he was about to tell her what was on his mind, but was rudely interrupted by the alarm going off on his phone signalling it was time for his conference call.

To her frustration, he snapped straight back into work mode, turning back to his computer and dialling a number on his phone, launching straight into his business spiel as soon as the person on the other end of the line picked up.

Despite her residual nerves, Cara still experienced the familiar little frisson of exhilaration that swept through her whenever she heard him do that. He'd set up a small desk for her next to his the day after he'd offered her the trial, which meant there was no getting away from the sound of his voice with its smooth, re-assuring intonation.

He really was a very impressive businessman, even if he was a bit of a bear to work for.

Forcing her mind away from thinking about how uplifting it would be to have someone as passionate and dedicated as Max for a boyfriend—especially after the demeaning experience of her last relationship—she fired up her laptop and started in on the work he'd given her to take care of today.

After a few minutes, her thoughts drifted back to the fateful phone call she'd taken earlier, before their confrontation, and she felt a twitch of nerves in her stomach. It had been a friend calling to let her know about a possible flat coming onto the rental market—which was why she'd broken her rule and answered the call. If she managed to get there early enough she might just be able to snag it, which was now a real possibility thanks to Max's sudden announcement about leaving work at four o'clock.

Come to think of it, she was a little surprised about him finishing early to meet a friend in town. He'd never done that before, always continuing to work as she packed up for the day and—she strongly suspected—on into the evening. That would certainly account for the dark circles under his eyes. And his irascible mood.

The man appeared to be a workaholic.

After an hour of working through some truly tedious data inputting, Cara got up to make them both a hot drink, aware that Max must be parched by now from having to talk almost continuously since he'd begun his call.

Returning with the drinks, she sat back down at her desk to see she had an email from the friend that had called her earlier about the flat for rent.

Hmm. That couldn't be a good sign; she'd already mailed the details through earlier.

With a sinking feeling, she opened it up and scanned the text, her previously restored mood slipping away.

The flat had already been let.

An irrational impulse to cry gripped her and she got up quickly and made for the bathroom before the tears came, desperate to hide her despondency from Max.

Staring into the mirror, she attempted to talk herself down from her gloom. Her friend Sarah had offered to put her up on her sofa for a few days, so she at least had somewhere to stay in the interim. The only trouble was, her friend lived in a tiny place that she shared with her party animal boyfriend and he wouldn't want her hanging around, playing gooseberry, for too long.

The mere idea of renting with strangers at the ripe old age of twenty-seven horrified her, so she was going to have to be prepared to lower her standards to be in with a chance of finding another one-bedroom flat that she could afford in central London.

That was okay; she could do that. Hopefully, something would come up soon and then she'd be able to make some positive changes and get fully back on her feet.

Surely it was time for things to start going her way now?

CHAPTER THREE

AFTER MAKING UP the excuse about seeing a friend on Friday night in order to let Cara leave early, Max decided that he might as well phone around to see if anyone was available for a pint after work and actually surprised himself by having an enjoyable night out with some friends that he hadn't seen for a while.

He'd spent the rest of the weekend working, only breaking to eat his way through the entire contents of the fridge that Cara had stocked for him. Despite his initial disdain at her choices, he found he actually rather enjoyed trying the things she'd bought. They certainly beat the mediocre takeaways he'd been living on for the past few months.

Perhaps it *was* useful for him to have someone else around the house for a while, as Poppy had suggested the last time they'd seen each other. He'd baulked at her proposal that he should get back out on the dating scene though—he definitely wasn't ready for that, and honestly couldn't imagine ever being ready.

He and Jemima had been a couple since meeting at the beginning of their first year at university, their initial connection so immediate and intense they'd missed lectures for three days running to stay in bed together. They'd moved in with each other directly after graduating, making a home for themselves first in Manchester, then in London. After spending so much of his youth being moved from city to city, school to school, by his bohemian mother—until he finally put his foot down and forced her to send him to boarding school—it had been a huge relief to finally feel in control of his own life. To belong somewhere, with someone who wouldn't ask him to give up the life and friends he'd painstakingly carved out for himself—just *one* more time.

Jemima had understood his need for stability and had put up with his aversion to change with sympathetic acceptance and generous bonhomie. His life had been comfortably settled and he'd been deeply content—until she'd died, leaving him marooned and devastated by grief.

The idea of finding someone he could love as much as Jem seemed ludicrous. No one could ever replace his wife and it wouldn't be fair to let them try.

No, he would be fine on his own; he had his business and his friends and that would be enough for him.

Walking past the flower arrangement that Cara had left on the hall table on his way to sort through yesterday's junk mail, he had a memory flash of the expression on her face when he'd bawled her out in the kitchen the other day.

His chest tightened uncomfortably at the memory.

He needed to stop beating himself up about that now. He'd made amends for what had happened, even if she hadn't seemed entirely back to her happy, bright-eyed self again by the time she'd left on Friday afternoon. But at least he hadn't needed to delve into the murky waters of how they were both *feeling* about what had happened. He'd had enough of that kind of thing after forcing himself through the interminable sessions with grief counsellors after Jemima's death; he certainly didn't need to put himself through that discomfort again for something as inconsequential as a spat with his employee.

Fortunately, Cara seemed as reluctant to talk about it all as he was.

Rubbing a hand over his face, he gave a snort of disbelief about where his thoughts had taken him. Again. Surely it wasn't normal to be spending his weekend thinking about his PA.

Hmm.

His initial concerns about her being an unwanted distraction seemed to be coming to fruition, which was a worry. Still, there were only a few more weeks left of the promised trial period, then he'd be free of her. Until then he was going to have to keep his head in the game, otherwise the business was going to suffer. And that wasn't something he was prepared to let happen.

Monday morning rushed around, bringing with it bright sunshine that flooded the house and warmed the still, cool air, lifting his spirits a little.

Max had just sat down at his desk with his first cup of coffee of the day when there was a ring on the doorbell.

Cara.

Swinging open the door to let her in, he was taken aback to see her looking as if she hadn't slept a wink all night. There were dark circles around her puffy eyes and her skin was pallid and dull-looking. It seemed to pain her to even raise a smile for him.

Was she hung-over?

His earlier positivity vanished, to be replaced by a feeling of disquiet.

'Did you have a good weekend?' he asked as she walked into the house and hung up her coat.

She gave him a wan smile. 'Not bad, thanks. It was certainly a busy one. I didn't get much sleep.'

Hmm. So she had been out partying, by the sound of it.

Despite his concerns, Cara appeared to work hard all day and he only caught her yawning once whilst making them both a strong cup of coffee in the kitchen, mid-afternoon.

At the end of the day, she waved her usual cheery goodbye, though there was less enthusiasm in her smile than she normally displayed at knocking-off time.

To his horror, she turned up in the same state the following day.

And the next.

In fact, on Thursday, when he opened the door, he could have sworn he caught the smell of alcohol on her as she dashed past him into the house. She certainly looked as though she could have been up drinking all night and plainly hadn't taken a shower that morning, her hair hanging greasy and limp in a severely pulled back ponytail.

Her work was beginning to suffer too, in increments. Each day he found he had to pick her up on more and more things she'd missed or got wrong, noticing that her once pristine fingernails were getting shorter and more ragged as time went on.

Clearly she was letting whatever was happening in her personal life get in the way of her work and that was unacceptable.

His previous feelings of magnanimity about having her around had all but vanished by Thursday afternoon and he was seriously considering having a word with her about her performance. The only reason he hadn't done so already was because he'd been so busy with back-to-back conference calls this week and in deference to Poppy he'd decided to give Cara the benefit of the doubt and put her slip-ups down to a couple of off days.

But he decided that enough was enough when he found her with her head propped on her arms, fast asleep, on the kitchen table when she was supposed to be making them both a hot drink.

Resentment bubbled up from his gut as he watched her peaceful form gently rise and fall as she slumbered on, totally oblivious to his incensed presence behind her. He'd been feeling guilty all weekend about how he'd spoken to her on Friday and here she was, only a few days later, turning up unfit for work.

His concern that her presence here would cause more harm than good had just been ratified.

'Wakey, wakey, Sleeping Beauty!' he said loudly, feeling a swell of angry satisfaction as she leapt up from the table and spun around to look at him, her face pink and creased on one side where it had rested against her arm.

'Oh! Whoa! Was I sleeping?' she mumbled, blinking hard.

Crossing his arms, he gave her a hard stare. 'Like a baby.'

She rubbed a hand across her eyes, smudging her make-up across her face. 'I'm so sorry—I only put my head down to rest for a moment while I was waiting for the kettle to boil and I must have drifted off.'

'Perhaps you should start going to bed at a more reasonable time then,' he ground out, his hands starting to shake as adrenaline kicked its way through his veins. 'I didn't hire you as a charity case, Cara. For the money I'm paying, I expected much more from you. You had me convinced you were up to the job in the first couple of days, but it's become clear over the last few that you're not.' He took a breath as he made peace with what he was about to say. 'I'm going to have to let you go. I can't carry someone who's going to get drunk every night and turn up unfit to work.'

Her eyes were wide now and she was mouthing at him as if her response had got stuck in her throat.

Shaking off the stab of conscience that had begun to poke him in the back, he pointed a finger at her. 'And you can hold the "It'll never happen again" routine,' he bit out. 'I'm not an idiot, though I feel like one for letting you take me in like this.'

To his surprise, instead of the tears he was readying himself for, her expression morphed into one of acute fury and she raised her own shaking finger back at him.

'I do not get drunk every night. For your information, I'm homeless at the moment and sleeping on a friend's couch, which doesn't work well for her insomniac boyfriend, who likes to party and play computer games late into the night and who came home drunk and spilled an entire can of beer over me while I was trying to sleep and who then hogged the bathroom this morning so I couldn't get in there for a shower.'

Her face had grown redder and redder throughout this speech and all he could do was stand there and stare at her, paralysed by surprise as she jabbed her finger at him with rage flashing in her eyes.

'I've worked my butt off for you, taking your irascible moods on the chin and getting on with it, but I'm not going to let you treat me like some nonentity waster. I'm a real person with real feelings, Max. I tried to make this work—you have no idea how hard I've been trying—but I guess this is just life's way of telling me that I'm done here in London.' She threw up her hands and took a deep shaky breath. 'After all the work I put into building myself a career here that I was so proud of—'

Taking in the look of utter frustration on her face, he felt his anger begin to drain away, only to be replaced with an uncomfortable twist of shame.

She was right, of course—he had been really unfriendly and probably very difficult to work with, and she was clearly dealing with some testing personal circumstances, which he'd made sure to blithely ignore.

He frowned and sighed heavily, torn about what to do next. While he could do without any extra problems at the moment, he couldn't bring himself to turn her away now he knew what she was dealing with. Because, despite it all, he admired her for standing up for herself.

Cara willed her heart to stop pounding like a pneumatic drill as she waited to see what Max would say next.

Had she really just shouted at him like that?

It was so unlike her to let her anger get the better of her, but something inside her had snapped at the unfairness of it all and she hadn't been able to hold back.

After spending the past few days using every ounce of energy keeping up the fake smile and pretending she could cope with the punishing days with Max on so little sleep, she'd hit a wall.

Hard.

The mix of panic, frustration and chronic tiredness had released something inside her and in those moments after she'd let the words fly she had the strangest sensation of the ground shifting under her feet. She was painfully aware that she'd probably just thrown away any hope of keeping this job, but at the same time she was immensely proud of herself for not allowing him to dismiss her like that. As if she was worth nothing.

Because she *wasn't*.

She deserved to be treated with more respect and she'd learnt by now that she wasn't going to get that from Max by meekly taking the insults he so callously dished out.

At her last place of work, in a fug of naïve disbelief,

she'd allowed those witches to strip her of her pride, but there was no way she was letting Max do that to her, too.

No matter what it cost her.

She could get another job—and she would, eventually—but she'd never be able to respect herself again if she didn't stand up to him now.

Her heart raced as she watched a range of expressions run across Max's face. The fact that he hadn't immediately repeated his dismissal gave her hope that there might be a slim chance he'd reverse his decision to fire her.

Moving her hands behind her back, she crossed her fingers for a miracle, feeling a bead of sweat run down her spine.

Sighing hard, Max ran a hand through the front of his hair, pushing it out of his eyes and looking at her with his usual expression of ill-concealed irritation.

'I'm guessing you became homeless on Friday, which is when the mistakes started to happen?' he asked finally.

She nodded, aware of the tension in her shoulders as she held her nerve. 'I spent all day on Sunday moving my furniture into storage. I've been staying with my friend Sarah and her boyfriend ever since.'

'But that can't carry on,' he said with finality to his voice.

Swallowing hard, she tipped up her chin. 'No. I know. I've tried to view so many places to rent in the last week, but they seem to go the second they're advertised. I can't get to them fast enough.'

He crossed his arms. 'And you have nowhere else to stay in London? No boyfriend? No family?'

Shaking her head, she straightened her posture, determined to hang on to her poise. She wouldn't look away, not now she'd been brave enough to take him on. If she was going to be fired, she was going down with her head held high. 'My parents live in Cornwall and none of my other friends in London have room to put me up.' She shifted uncomfortably on the spot and swallowed back the lingering hurt at the memory of her last disastrous relationship. 'I've been single for a few months now.'

He stared back at her, his eyes hooded and his brow drawn down.

A world of emotions rattled through her as she waited to hear his verdict.

'Okay. You can stay here until you find a flat to rent.'

She gawped at him, wondering whether her brain was playing tricks on her. 'I'm sorry—*what*?'

'I said—you can stay here,' he said slowly, enunciating every word. 'I have plenty of spare rooms. I'm on the top floor so you could have the whole middle floor to yourself.'

'*Really?*'

He bristled, rolling his eyes up to the ceiling and letting out a frustrated snort. 'Yes, really. I'm not just making this up to see your impression of a goldfish.'

She stared at him even harder. Had he just made a *joke*? That was definitely a first.

Unfolding his arms, he batted a hand through the air. 'I'm sure it won't take you long to find somewhere else and until then I need you turning up to work fully rested and back to your efficient, capable self.'

Her eyes were so wide now she felt sure she must look as if she was wearing a pair of those joke goggle-eye glasses.

He was admitting to her being good at her job too now? Wonders would never cease.

But she was allowing these revelations to distract her from the decision she needed to make. Could she really live in the same house as her boss? Even if it was only for a short time.

Right now, it didn't feel as though she had much of a choice. The thought of spending even one more night in Party Central made her heart sink. If she turned Max down on his offer, that was the only other viable option—save staying in a hotel she couldn't afford or renting a place a long way out and spending her life commuting in. Neither of them were appealing options.

But could she really live here with him? The mere idea of it made her insides flutter and it wasn't just because he was a bit of a difficult character. During the week and a half that she'd known him, she'd become increasingly jittery in his presence, feeling a tickle of excitement run up her spine every time she caught his scent in the air or even just watched him move around his territory like some kind of lean, mean, business machine. Not that he'd ever given her a reason to think she was in any kind of danger being there alone with him. Clearly, he had no interest in her romantically. If anything, she'd felt it had been the total opposite for him, as if he didn't think of her as a woman at all, only a phone-answering, data-sorting robot.

So she was pretty sure he didn't have an ulterior motive behind his suggestion that she should stay in his house.

Unfortunately.

Naughty, naughty Cara.

'Well, if you're sure it won't be too much of an inconvenience to you,' she said slowly.

'No. It's fine,' he answered curtly. 'We'll have to make sure to respect each other's privacy, but it's a big place so that shouldn't be a problem. All the rooms have locks on them, in case you're worried.'

Her pulse picked up as a host of X-rated images rushed through her head.

Slam a lid on that, you maniac.

'I'm not worried,' she squeaked.

He nodded.

'And your girlfriend won't mind me staying here?' she asked carefully.

'I don't have a girlfriend.'

'Or your w—?' she began to ask, just in case.

'I'm single,' he cut in with a curt snap to his voice.

Okay, so the subject of his relationships was out of bounds then.

She was surprised to hear that he wasn't attached in any way, though. Surely someone with his money, looks and smarts would have women lining up around the block for the pleasure of his company. Although, come to think of it, based on her run-ins with him so far, she could see how his acerbic temperament might be a problem for some people.

'Right, I may as well show you your room now,' Max said, snapping her out of her meandering thoughts. 'Clearly, you're not in a fit state to work this afternoon, so you may as well finish for the day.' He turned and walked out of the room, leaving her gaping at the empty space he'd left.

So that was it then—decision made.

'Oh! Okay.' She hustled to catch him up, feeling her joints complain as she moved. *Crikey.* She was tired. Her whole body ached from sleeping on a saggy sofa and performing on so little sleep for the past few days.

She followed him up the sweeping staircase to the next level and along the landing to the third door on the right.

Opening it up, he motioned for her to walk past him into the bedroom.

She tried not to breathe in his fresh, spicy scent as she did so, her nerves already shot from the rigours of the day.

It was, of course, the most beautifully appointed bedroom she'd ever been in.

Light flooded in through the large window, which was framed by long French grey curtains in a heavy silk. The rest of the furnishing was simple and elegant, in a way Cara had never been able to achieve in her own flat. The pieces that had been chosen clearly had heritage and fitted perfectly with the large airy room. His interior designer must have cost a pretty penny.

Tears welled in her eyes as she took in the original

ornate fireplace, which stood proudly opposite a beautiful king-sized iron-framed bed. Fighting the urge to collapse onto it in relief and bury herself in the soft, plump-looking duvet, she blinked hard, then turned to face Max, who was hanging back by the door with a distracted frown on his face.

'This is a beautiful room—thank you,' she said, acutely aware of the tremor in her voice.

Max's frown deepened, but he didn't comment on it. 'You're welcome. You should go over to your friend's house and get your things now, then you'll have time to settle in. We'll start over again tomorrow.'

'Okay, good idea.'

'I'll leave you to it then,' he said, turning to go.

'Max?'

He turned back. 'Yes?'

'I'm really grateful—for letting me stay here.'

'No problem,' he said, turning briskly on the spot and walking away, leaving her staring after him with her heart in her mouth.

Well, she certainly hadn't expected this when she'd woken up this morning reeking of stale beer.

Sinking down gratefully onto the bed, she finally allowed her tense muscles to relax, feeling the tiredness rush back, deep into her bones.

How was she ever going to be able to drag herself away from this beautiful room when she managed to find a place of her own to rent?

More to the point, was she really going to be able to live in the same house as Max without going totally insane?

Steeling herself to make the journey over to Sarah's house and pick up her things, she rocked herself up off the bed of her dreams and onto her feet and took a deep, resolute breath.

There was only one way to find out.

CHAPTER FOUR

IF SOMEONE HAD asked Max to explain exactly what had prompted him to suggest that Cara move in, he was pretty sure he'd have been stumped for an answer.

All he knew was that he couldn't let things go on the way they were. Judging by her outburst, she was clearly struggling to cope with all that life had thrown at her recently and it was no skin off his nose to let her stay for a few nights in one of the empty bedrooms.

He had enough of them, after all.

Also, as a good friend of her cousin's he felt a responsibility to make sure that Cara was okay whilst Poppy was away and unable to help her herself. He knew from experience that good friends were essential when life decided to throw its twisted cruelty your way, and he was acutely aware that it was the support and encouragement of his friends that had helped him find his way out of the darkness after Jemima died.

Watching Cara working hard the next day, he was glad she was still around. When she was on good form, she was an asset to the business and, truthfully, it had become comforting for him to have another person around—it stopped him from *thinking* so much in the resounding silence of the house.

They hadn't talked about what had happened again, which was a relief. He just wanted everything to get back to the way it had been with the minimum of fuss. With that in mind, he was a little concerned about what it would be like having her around at the weekend. He'd probably end up working, like he always did, so he wasn't too worried about the daytime, but they'd need to make sure they gave each other enough space in the evenings so they didn't end up biting each other's heads off again.

With any luck, she'd be out a lot of the time anyway, flat-hunting or seeing friends.

At six o'clock he leant back in his chair and stretched his arms above his head, working the kinks out of his tight muscles.

'Time to finish for the day, Cara,' he said to the side of her head.

She glanced round at him, the expression in her eyes far away, as if she was in the middle of a thought.

'Um, okay. I'll just finish this.' She tapped on her keyboard for a few more seconds before closing the laptop with a flourish.

'Okay then. Bring on the weekend.' She flashed him a cheeky smile, which gave him pause.

'You're not thinking of bringing the party to this house, I hope.'

Quickly switching to a solemn expression, she gave a shake of her head. 'Of course not. That's not what I meant.'

'Hmm.'

The corner of her mouth twitched upwards. 'You seem to have a really skewed impression of me. I don't go in for heavy drinking and partying—it's really not my style.'

'Okay.' He held up both hands. 'Not that it's any of my business; you can stay out all night at the weekends, for all I care,' he said, aware of a strange plummeting sensation in his chest as images of what she might get up to out on the town flashed through his head.

Good God, man—you're not her keeper.

'As long as your work doesn't suffer,' he added quickly.

'Actually,' she said, slouching back in her seat and hooking her slender arm over the back of her chair, 'I was thinking about cooking you a meal tonight, to say thank you for letting me stay.'

He wasn't sure why, but the thought of that made him uncomfortable. Perhaps because it would blur the lines between employee and friend too much.

'That's kind, but I have plans tonight,' he lied, racking his brain to remember what his friend Dan had said about his availability this weekend. Even if he was busy he was sure he could rustle up a dinner invitation somewhere else, to let Cara off the hook without any bad feelings.

'And you don't need to thank me for letting you stay here. It's what any decent human being would have done.'

Her face seemed to fall a little and she drew her arm back in towards her body, sliding her hands between her knees so that her shoulders hunched inwards. 'Oh, okay, well, I'm just going to pop out and shop for my own dinner, so I'll see you shortly,' she said, ramping her smile back up again and wheeling her chair away from the desk with her feet.

'Actually, I'm heading out myself in a minute and I'll probably be back late, so I'll see you tomorrow.'

Her smile froze. 'Right. Well, have a good night.'

This was ridiculous. The last thing he'd wanted was for them both to feel awkward about living under the same roof.

He let out a long sigh and pushed his hair away from his face. 'Look, Cara, don't think you have to hang out with me while you're staying here. We don't need to be in each other's pockets the whole time. Feel free to do your own thing.'

Clearly he'd been a bit brusque because she recoiled a little. 'I understand,' she said, getting up and awkwardly pushing her chair back under her desk. 'Have a good night!' she said in that overly chirpy way she had, which he was beginning to learn meant he'd offended her.

Not waiting for his reply, she turned her back on him and walked straight out of the room, her shoulders stiff.

Great. This was exactly what he'd hoped to avoid.

He scrubbed a hand over his face. Maybe it had been a mistake to ask her to stay.

But he couldn't kick her out now.

All he could do was cross his fingers and hope she'd find herself another place to live soon.

* * *

To his surprise, he didn't see much of Cara over the next couple of days. She'd obviously taken his suggestion about giving each other space to heart and was avoiding being in the house with him as much as possible.

The extremity of her desertion grated on his nerves.

What was it that made it impossible for them to understand each other? They were very different in temperament, of course, which didn't help, but it was more than that. It was as if there was some kind of meaning-altering force field between them.

On Sunday, when the silence in the house got too much for him, he went out for a long walk around Hyde Park. He stopped at the café next to the water for lunch, something he and Jemima had done most Sundays, fighting against the painful undertow of nostalgia that dragged at him as he sat there alone. It was all so intensely familiar.

All except for the empty seat in front of him.

He snorted into his drink, disgusted with himself for being so pathetic. He should consider himself lucky. He was the one who got to have a future, unlike his big-hearted, selfless wife. The woman who everyone had loved. One of the few people, in his opinion, who had truly deserved a long and happy life.

Arriving home mid-afternoon, he walked in to find the undertones of Cara's perfume hanging in the air.

So she was back then.

Closing his eyes, he imagined he could actually sense her presence in the atmosphere, like a low hum of white noise.

Or was he being overly sensitive?

Probably.

From the moment she'd agreed to move in he'd experienced a strange undercurrent of apprehension and it seemed to be affecting his state of mind.

After stowing his shoes and coat in the cloakroom, he went into the living room to find that a large display of flowers had been placed on top of the grand piano. He bristled, remembering the way he'd felt the last time Cara had started to mess with his environment.

Sighing, he rubbed a hand through his hair, attempting to release the tension in his scalp. They were just flowers. He really needed to chill out or he was going to drive himself insane. Jemima would have laughed if she'd seen how strung-out he was over something so inconsequential. He could almost hear her teasing voice ringing in his ears.

A noise startled him and he whipped round to see Cara standing in the doorway to the room, dressed in worn jeans and a sloppy sweater, her face scrubbed of make-up and her bright blue eyes luminous in the soft afternoon light. To his overwrought brain, she seemed to radiate an ethereal kind of beauty, her long hair lying in soft, undulating waves around her face and her creamy skin radiant with health. He experienced a strangely intense moment of confusion, and he realised that somewhere in the depths of his screwed-up consciousness he'd half expected it to be Jemima standing there instead—which was why his, 'Hello,' came out more gruffly than he'd intended.

Her welcoming smile faltered and she glanced down

at her fingernails and frowned, as if fighting an impulse to chew on them, but when she looked back up her smile was firmly back in place.

'Isn't it a beautiful day?' She tipped her head towards the piano behind him. 'I hope you don't mind, but the spring sunshine inspired me to put fresh flowers in most of the rooms—not your bedroom, of course; I didn't go in there,' she added quickly. 'The house seemed to be crying out for a bit of life and colour and I wanted to do something to say thank you for letting me stay, even though you said I didn't need to.'

'Sure. That's fine,' was all he could muster. For some reason his blood was flying through his veins and he felt so hot he thought he might spontaneously combust at any second.

'Oh, and I stripped and remade the bed in the room next to yours,' she added casually. 'It looked like the cleaners had missed it. I gave it a good vacuum, too; it was really dusty.'

The heat was swept away by a flood of icy panic. 'You *what*?'

The ferocity in his tone obviously alarmed her because she flinched and blinked hard.

But hurting Cara's feelings was the least of his worries right then.

Not waiting for her reply, he pushed past her and raced up the stairs, aware of his heart thumping painfully in his chest as he willed it not to be so.

Please don't let her have destroyed that room.

Reaching the landing on the top floor, he flung open the door and stared into the now immaculate bedroom, the stringent scent of cleaning fluid clogging his throat and making his stomach roll.

She'd stripped it bare.

Everything he'd been protecting from the past had been torn off or wiped away. The bed, as she'd said, now had fresh linen on it.

He heard her laboured breath behind him as she made it up to the landing and whipped round to face her.

'Where are the sheets from the bed, Cara?' he demanded, well past the point of being able to conceal his anger.

Her face was drained of all colour. 'What did I do wrong?'

'The *sheets*, Cara—where are the *sheets*?'

'I washed them,' she whispered, unable to meet his eyes. 'They're in the dryer.'

That was it then. Jemima's room was ruined.

Bitterness welled in his gut as he took in her wide-eyed bewilderment. The woman was a walking disaster area and she'd caused nothing but trouble since she got here.

A rage he couldn't contain made him pace towards her.

'Why do you have to meddle with everything? Hmm? What is it with you? This need to please all the time isn't natural. In fact it's downright pathetic. Just keep your hands off my personal stuff, okay? Is that really too much to ask?'

She seemed frozen to the spot as she stared at him with glassy eyes, her jaw clamped so tight he could see the muscle flickering under the pressure, but, instead of shouting back this time, she dragged in a sharp, painful-sounding breath before turning on the spot and walking out of the room.

He listened to her heavy footsteps on the stairs and then the slam of her bedroom door, wincing as the sound reverberated through his aching head. Staring down at the soulless bed, he allowed the heat of his bitterness and anger and shame to wash through him, leaving behind an icy numbness in its wake.

Then he closed his eyes, dropped his chin to his chest and sank down onto the last place he'd been truly happy.

Oh, God, please don't let this be happening to me. Again.

Cara wrapped her arms around her middle and pressed her forehead against the cool wall of her bedroom, waiting for the dizziness and nausea to subside so she could pack up her things and leave.

What was it with her? She seemed destined to put herself in a position of weakness, where the only option left to her was to give up and run away.

Which she really didn't want to do again.

But she had to protect herself. She couldn't be around someone so toxic—someone who clearly thought so little of her. Even Ewan hadn't been that cruel to her when he'd left her after she'd failed to live up to his exacting standards. She'd never seen a look of such pure disgust on anyone's face before. The mere memory of it made the dizziness worse.

There was no way she was staying in a place where she'd be liable to see that look again. She'd rather go home and admit to her parents that she'd failed and deal with their badly concealed disappointment than stay here with Max any longer.

She'd never met anyone with such a quick temper. What was his problem, anyway? He appeared to have everything here: the security of a beautiful house in one of the most sought-after areas of London, a thriving business, friends who invited him out for dinner, and he clearly had pots of cash to cushion his easy, comfortable life. In fact, the more she thought about it, the more incensed she became.

Who was he to speak to her like that? Sure, there had been a couple of little bumps in the road when she'd not exactly been at her best, but she'd worked above and beyond the call of duty for the rest of the time. And she'd been trying to do something nice for him in making the house look good—pretty much the only thing she could think of to offer as a thank you to a man who seemed to have everything. What had been so awful about that? She knew she could be a bit over the top in trying to please people sometimes, but this hadn't been a big thing. It was just an empty guest room that had been overlooked.

Wasn't it?

The extremity of his reaction niggled at her.

Surely just giving it a quick clean didn't deserve that angry reaction.

No.

He was a control freak bully and she needed to get away from him.

As soon as she was sure the dizziness had passed,

she carefully packed up all her things and zipped them into her suitcase, fighting with all her might against the tight pressure in her throat and the itchy heat in her eyes.

She'd known this opportunity had to be too good to be true—the job, working with someone as impressive as Max and definitely being invited to stay in this amazing house.

But she wasn't going to skulk away. If she didn't face up to Max one last time with her head held high she'd regret it for the rest of her life. He wasn't going to run her out of here; she was going to leave in her time and on her terms.

Taking a deep breath, she rolled her shoulders back and fixed the bland look of calm she'd become so practised at onto her face.

Okay. Time for one last confrontation.

She found Max in the guest room where she'd left him, sitting on the bed with his head in his hands, his hunched shoulders stretching his T-shirt tight against his broad back.

As she walked into the room, he looked up at her with an expression of such torment on his face that it made her stop in her tracks.

What was going on? She'd expected him to still be angry, but instead he looked—*beaten*.

Did he regret what he'd said to her?

Giving herself a mental shake, she took another deliberate step towards him. It didn't matter; there wasn't anything he could say to make up for the cruelty of his last statement anyway. This wasn't the first time he'd treated her with such brutal disdain and she wasn't going to put up with it any longer.

Forcing back her shoulders, she took one final step closer to him, feeling her legs shaking with tension.

'This isn't going to work, Max. I can't live in a place where I'm constantly afraid of doing the wrong thing and making you angry. I don't know what I did that was so bad, or what's going on with you to make you react like that, but I'm not going to let you destroy what's left of my confidence. I'm not going to be a victim any more.' She took a deep, shuddering breath. 'So I'm leaving now. And that goes for the job, too.'

Her heart gave a lurch at the flash of contrition in his eyes, but she knew she had to be strong and walk away for her own good.

'Goodbye, Max, and good luck.'

As she turned to go, fighting against the tears that threatened to give her away, she thought she heard the bedsprings creak as if he'd stood up, but didn't turn round to find out.

She was halfway down the stairs when she heard Max's voice behind her. 'Wait, Cara!'

Spinning round, she held up a hand to stop him from coming any closer, intensely aware that, despite her anger with him, there was a small part of her that was desperate to hear him say something nice to her, to persuade her that he wasn't the monster he seemed to be. 'I can't walk on eggshells around you any more, Max; I don't think my heart will stand it.'

In any way, shape or form.

He slumped down onto the top step and put his elbows on his knees, his whole posture defeated. 'Don't go,' he said quietly.

'I have to.'

Looking up, he fixed her with a glassy stare. 'I know I've been a nightmare to be around recently—' He frowned and shook his head. 'It's not you, Cara—it's one hundred per cent me. Please, at least hear me out. I need to tell you what's going on so you don't leave thinking any of this is your fault.' He sighed and rubbed a hand through his hair. 'That's the last thing I want to happen.'

She paused. Even if she still chose to leave after hearing him out, at least she'd know *why* it hadn't worked and be able to make peace with her decision to walk away.

The silence stretched to breaking point between them. 'Okay,' she said.

He nodded. 'Thank you.' Getting up from the step, he gestured down the stairs. 'Let's go into the sitting room.'

Once there, she perched on the edge of the sofa and waited for him to take the chair opposite, but he surprised her by sitting next to her instead, sinking back into the cushions with a long guttural sigh which managed to touch every nerve-ending in her body.

'This is going to make me sound mentally unstable.'

She turned to frown at him. 'Oka-ay…' she said, failing to keep her apprehension out of her voice.

'That bed hasn't been changed since my wife, Jemima, died a year and a half ago.'

Hot horror slid through her, her skin prickling as if

she were being stabbed with a thousand needles. 'But I thought you said—' She shook her suddenly fuzzy head. 'You never said—' Words, it seemed, had totally failed her. Everything she knew about him slipped sickeningly into place: the ever-fluctuating moods, the reluctance to talk about his personal life, his anger at her meddling with things in his house.

His *wife's* house.

Looking away, he stared at the wall opposite, sitting forward with clenched fists as if he was steeling himself to get it all out in the open.

'I couldn't bring myself to change it.' He paused and she saw his shoulders rise then fall as he took a deep breath. 'The bed, I mean. It still smelled faintly like her. I let her mother take all her clothes and other personal effects—what would I have done with them?—but the bed was mine. The last place we'd been together before I lost her—' he took another breath, pushing back his hunched shoulders '—before she died.'

'Oh, God, Max… I'm so, so sorry. I had no idea.'

He huffed out a dry laugh. 'How could you? I did everything I could to avoid talking to you about it.' He grimaced. 'Because, to be honest, I've done enough talking about it to last me a lifetime. I guess, in my twisted imagination, I thought if you didn't know, I could pretend it hadn't happened when you were around. Outside of work, you're the first normal, unconnected thing I've had in my life since I lost her and I guess I was hanging on to that.'

He turned to look at her again. 'I should have told you, Cara, especially after you moved in, but I couldn't find a way to bring it up without—' He paused and swallowed hard, the look in his eyes so wretched that, without thinking, she reached out and laid a hand on his bare forearm.

He frowned down at where their bodies connected and the air seemed to crackle around them.

Disconcerted by the heat of him beneath her fingertips, she withdrew her hand and laid it back on her lap.

'It's kind of you to consider me *normal*,' she said, flipping him a grin, hoping the levity might go some way to smoothing out the sudden weird tension between them.

He gave a gentle snort, as if to acknowledge her pathetic attempt at humour.

Why had she never recognised his behaviour as grief before? Now she knew to look for it, it was starkly discernible in the deep frown lines in his face and the haunted look in his eyes.

But she'd been so caught up in her own private universe of problems she hadn't even considered *why* Max seemed so bitter all the time.

She'd thought he had everything.

How wrong she'd been.

They sat in silence for a while, the only sound in the room the soothing *tick-tock* of the carriage clock on the mantelpiece, like a steady heartbeat in the chaos.

'How did she die?' Cara asked eventually. She was pretty sure he wouldn't be keen to revisit this conversation and she wanted to have all the information from this point onwards so she could avoid any future blunders.

The familiarity of the question seemed to rouse him. 'She had a subarachnoid haemorrhage—it's where a blood vessel in the brain bursts—' he added, when she frowned at him in confusion. 'On our one-year wedding anniversary. It happened totally out of the blue. I was late for our celebration dinner and I got a phone message saying she'd collapsed in the restaurant. By the time I got to the hospital she had such extensive brain damage she didn't even recognise me. She died two weeks later. I never got to say goodbye properly.' He snorted gently. 'The last thing I said to her before it happened was "Stop being such a nag; I won't be late," when I left her in bed that morning and went to work.'

Cara had to swallow past the tightness in her throat before she could speak. 'That's why you didn't want me to leave here with us on bad terms.' She put a hand back onto his arm and gave it an ineffectual rub, feeling completely out of her depth. 'Oh, Max, I'm so sorry. What a horrible thing to happen.'

He leant back against the cushions, breaking the contact of her touch, and stared up at the ceiling. 'I often wonder whether I would have noticed some signs if I'd paid more attention to her. If I hadn't been so caught up with work—'

She couldn't think of a single thing to say to make him feel better—though maybe there wasn't anything she could say. Sometimes you didn't need answers or solutions; you just needed someone to listen and agree with you about how cruel life could be.

He turned to look at her, his mouth drawn into a tight line.

'Look, Cara, I can see that you wanting to help comes from a good place. You're a kind and decent person—much more decent than I am.' He gave her a pained smile, which she returned. 'I've been on my own here for so long I've clearly become very selfish with my personal space.' He rubbed a hand across his brow. 'And this was Jemima's house—she was the one who chose how to decorate it and made it a home for us.' He turned to make full eye contact with her again, his expression apologetic. 'It's taking a bit of adjusting to, having someone else around. Despite evidence to the contrary, I really appreciate the thoughtful gestures you've made.'

His reference to her *gestures* only made the heavy feeling in her stomach worse.

'I'm really sorry, Max. I can totally understand why you'd find it hard to see me meddling with Jemima's things. I think I was so excited by the idea of living in such a beautiful house that I got a bit carried away. I forgot I was just a visitor here and that it's your home. That was selfish of *me*.'

He shook his head. 'I don't want you to feel like that. While you're here it's your home, too.'

She frowned and turned away to stare down at the floor, distracted for a moment by how scratty and out of place her old slippers looked against the rich cream-coloured wool carpet.

That was exactly the problem. It wasn't her home and it never would be. She didn't really *fit* here.

For some reason that made her feel more depressed than she had since the day she'd left her last job.

'Have you had any luck with finding a flat to rent?' he asked, breaking the silence that had fallen like a suffocating layer of dust between them.

'Not yet, but I have an appointment to view somewhere tomorrow and there are new places coming up all the time. I'll find something soon, I'm sure of it,' she said, plastering what must have been the worst fake smile she'd ever mustered onto her face.

He nodded slowly, but didn't say anything.

Twitching with discomfort now, she stood up. 'I should go.'

He frowned at her in confusion. 'What do you mean? Where are you going?'

'Back to Sarah's. I think that would be best.'

Standing up, too, he put out a hand as if to touch her, but stopped himself and shoved it into the back pocket of his jeans instead.

'Look, don't leave. I promise to be less of an ogre. I let my anger get the better of me, which was unfair.'

'I don't know, Max—' She couldn't stay here now. Could she?

Obviously seeing the hesitation on her face, he leant forward and waited until she made eye contact. 'I like having you around.' There was a teasing lightness in his expression that made her feel as if he was finally showing her the real Max. The one who had been hiding inside layers of brusque aloofness and icy calm for the past few weeks.

Warmth pooled, deep in her body. 'Really? I feel like I've made nothing but a nuisance of myself since I got here.'

He gave another snort and the first proper smile she'd seen in a while. It made his whole face light up and the sight of it sent a rush of warm pleasure across her skin. 'It's certainly been *eventful* having you here.'

She couldn't help but return his grin, despite the feeling that she was somehow losing control of herself.

'Stay. Please.'

Her heart turned over at the expression on his face. It was something she'd never seen before. Against all the odds, he looked *hopeful*.

Despite a warning voice in the back of her head, she knew there was no way she could walk out of the door now that he'd laid himself bare. She could see that the extreme mood swings were coming from a place of deep pain and the very last thing he needed was to be left alone with just his tormenting memories for company in this big empty house.

It appeared as though they needed each other.

The levelling of the emotional stakes galvanised her.

'Okay,' she said, giving him a reassuring smile. 'I'll stay. On one condition.'

'And that is?'

'That you *talk* to me when you feel the gloom descending—like a *person*, not just an employee. And let me help if I can.' She crossed her arms and raised a challenging eyebrow.

He huffed out a laugh. 'And how do you propose to help?'

'I don't know. Perhaps I can jolly you out of your moods, if you give me the chance.'

'*Jolly*. That's a fitting word for you.'

'Yeah, well, someone has to raise the positivity levels in this house of doom.' She stilled, wondering whether she'd gone a step too far, but when she dared to peek at him he was smiling, albeit in a rather bemused way.

A sense of relief washed over her. The last thing she wanted to do was read the situation wrong now they'd had a breakthrough. In fact, she really ought to push for a treaty to make things crystal clear between them.

'Look, at the risk of micromanaging the situation, can we agree that from this point on you'll be totally straight with me, and in return I promise to be totally straight with you?'

He gave her a puzzled look. 'Why? Is there something you need to tell me?'

She considered admitting she'd lied about why she'd left her last job and dismissed it immediately. There was no point going over that right now; it had no relevance to this and it would make her sound totally pathetic compared to what he'd been through.

'No, no! Nothing! It was just a turn of phrase.'

He snorted gently, rolling his eyes upward, his mouth lifting at the corner. 'Okay then, Miss Fix-it, total honesty it is. You've got yourself a deal.'

CHAPTER FIVE

JUST AS MAX thought he'd had enough drama to last him a lifetime, things took another alarming turn, only this time it was the business that threatened to walk away from him.

Opening his email first thing on Monday morning, he found a missive from his longest standing and most profitable client, letting him know that they were considering taking their business elsewhere.

Cara walked in with their coffee just as he'd finished reading it and the concern on her face made it clear how rattled he must look.

'Max? What's wrong?'

'Our biggest client is threatening to terminate our contract with them.'

Her eyes grew larger. 'Why?'

'I'm guessing one of our competitors has been sniffing around, making eyes at them and I've been putting off going to the meetings they've been trying to arrange for a while now. I haven't had the time to give them the same level of attention as before, so their head's been turned.'

'Is it salvageable?'

'Yes. If I go up there today and show them exactly why they should stay with me.'

'Okay.' She moved swiftly over to her desk and opened up her internet browser, her nails rattling against her keyboard as she typed in an enquiry. 'There's a train to Manchester in forty minutes. You go and pack some stuff; I'll call a cab and book you a seat. You can speak to me from the train about anything that needs handling today.'

He sighed and rubbed a hand through his hair, feeling the tension mounting in his scalp. 'It's going to take more than an afternoon to get this sorted. I'll probably need to be up there for most of the week.'

'Then stay as long as you need.'

Shaking his head, he batted a hand towards his computer. 'I have that proposal to finish for the end of Thursday, not to mention the monstrous list of things to tackle for all the other clients this week.'

'Leave it with me. If you set me up with a folder of your previous proposals and give me the questions you need answering, I'll put some sections together for you, so you'll only need to check and edit them as we go. And don't worry about the other clients; I can handle the majority of enquiries and rearrange anything that isn't urgent for next week. I'll only contact you with the really important stuff.'

'Are you sure you can handle that? It's a lot to leave you with at such short notice.'

'I'll be fine.' She seemed so eager he didn't have the heart to argue.

In all honesty, it was going to be tough for him to let go of his tight grip on the business and trust that this would work out, but he knew he didn't have a choice—there was no way he was letting this contract slip through his fingers. He really couldn't afford to lose this firm's loyalty at this point in his business's infancy; it would make him look weak to competitors as well as potential new clients, and presenting a confident front was everything in this game.

'Okay.' He stood up and gathered his laptop and charger together before making for the door. 'Thanks, Cara. I'll get my stuff together and call you from the train.'

Turning back, he saw she was standing stiffly with her hands clasped in front of her, her eyes wide and her cheeks flushed.

Pausing for a moment, he wondered whether he was asking too much of her, but quickly dismissed it. She'd chosen to stay and she knew what she was getting herself into.

They were in it together now.

To his relief, Cara successfully held the fort back in London whilst he was away, routinely emailing him sections of completed work to be used in the business proposal that he wrote in the evenings in time to make the deadline. She seemed to have a real flair for picking out relevant information and had made an excellent job of copying his language style.

She also saved his hide by sending flowers and a card in his name to his mother for her birthday, which he was ashamed to discover he'd forgotten all about in his panic about losing the client.

Damaging the precarious cordiality that he and his mother had tentatively built up after working through their differences over the past few years would have been just as bad, and he was immensely grateful to Cara for her forethought and care.

She really was excellent at her job.

In fact, after receiving compliments from clients about how responsive and professional she'd been when they'd contacted her with enquiries and complications to be dealt with, he was beginning to realise that he'd actually been very fortunate to secure her services. He felt sure, if she wanted to, she could walk into a job with a much better salary with her eyes shut.

Which made him wonder again why she hadn't.

Whatever the reason, the idea of losing her excellent skill base now made him uneasy. Even though he'd been certain he'd want to let her go at the end of the trial month, he was now beginning to think that that would be a huge mistake.

He had some serious thinking to do.

If he was honest, he reflected on Thursday evening, sitting alone in the hotel's busy restaurant, having time and space away from Cara and the house had been a relief. He'd been glad of the opportunity to get his head together after their confrontation. She was the first person, outside his close circle of friends, that he'd talked to in any detail about what had happened to Jemima and it had changed the atmosphere between them. To Cara's credit, she hadn't trotted out platitudes to try and make him feel better and he was grateful to her for that, but he felt a little awkward about how much of himself he'd exposed.

Conversely, though, it also felt as though a weight that he'd not noticed carrying had been lifted from his shoulders. Not just because he'd finally told Cara about Jem—which he'd begun to feel weirdly seedy about, as if he was keeping a dirty secret from her—but also because it had got to the point where he'd become irrationally superstitious about clearing out the room, as though all his memories of Jemima would be wiped away if he touched it. Which, of course, they hadn't been—she was still firmly embedded there in his head and his heart. So, even though he'd been angry and upset with Cara at the time, in retrospect, it had been a healthy thing for that decision to be wrenched out of his hands.

It felt as though he'd taken a step further into the light.

Cara was out when he arrived back at Friday lunchtime, still buzzed with elation from keeping the client, so he went to unpack his bags upstairs, return a few phone calls and take a shower before coming back down.

Walking into the kitchen, he spotted her standing by the sink with her back to him, washing a mug. He stopped to watch her for a moment, smiling as he realised she was singing softly to herself, her slim hips swaying in time to the rhythm of the song. She had a beautiful voice, lyrical and sweet, and a strange, intense warmth wound through him as he stood there listening to her. It had been a long time since anyone had sung in this house and there was something so pure and uplifting about it a shiver ran down his spine, inexplicably chased by a deep pull of longing.

Though not for Cara, surely? But for a time when his life had fewer sharp edges. A simpler time. A happier one.

Shaking himself out of this unsettling observation, he moved quickly into the room so she wouldn't think he'd been standing there spying on her.

'Hi, Cara.'

She jumped and gasped, spinning round to face him, her hand pressed to her chest. She looked fresh and well rested, but there was a wary expression in her eyes.

'Max! I didn't hear you come in.'

'I was upstairs, taking a shower and returning some urgent calls. I got back about an hour ago.'

She nodded, her professional face quickly restored. 'How was Manchester?'

'Good. We got them back on board. How have things been here?'

'That's great! Things have been fine here. It's certainly been very quiet without you.'

By 'quiet' he suspected she actually meant less fraught with angry outbursts.

There was an uncomfortable silence while she fussed about with the tea towel, hooking it carefully over the handle of the cooker door and smoothing it until it lay perfectly straight.

Tearing his eyes away from the rather disconcerting sight of her stroking her hands slowly up and down the offending article, he walked over to where the kettle sat on the work surface and flicked it on to boil. He was unsettled to find that things still felt awkward between them when they were face to face—not that he should be surprised that they were. Their last non-work conversation had been a pretty heavy one, after all.

Evidently he needed to make more of an effort to be friendly now if he was going to be in with a chance of persuading her to stay after the month's trial was up.

The thought of going back to being alone in this house certainly wasn't a comforting one any more. If he was honest, it had been heartening to know that Cara would be here when he got back. Now that the black hole of Jemima's room had been destroyed and he'd fully opened the door to Cara, the loneliness he'd previously managed to keep at bay had walked right in.

Turning to face her again, he leant back against the counter and crossed his arms.

'I wanted to talk to you about the quality of the work you've been producing.'

Her face seemed to pale and he realised he could have phrased that better. He'd never been good at letting his colleagues know when he was pleased with their work—or Jemima when he was proud of something she'd achieved, he realised with a stab of pain— but after Cara had given it to him straight about how it affected her, he was determined to get better at it.

'What I mean is—I'm really impressed with the way you've handled the work here this week while I've been away,' he amended.

'Oh! Good. Thank you.' The pride in her wobbly smile made his breath catch.

He nodded and gave a little cough to release the peculiar tension in his throat, turning back to the counter to grab a mug for his drink and give them both a moment to regroup. There was a brightly coloured card propped up next to the mug tree and he picked it up as a distraction while he waited for the kettle to finish boiling and glanced at what was written inside.

'You didn't tell me it was your birthday,' he said, turning to face her again, feeling an unsettling mixture of surprise and dismay at her not mentioning something as important as that to him.

Colour rushed to her cheeks. 'Oh, sorry! I didn't mean to leave that lying around.' She walked over and took the card from his hand, leaning against the worktop next to him and enveloping him in her familiar floral scent. She tapped the corner of the card gently against her palm and he watched, hypnotised by the action. 'It was on Wednesday. As you were away I didn't think it was worth mentioning.' She looked up at him from under her lashes. 'Don't worry—I didn't have a wild house party here while you were away, only a couple of friends over for dinner and we made sure to tidy up afterwards.'

Fighting a strange disquiet, he flapped a dismissive hand at her. 'Cara, it's okay for you to keep some of your things in the communal areas and have friends over for your birthday, for God's sake. I don't expect the place to be pristine the whole time.'

'Still. I meant to put this up in my room with the others.'

Despite their pact to be more open with each other, it was evidently going to take a lot more time and effort to get her to relax around him.

Maybe he should present her with some kind of peace offering. In fact, thinking about it, her birthday could provide the perfect excuse.

He'd seen her reading an article about a new play in a magazine one lunchtime last week, and when he picked it up later he noticed she'd put a ring around the box office number, as if to remind herself to book tickets.

After dispatching her back to the office with a list of clients to chase up about invoices, he called the theatre, only to find the play had sold out weeks ago. Not prepared to be defeated that easily, he placed a call to his friend James, who was a long-time benefactor of the theatre.

'Hey, man, how are things?' his friend asked as soon as he picked up.

'Great. Business is booming. How about you?'

'Life's good. Penny's pregnant again,' James said with pleasure in his voice.

Max ignored the twinge of pain in his chest. 'That's great. Congratulations.'

'Thanks. Let's just hope this one's going to give us less trouble arriving into the world.'

'You're certainly owed an easy birth after the last time.'

'You could say that. Anyway, what can I do for you, my friend?'

'I wanted to get hold of tickets for that new play at the Apollo Theatre for tonight's performance. It's my PA's birthday and I wanted to treat her, but it's sold out. Can you help me with that?'

'Your PA, huh?' There was a twist of wryness in James's voice that shot a prickle straight up his spine.

'Yeah. My PA,' he repeated with added terseness born of discomfort.

His friend chuckled. 'No problem. I'll call and get them to put some tickets aside for you for the VIP box. I saw it last week—it's great—but it starts early, at five, so you'll need to get a move on.' There was a loaded pause. 'It's good to hear you're getting out again.'

Max bristled again. 'I go out.'

'But not with women. Not since Jemima passed away.'

He sighed, beginning to wish he hadn't called now. 'It's not a date. She's my *PA*.'

James chuckled again. 'Well, she's lucky to have you for an *employer*. These tickets are like gold dust.'

'Thanks, I owe you one,' Max said, fighting hard to keep the growl out of his voice. To his annoyance, he felt rattled by what his friend was insinuating. It wasn't stepping over the line to do something like this for Cara, was it?

'Don't worry about it,' James said.

Max wasn't sure for a moment whether he'd voiced his concerns out loud and James was answering that question or whether he was just talking about paying him back the favour.

'Thanks, James, I've got to go,' he muttered, wanting to end the call so he could walk around and loosen off this weird tension in his chest.

'No worries.'

Max put the phone down, wondering again whether this gesture was a step too far.

No. She'd worked hard for him, under some testing circumstances and he wanted her to know that he appreciated it. If he wanted to retain her services—and he was pretty sure now that he did—he was going to have to make sure she knew how much she was valued here so she didn't go looking for another job.

Cara was back at her desk, busily typing away on her laptop, when he walked into the room they used as an office. Leaning against the edge of her desk, he waited until she'd finished and turned to face him.

'I'm nearly done here,' she said, only holding eye contact for a moment before glancing back at her computer.

'Great, because a friend of mine just called to say he has two spare tickets to that new play at the Apollo and I was thinking I could take you as a thank you for holding the fort so effectively whilst I've been away. And for missing your birthday.'

She stared at him as if she thought she might have misheard. 'I'm sorry?'

He smiled at her baffled expression, feeling a kink of pleasure at her reaction. 'We'll need to leave in the next few minutes if we're going to make it into town in time to catch the beginning.' He stood up and she blinked in surprise.

'You and *me*? Right *now*?'

'Yes. You don't have other plans, do you?'

'Um, no.'

He nodded. 'Great.'

Gesturing up and down her body, she frowned, looking a little flustered. 'But I can't go dressed like this.'

He glanced at her jeans and T-shirt, trying not to let his eyes linger on the way they fitted her trim, slender body. 'You're going to have to change quickly then,' he said, pulling his mobile out of his pocket and dialling the number for the taxi.

Cara chattered away in the cab all the way there about how the play had been given rave reviews after its preview performance and how people were already paying crazy money on auction websites for re-sold tickets to see it. Her enthusiasm was contagious and, stepping out of the car, he was surprised to find he was actually looking forward to seeing it.

The theatre was a recently renovated grand art deco building slap-bang in the middle of Soho, a short stroll from the hectic retail circus of Oxford Street.

It had been a while since he'd made it into town on a Friday night and even longer since he'd been to see any kind of live show. When he and Jemima had moved to London they'd been full of enthusiasm about how they'd be living in the heart of the action and would be able to go out every other night to see the most cutting-edge performances and mind-expanding lectures. They were going to become paragons of good taste and spectacularly cultured to boot.

And then real life had taken over and they'd become

increasingly buried under the weight of work stress and life tiredness as the years went by and had barely made it out to anything at all. It had been fine when they'd had each other for company, but he was aware that he needed to make more of an effort to get out and be sociable now he was on his own.

Not that he'd been a total recluse since Jem had died; he'd been out with friends—Poppy being his most regular pub partner—but he'd done it in a cocoon of grief, always feeling slightly detached from what was going on around him.

Doing this with Cara meant he was having to make an effort again. Which was a good thing. It felt healthy. Perhaps that was why he was feeling more upbeat than he had in a while—as if there was life beyond the narrow world he'd been living in for the past year and a half.

After paying the taxi driver, they jogged straight to the box office for their tickets, then through the empty lobby to the auditorium to find their seats in the VIP box, the usher giving them a pointed look as she closed the doors firmly behind them. It seemed they'd only just made it. This theory was borne out by the dimming of the lights and the grand swish of the curtain opening just as they folded themselves into their seats.

Max turned to find Cara with her mouth comically open and an expression that clearly said *I can't believe we've just casually nipped into the best seats in the house.* He flashed her a quick smile, enjoying her pleasure and the sense of satisfaction at doing something good here, before settling back into his plush red velvet chair, his heart beating heavily in his chest.

A waft of her perfume hit his nose as she reached up to adjust her ponytail, which made his heart beat even harder—perhaps from the sudden sensory overload. Taking a deep breath, he concentrated on bringing his breathing back to normal and focused on the action on stage, determined to put all other thoughts aside for the meantime and try to enjoy whatever this turned out to be.

Cara was immensely relieved when the play stood up to her enthusiastic anticipation. It would have been pretty embarrassing if it had been a real flop after all the fuss she'd made about it on the way there. Every time she heard Max chuckle at one of the jokes she experienced a warm flutter of pleasure in her stomach.

Max bringing her here to the theatre had thrown her for a complete loop. Even though he'd finally let her into his head last weekend, she'd expected him to go back to being distant with her again once he came back from Manchester. But instead he'd surprised her by complimenting her, then not only getting tickets to the hottest play in London, but bringing her here himself as a reward for working hard.

Dumbfounded was not the word.

Not that she was complaining.

Sneaking a glance at him, she thought she'd never seen him looking so relaxed. She could hardly believe he was the same man who had opened the door to her on the first day they'd met. He seemed larger now somehow, as if he'd straightened up and filled out in the time since she'd last seen him. That had to be all in her head, of course, but he certainly seemed more *real* now that she knew what drove his rage. In fact it was incredible how differently she felt now she knew what sort of horror he'd been through—losing someone he loved in such a senseless way.

No wonder he was so angry at the world.

Selfishly, it was a massive relief to know that none of his dark moods had been about her performance—apart from when she'd fallen asleep on the kitchen table during business hours, of course.

After he'd left for Manchester, she'd had a minor panic attack about how she was going to cope on her own, terrified of making a mistake that would impact negatively on the business, but, after giving herself a good talking-to in the mirror, she'd pulled it together and got on with the job in hand. And she'd been fine. More than fine. In fact she'd actually started to enjoy her job again as she relaxed into the role and reasserted her working practices.

Truth be told, before she'd started working for Max, she didn't know whether she'd be able to hold her nerve in a business environment any more. He'd been a hard taskmaster but she knew she'd benefited from that, discovering that she had the strength to stand up for herself when it counted. She'd been tested to her limits and she'd come through the other side and that, to her, had been her biggest achievement in a very long time.

She felt proud of herself again.

As the first half drew to a close she became increas-

ingly conscious of the heat radiating from Max's powerful body and his arm that pressed up against hers as
he leaned into the armrest. Her skin felt hot and prickly
where it touched his, as if he was giving off an electric charge, and it was sending little currents of energy
through the most disconcerting places in her body.

It seemed her crush on him had grown right along
with her respect and she was agonisingly aware of how
easy it would be to fall for him if she let herself.

Which she wasn't going to do. He was clearly still
in love with his wife and there was no way she could
compete with a ghost.

Only pain and heartache lay that way.

As soon as the curtain swished closed and the lights
came on to signal the intermission she sprang up from
her seat, eager to break their physical connection as
soon as possible.

'Let's grab a drink,' Max said, leaning in close so
she could hear him over the noise of audience chatter,
his breath tickling the hairs around her ear.

'Good idea.' She was eager to move now to release
the pent-up energy that was making her heart race.

Max gestured for her to go first, staying close behind
her as they walked down the stairs towards the bar, his
dominating presence like a looming shadow at her back.

They joined the rest of the audience at the bottom of
the stairs and she pushed her way through the shouty
crowd of people towards the shiny black-lacquered bar,
which was already six people deep with waiting customers.

'Hmm, this could take a while,' she said to Max as they came to a stop at the outskirts of the throng.

'Don't worry, I'll get the drinks,' he said, walking around the perimeter of the group as if gauging the best place to make a start. 'Glass of wine?' he asked.

'Red please.'

'Okay, I'm going in,' he said, taking an audible breath and turning to the side to shoulder through a small gap between two groups of chatting people with their backs to each other.

Cara watched in fascinated awe as Max made it to the bar in record time, flipping a friendly smile as he sidled through the crowd and charming a group of women into letting him into a small gap at the counter next to them.

After making sure his newly made friends were served first, he placed his order with the barman and was back a few moments later, two glasses of red wine held aloft in a gesture of celebration.

'Wow, nice work,' Cara said, accepting a glass and trying not to grin like a loon. 'I've never seen anyone work a bar crowd like that before.'

Max shrugged and took a sip of wine, pinning a look of exaggerated nonchalance onto his face. 'I have hidden depths.'

She started to laugh, but it dried in her throat as she locked eyes with someone on the other side of the room.

Someone she thought she'd never see again.

Swallowing hard, she dragged her gaze back to Max and dredged up a smile, grasping for cool so she wouldn't have to explain her sudden change in mood.

But it was not to be. The man was too astute for his own good.

'Are you okay? You look like you've seen a ghost,' he said, his intelligent eyes flashing with concern.

Damn and blast. This was the last thing she wanted to have to deal with tonight.

'Fine,' she squeaked, her cheeks growing hot under the intensity of his gaze.

'Cara. I thought we'd agreed to be straight with each other from now on.'

Sighing, she nodded towards the other side of the bar. 'That guy over there is an old friend of mine.'

He frowned as she failed to keep the hurt out of her voice and she internally kicked herself for being so transparent.

'He can't be a very good friend if you're ignoring each other.'

She sighed and tapped at the floor with the toe of her shoe. 'It's complicated.'

He raised his eyebrows, waiting for her to go on.

After pausing for a moment, she decided there was no point in trying to gloss over it. 'The thing is—his fiancée has a problem with me.'

'Really? Why?'

'Because I'm female.'

He folded his arms. 'She's the jealous type, huh?'

'Yeah. And no matter how much Jack's tried to convince her that our friendship is purely platonic, she won't believe him. So I've been confined to the rubbish heap of Friends Lost and Passed Over.' She huffed out a sigh. 'I can't really blame him for making that choice, though. He loves her and I want him to be happy, and if that means we can't be friends any more then so be it.'

The look of bewildered outrage in Max's expression made the breath catch in her throat and she practically stopped breathing altogether as he reached out and stroked his hand down her arm in a show of solidarity, his touch sending tingles of pure pleasure through every nerve in her body.

Staring up into his handsome face, she wondered again what it would feel like to have someone like Max for a partner. To know that he was on her side and that he had her back, no matter what happened.

But she was kidding herself. He was never going to offer her the chance to find out. She was his employee and she'd do well to remember that.

Tearing her gaze away from him, she glanced back across the room to where the fiancée in question had now appeared by Jack's side. From a distance they appeared to be having a heated discussion about something, their heads close together as they gesticulated at each other. As she watched, they suddenly sprang apart and Jack turned to catch her eye again, already moving towards where she and Max were standing.

He was coming over.

Her body tensed with apprehension and she jumped in surprise as Max put his hand on her arm again, then increased his grip, as if readying himself to spirit her away from a painful confrontation.

'Cara! It's been ages,' Jack said as he came to a stop in front of her, looking just as boyishly handsome as ever, with his lopsided grin and great mop of wavy blond hair.

'It has, Jack.'

'How are you?' he asked, looking a little shame-faced now, as well he should. They'd become good friends after meeting at their first jobs after university and had been close once, spending weekends at each other's houses and standing in as 'plus ones' at weddings and parties if either of them were single and in need of support.

There had been a time when she'd wondered whether they'd end up together, but as time had passed it became obvious that wasn't meant to be. He was a great guy, but the chemistry just wasn't there for her—or for him, it seemed. But seeing him here now reminded her just how much she missed his friendship. She could have really done with his support after Ewan sauntered away from their relationship in search of someone with less emotional baggage, but it had been at that point that his fiancée had issued her ultimatum, and Cara had well and truly been the loser in that contest.

Not that she blamed him for choosing Amber. She had to respect his loyalty to the woman he loved.

'I'm great, Jack, thanks. How are you—' she paused and flicked her gaze to his fiancée, who had now appeared at his side '—both?' Somehow she managed to dredge up a smile for the woman. 'Hi, Amber.'

'Hi, Cara, we're great, thanks,' Amber said, acerbity dripping from every word as she pointedly wrapped a possessive arm around Jack's waist. Turning to look at Max, she gave him a subtle, but telling, once-over.

'And who's this?'

'This is Max…' Cara took a breath, about to say *my boss*, when Max cut her off to lean in and shake hands with Amber.

'It's lovely to meet you, Amber,' he said in the same smooth tone she'd heard him use to appease clients.

It worked just as well on Amber because her cheeks flooded with colour and she actually fluttered her lashes at him. Turning back to Cara, she gave her a cool smile, her expression puzzled, as if she was trying to work out how she'd got her hands on someone as impressive as Max.

'Did Jack tell you—our wedding's on Sunday so this evening is our last hurrah before married life?' Amber's eyes twinkled with malice. 'Jack's firm is very well reputed in the City and people practically throw invitations at him every day,' she said, her tone breezy but her eyes hard, as though she was challenging Cara to beat her with something better than that.

Which, of course, she had no hope of doing.

Pushing away the thump of humiliation, Cara forced her mouth into the shape of a smile.

'That's wonderful—congratulations! I had no idea the wedding was so soon.'

Amber leaned in and gave her a pitying smile. 'We've kept it a small affair, which is why we couldn't send you an invitation, Cara.'

Max shifted next to her, pulling her a bit tighter against him in the process and surprising her again by rubbing her arm in support. She wondered whether he could feel how fast her pulse was racing through her body with him holding her so close.

'But we had two spaces open up this week,' Jack said suddenly and a little too loudly, as if he'd finally decided to step out of his fiancée's shadow and take control. 'My cousin and her husband have had to drop out to visit sick family abroad. If you're not busy you could come in their place.'

Judging by the look on Amber's face, she obviously hadn't had this in mind when she'd agreed to be dragged over here.

'It would be great if you could make it,' Jack pressed, his expression open, almost pleading now. It seemed that he genuinely wanted her to be there. Perhaps this was his way of making things up to her after cutting her out of his life so brutally. At least that was something.

But she couldn't say yes when the invitation was for both her and Max and she hated the idea of turning up and spending the day on her own amongst all those happy couples.

Before she could open her mouth to make up an excuse and turn them down, Max leaned in and said, 'Thank you—we'd love to come.'

She swivelled her head to gape at him, almost giving herself whiplash in the process, stunned to find a look of cool certainty on his face.

'Are you sure we're not busy?' she said pointedly, raising both eyebrows at him.

'I'm sure,' he replied with a firm nod.

Turning back to Jack, she gave him what must have

been the weirdest-looking smile. 'Okay—er—' she swallowed '—then we'd love to come. Thanks.'

'That's great,' Jack said, giving her a look that both said *I'm sorry for everything* and *thank you*.

'We'd better go and get a drink before the performance starts again,' Amber said with steel in her voice, her patience clearly used up now.

'I'll text you with the details, Cara,' Jack said as Amber drew him away.

'Okay, see you on Sunday,' Cara said weakly to their disappearing figures.

As soon as they were out of earshot she turned to stare at Max, no doubt doing her impression of a goldfish again.

'He's a brave man,' was all Max said in reply.

'You realise they think we're a couple?'

He nodded, a fierce intensity in his eyes causing a delicious shiver to rush down her spine. 'I know, but I wanted to see the look on that awful woman's face when we said yes, and I have no problem pretending to be your partner if it's going to smooth the way back to a friendship with Jack for you.'

Max as her partner. Just the thought of it made her quiver right down to her toes.

'That's—' she searched for the right words '—game of you.'

'It'll be my pleasure.'

There was an odd moment where the noises around her seemed to get very loud in her ears. Tearing her gaze away from his, she gulped down the last of her wine and wrapped her hands around the glass in order to prevent herself from chewing on her nails.

Okay. Well, that happened.

Who knew that Max would turn out to be her knight in shining armour?

CHAPTER SIX

MAX HAD NO idea where this strange possessiveness towards Cara had sprung from, but he hadn't been about to let that awful woman, Amber, treat her with so little respect. She deserved more than that. Much more. And while she was working for him he was going to make sure she got it.

Which meant he was now going to be escorting her to a wedding—the kind of event he'd sworn to avoid after Jemima died. The thought of being back in a church, watching a couple with their whole lives ahead of them begin their journey together, made his stomach clench with unease.

One year—that was all he'd been allowed with his wife. One lousy year. It made him want to spit with rage at the world. Why her? Why them?

Still, at least he didn't know the happy couple and would be able to keep a low profile at the wedding, hiding his bitterness behind a bland smile. He didn't need to engage. He'd just be there to support Cara; that was all.

After the play finished they travelled home in silence, a stark contrast to their journey there, but he was glad of the quiet. Perversely, it felt as though he and Cara had grown closer during that short time, the confrontation and subsequent solidarity banding them together like teammates.

Which of course they were, he reminded himself as he opened the front door to his house and ushered her inside, at least when it came to the business.

Cara's phone beeped as she shrugged off her coat and she plucked it out of her handbag and read the message, her smile dropping by degrees as she scanned the text.

'Problem?' he asked, an uncomfortable sense of foreboding pricking at the edge of his mind. It had taken him a long time to be able to answer the phone without feeling the crush of anxiety he'd been plagued with after the call telling him his wife had collapsed and had been rushed into hospital.

He took a step closer to her, glad she was here to distract him from the lingering bad memories.

Glancing up, she gave him a sheepish look. 'It's a text from Jack with the details of the wedding.'

'Oh, right.' He stepped back, relief flowing through him, but Cara didn't appear to relax. Instead her grimace only deepened.

'Um. Apparently it's in Leicestershire. Which is a two and a half hour drive from here. So we'll need to stay overnight.' She wrinkled her nose, the apology clear on her face.

Great. Just what had he let himself in for here?

'No problem,' he forced himself to say, holding back

the irritation he felt at the news. It wasn't Cara's fault and he was the one who had pushed for this to happen.

More fool him.

'Really? You don't mind?' she asked, relief clear in her tone.

'No, it's fine,' he lied, trying not to think about all the hours he'd have to spend away from his desk so he could make nice with a bunch of strangers.

'Great, then I'll book us a couple of rooms in the B&B that Jack suggested,' she said, her smile returning.

'You do that.' He gave her a firm nod and hid a yawn behind his hand. 'I'm heading off to bed,' he said, feeling the stress of the week finally catching up with him. 'See you in the morning, Cara. And Happy Birthday.'

Cara disappeared for most of the next day, apparently going to look at potential flats to rent, then retiring to bed early, citing exhaustion from the busy, but fruitless, day.

After the tension of Friday night, Max was glad of the respite and spent most of his time working through the backlog of emails he'd accumulated after his week away.

Sunday finally rolled around and he woke early, staring into the cool empty air next to him and experiencing the usual ache of hollowness in his chest, before pulling himself together and hoisting his carcass out of bed and straight into the shower.

The wedding was at midday so at least he had a couple of hours to psych himself up before they had to head over to the Leicestershire estate where it was being held.

The sun was out and glinting off the polished windows of the houses opposite when he pulled his curtains open, momentarily blinding him with its brightness. It was definitely a day for being outdoors.

He'd barely breathed fresh air in the past week, only moving between office and hotel, and the thought of feeling the warm sun on his skin spurred him into action. He pulled on his running gear, something he'd not done for over a year and a half, and went for a long run, welcoming the numbing pain as he worked his lethargic muscles hard, followed by the rewarding rush of serotonin as it chased its way through his veins. After a while it felt as though he was flying along the pavement, the worries and stresses of the past week pushed to the very back of his mind by the punishing exercise.

For the first time in a long while he felt as if he were truly awake.

Cara appeared to be up and about when he limped back into his kitchen for a long drink of water, his senses perking up as he breathed in the comforting smell of the coffee she'd been drinking, threaded with the flowery scent of her perfume.

Glancing up at the clock as he knocked back his second glass of water, he was shocked to see it was already nearly nine o'clock, which meant he really ought to get a move on if he was going to be ready to leave for the wedding on time.

Turning back from loading his glass into the dishwasher, he was brought up short by the sight of Cara standing in the hallway just outside the kitchen door, watching him. She'd twisted her long hair up into some sort of complicated-looking hairstyle and her dark eyes sparkled with glittery make-up. The elegant silver strapless dress she wore fitted her body perfectly, moulding itself to her gentle curves and making her seem taller and—something else. More mature, perhaps? More sophisticated?

Whatever it was, she looked completely and utterly beautiful.

Realising he was standing there gawping at her like some crass teenage boy, he cleared his suddenly dry throat and dredged up a smile which he hoped didn't look as lascivious as it felt.

'Hey, you look like you're dressed for a wedding,' he said, cringing inside at how pathetic that sounded.

She smiled. 'And you don't. I hope you're not thinking of going like that because I'm pretty sure it didn't say "sports casual" on the invitation.' Her amused gaze raked up and down his body, her eyebrows rising at the sight of his sweat-soaked running gear.

He returned her grin, finding it strangely difficult to keep it natural-looking. His whole face felt as if he'd had his head stuck in the freezer. What was wrong with him? A bit of sunshine and a fancy dress and his mind was in a spin.

'I'd better go and take a shower; otherwise we're going to be late,' he said, already walking towards the door.

'Could you do me a favour before you go?' she asked, colour rising in her cheeks.

'Er…sure. As long as it's not going to cost me anything,' he joked, coming to a stop in front of her. In her heels she was nearly as tall as him, making it easier to directly meet her gaze. She had such amazing eyes: bright and clear with vitality and intellect. The make-up and hair made him think of Audrey Hepburn in *Breakfast at Tiffany's*.

'Could you do up the buttons on the back of my dress?' she asked, her voice sounding unusually breathy, as if it had taken a lot for her to ask for his help.

'Sure,' he said, waiting for her to turn around and present her back to him. His breath caught as he took in the long, elegant line of her spine as it disappeared into the base of her dress. There were three buttons that held the top half of it together, with a large piece cut out at the bottom, which would leave her creamy skin and the gentle swells of muscle at the base of her back exposed.

Heaven help him.

Hands feeling as if they'd been trapped in the freezer, too, he fiddled around with the buttons, feeling the warmth of her skin heat the tips of his fingers. Hot barbs of awareness tracked along his nerves and embedded themselves deep in his body and his breath came out in short ragged gasps, which he'd like to think was an after-effect of the hard exercise, but was more likely to be down to his close proximity to a woman's body, after his had been starved of attention for the past year and a half.

'There you go,' he said, snapping the final button into its hole with a sigh of relief. 'I'll be back down in fifteen.'

And with that he made his escape.

* * *

Wow. This felt weird, being at Jack's wedding—a friend she thought she'd never see again—with Max—her recalcitrant boss—as her escort. The whole world seemed to have flipped on its head. If someone had told her a week ago that this was going to happen she would have given them a polite smile whilst slowly backing away.

But here she was, swaying unsteadily in the only pair of high heels she owned, with Max at her side. The man who could give Hollywood's top leading men a run for their money in the charisma department.

There had been a moment in the kitchen, after he'd turned around and noticed her, when she thought she'd seen something in his eyes. Something that had never been there before. Something like desire.

And then when he'd helped her with her dress it had felt as though the air had crackled and jumped between them. The bloom of his breath on her neck had made her knees weak and her heart race. She could have sworn his voice had held a rougher undertone than she was used to hearing as he excused himself.

But she knew she was kidding herself if she thought she should read more than friendly interest into his actions.

They had Radio Four on for the entire journey up to Leicestershire, listening in rapt silence to a segment on finance, then chuckling along to a radio play. Cara was surprised by how easy it was to sit beside Max and how relaxed and drawn into their shared enjoyment of the programme she was. So much so, that it was to her great surprise that they pulled into the small car park of the church where the wedding was taking place, seemingly only a short time after leaving London.

The sunshine that had poured in through her bedroom window that morning had decided to stick around for the rest of the day, disposing of the insubstantial candyfloss clouds of the morning to reveal the most intensely blue sky she'd ever seen.

All around her, newly blooming spring flowers bopped their heads in time to the rhythm of the light spring breeze, their gaudy colours a striking counterpoint to the verdant green of the lawns surrounding them.

Taking a deep breath, she drew the sweet, fresh air deep into her lungs. This should mark a new beginning in her life, she decided. The start of the next chapter, where the foundations she'd laid in the past few weeks would hopefully prove strong enough to support her from this point onwards.

'It's nearly twelve o'clock; we should go in,' Max said with regret in his voice as he cast his gaze around their beautiful surroundings.

Attempting to keep her eyes up and off the tantalising view of his rear in the well-cut designer suit he'd chosen to wear today, she tripped into the church after him, shivering slightly at the change in temperature as they walked out of the sunshine and into the nave.

Most of the pews were already full, so they hung back for a moment to be directed to a seat by one of the ushers.

And that was when the day took a definite turn for the worse.

Her world seemed to spin on its axis, rolling her stomach along with it, as her former and current life lined up on a collision course. One of the PAs who had belonged to the Cobra Clique was standing down by the altar, her long blond hair slithering down her back as she threw her head back and laughed at something that the man standing next to her said.

Taking a deep breath, Cara willed herself not to panic, but her distress must have shown plainly on her face because Max turned to glance in the direction she was staring and said, 'Cara? What's wrong?'

'Ah…nothing.' She flapped a dismissive hand at him, feeling her cheeks flame with heat, and took a step backwards, hoping the stone pillar would shield her. But serendipity refused to smile as the woman turned towards them, catching her eye, her pupils flaring in recognition and her gaze moving, as if in slow motion, from Cara to Max and back again. And the look on her face plainly said she wasn't going to miss this golden opportunity to make more trouble for her.

Looking around her wildly, Cara's heart sank as she realised there was nowhere to run, nowhere to hide.

It was usually at this point in a film that the leading lady would pull the guy she was with towards her and kiss him hard to distract him from the oncoming danger, but she knew, as she stared with regret at Max's full, inviting mouth, that there was no way she could do that. He'd probably choke in shock, then fire her on the spot if she even attempted it. It wouldn't just put her job in jeopardy—it would blow it to smithereens.

There was only one thing left to do.

'Max, I need to tell you something.'

He frowned at her, his eyes darkening as he caught on to her worried tone.

'What's wrong?'

'I—er—'

'Cara?' He looked really alarmed now and she shook her head, trying to clear it. She needed to keep her cool or she'd end up looking even more of an idiot.

'I wasn't entirely straight with you about why I left my last job. Truth is—' she took a breath '—I didn't take redundancy.'

He blinked, then frowned. 'So you were fired?'

'No. I—'

'What did you do, Cara? What are you trying to tell me?' His voice held a tinge of the old Max now—the one who didn't suffer fools.

'Okay—' She closed her eyes and held up a hand. 'Look, just give me a minute and I'll explain. The thing is—' Locking her shaking hands together, she took a steadying breath. 'I was bullied by a gang of women there who made my life a living hell and I handed in my notice before my boss could fire me for incompetence as a result of it,' she said, mortified by the tremor in her voice.

When she opened her eyes to look at him, the expression of angry disbelief on his face made her want to melt into a puddle of shame.

'What?'

She swallowed past the tightness in her throat. 'I had no choice but to leave.'

He shook his head in confusion. 'Why didn't you tell me?'

Out of the corner of her eye she saw her nemesis approaching and felt every hair on her body stand to attention. The woman was only ten steps away, at most.

'And why are you telling me this now?' he pressed.

'Because one of the women is here at the wedding and she'll probably tell you a pack of lies to make me look bad. I didn't exactly leave graciously. There was a jug of cold coffee and some very white blouses involved.' She cringed at the desperation in her voice, but Max just turned to glare in the direction she'd been avoiding, then let out a sharp huff of breath.

'Come outside for a minute.'

Wrapping his hand around her arm, he propelled her back out through the doors of the church and down the steps, coming to a sudden halt under the looming shadow of the clock tower, where he released her. Crossing his arms, he looked down at her with an expression of such exasperation it made her quake in her stilettos.

'Why didn't you mention this to me before?' he asked, shoving back the hair that had fallen across his forehead during their short journey, only drawing more attention to his piercing gaze.

Sticking her chin in the air, she crossed her own arms, determined to stand up for herself. 'I really wanted to work with you and I thought you might not hire me if you knew the truth. It didn't exactly look good on my CV that I'd only stuck it out there for three months before admitting defeat.'

'So you thought you had to lie to me to get the job?'

She held up her hands in apology. 'I know I should have told you the truth, but I'd already messed up other job interviews because I was so nervous and ashamed of myself for being so weak.' She hugged her arms around her again. 'I didn't want you to think badly of me. Anyway, at the time you barely wanted to talk to me about the work I had to do, let alone anything of a personal nature, so I thought it best to keep it to myself.' She looked at him steadily, craving his understanding. 'You can be pretty intimidating, you know.'

She was saved from having to further explain herself by one of the ushers loudly asking the stragglers outside to please go into the church and take their seats because the bride had arrived.

From the look on Max's face she wasn't sure whether he was going to walk away and leave her standing there like a total lemon on her own or turn around and punch the wall. She didn't fancy watching either scenario play out.

To her surprise, he let out a long, frustrated sigh and looked towards the gaggle of people filing into the church.

'We can't talk about this now or we'll be walking in with the bridal party, and there's no way I'd pass for a bridesmaid,' he said stiffly.

She stared at him. 'You mean you're not going to leave?'

'No, I'm not going to leave,' he said crossly. 'We'll talk more about this after the ceremony.'

And with that he put his hand firmly against the middle of her back and ushered her inside.

Sliding into the polished wooden pew next to Max and surreptitiously wiping her damp palms on her dress, she glanced at him out of the corner of her eye. From the set of his shoulders she could tell he wasn't likely to let *this* go with a casual wave of his hand.

In fact she'd bet everything she had left that he was really going to fire her this time.

Frustration churned in her stomach. After all the progress she'd made in getting back on her feet, and persuading Max to finally trust her, was it really going to end like this?

Looking along the pews, she saw that her nemesis was sitting on the other side of the church, a wide smile on her face as she watched the ceremony unfold. At least that threat had been neutralised. There wasn't anything left that she could do to hurt her.

She hoped.

Rage unfurled within Cara at the unfairness of it all. Why did this woman get to enjoy herself when she had to sit here worrying about her future?

As she watched Amber make her stately way up the aisle towards a rather nervous-looking Jack, she could barely concentrate for wondering what Max was going to say to her once they were facing each other over their garlic mushrooms at the lunch afterwards. There was no way she was going to be able to force down a bite of food until they'd resolved this.

Oh, get a grip, Cara.

When she dared take a peek at him from the corner of her eye again, he seemed to be grimly staring straight ahead. Forcing herself to relax, she uncrossed her legs, then her arms and sat up straighter, determined not to appear anxious or pitiful. She knew what she had to do. There would be no gratuitous begging or bartering for a reprieve. She would hold her head high throughout it all and calmly state her case.

And until she had that opportunity she was going to damn well enjoy watching her friend get married.

Judging by her rigid posture and ashen complexion, Cara really didn't appear to be enjoying the ceremony, which only increased Max's discomfort at being there, too. Not that he blamed her in any way for it. He'd chosen to come here with her after all. Though, from the sound of it, she must be regretting bringing him along now.

Had he really been so unapproachable that she'd chosen to lie to his face instead of admitting to having a rough time at her last place of work?

He sighed inwardly.

She was absolutely right, though. Again. He could be intimidating. And he'd been at the peak of his remoteness when she'd first arrived on his doorstep and asked him for a job. He also knew that if she'd mentioned the personal issues that had been intrinsic to her leaving her last job when they'd first met it would have given him pause enough to turn her away. He hadn't wanted any kind of complication at that point.

But he was so glad now that he hadn't.

Somehow, in her innocent passive-aggressive way, she'd managed to push his buttons and, even though he'd fought it at the time, that was exactly what he'd needed.

She was what he'd needed.

After the ceremony finished they were immediately ushered out of the church and straight up the sweeping manicured driveway to the front of a grand Georgian house where an enormous canvas marquee had been set up next to the orangery.

A small affair, his foot.

As soon as they stepped inside they had toxic-coloured cocktails thrust upon them and were politely but firmly asked to make their way back outside again to the linen-draped tables on the terrace next to the house.

'This is like a military operation,' he muttered to Cara, who had walked quietly next to him since they'd left the church, her face pale and her expression serious. She gave him a weak smile, her eyes darting from side to side as if she was seriously contemplating making a run for it and scoping out the best means of escape.

He sighed. 'Come and sit down over here where it's quiet,' he said, looping his arm through hers and guiding her towards one of the empty tables nearest the house.

To his frustration she stiffened, then slipped out of his steadying grip and folded her arms across her chest instead, her shoulders rigid and her chin firmly up as they walked. Just as they picked their way over the last bit of gravelled path to reach the table she stumbled and on reflex he quickly moved in to catch her.

'Are you okay?' he asked, placing a hand on the exposed part of her back, feeling the heat of her body warm the palm of his hand and send an echoing sensation through his entire abdomen.

His touch seemed to undo something in her and she collapsed into the nearest chair and gave him such a fearful look his heart jumped into his throat.

'I'm sorry for lying to you, Max. Please don't fire me. If I lose this job I'll have to move back to Cornwall and I really, really don't want to leave London. It's my home and I love it. I can't imagine living anywhere else now. And I really like working for you.' Swallowing hard, she gave him a small quavering smile. 'I swear I will never lie to you again. Believe it or not, I usually have a rock-solid moral compass and if I hadn't felt backed into a corner I never would have twisted the truth. I was on the cusp of losing everything and I was desperate, Max. Totally. Desperate.' She punctuated each of the last words with a slap of her hand on the table.

'Cara, I'm not going to fire you.'

How could she think that he would? Good grief, had he done such a number on her that she'd think he'd be capable of something as heartless as that?

'You're not?' Her eyes shone in the reflected brightness thrown up by the white tablecloth and he looked away while she blinked back threatening tears.

'Of course not.' He shifted forward in his seat, closer to her. 'You well and truly proved your worth to the business last week.' He waited till she looked at him again. 'I have to admit, I'm hurt that you thought I'd fire you for admitting to being bullied.' He leaned back in his chair with a sigh. 'God, you must think I'm a real tool if you seriously believed I'd do something like that.'

'It's just—you can be a bit…fierce…sometimes. And

I didn't want to show any weakness.' She visibly cringed as she said it, and his insides plummeted.

'Tell me more about what happened at your last job,' he said quietly, wanting to get things completely straight between them, but not wanting to spook her further in the process.

Her gaze slid away. 'It's not a happy tale, or something I'm particularly proud of.'

'No. I got that impression.'

'Okay, I'll tell you, but please don't judge me too harshly. Things like this always look so simple and manageable from a distance, but when you're in the thick of it, it's incredibly difficult to think straight without letting your emotions get in the way.'

He held up his hands, palms forward, and affected a non-judgemental expression.

She nodded and sat up straighter. 'I thought I'd hit the jackpot when I was offered that position. Ugh! What an idiot,' she said, her self-conscious grimace making him want to move closer to her, to draw her towards him and smooth out the kinks of her pain. But he couldn't do that. It wasn't his place.

So he just nodded and waited for her to continue.

'When I started as Executive Assistant to the CEO of LED Software I had no idea about the office politics that were going on there. But it didn't take me long to find out. Apparently one of the other PAs had expected to be a shoo-in for my job and was *very* unimpressed when they gave it to me. She made it her mission from my first day to make my life miserable. As one of the longest-standing members of staff—and a very, er, *strong* personality—she had the allegiance of all the other PAs and a lot of the other members of staff and they ganged up on me. At first I thought I was going mad. I'd make diary appointments for my boss with other high-ranking members of staff in the company, which their PAs would claim to have no knowledge of by the time I sent him along for the meeting. Or the notes I'd print out for an important phone call with the Executive Board would go missing from his desk right before it took place and he'd have to take it unbriefed.' She tapped her fingers on the table. 'That did not go down well. My boss was a very proud guy and he expected things to be perfect.'

'I can relate to that,' Max said, forcing compassion into his smile despite the tug of disquiet in his gut. He was just as guilty when it came to perfectionism.

But, instead of admonishing him, she smiled back.

'Lots of other little things like that happened,' she continued, rubbing a hand across her forehead, 'which made me look incompetent, but I couldn't prove that someone was interfering with my work and when I mentioned it to my boss he'd wave away my concerns and suggest I was slipping up on the job and blaming others to cover my back. I let the stress of it get to me and started making real mistakes, things I never would have let slip at the last place I worked. It rattled me, to the point where I started believing I wasn't cut out for the job. I wasn't sleeping properly with the stress of it and I ended up breaking down one day in front of my boss. And that—' she clicked her fingers '—was the end of our working relationship. He seemed to lose all respect for me after that and started giving the other PAs things that were my job to do.'

Max snorted in frustration. 'The guy sounds like an idiot.'

She gave him a wan smile. 'I was the idiot. I only found out what was really going on when I overheard a couple of the PAs laughing about it in the ladies' bathroom.'

Her eyes were dark with an expression he couldn't quite read now. Was it anger? Resentment? It certainly didn't look like self-pity.

'So you left,' he prompted.

She took a sip of her drink and he did the same, grimacing at the claggy sweetness of the cocktail.

'I had to,' she said. 'My professional reputation was at stake, not to mention my sanity. I couldn't afford to be fired; it would have looked awful on my CV. Not to mention how upset my parents would have been. They're desperate for me to have a successful career. They never had the opportunity to get a good education or well-paid job themselves so they scrimped and saved for years to put me through private school. It's a point of pride for my dad in particular. Apparently he never shuts up to his friends about me working with "the movers and shakers in the Big Smoke".' She shot him an embarrassed grimace.

He smiled. 'You're lucky—my mother couldn't give two hoots whether I'm successful or not. She's not what you'd call an engaged parent.'

Her brow furrowed in sympathy. 'And your father?'

'I never met him.' He leant back with a sigh. 'My

mother fell pregnant with me when she was sixteen and still maintains that she doesn't know who he was. She was pretty wild in her youth and constantly moved us around the country. Barely a term at school would go by before she had us packing up and moving on. She couldn't bear to stay in the same place for long. Not that she's exactly settled now.'

Her gaze was sympathetic. 'That must have been tough when you were young.'

He shrugged. 'It was a bit. I never got to keep the friends I made for very long.'

He thought about how his unsettled youth had impacted on the way he liked to live now. He still didn't like change, even all these years later; it made him tetchy and short-tempered. Which was something Cara had got to know all about recently.

Keen to pull his mind away from his own shortcomings, he leaned forward in his seat and recaptured eye contact with her. 'So what happened when you handed in your notice?'

She started at the sudden flip in subject back to her and twisted the stem of her glass in her fingers, looking away from his gaze and focusing on the garish liquid as it swirled up towards the rim. 'My boss didn't even bat an eyelid, just tossed my letter of resignation onto his desk and went back to the email he was typing, which confirmed just how insignificant I was to him. I took a couple of weeks to get my head straight after that, but I needed another job. I've never earned enough to build up any savings and my landlord chose that moment to hoick my rent up. I sent my CV out everywhere and got a few interviews, but every one I attended was a washout. It was as if they could sense the cloud of failure that hung around me like a bad smell.'

'And that's when Poppy sent you to me.'

Wrinkling her nose, she gave him a rueful smile. 'I told her a bit about what had happened before she went off to shoot her latest project and she must have thought the two of us could help each other out because she emailed me to suggest I try you for a job. She made it sound as if you were desperate for help and it seemed like fate that I should work for you.'

'Desperate, huh?' He leant back in his seat and raised an eyebrow, feeling amusement tug at his mouth. That was textbook Poppy. 'Well, I have to admit it's been good for me, having you around. It's certainly kept me on my toes.'

'Yeah, there's never a dull moment when I'm around, huh?'

The air seemed to grow thick between them as their eyes met and he watched in arrested fascination as her cheeks flamed with colour.

Sliding her gaze away, she stared down at the table, clutching her glass, her chewed nails in plain view. He'd known it the whole time, of course, that she was fighting against some inner trauma, as her nerve and buoyancy deteriorated in the face of his brittle moods. Her increasingly ragged nails had been the indicator he'd been determined to ignore.

But not any more.

A string quartet suddenly started up on the terrace behind them and he winced as the sound assaulted his ears. He'd never liked the sound of violins and an instrument such as that should never be used to play soft rock covers. It was a crime against humanity.

'Come on, let's take a walk around the grounds and clear our heads,' he said, standing up and holding out his hand to help her up from the chair.

She looked at it with that little frown that always made something twist in his chest, before giving a firm nod and putting her hand in his.

CHAPTER SEVEN

A WALK WAS exactly what Cara needed to clear her head.

She couldn't quite believe she'd just spilled her guts to Max like that, but it was a massive relief to have it all out in the open, even if she did still feel shaky with the effort of holding herself together.

Of course, seeing the concern on his handsome face had only made her ridiculous crush on him deepen, and she was beginning to worry about how she was going to cope with seeing him every day, knowing that they'd never be anything more than colleagues or, at the very most, friends.

A twinkling light in the distance danced in her peripheral vision and she stopped and turned to see what it was, feeling her heels sink into the soft earth beneath her feet. Pulling her shoes off, she hooked her fingers into the straps before running to catch up with Max, who was now a few paces ahead of her, seemingly caught up in his own world, his head dipped as a frown played across his brow.

'Hey, do you fancy walking to that lake over there?' she asked him.

'Hmm?' His eyes looked unfocused, as if his thoughts were miles away. 'Yes, okay.'

The sudden detachment worried her. 'Is everything okay?' Perhaps, now he'd had more time to reflect on what she'd told him, he was starting to regret getting involved in her messed up life.

She took a breath. 'Do you want to head back to London? I wouldn't blame you if you did.'

Turning to look her in the eye again, he blinked, as though casting away whatever was bothering him. 'No, no. I'm fine.' His gaze flicked towards the lake, then back to her again and he gave her a tense smile. 'Yeah, let's walk that way.'

It only took them a couple of minutes to get there, now that she was in bare feet, and they stopped at the lakeshore and looked out across the water to the dark, impenetrable-looking forest on the other side.

'It's a beautiful setting they've chosen,' Cara said, to fill the heavy silence that had fallen between them.

'Yes, it's lovely.' Max bent down and picked up a smooth flat stone, running his fingertips across its surface. 'This looks like a good skimmer.' He shrugged off his jacket and rolled up the sleeves of his shirt, revealing his muscular forearms.

Cara stared at them, her mouth drying at the sight. There was something so real, so virile about the image of his tanned skin, with its smattering of dark hair, in stark contrast to the crisp white cotton of his formal shirt. As if he was revealing the *man* inside the businessman.

Supressing a powerful desire to reach out and trace

her fingers across the dips and swells of his muscles, she took a step away to give him plenty of room as he drew his elbow back and bent low, then flung the stone hard across the water.

A deep, satisfied chuckle rumbled from his chest as the stone bounced three times across the still surface, spinning out rings of gentle ripples in its wake, before sinking without a trace into the middle of the lake.

He turned to face her with a grin, his eyes alive with glee, and she couldn't help but smile back.

'Impressive.'

He blew on his fingers and pretended to polish them on his shirt. 'I'm a natural. What can I say?'

Seeing his delight at the achievement, she had a strong desire to get in on the fun. Perhaps it would help distract her from thinking about how alone they were out here on the edge of the lake. 'Does your natural talent stretch to teaching me how to do that?'

'You've never skimmed a stone?' He looked so over-the-top incredulous she couldn't help but laugh.

'Never.'

'Didn't you say your parents live in Cornwall? Surely there's plenty of opportunities to be near water there.'

She snorted and took a step backwards, staring down at the muddy grass at their feet. 'Yeah, if you live near the coast, which they don't. I never learnt to drive when I was living there and my parents didn't take me to the beach that much when I was young. My dad's always suffered with a bad back from the heavy lifting he has to do at work, so he never got involved in anything of a physical nature. And my mum's a real homebody. She's suffered with agoraphobia for years.'

She heard him let out a low exhalation of breath and glanced up to find an expression of real sympathy in his eyes. 'I'm sorry to hear that. That must have been hard for you as a kid,' he said softly.

Shrugging one shoulder, she gave a nod to acknowledge his concern, remembering the feeling of being trapped inside four small walls when she was living at home, with nowhere to escape to. Going to school every day had actually been a welcome escape from it and as soon as she'd finished her studies she'd high-tailed it to London.

'Yeah, it was a bit. My parents are good people, though. They threw all their energy into raising me. And they made sure to let me know how loved I was.' Which was the absolute truth, she realised with a sting of shame, because she'd distanced herself from them since leaving home in an attempt to leave her stultifying life there behind her. But she'd left them behind, too. They didn't deserve that. A visit was well overdue and she made a pact with herself to call them and arrange a date to see them as soon as she got back to London.

Max nodded, seemingly satisfied that she didn't need any more consoling, and broke eye contact to lean down and pick up another flat pebble.

She watched him weigh it in his palm, as if checking it was worth the effort of throwing it. Everything he did was measured and thorough like that, which was probably why he was such a successful businessman.

'Here, this looks like a good one. It's nice and flat

with a decent weight to it so it'll fly and not sink immediately.' He turned it over in his hand. 'You need to get it to ride the air for a while before it comes down and maintain enough lift to jump.'

He held it out to her and she took it and looked at it with a frown. 'Is there a proper way to hold it?'

'I find the best way is to pinch it between my first finger and thumb. Like this.' He picked up another stone and demonstrated.

She copied the positioning in her own hand then gave him a confident nod, drew back her arm and threw it as hard as she could.

It landed in the lake with a *plop* and sank immediately.

'Darn it! What did I do wrong?' she asked, annoyed with herself for failing so badly.

'Don't worry; it can take a bit of practice to get your technique right. You need to get lower to the ground and swing your arm in a horizontal arc. When it feels like the stone could fly straight forward and parallel with the water, loosen the grip with your thumb and let it roll, snapping your finger forwards hard.'

'Huh. You make it sound so easy.'

He grinned and raised his eyebrows. 'Try again.'

Picking up a good-looking candidate, she positioned the stone between her finger and thumb and was just about to throw it when Max said, 'Stop!'

Glancing round at him with a grimace of frustration, she saw he was frowning and shaking his head.

'You need to swing your arm at a lower angle. Like this.'

Before she could react, he'd moved to stand directly behind her, putting his left hand on her hip and wrapping his right hand around the hand she was holding the stone in. Her heart nearly leapt out of her chest at the firmness of his touch and started hammering away, forcing the blood through her body at a much higher rate than was reasonable for such low-level exercise.

As he drew their arms backwards the movement made her shoulder press against the hard wall of his chest and she was mightily glad that he couldn't see her face at that precise moment. She was pretty sure it must look a real picture.

'Okay, on three we'll throw it together.' His mouth was so close to her ear she felt his breath tickle the downy little hairs on the outer whorl.

'One…two…three!'

They moved their linked hands in a sweeping arc, Cara feeling the power of Max's body push against her as the momentum of the move forced them forwards. She was so distracted by being engulfed in his arms she nearly didn't see the stone bounce a couple of times before it sank beneath the water.

'Woo-hoo!' Max shouted, releasing her to take a step back and raise his hand, waiting for her to give him a high five.

The sudden loss of his touch left her feeling strangely light and disorientated—but now was not the time to go to pieces. Mentally pulling herself together, she swung her hand up to meet his, their palms slapping loudly as they connected, then bent down straight away, pretending to search the ground for another missile.

'Who taught you to skim stones? A brother?' she asked casually, grimacing at the quaver in her voice, before grabbing another good-looking pebble and righting herself.

He'd stooped to pick up his own stone and glanced round at her as he straightened up. 'No. I'm an only child. I think once my mother realised how much hard work it was raising me she was determined not to have any more kids.' He raised a disparaging eyebrow then turned away to fling the stone across the lake, managing five bounces this time. He nodded with satisfaction. 'I used to mountain bike over to a nearby reservoir with a friend from boarding school at the weekends and we'd have competitions to see who could get their stone the furthest,' he said, already searching the ground for another likely skimmer, his movements surprisingly lithe considering the size of his powerful body.

A sudden need to get this right overwhelmed her.

She wasn't usually a superstitious person, but she imagined she could sense the power in this one simple challenge. If she got this stone to bounce by herself, maybe, just maybe, everything would be okay.

She was throwing this for her pride and the return of her strength. To prove to Max—but mostly to herself—that she was resilient and capable and—dare she even suggest it?—brave enough to try something new, even if there was a good chance she'd fail spectacularly and end up looking foolish again.

Harnessing the power of positive thought, she drew back her hand, took a second to centre herself, then flung the stone hard across the water, snapping her finger like he'd taught her and holding her breath as she watched it sail through the air.

It dropped low about fifteen feet out and for a second she thought she'd messed it up, but her spirits soared as she saw it bounce twice before disappearing.

Spinning round to make a celebratory face at Max, she was gratified to see him nod in exaggerated approval, a smile playing about his lips.

'Good job! You're a quick study; but then we already knew that about you.'

The compliment made her insides flare with warmth and she let out a laugh of delight, elation twisting through her as she saw him grin back.

Their gazes snagged and held, his pupils dilating till his eyes looked nearly black in the bright afternoon light.

A wave of electric heat spread through her at the sight of it, but the laughter died in her throat as he turned abruptly away and stared off towards the house instead, folding his arms so tightly against his chest she could make out the shape of his muscles under his shirt.

He cleared his throat. 'You know, this place is just like the venue where Jemima and I got married,' he said, so casually she wondered how much emotion he'd had to rein in, in order to say it.

Ugh. What a selfish dolt she was. Here she'd been worrying about what he thought of her and her tales of woe, when he was doing battle with his own demons.

It had occurred to her earlier that morning, as she'd struggled to do up her dress, that attending a wedding could be problematic for him, but she'd forgotten all about it after the incident in the kitchen, her thoughts distracted by the unnerving tension that had crackled between them ever since.

Or what she'd thought was tension.

Perhaps it had been apprehension on his part.

And then, when he'd mentioned how transient and lonely his youth had been over drinks earlier, it had brought it home to her why Jemima's death had hit him so hard. It sounded as if she'd been the person anchoring his life after years of feeling adrift and insecure. And this place reminded him of everything he'd lost.

No wonder he seemed so unsettled.

He'd still come here to help her out, though, despite his discomfort at being at this kind of event, which was a decent and kind thing for him to do and way beyond the call of duty as her boss. Her heart did a slow flip in her chest as she realised exactly what it must have cost him to agree to come.

'I'm sorry for dragging you here today. I didn't think about how hard it would be for you. After losing Jemima.'

He put his hand on her arm and waited for her to look at him before speaking. 'You have nothing to apologise for. *Nothing*. I wanted to come here to support you because you've done nothing but support me for the last few weeks. It's my turn to look after you today.' He was looking directly at her now and the fierce intensity in his eyes made a delicious shiver zip down her spine.

'Honestly, I thought it would be awful coming here,' he said, casting his gaze back towards the house again, 'but it's not been the trial I thought it'd be. In fact—'

he ran a hand over his hair and let out a low breath '—it's been good for me to confront a situation like this. I've been missing out on so much life since Jem died and it's time I pulled my head out of the sand and faced the world again.'

Cara swallowed hard, ensnared in the emotion of the moment, her heart thudding against her chest and her breath rasping in her dry throat. Looking at Max now, she realised that the ever-present frown was nowhere to be seen for once. Instead, there was light in his eyes and something else...

They stood, frozen in the moment, as the gentle spring wind wrapped around them and the birds sang enthusiastically above their heads.

It would be so easy to push up onto tiptoe and slide her hands around his neck. To press her lips against his and feel the heat and masculine strength of him, to slide her tongue into his mouth and taste him. She ached to feel his breath against her skin and his hands in her hair, her whole body tingling with the sensory expectation of it.

She wanted to be the one to remind him what living could be like, if only he'd let her.

To her disappointment, Max broke eye contact with her and nodded towards the marquee behind them. 'We should probably get back before they send out a search party. We don't want to find ourselves in trouble for messing with Amber's schedule of events and being frogmarched to our seats,' he said lightly, though his voice sounded gruffer than normal.

Had he seen it in her face? The longing. She hoped

not. The thought of her infatuation putting their fragile relationship under any more strain made her insides squirm.

Anyway, that tension-filled moment had probably been him thinking about Jemima again.

Not her.

They walked in silence back to the marquee, the bright sun pleasantly warm on the back of her neck and bare shoulders, but her insides icy cold.

Despite their little detour, they weren't the last to sit down. It was with a sigh of relief that Cara slumped into her seat and reached for the bottle of white wine on the table, more than ready to blot out the ache of disappointment that had been present ever since he'd suggested they give up their truancy from the festivities and head back into the fray.

It wasn't that she didn't want to be here exactly; it was just that it had been so much fun hanging out with him. Just the two of them together, like friends. Or something.

Knocking back half a glass of wine in one go, she refilled it before offering the bottle to Max.

He was looking at her with bemusement, one eyebrow raised. 'Thirsty?'

Heat flared across her cheeks. 'Just getting in the party mood,' she said, forcing a nonchalant smile. 'It looks like we have some catching up to do.'

The raucous chatter and laughter in the room suggested that people were already pretty tiddly on the cocktails they'd been served.

'Okay, well, I'm going to stick to water if I have to

drive to the bed and breakfast place later. I think one of us should stay sober enough to find our way there at the end of the night. I don't fancy kipping in the car.'

She gave him an awkward grin as the thought of sleeping in such close proximity to him made more heat rush to her face.

Picking up her glass, she took another long sip of wine to cover her distress.

Oh, good grief. It was going to be a long night.

The meal was surprisingly tasty, considering how many people were being catered for, and Cara began to relax as the wine did its work. She quickly found herself in a conversation with the lady to her right, who turned out to be Amber's second cousin and an estate agent in Angel, about the dearth of affordable housing to rent in London. By the end of dessert, the woman had promised to give Cara first dibs on a lovely-sounding one-bedroom flat that was just about to come onto her books. And that proved to Cara, without a shadow of a doubt, that you just had to be in the right place at the right time to get lucky.

Turning to say this exact thing to Max, she was disturbed to find he'd finished his conversation with the man next to him and was frowning down at the tablecloth.

'Sorry for ignoring you,' she said, worried he was getting sucked down into dark thoughts again with all the celebrating going on around him.

He gave her a tense smile and pushed his chair away from the table. 'You weren't. I overheard your conversation about finding a flat; that's great news—you should definitely get her number and follow that up,' he said, standing and tapping the back of his chair. 'I'm going to find the bathrooms. I'll be back in a minute.'

She watched him stride away with a lump in her throat. Was he upset about the prospect of her moving out? She dismissed the notion immediately. No, he couldn't be. He must be craving his space again by now. Even though she'd loved living there, she knew it was time to move out. Especially now that her feelings for him had twisted themselves into something new. Something dangerous.

'That's a good one you've got there—very sexy,' Amber's second cousin muttered into her ear, pulling back to waggle her eyebrows suggestively, only making the lump in Cara's throat grow in size.

Unable to speak, she gave the woman what she hoped looked like a gracious smile.

'Hi, Cara.'

The voice behind her made her jump in her seat and she swivelled round, only to find herself staring into the eyes of the woman she'd been trying to avoid since spotting her in the church earlier.

Her meal rolled uncomfortably in her stomach.

'Hi, Lucy.'

Instead of the look of cool disdain Cara was expecting, she was surprised to see Lucy bite her lip, her expression wary.

'How are you?' Lucy asked falteringly, as if afraid to hear the answer.

'Fine, thank you.' Cara kept her voice deliberately

neutral, just in case this was an opening gambit to get her to admit to something she really didn't want to say.

'Can I talk to you for a moment?'

Cara swallowed her anxiety and gestured towards the chair Max had vacated, wondering what on earth this woman could have to say to her. Whatever it was, it was better to get it over with now so she didn't spend the rest of the night looking over her shoulder. Straightening her back, she steeled herself to deal with anything she could throw at her.

Lucy sat on the edge of the seat, as close as she could get to Cara without touching her, and laid her hands on her lap before taking a deep breath. 'I wanted to come over and apologise as soon as I could so there wasn't any kind of atmosphere between us today.'

Cara stared at her. 'I'm sorry? Did you say *apologise*?'

Lucy crossed her legs, then uncrossed them again, her cheeks flooding with colour. 'Yes… I'm really sorry about the way you were treated at LED. I feel awful about it. I let Michelle bully me into taking her side—because I knew she'd turn on me, too, if I stood up for you—and I was pathetic enough to let her. I want you to know that I didn't do any of those awful things to you, but I didn't stop it either.' She shook her head and let out a low sigh. 'I feel awful about it, Cara, truly.'

At that moment Cara felt a pair of hands land lightly on her shoulders. Twisting her head round, she saw that Max had returned and was standing over her like some kind of dark guardian angel.

'Everything okay, Cara?' From the cool tone in his

voice she suspected he'd be more than willing to step in and eject Lucy from her seat if she asked him to.

'Fine, thanks, Max. This is Lucy. She came over to apologise for her *unfriendliness* at the last place I worked.'

'Is that so?'

Cara couldn't see the expression on his face from that angle but, from the sound of his voice and the way Lucy seemed to shrink back in her chair, she guessed it wasn't a very friendly one.

Lucy cleared her throat awkwardly. 'Yes, I feel dreadful about the whole thing. It was horrible working there. In fact, I left the week after you did. I couldn't stand the smug look on Michelle's face any more. Although—' she leaned forward in a conspiratorial manner '—I heard from one of the other girls that she only lasted a month before he got rid of her. She couldn't hack it, apparently.' She snorted. 'That's karma in action, right there.' Clearly feeling she'd said her piece, Lucy stood up so that Max could have his chair back and took a small step away from them. 'Anyway, I'd better get back to my table; apparently there's coffee on the way and I'm desperate for some. Those cocktails were evil, weren't they?'

'Why are you here today?' Cara asked before she could turn and leave, intrigued by the coincidence.

'I'm Jack's—the groom's—new PA.'

Cara couldn't help but laugh at life's weird little twist. 'Really?'

'Yeah, he's a great boss, really lovely to work for.' She leant forward again and said in a quiet voice, 'I don't think Amber likes me very much, though; she didn't seem very pleased to see me here.'

'I wouldn't take that too personally,' Cara said, giving her a reassuring smile. 'She's an intensely protective person.' She put a hand on Lucy's arm. 'Thanks for being brave enough to come over and apologise, Lucy; I really appreciate the gesture.'

Lucy gave her one last smile, and Max a slightly terrified grimace, before retreating to her table.

Max sat back down in his chair, giving her an impressed nod. 'Nicely handled.'

Warm pleasure coursed through her as she took in the look of approval in his eyes. Feeling a little flustered by it, she picked up her glass of wine to take a big gulp, but judged the tilt badly and some escaped from the side of the rim and dribbled down her chin. Before she had time to react, Max whipped his napkin under her jaw and caught the rogue droplets with it, stopping them from splashing onto her dress.

'Smooth!' she said, laughing in surprise.

'I have moves,' he replied, his eyes twinkling and his mouth twitching into a warm smile.

A wave of heat engulfed her and her stomach did a full-on somersault.

Oh, no, what was *happening* to her?

Heart racing, she finally allowed the truth to filter through to her consciousness.

It was, of course, the very last thing she needed to happen.

She was falling in love with him.

CHAPTER EIGHT

AFTER THE MEAL and speeches, all the guests were encouraged to go through to the house, where a bar had been set up under the sweeping staircase in the hall and a DJ in the ballroom was playing ambient tunes in the hope of drawing the guests in there to sit around the tables that surrounded the dance floor.

Waiting at the bar to grab them both a caffeinated soft drink to give them some energy for the rest of the evening's events, Max allowed his thoughts to jump back over the day.

He'd had fun at the lake with Cara, which had taken him by surprise, because the last thing he'd expected when he'd got up that morning was that he would enjoy himself today.

But Cara had a way of finding the joy in things.

In fact, he'd been so caught up in the pleasure of showing her how to skim stones, he hadn't thought about what he was doing until his hand was on the soft curve of her hip and his body was pressed up close to hers, the familiar floral scent of her perfume in his nose and the heat of her warming his skin. He'd hidden his instinctive response to it well enough, he thought, using the excessive rush of adrenaline to hurl more stones across the water.

And then she'd been so delighted when she'd managed to skim that stone by herself he'd felt a mad urge to wrap his arms around her again in celebration and experience the moment with her.

But that time he'd managed to rein himself in, randomly talking about his own wedding to break the tension, only to feel a different kind of self-reproach when Cara assumed his indiscriminate jump to the subject was down to him feeling gloomy about his situation.

Which it really hadn't been.

Returning with the drinks to where he'd left Cara standing just inside the ballroom, he handed one to her and smiled when she received it with a grimace of relieved thanks. The main lights in the room were set low and a large glitter ball revolved slowly from the ceiling, scattering the floor and walls with shards of silver light. Max watched them dance over Cara's face in fascination, thinking that she looked like some kind of ethereal seraph, with her bright eyes and pale creamy skin against the glowing silver of her dress.

A strange elation twisted through him, triggering a lifting sensation throughout his whole body—as if all the things that had dragged him down in the past eighteen months were losing their weight and slowly drifting upwards. The sadness he'd expected to keep on hitting him throughout the day was still notably absent, and instead there was a weird sense of rightness about being here.

With her.

Catching her giving him a quizzical look, he was just about to ask if she wanted to take another walk outside so they could hear each other speak when Jack and Amber walked past them and onto the empty dance floor. Noticing their presence, the DJ cued up a new track as a surge of guests crowded into the room, evidently following the happy couple in to watch their first dance as husband and wife.

Max found himself jostled closer to Cara as the edges of the dance floor filled up and he instinctively put an arm around her to stop her from being shoved around, too. She turned to look at him, the expression in her eyes startled at first, but then sparking with understanding when he nodded towards a gap in the crowd a little along from them.

He guided them towards it, feeling her hips sway against his as they moved, and had to will his attention-starved body not to respond.

Once in the space, he let her go, relaxing his arm to his side, and could have sworn he saw her shoulders drop a little as if she'd been holding herself rigid.

Feeling a little disconcerted by her obvious discomfort at him touching her again, he watched the happy couple blindly as they twirled around the dance floor, going through the motions of the ballroom dance they'd plainly been practising for the past few months.

Had he overstepped the mark by manhandling her like that? He'd not meant to make her uncomfortable but they were supposed to be there as a couple, so it wasn't as though it wasn't within his remit to act that way around her.

Ugh. There was no point in beating himself up about it. He'd just have to be more careful about the way he touched her, or not, for the rest of the evening.

As soon as the dance finished, other couples joined the newlyweds on the dance floor and, spotting Cara, Jack broke away from Amber and made his way over to them.

'Cara, I'm so glad you made it!' he said, stooping down to pull her into a bear hug, making her squeal with laughter as he spun her around before placing her back down again.

Cara pulled away from him, her cheeks flushed, and rubbed his arm affectionately. 'Congratulations. And thank you for inviting us. It's a beautiful wedding.'

'I'm glad you're having a good time,' Jack replied, smiling into her eyes. 'Want to dance with me, for old times' sake?' he said, already taking her arm and leading her away from Max onto the dance floor. 'You don't mind if I steal her away for a minute, do you, Max?' he tossed over his shoulder, plainly not at all interested in Max's real opinion on the matter.

Not that Max *should* mind.

Watching Cara laugh at something that Jack whispered into her ear as he began to move her around the dance floor, Max was hit by an unreasonable surge of irritation and had to force himself to relax his arms and let them hang by his sides instead of balling them into tight fists. What the heck was going on with him today? How messed up was he to be jealous of a new groom, who was clearly infatuated with his wife, just because he was dancing with Cara? It must be because the guy seemed to have everything—a wife who loved him, a successful career with colleagues who respected him, Cara as a friend…

The track came to a close and a new, slower one started up. Before he could check himself, Max strode across to where Jack and Cara were just breaking apart.

'You don't mind if I cut in now, do you?' he said to Jack, intensely conscious that his words had come out as more of a statement than a question.

Jack's eyebrows rose infinitesimally at Max's less than gracious tone, but he smiled at Cara and swept a hand to encompass them both. 'Be my guest.' Leaning forward, he kissed Cara on the cheek before moving away from her. 'It's great to see you so happy. You know, you're actually glowing.' He slapped Max on the back. 'You're obviously good for her, Max. Look after her, okay? She's a good one,' he said. 'But watch your feet; she's a bit of a toe-stamper,' he added, ducking out of the way as Cara swiped a hand at him and walked off laughing.

Turning back, Cara fixed Max with an awkward smile, then leaned in to speak into his ear. 'Sorry about that. I didn't want to admit to the truth about us and break the mood.'

Max nodded, his shoulders suddenly stiff, surprised to find he was disappointed to hear her say that her glow was nothing to do with him.

Don't be ridiculous, you fool—how could it be?

His feelings must have shown on his face because she

took a small step away from him and said, 'You don't really need to dance with me, but thanks for the gesture.'

He shrugged. 'It's no problem. You seemed to be enjoying yourself and I was anticipating Jack being commandeered at any second by Amber or another relative wanting his attention so I thought I'd jump in,' he replied, feeling the hairs that had escaped from her up-do tickle his nose as he leaned in close to her.

She looked at him for the longest moment, something flickering behind her eyes, before giving him a small nod and a smile. 'Okay then, I'd love to dance.'

Holding her as loosely as he could in his arms, he guided her around the dance floor, leading her in a basic waltz and finding pleasure in the way she responded to his lead, copying his movements with a real sense that she trusted him not to make a false step. His blood roared through his veins as his heart worked overtime to keep him cool in the accumulated heat of the bodies that surrounded them. Or was it the feeling of her in his arms that was doing that to him?

He felt her back shift against his palm and turned to see she was waving to Lucy, the woman who had come over to apologise to her at dinner.

A sense of admiration swept thorough him as he reflected on how well she'd handled that situation. When he'd returned to the table, after needing to take a breath of air and talk himself down from a strange feeling of despondency when he heard she was likely to find a new place to live soon, and seen them talking, he'd feared the worst. An intense urge to step in and protect her had grabbed him by the throat, making him move fast and put his hands on her, to let her know he had her back if she needed him.

She hadn't, though. In fact she'd shown real strength and finesse with her response. Another example of why she was so good at her job. And why he respected her so much as a person. Why he liked her—

Halting his thoughts right there, he guided her over to the side of the dance floor as the music changed into retro pop and drew away from her, feeling oddly bereft at the loss of her warm body so close to his own.

The room was spinning.

And it wasn't from the alcohol she'd consumed earlier or even the overwhelming heat and noise—it was because of Max. Being so close to him, feeling the strength of his will as he whirled her around the dance floor had sent her senses into a nosedive.

'Max, do you mind if we go outside for a minute? I need some air.'

The look her gave her was one of pure alarm. 'Are you all right?'

'I'm fine, just a bit hot,' she said, flapping a hand ineffectually in front of her face.

Giving her a curt nod, he motioned for her to walk out of the ballroom in front of him, shadowing her closely as she pushed her way through the crowd of people in the hallway and out into the blissfully cool evening air.

Slumping down onto a cold stone bench pushed up against the front of the house, she let out a deep sigh of relief as the fresh air pricked at her hot skin.

'I'm going to fetch you a drink of water,' Max said, standing over her, his face a picture of concern. 'Stay here.'

She watched him go, her stomach sinking with embarrassment, wondering how she was ever going to explain herself if she didn't manage to pull it together.

Putting her head in her hands, she breathed in the echo of Max's scent on her skin, its musky undertones making her heart trip over itself.

'Are you okay there?'

The deep voice made her start and she looked up to see one of the male guests looking down at her, his brow creased in worry. She seemed to remember Amber's second cousin pointing him out as Amber's youngest brother and the black sheep of the family. *Womaniser* was the word she'd used.

Sitting up straighter in her seat, she gave him a friendly but dispassionate smile. 'I'm fine, thanks, just a bit hot from dancing.'

Instead of nodding and walking away, he sat down next to her and held out his hand. 'I'm Frank, Amber's black sheep of a brother,' he said with a twinkle in his eye.

She couldn't help but laugh as she shook his hand. 'I'm Cara.'

'I don't know whether anyone's told you this today, Cara, but you look beautiful in that dress,' he said, his voice smooth like melted chocolate. He wanted her. She could see it in his face.

Cara was just about to open her mouth to politely brush him off when a shadow fell across them. Looking up, she saw that Max had returned with her glass of water and was standing over them with a strange look on his face.

'Here's your drink, Cara,' he said, handing it over and giving Frank a curt nod.

Frank must have seen something in Max's expression because he got up quickly and took a step away from them both. 'Okay, well, it looks like your boyfriend's got this, so I'll say good evening. Have a good one, Cara,' he said, flashing her a disappointed smile as he backed away, then turning on his heel to disappear into the dark garden.

'Sorry,' Max said gruffly, 'I didn't mean to scare him off.' He didn't look particularly sorry, though, she noted as he sat down next to her and laid his arm across the back of the bench. In fact, if anything, he seemed pleased that the guy had gone. Turning to look him directly in the eye, her stomach gave a flutter of nerves as something flickered in his eyes. Something fierce and disconcerting.

Telling herself she must be seeing things, she forced a composed smile onto her face. 'It's okay; he wasn't my type anyway.'

Not like you.

Pushing the rogue thought away, she took a long sip of the water he'd fetched to cover her nerves. What was she doing, letting herself imagine there was something developing between them?

'Thanks for the water. I didn't mean to worry you. I'm feeling better now I'm in the fresh air.'

Despite her claims, he was still looking at her with that strange expression in his eyes.

'Why are you single?' he asked suddenly, making her blink at him in surprise.

'Oh, you know…'

He frowned. 'It's not because I've been working you too hard, is it?'

'No, no!' She shook her head. 'It's through personal choice.'

His frown deepened, as if he didn't quite believe her.

She swallowed before expanding on her answer, linking her fingers tightly together around the glass. 'I decided to take a break from dating for a while. My last relationship was a bit of a disaster.'

He relaxed back against the bench. 'How so?'

'The whole fiasco at LED pretty much ruined it. After I started having trouble coping with what was going on at work I got a bit down and it made me withdraw into myself. My ex-boyfriend, Ewan, got fed up with me being so…er…*unresponsive*.' She cringed. 'That's why I've been trying so hard to stay positive. I know how it can get boring, having people around who feel sorry for themselves all the time.'

He ran his hand through his hair, letting out a long, low sigh.

Heat rushed through her as she realised how Max might have interpreted what she'd just said. 'I didn't mean… I wasn't talking about you.'

He snorted gently and flashed her a smile. 'I didn't think you were. I was frustrated on your behalf. I can't believe the guy was stupid enough to treat you like that.'

'Yeah, well, it's in the past now. To be honest, that relationship was always doomed to fail. He was a little too self-centred for my liking. He made it pretty obvious he thought I wasn't good enough for him.'

'Not good enough! That's the most ridiculous thing I ever heard,' he snapped out, the ferocity in his tone telling her he had a lot more he wanted to say on the matter, but for the sake of propriety was keeping it to himself.

She smiled at him, her heart rising to her throat. 'It's okay. It doesn't bother me any more.' And it really didn't, she realised with a sense of satisfaction. Her experiences since breaking up with Ewan had taught her that her real self-worth came from her own actions and achievements, not pleasing someone else.

Putting the empty glass onto the ground by the bench, she tried to hide a yawn of tiredness behind her hand. It had been a long and intense day.

'Do you want to get out of here?' Max asked quietly.

Clearly she hadn't been able to hide her exhaustion from him.

Looking at him with a smile of gratitude, she nodded her head. 'I wouldn't mind. I don't think I've got the energy for any more dancing.'

He stood up. 'Okay, I'll go and fetch the car.'

'I'll just pop back in and say goodbye to Jack and Amber and I'll meet you back here,' she said, gesturing to the pull-in place at the end of the sweeping driveway.

He nodded, before turning on his heel and heading off towards where they'd left the car parked by the estate's church.

She watched him disappear into the darkness, with his

jacket slung over his arm and the white shirt stretched across his broad shoulders glowing in the moonlight, before he dipped out of sight.

After saying a hurried goodbye to the now rather inebriated newlyweds, she came out to find Max waiting for her in the car and jumped in gratefully, sinking back into the soft leather seat with a sigh. Now she knew that bed wasn't far away, she was desperate to escape to her room and finally be able to relax away from Max's unsettling presence.

It only took them five minutes to drive to the B&B she'd booked them into and as luck would have it there was a convenient parking space right outside the pretty thatched cottage.

'We're in the annexe at the back,' she said to Max as he hauled their overnight bags out of the boot. 'They gave me a key code to open the door so we won't need to disturb them.'

'Great,' Max said, hoisting the bags onto his back and following her down the path of the colourful country cottage garden towards the rear of the house. The air smelled sweetly of the honeysuckle that wound itself around a large wooden arch leading through to the back garden where their accommodation was housed, and Cara breathed it in with a great sense of pleasure. The place felt almost magical, shrouded as it was in the velvety darkness of the night.

Cara tapped the code into the keypad next to the small oak door that led directly into the annexe and flipped on the lights as soon as they were inside, illuminating a beautifully presented hallway with its simple country-style furniture and heritage-coloured décor. Two open bedroom doors stood opposite each other and there was a small bathroom at the back, which they would share.

'I hope this is okay. All the local hotels were fully booked and Jack said this was the place his cousin and her family were going to stay in, so the owners were pleased to swap the booking to us, considering it was such a last-minute cancellation.'

Max nodded, looking around at the layout, his expression neutral. 'It's great.'

The hallway was so small they were standing much closer to each other than Cara was entirely comfortable with. Max moved past her to drop his bag into one of the rooms and his musky scent hit her senses, making her whole body quiver with longing. The thought of him being just a few feet away from her was going to make it very difficult to sleep, despite how tired she was.

After dropping her bag into the other room, Max walked back into the hallway and stood in front of her, a small frown playing across his face. 'Are you feeling okay now?'

She smiled, the effort making her cheeks ache. 'I'm fine.' She took a nervous step backwards, and jumped a little as her back hit the wall behind her. 'Thank you so much for coming with me. I really appreciate it.'

He was looking at her with that fierce expression in his eyes again and a heavy, tingly heat slid from her throat, deep into her belly, sending electric currents of need to every nerve-ending in her body. For some reason she was finding it hard to breathe.

'It was my pleasure, Cara,' he said, his voice gruff as if he was having trouble with his own airways. 'You know, that guy you were talking to earlier was right. You do look beautiful in that dress.'

She stared at him, a disorientating mixture of excitement and confusion swirling around her head.

His gaze flicked away from hers for a second and when his eyes returned to hers the fierce look had gone and was replaced with a friendly twinkle. 'It occurred to me that you might have a bit of trouble getting out it—after needing my help to do it up this morning. Want me to undo the buttons for you?'

What was this?

Cara knew what she wanted it to be: for Max to want the same thing that she did—to alleviate this unbearable need to touch and kiss and hold him. To slide off all their clothes and lose themselves in each other's body.

To love him.

Did he want that, too?

Could he?

Her heart was beating so hard and fast, all she could hear and feel was the hot pulse of her blood through her body.

'That would be great. Thank you,' she managed to force past her dry throat.

She rotated on the spot until her back was to him, her whole body vibrating with tension as she felt his fingers graze her skin as he released each of the buttons in turn.

As soon as the last one popped free, she trapped the now loose dress against her body and turned to face him again, trying to summon an expression that wouldn't give her feelings away.

He looked at her for the longest time, his eyes wide and dark and his breathing shallow.

She watched him flick his tongue between his lips and something snapped inside her. Unable to stand the tension any longer, she rocked forward on her toes and tipped her head up, pressing her mouth to his. His lips were firm under hers and his scent enveloped her, wrapping round her senses, only adding to her violent pull of need to deepen the kiss.

Until she realised he wasn't kissing her back.

He hadn't moved away from her, but she could feel how tense he was under her touch. As if he was holding himself rigid.

She stilled, one hand anchoring herself against his broad shoulder, the other still holding her dress tightly against her body, and pulled away, eyes screwed shut, her stomach plummeting to her shoes at his lack of response.

What had she *done*?

When she dared open her eyes, he was looking at her with such an expression of torment that she had to close them again.

'I'm sorry. So, so sorry,' she whispered, her throat locking up and her face burning with mortification.

'Cara—' He sounded troubled. Aggrieved. Exasperated.

Stumbling away from him, her back hit the wall again and she felt her way blindly into her bedroom and slammed the door shut, leaning back on it as if it would keep out the horror of the past few seconds.

Which, of course, it wouldn't.

What must he think of her? All he'd done was offer to help her with her dress and she'd thrown herself at him. What had possessed her to do that when she knew he wasn't over losing his wife? How could she have thought he wanted anything more to develop between them?

She was a fool.

And she couldn't even blame it on alcohol because she'd been drinking soft drinks for the past couple of hours.

She jumped in fright as she felt Max knock on the door, the vibration of it echoing through her tightly strung body. She knew she had to face him. To apologise and try to find some way to make things right again.

Struggling to get her breathing under control, she stepped away from the door and opened it, forcing herself to look up into Max's face with as much cool confidence as she could muster.

Before he could say anything, she held up a hand. 'I really am sorry… I don't know what happened. It won't ever happen ag—'

But, before she could finish the sentence, he took a step towards her, the expression in his eyes wild and intense as he slid his hand into her hair, drawing her forward and pressing his lips against hers.

They stumbled into the room, off balance, as their mouths crashed together. Electric heat exploded deep within her and she heard him groan with pleasure when she pressed her body hard into his. She could feel the urgency in him as he pushed her back against the wall, his hard body trapping her there as he fervently explored her mouth with his own, his tongue sliding firmly against hers. Taking a step back, he pulled his shirt over his head in one swift movement and dropped it onto the floor next to them.

'Are you sure you want this, Cara?' he asked, his voice guttural and low as she feverishly ran her hands over the dips and swells of his chest in dazed wonder.

'Yes.'

She smiled as he exhaled in relief and brought his mouth back down to hers, sliding his hands down to her thighs so he could pick her up and carry her over to the bed.

Then there was no more talking, just the feel of his solid body pressed hard against hers and the slide and twist of his muscles under his soft skin and—sensation—a riot of sensation that she sunk into and lost herself in. Her body had craved this for so long it was a sweet, beautiful relief to finally have what she wanted.

What she needed.

In those moments there was no past and no future; they were purely living for the moment.

And it was absolutely perfect.

CHAPTER NINE

MAX AWOKE FROM such a deep sleep it took him a while to realise that he wasn't in his own bed.

And that he wasn't alone.

Cara's warm body was pressed up against his back, her arm draped heavily over his hip and her head tucked in between his shoulder blades. He could feel her breath against his skin and hear her gentle exhalations.

Memories from the night they'd just spent together flitted through his head like a film on fast-forward, the intensity of them making his skin tingle and his blood pound through his body. It had been amazing. More than amazing. It had rocked his world.

It had felt so good holding her in his arms, feeling her respond so willingly to his demands and clearly enjoying making her own on him.

But, lying here now, he knew it had been a mistake.

It was too soon after losing his wife to be feeling like that. It felt wrong—somehow seedy and inappropriate. Greedy.

He'd had his shot at love and it wasn't right that he should get another one. Especially not so soon after losing Jemima. In the cold light of day it seemed tasteless somehow, as if he hadn't paid his dues.

He'd been in such a fog of need all day yesterday that he'd pushed all the rational arguments to the back of his head and just taken what he'd wanted, which had been totally unfair on Cara.

He wasn't ready to give himself over to a relationship again. And he knew that Cara would need more from him than he was able to give. She'd want the fairy tale, and he was no Prince Charming.

The worst thing was: he'd known that this was going to happen. From the moment he'd set eyes on her. He'd been attracted to her, even though he'd pretended to himself that he wasn't. And he'd only made things worse for himself by keeping her at arm's length. The more he'd told himself *no*, the more he'd wanted her. That was why he'd really thought it best to get rid of her quickly, before anything could happen between them. And then, once it became clear there was no hiding from the fact she was a positive force in his life, he'd pretended to himself that he wanted her to stay purely for her skills as a PA.

Idiot.

It had well and truly backfired on him.

This was precisely why he'd stopped himself from becoming friends with her at the beginning. He'd known it would guide them down a dangerous path.

His concerns hadn't stopped him from knocking on her door after she'd run away from him last night, though. Even after it had taken everything he'd had not to respond to that first kiss. But she'd looked so hurt, so devastatingly bereft that he'd found himself chasing after her to try and put it right. And, judging by her reaction when he'd been unable to hold back a second time and stop himself from kissing her, she'd been just as desperate as him for it to happen. In fact, the small, encouraging noises that had driven him wild made him think she'd wanted it for a while.

And, as his penance, he was now going to have to explain to her why it could never happen again.

Drawing away from her as gently as he could so as not to wake her, he swung his legs out of bed and sat on the edge, putting his head in his hands, trying to figure out what to do next. He wasn't going to just leave her here in the middle of rural Leicestershire with no transport, but the thought of having to sit through the whole car journey home with her after explaining why last night had been a mistake filled him with dread.

He jumped as a slender arm snaked round his middle and Cara kissed down the length of his spine, before pulling herself up to sit behind him with her legs on either side of his body, her breasts pressing into his back.

'Good morning,' she said, her voice guttural with sleep.

Fighting to keep his body from responding to her, he put his hand on the arm that was wrapped around his middle and gently prised it away.

'Are you okay?' she asked, her tone sounding worried now.

'Fine.' He stood up and grabbed his trousers, pulling them on roughly before turning back to her.

She'd tugged the sheet around her and was looking

up at him with such an expression of concern he nearly reached for her.

Steeling himself against the impulse, he shoved his hands in his pockets and looked at her with as much cool determination as he could muster.

'This was wrong, Cara. Us, doing this.'

'What?' Her eyes widened in confused surprise.

'I'm sorry. I shouldn't have let it happen. I got caught up in the moment, which was selfish of me.'

Her expression changed in an instant to one of panic. 'No.' She held out her hands beseechingly. 'Please don't be sorry about it. I wanted it to happen, too.'

He swallowed hard, tearing his eyes away from her worried gaze. 'I can't give you what you want long-term, Cara.'

Pulling the sheet tighter around her body, she frowned at him. 'You don't know what I want.'

He smiled sadly. 'Yes, I do. You want this to turn into something serious, but I don't. I'm happy with my life the way it is.'

'You're *happy*?' She looked incredulous.

He rubbed his hand over his face in irritation. 'Yes, Cara, I'm happy,' he said, but he felt the lie land heavily in his gut.

'But what we had last night—and all day yesterday— I didn't imagine it.' She shook her head as if trying to throw off any niggling doubts. 'It was so good. It felt right between us, Max. Surely you felt that, too.'

He looked at her steadily, already hating himself for what he was about to say. 'No. Sorry.' He scrubbed a hand through his hair. 'Look, I was feeling lonely and you happened to be there. I feel awful about it and I won't blame you for being angry.'

She didn't believe him; he could see it in her eyes.

'I understand why you're panicking,' she said, holding out her hands in a pleading gesture, 'because we've just changed the nature of our relationship and it's a scary thing, taking things a step further, especially after what happened to Jemima...'

'See, that's the thing, Cara. I've been through that once and I'm not prepared to put myself through something like that again.'

'But it was so random—'

'The type of illness isn't the point here. It's the idea of pouring all your love into one person, only to lose them in the blink of an eye. I can go through that again.'

'But you can't cut yourself off from the world, Max. It'll drive you insane.'

He took a pace forward and folded his arms across his chest. 'You want to know what really drives me insane—that my wife was lying there in hospital with the life draining out of her and there wasn't a thing I could do about it. Not one damn thing. I promised her I'd look after her through thick and thin. I failed, Cara.' His throat felt tight with emotion he didn't want to feel any more.

'You didn't fail.'

He rubbed a hand over his eyes, taking a deep breath to loosen off the tension in his chest. 'I'm a fixer, Cara, but I couldn't fix that.'

'There wasn't anything you could have done.'

'I could have paid her more attention.'

'I'm sure she knew how much you loved her.'

And there was the rub. He did love Jemima. Too much to have room for anyone else in his heart.

'Yes, I think she did. But that doesn't change anything between you and me. I don't want this, Cara,' he said, waggling a finger between the two of them.

She stared at him in disbelief. 'So that's it? You've made up your mind and there's nothing I can do to change it?'

'Yes.'

Tipping up her chin, she looked him dead in the eye. 'Do you still want me to work for you?' she asked, her voice breaking with emotion.

Did he? His working life had been a lot less stressful since she'd been around, but what had just happened between them would make his personal life a lot more complicated. They were between a rock and a hard place. 'Yes. But I'll understand if it's too uncomfortable for you to stay.'

'So you'd let me just walk away?'

He sighed. 'If that's what you want.'

The look she gave him chilled him to the bone. 'You know, I don't believe for a second that Jemima would have wanted you to mourn her for the rest of your life. I think she'd have wanted you to be happy. You need to stop hiding behind her death and face the world again. Like you said you were going to yesterday. What happened to that, Max? Hmm? What happened to *you*? Jemima might not be alive any more, but *you* are and you need to stop punishing yourself for that and start living again.'

'I'm not ready—'

'You know, I love you, Max,' she broke in loudly, her eyes shining with tears.

He took a sharp intake of breath as the words cut through him. No. He didn't want to hear that from her right now. She was trying to emotionally manipulate him into doing something he didn't want to do.

'How can you love me?' Anger made his voice shake. 'We barely know each other.'

'I know you, Max,' she said calmly, her voice rich with emotion.

'You might think you do because I've told you a few personal things about myself recently, but that doesn't mean you get who I am and what I want.'

'Do you know what you want? Because it seems to me you're stopping yourself from being happy on purpose. You enjoyed being with me yesterday, Max, I know it.'

'I did enjoy it, but not in the way you think. It was good to get out of the house and have some fun, but that's all it was, Cara, *fun*.'

She shook her head, her body visibly shaking now. 'I don't believe you.'

'Fine. Don't believe me. Keep living in your perfect little imaginary world where everything is jolly and works out for the best, but don't expect me to show up.'

She reacted as if his words had physically hurt her, jolting back and hugging her arms around herself. 'How can you say that to me?'

Guilt wrapped around him and squeezed hard. She was right; it was a low blow after what he'd already put her through, but he was being cruel to be kind. Sinking onto the edge of the bed, he held up a pacifying hand. 'You see, I'm messed up, Cara. It's too soon for me. I'm not ready for another serious relationship. Maybe I'll never be ready. And it's not fair to ask you to wait for me.'

Her shoulders stiffened, as if she was fighting to keep them from slumping. 'Okay. If that's the way you feel,' she clipped out.

'It is, Cara. I'm sorry.'

The look she gave him was one of such disappointed disdain he recoiled a little.

'Well, then, I guess it's time for me to leave.' She shuffled to the edge of the bed. 'I'm not going to stick around here and let you treat me like I mean nothing to you. I'm worth more than that, Max, and if you can't appreciate that, then that's your loss.' With the sheet still wrapped firmly around her, she stood up and faced him, her eyes dark with anger. 'You can give me a lift to the nearest train station and I'll make my own way back to London.' Turning away from him, she walked over to where her overnight bag sat on the floor.

'Cara, don't be ridiculous—' he started to say, his tone sounding so insincere he cringed inwardly.

Swivelling on the spot, she pointed a shaking finger at him. 'Don't you dare say I'm the one being ridiculous. I'm catching the train. Please go and get changed in your own room. I'll meet you by the car in fifteen minutes.'

'Cara—' He tried to protest, moving towards her, but it was useless. He had nothing left to say.

There was no way to make this better.

'Okay,' he said quietly.

He watched her grab her wash kit from her bag, his gut twisting with unease.

Turning back, she gave him a jerky nod and then, staring resolutely ahead, went to stride past him to the bathroom.

Acting on pure impulse, he put out a hand to stop her, wrapping his fingers around her arm to prevent her from going any further. He could feel her shaking under his grip and he rubbed her arm gently, trying to imbue how sorry he was through the power of his touch.

She put her hand over his and for a second he thought she was going to squeeze his hand with understanding, but instead she pulled his fingers away from her arm and, without giving him another look, walked away.

Cara waited until Max's car had pulled away from the train station before sinking onto the bench next to the ticket office and putting her head in her hands, finally letting the tears stream down her face.

She'd spent the whole car journey there—which had only taken about ten minutes but had felt like ten painful hours—holding her head high and fighting back the hot pressure in her throat and behind her eyes.

They hadn't uttered one word to each other since he'd started the engine and she was grateful for that, because she knew if she'd had to speak there was no way she'd be able to hold it together.

It seemed they'd come full circle, with him withdrawing so far into himself he might as well have been a machine and her not wanting to show him any weakness.

What a mess.

And she'd told him she loved him.

Her chest cramped hard at the memory. When the words left her mouth, she hadn't known what sort of reaction to expect; in fact she hadn't even known she was going to say them until they'd rolled off her tongue, but she was still shocked by the flare of anger she'd seen in his eyes.

He'd thought she was trying to manipulate him, when that had been the last thing on her mind at the time. She'd wanted him to know he was loved and there could be a future for them if he wanted it.

Thinking about it now, though, she realised she had been trying to shock him into action. To reach something deep inside him that he'd been fiercely protecting ever since Jemima had died. It wasn't surprising he'd reacted the way he had, though. She couldn't begin to imagine the pain of losing a spouse, but she understood the pain of losing someone you loved in the blink of an eye or, in this case, in the time it took to say three small words.

Fury and frustration swirled in her gut, her empty stomach on the edge of nausea. How could she have let herself fall for a man who was still grieving for his wife and had no space left in his heart for her?

Clearly she was a glutton for punishment. And, because of that, she'd now not only lost her heart, she'd lost her home and her job, as well.

* * *

Back in London three hours later, she let herself wearily into Max's house, her nerves prickling at the thought of him being there.

Part of her wanted to see him—some mad voice in the back of her head had been whispering about him changing his mind after having time to reflect on what she'd said—but the other, sane part told her she was being naïve.

Walking into the kitchen, she saw that a note had been left in the middle of the table with her name written on it in Max's neat handwriting.

Picking it up with a trembling hand, she read the words, her stomach twisting with pain and her sight blurring with tears as she took in the news that he'd gone to Ireland a couple of days early for his meeting there, to give them a bit of space.

He wasn't interested in giving them another chance.

It was over.

Slumping into the nearest chair, she willed herself not to cry again. There was no point; she wasn't going to solve anything by sitting here feeling sorry for herself.

She had to look after herself now.

Her life had no foundations any more; it was listing at a dangerous angle and at some point in the near future it could crash to the ground if she didn't do something drastic to shore it up.

She'd *so* wanted to belong here with him, but this house wasn't her home and Max wasn't her husband.

His heart belonged to someone else.

She hated the fact she was jealous of a ghost, and not

just because Jemima had been beautiful and talented, but because Max loved her with a fierceness she could barely comprehend.

How could she ever compete with that?

The stone-cold truth was: she couldn't.

And she couldn't stay here a moment longer either.

After carefully folding her clothes into her suitcase, she phoned Sarah to ask whether she could sleep on her couch again, just until she'd moved into the flat that Amber's cousin had promised to let to her.

'Sure, you'd be welcome to stay with us again,' Sarah said, after finally coaxing out the reason for her needing a place to escape to so soon after moving into Max's house. 'But you might want to try Anna. She's going to be away in the States for a couple of weeks from tomorrow and I bet she'd love you to housesit for her.'

One phone call to their friend Anna later and she had a new place to live for the next couple of weeks. So that was her accommodation sorted. Now it was just the small matter of finding a new job.

She'd received an email last week from one of the firms that she'd sent a job application to, offering her an interview, but hadn't had time to respond to it, being so busy keeping the business afloat while Max was in Manchester. After firing off an email accepting an interview for the Tuesday of that week, she turned her thoughts to her current job.

Even though she was angry and upset with Max, there was no way she was just going to abandon the business without finding someone to take over the role she'd carved out for herself. Max might not want her around, but he was still going to need a PA. The meeting he had with a large corporation in Ireland later this week was an exciting prospect and if he managed to land their business he was going to need to hire more staff, pronto.

So this week it looked as if she was going to be both interviewer and interviewee.

The thought of it both exhausted and saddened her.

But she'd made her bed when she'd shared hers with Max, and now she was going to have to lie in it.

CHAPTER TEN

MAX HAD THOUGHT he was okay with the decision to walk away from a relationship with Cara, but his subconscious seemed to have other ideas when he woke up in a cold sweat for the third day running after dreaming that Cara was locked in the house whilst it burnt to the ground and he couldn't find any way to get her out.

Even after he'd been up for a while and looked through his emails, he still couldn't get rid of the haunting image of Cara's face contorted with terror as the flames licked around her. Despite the rational part of his brain telling him it wasn't real, he couldn't shake the feeling that he'd failed her.

Because, of course, he had, he finally accepted, as he sat down to eat his breakfast in the hotel restaurant before his meeting. She'd laid herself bare for him, both figuratively and literally, and he'd abused her trust by treating her as if she meant nothing to him.

Which wasn't the case at all.

He sighed and rubbed a hand over his tired eyes. The last thing he should be doing right now was worrying about how he'd treated Cara when he was about to walk into one of the biggest corporations in Ireland and convince them to give him their business. This was exactly what he'd feared would happen when he'd first agreed to let her work for him—that the business might suffer. Though, to be fair to Cara, this mess was of his own making.

Feeling his phone vibrate, he lifted it out of his pocket and tapped on the icon to open his text messages. It was from Cara.

With his pulse thumping hard in his throat, he read what she'd written. It simply said:

Good luck today. I'll be thinking of you.

A heavy pressure built in his chest as he read the words through for a second time.

She was thinking about him.

Those few simple words undid something in him and a wave of pure anguish crashed through his body, stealing his breath and making his vision blur. Despite how he'd treated her, she was still looking out for him.

She wanted him to know that he wasn't alone.

That was so like Cara. She was such a good person: selfless and kind, but also brave and honourable. Jemima would have loved her.

Taking a deep breath, he mentally pulled himself together. Now was not the time to lose the plot. He had some serious business to attend to and he wasn't about to let all the work that he and Cara had put into making this opportunity happen go to waste.

* * *

Fourteen hours later Max flopped onto his hotel bed, totally exhausted after spending the whole day selling himself to the prospective clients, then taking them out for a celebratory dinner to mark their partnership when they signed on the dotted line to buy his company's services.

He'd done it; he'd closed the deal—and a very profitable deal it was, too—which meant he could now comfortably grow the business and hire a team of people to work for him.

His life was moving on.

A strong urge to call Cara and let her know he'd been successful had him sitting up and reaching for his phone, but he stopped himself from tapping on her name at the last second. He couldn't call her this late at night without it *meaning* something.

Frustration rattled through him, swiftly followed by such an intense wave of despondency it took his breath away. He needed to talk to someone. Right now.

Scrolling through his contacts, he found the name he wanted and pressed *call*, his hands twitching with impatience as he listened to the long drones of the dialling tone.

'Max? Is everything okay?' said a sleepy voice on the other end of the line.

'Hi, Poppy, sorry—I forgot it'd be so late where you are,' he lied.

'No problem,' his friend replied, her voice strained as if she was struggling to sit up in bed. 'What's up? Is everything okay?'

'Yes. Fine. Everything's fine. I won a pivotal contract for the business today so I'm really happy,' he said, acutely aware of how flat his voice sounded despite his best efforts to sound upbeat.

Apparently it didn't fool Poppy either. 'You don't *sound* really happy, Max. Are you sure there isn't something else bothering you?'

His friend was too astute for her own good. But then she'd seen him at his lowest after Jemima died and had taken many a late night call from him throughout that dark time. He hadn't called her in a while though, so it wasn't entirely surprising that she thought something was wrong now.

'Er—' He ran a hand through his hair and sighed, feeling exhaustion drag at him. 'No, I'm—' But he couldn't say it. He wasn't fine. In fact he was far from it.

A blast of rage came out of nowhere and he gripped his phone hard, fighting for control.

It was a losing battle.

'You did it on purpose, didn't you? Sent Cara to me so I'd fall in love with her,' he said angrily, blood pumping hard through his body, and he leapt up from the bed and started to pace the room.

His heart gave an extra hard thump as the stunned silence at the other end of the line penetrated through his anger, bringing home to him exactly what he'd just said.

'Are you in love with her?' Poppy asked quietly, as if not wanting to break the spell.

He slapped the wall hard, feeling a sick satisfaction at the sting of pain in the palm of his hand. 'Jemima's only been dead for a year and a half.'

'That has nothing to do with it, and it wasn't what I asked you.'

He sighed and slumped back down onto the bed, battling to deal with the disorientating mass of emotions swirling though his head. 'I don't know, Poppy,' he said finally. 'I don't know.'

'If you don't know, that probably means that you are but you're too pig-headed to admit it to yourself.'

He couldn't help but laugh. His friend knew him so well.

'Is she in love with you?' Poppy asked.

'She says she is.'

He could almost feel his friend smiling on the other end of the phone.

Damn her.

'Look, I've got to go,' he said, 'I've had a very long day and my flight back to London leaves at six o'clock in the morning,' he finished, not wanting to protract this uncomfortable conversation any longer. 'I'll call you tomorrow after I've had some sleep and got my head straight, okay?'

'Okay.' There was a pause. 'You deserve to be happy though, Max, you know that, don't you? It's what Jemima would have wanted.'

He cut the call and threw the phone onto the bed, staring sightlessly at the blank wall in front of him.

Did he deserve to be happy, after the way he'd acted? Was he worthy of a second chance?

There was only one person who could answer that question.

* * *

The house was quiet when he arrived home at eight-thirty the next morning. Eerily so.

Cara should have been up by now, having breakfast and getting ready for the day—if she was there.

His stomach sank with dread as he considered the possibility that she wasn't. That she'd taken him at his word and walked away. Not that he could blame her.

Racing up the stairs, he came to an abrupt halt in front of her open bedroom door and peered inside. It was immaculate. And empty. As if she'd never been there.

Uncomfortable heat swamped him as he made his way slowly back down to the kitchen. Perhaps she hadn't gone. Perhaps she'd had a tidying spree in her room, then gone out early to grab some breakfast or something.

But he knew that none of these guesses were right when he spotted her keys to the house and the company mobile he'd given her to use for all their communications sitting in the middle of the kitchen table.

The silence of the house seemed to press in on him, crushing his chest, and he slumped onto the nearest chair and put his head in his hands.

This was all wrong. *All* of it.

He didn't want to stay in this house any longer; it was like living in a tomb. Or a shrine. Whatever it was, it felt wrong for him to be here now. Memories of the life he'd had here with Jemima were holding him back, preventing him from moving on and finding happiness again. Deep down, he knew Jem wouldn't have wanted that for him. He certainly wouldn't have wanted her to mourn him for the rest of her life.

She'd want him to be happy.

Like he had been on Sunday night.

He was in love with Cara.

Groaning loudly into his hands, he shook his head, unable to believe what a total idiot he'd been.

Memories of Cara flashed through his mind: her generous smile and kind gestures. Her standing up to him when it mattered to her most. Telling him she loved him.

His heart swelled with emotion, sending his blood coursing through his body and making it sing in his ears.

So this was living. How he'd missed it.

A loud ring on the doorbell made him jump.

Cara.

It had to be Cara, arriving promptly at nine o'clock for work like she always did.

Please, let it be her.

Tension tightened his muscles as he paced towards the door and flung it open, ready to say what he needed to say to her now. To be honest with her. To let her know how much he loved her and wanted her in his life.

'Max Firebrace?'

Instead of Cara standing on his doorstep, there was a tall, red-haired woman in a suit giving him a broad smile.

'Yes. Who are you?' he said impatiently, not wanting to deal with anything but his need to speak to Cara right then.

She held out a hand. 'I'm Donna, your new PA.'

The air seemed to freeze around him. *'What?'*

The smile she gave him was one of tolerant fortitude. 'Cara said you might be surprised to see me because you've been in Ireland all week.'

'Cara sent you here?'

'Yes, she interviewed me yesterday and said I should start today.'

He stared at her, stunned. 'Where is Cara?'

Donna looked confused. 'Er... I don't know. I wasn't expecting her to be here. She said something about starting a new job for a firm in the City next week. We spent all of yesterday afternoon getting me up to speed with the things I need to do to fulfil the role and went through the systems you use here, so I assumed she'd already served her notice.'

So that was it then. He was too late to save the situation. She was gone.

'You'd better come in,' he muttered, frustration tugging hard at his insides.

'So will we be working here the whole time? It's a beautiful house,' Donna said brightly, looking around the hall.

'No. I'm going to rent an office soon,' he said distractedly, his voice rough with panic.

How was he going to find her? He didn't have any contact details for her friends or her personal mobile number; she'd always used the company one to call or text him. He could try Poppy, but she'd probably be out filming in the middle of the desert right now and wouldn't want to be disturbed with phone calls.

A thought suddenly occurred to him. 'Donna? Did Cara interview you here?'

'No. I went to her flat.' She frowned. 'Although, come to think of it, I don't think it was her place; she didn't know which cupboard the sugar for my drink was kept in.'

He paced towards her, startling her with a rather manic smile.

'Okay, Donna. Your first job as my PA is to give me the address where you met Cara.'

At first Cara thought that the loud banging was part of her dream, but she started awake as the noise thundered through the flat again, seeming to shake the walls. Whoever was knocking really wanted to get her attention.

Pulling her big towelling dressing gown on over her sleep shorts and vest top, she stumbled to the door, still half-asleep. Perhaps the postman had a delivery for one of the other flats and they weren't in to receive it.

But it wasn't the postman.

It was Max.

Her vision tilted as she stumbled against the door in surprise and she hung on to the handle for dear life in an attempt to stop herself from falling towards him.

'Max! How did you find me?' she croaked, her voice completely useless in the face of his shocking presence.

She'd told herself that giving them both some space to breathe was the best thing she could do. After leaving his house on Monday she'd tried to push him out of her mind in an attempt to get through the dark, lonely days without him, but always, in the back of her mind, was the hope that he'd think about what she'd said and maybe, at some point in the future, want to look her up again.

But she hadn't expected it to happen so soon.

'My new PA, Donna, gave me the address,' he said, raising an eyebrow in chastisement, though the sparkle in his eyes told her he wasn't seriously angry with her for going ahead and hiring someone to take her place without his approval.

Telling herself not to get too excited in case he was only popping round to drop off something she'd accidentally left at the house, she motioned for him to come inside and led him through to the kitchen diner, turning to lean against the counter for support.

'You did say you'd understand if I couldn't work with you any more. After what happened,' she said.

He came to a stop a few feet away from her and propped himself against the table. 'I did.'

She took a breath and tipped up her chin. 'I'm not made of stone, Max. As much as I'd like to sweep what happened on Sunday under the carpet, I can't do that. I'm sorry.'

Letting out a long sigh, he shifted against the table. 'Don't be sorry. It wasn't your fault. It was mine. I was the one who knocked on your door when you had the strength to walk away.'

She snorted gently. 'That wasn't strength; it was cowardice.'

'You're not a coward, Cara; you just have a strong sense of self-preservation. You should consider it a gift.'

She stared down at the floor, aware of the heat of her humiliation rising to her face, not wanting him to see how weak and out of control she was right now.

'So you start a new job next week?' he asked quietly.

Forcing herself to look at him again, she gave him the most assertive smile she could muster. 'Yes, at a place in the City. It's a good company and the people were very friendly when they showed me around.'

'I bet you could handle just about anything after having to work for me.' He smiled, but she couldn't return it this time. The muscles in her face wouldn't move. They seemed to be frozen in place.

Gosh, this was awkward.

'You've been good for my confidence.' She flapped a hand at him and added, 'Work-wise,' when he raised his eyebrows in dispute. 'You were great at letting me know when I'd done a good job.'

'Only because you were brave enough to point out how bad I was at it.'

She managed a smile this time, albeit a rather wonky one. 'Well, whatever. I really appreciated it.'

There was a tense silence where they both looked away, as if psyching themselves up to tackle the real issues.

'Look, I'm not here to ask you to come back and work for me again,' Max said finally, running a hand over his hair.

'Oh. Okay,' she whispered, fighting back the tears. She would not break down in front of him. She *wouldn't*.

He frowned, as if worried about the way she'd reacted, and sighed loudly. 'Argh! I'm so bad at this.' He moved towards her but stopped a couple of feet away, holding up his hands. 'I wanted to tell you that I think I've finally made peace with what happened to Jemima. Despite my best efforts to remain a reclusive, twisted misery guts, I think I'm going to be okay now.' He took another step towards her, giving her a tentative smile. 'Thanks to you.'

Forcing down the lump in her throat, she smiled back. 'That's good to hear, Max. Really good. I'm happy that you're happy. And I do understand why you don't want me to come back and work for you. It must have been hard having me hanging around your house so much.'

'I'm going to sell the house, Cara.'

She stared at him in shock, her heart racing. 'What? But—how can you stand to leave it? That beautiful house.'

'I don't care about the house. I care about us.' This time he walked right up to her, so close she could feel the heat radiating from his body, and looked her directly in the eye. 'I'm ready to live again and I want to do it with you.'

'You—?'

'Want *you*, Cara.' His voice shook with emotion and she could see now that he was trembling.

'But—? I thought you said—when did you…?' Her voice petered out as her brain shut down in shock.

He half smiled, half frowned. 'Clearly I need to explain some things.' He took her hand and led her gently over to the sofa in the living area, guiding her to sit down next to him, keeping his fingers tightly locked with hers and capturing her gaze before speaking.

'When we slept together I felt like I'd betrayed a promise to Jemima.' He swallowed hard. 'After what happened to her I thought I had no right to be happy and start again when she couldn't do that. I truly thought I'd never love someone else the way I loved her, but then I realised I didn't need to. The love I feel for you is different—just as strong, but a different flavour. Does that make sense?'

He waited for her to nod shakily before continuing. 'I don't want to replicate Jemima or the way it was with her. I want to experience it all afresh with you. I'll always love Jem because she was a big part of my life for many years, but I can compartmentalise that now as part of my past.' He squeezed her fingers hard. 'You're my future.'

'Really?' Her throat was so tense with emotion she could hardly form the word.

'Yes. I love you, Cara.'

And she knew from the look on his face that he meant every word. He'd never given up anything of an emotional nature lightly and she understood what a superhuman effort it must have taken for him to come here and say all that to her.

Reaching out a hand, she ran her fingers across his cheek, desperate to smooth away any fears he might have. 'I love you, too.'

He closed his eyes and breathed out hard in relief before opening them again, looking more at peace than she'd ever seen him before. Lifting his own hand, he slid his fingers into her hair and drew her towards him, pressing his mouth to hers and kissing her long and hard.

She felt it right down to her toes.

Drawing away for a moment, he touched his forehead to hers and whispered, 'You make me so happy.'

And then, once again, there was no more talking. Just passion and joy and excitement for their bright new future together.

EPILOGUE

One year later

THE HOUSE THEY'D chosen to buy together was just the
sort of place Cara had dreamed of owning during her
romantic but practical twenties. It wasn't as grand or
impressive as the house in South Kensington, but it felt
exactly right for the two of them. And perhaps for any
future family that chose to come along.

Not that having children was on the cards *right* now.
Max was focusing hard on maintaining the expansion
of his Management Solutions business, which had been
flying ever since the Irish company awarded him their
contract, and Cara was happy in her new position as
Executive Assistant to the CEO of the company she'd
joined in the City. But they'd talked about the possibility
of it happening in the near future and had both agreed
it was something they wanted.

Life was good. And so was their relationship.

After worrying for the first few months that, despite
his assurances to the contrary, Max might still be in the
grip of grief and that they had some struggles ahead of

them, her fears had been assuaged as their partnership flourished and grew into something so strong and authentic she could barely breathe with happiness some days.

Max's anger had faded but his fierceness remained, which she now experienced as both a protective and supportive force in her life. Being a party to his sad past had taught her to count her blessings, and she did. Every single day.

Arriving home late after enjoying a quick Friday night drink with her colleagues, she let herself into their golden-bricked Victorian town house—which they'd chosen for the views of Victoria Park and its close location to the thriving bustle and buzz of Columbia Road with its weekly flower market and kitschy independent furniture shops—and stopped dead in the doorway, staring down at the floor.

It was covered in flowers, of all colours and varieties. Frowning at them in bewilderment, she realised they were arranged into the shape of a sweeping arrow pointing towards the living room.

'Max? I'm home. What's going on? It looks like spring has exploded in our hallway!'

Tiptoeing carefully over the flowers so as not to crush too many of them, she made her way towards the living room and peered nervously through the doorway, her heart skittering at the mystery of it.

What she saw inside took her breath away.

Every surface was covered in vibrantly coloured bouquets of spring flowers, displayed in all manner of receptacles: from antique vases to the measuring jug she used to make her porridge in the mornings. Even the light fitting had a large cutting of honeysuckle spiralling down from it, its sweet fragrance permeating the air. It reminded her of their first night together after Jack's wedding. Which quickly led her to memories of all the wonderful nights that had come after it, where she'd lain in Max's arms, breathing in the scent of his skin, barely able to believe how loved and cherished she felt.

And she was loved, as Max constantly reminded her, and her support and love for him had enabled him to finally say goodbye to Jemima and the past that had kept him ensnared for so long.

She'd unlocked his heart.

She was the key, he'd told her as he carried her, giggling, over the threshold into their house six months ago.

She'd finally found her home.

Their home.

He was standing next to the rose-strewn piano in the bay, looking at her with the same expression of fierce love and desire that always made her blood rush with heat.

'Hello, beautiful, did you have a good night?' he asked, walking towards where she stood, his smile bringing a mesmerising twinkle to his eyes.

'I did, thank you.' She swept a hand around the room, unable to stop herself from blurting, 'Max, what is this?'

The reverent expression on his face made her heart leap into her throat. 'This is me asking you to marry me,' he said, dropping to one knee in front of her and taking her hand in his, smiling at her gasp of surprise.

'This time last year I thought I'd never want to be married again—that I didn't deserve to be happy—but meeting you changed all that. You saved me, Cara.' Reaching into his pocket, he withdrew a small black velvet-covered box and flipped it open to reveal a beautiful flower-shaped diamond ring.

'I love you, and I want to spend the rest of my life loving you.' His eyes were alive with passion and hope. 'So what do you say—will you marry me?'

Heart pounding and her whole body shaking with excitement, she dropped onto her knees in front of him and gazed into his face, hardly able to believe the intensity of the love she felt for him.

'Yes,' she said simply, smiling into his eyes, letting him know how much she loved him back. 'Yes. I will.'

* * * * *

MILLS & BOON®

Cherish™

EXPERIENCE THE ULTIMATE RUSH OF FALLING IN LOVE

A sneak peek at next month's titles...

In stores from 14th January 2016:

- **A Deal to Mend Their Marriage** – Michelle Douglas and **Fortune's Perfect Valentine** – Stella Bagwell
- **Dr. Forget-Me-Not** – Marie Ferrarella and **Saved by the CEO** – Barbara Wallace

In stores from 28th January 2016:

- **A Soldier's Promise** – Karen Templeton and **Tempted by Her Tycoon Boss** – Jennie Adams
- **Pregnant with a Royal Baby!** – Susan Meier and **The Would-Be Daddy** – Jacqueline Diamond

---

1015_MB514

MILLS & BOON®

Man of the Year

Our winning cover star will be revealed next month!

**Don't miss out on your copy
– order from millsandboon.co.uk**

Read more about Man of the Year 2016 at

www.millsandboon.co.uk/moty2016

**Have you been following our
Man of the Year 2016 campaign?**
🐦 #MOTY2016

MILLS & BOON®

Want to get more from Mills & Boon?

Here's what's available to you if you join the exclusive **Mills & Boon eBook Club** today:

✦ *Convenience – choose your books each month*
✦ *Exclusive – receive your books a month before anywhere else*
✦ *Flexibility – change your subscription at any time*
✦ *Variety – gain access to eBook-only series*
✦ *Value – subscriptions from just £3.99 a month*

So visit **www.millsandboon.co.uk/esubs** today to be a part of this exclusive eBook Club!